PENGUIN CLASSICS

THE HISTORY OF MR POLLY

H. G. WELLS, the third son of a small shopkeeper, was born in
Bromley in 1866. After two years' apprenticeship in a draper's
shop, he became a pupil-teacher at Midhurst Grammar School
and won a scholarship to study under T. H. Huxley at the Normal
School of Science, South Kensington. He taught biology before
becoming a professional writer and journalist. He wrote more
than a hundred books, including novels, essays, histories and
programmes for world regeneration.

Wells, who rose from obscurity to world fame, had an emotion-
ally and intellectually turbulent life. His prophetic imagination
was first displayed in pioneering works of science fiction such as
The Time Machine (1895), *The Island of Doctor Moreau* (1896),
The Invisible Man (1897) and *The War of the Worlds* (1898).
Later he became an apostle of socialism, science and progress,
whose anticipations of a future world state include *The Shape of
Things to Come* (1933). His controversial views on sexual equality
and women's rights were expressed in the novels *Ann Veronica*
(1909) and *The New Machiavelli* (1911). He was, in Bertrand
Russell's words, 'an important liberator of thought and action'.

Wells drew on his own early struggles in many of his best
novels, including *Love and Mr Lewisham* (1900), *Kipps* (1905),
Tono-Bungay (1909) and *The History of Mr Polly* (1910). His
educational works, some written in collaboration, include *The
Outline of History* (1920) and *The Science of Life* (1930). His
Experiment in Autobiography (2 vols, 1934) reviews his world.
He died in London in 1946.

JOHN SUTHERLAND is emeritus Lord Northcliffe Professor of
Modern English Literature at University College London and a
visiting professor of Literature at the California Institute of Technology. He is the author of many books and has edited many
volumes of Trollope's works. For Penguin Classics he has edited
Phineas Finn, *Rachel Ray*, Thackeray's *Henry Esmond* and H. G.
Wells's *The History of Mr Polly*. For Viking Penguin he has
written *Stephen Spender: The Authorized Biography*.

T0200827

SIMON J. JAMES is Lecturer in Victorian Literature at the University of Durham, and a graduate of the University of Cambridge. He is the author of *Unsettled Accounts: Money and Narrative Form in the Novels of George Gissing* (Anthem, 2003) and of articles on Gissing, H. G. Wells and Charles Dickens. He is the editor of Volume 2 of the *Collected Works of George Gissing on Charles Dickens* and of three other Penguin Wells titles.

H. G. WELLS

The History of Mr Polly

Edited by SIMON J. JAMES
with an Introduction by JOHN SUTHERLAND
and Notes by JOHN SUTHERLAND *and* SIMON J. JAMES

PENGUIN BOOKS

PENGUIN CLASSICS

Published by the Penguin Group
Penguin Books Ltd, 80 Strand, London WC2R ORL, England
Penguin Group (USA) Inc., 375 Hudson Street, New York, New York 10014, USA
Penguin Group (Canada), 10 Alcorn Avenue, Toronto, Ontario, Canada M4V 3B2
(a division of Pearson Penguin Canada Inc.)
Penguin Ireland, 25 St Stephen's Green, Dublin 2, Ireland
(a division of Penguin Books Ltd)
Penguin Group (Australia), 250 Camberwell Road,
Camberwell, Victoria 3124, Australia (a division of Pearson Australia Group Pty Ltd)
Penguin Books India Pvt Ltd, 11 Community Centre,
Panchsheel Park, New Delhi – 110 017, India
Penguin Group (NZ), cnr Airborne and Rosedale Roads, Albany,
Auckland 1310, New Zealand (a division of Pearson New Zealand Ltd)
Penguin Books (South Africa) (Pty) Ltd, 24 Sturdee Avenue,
Rosebank 2196, South Africa

Penguin Books Ltd, Registered Offices: 80 Strand, London WC2R ORL, England

www.penguin.com

First published 1910
This edition first published in Penguin Classics 2005

022

Text copyright © the Literary Executors of the Estate of H. G. Wells
Biographical Note, Further Reading, Note on the Text
copyright © Simon J. James, 2005
Introduction copyright © John Sutherland, 2005
Notes copyright © John Sutherland and Simon J. James, 2005
All rights reserved

The moral right of the editors has been asserted

Set in 10.25/12.25 pt PostScript Adobe Sabon
Typeset by Rowland Phototypesetting Ltd, Bury St Edmunds, Suffolk
Printed and bound in Great Britain by Clays Ltd, Elcograf S.p.A.

ISBN-13: 978-0-141-44107-8

www.greenpenguin.co.uk

MIX
Paper from
responsible sources
FSC
www.fsc.org
FSC® C018179

Penguin Books is committed to a sustainable
future for our business, our readers and our planet.
This book is made from Forest Stewardship
Council™ certified paper.

CONTENTS

Biographical Note

Herbert George Wells was born on 21 September 1866 at Bromley, Kent, a small market town soon to be swallowed up by the suburban growth of outer London. His father, formerly a professional gardener and a county cricketer renowned for his fast bowling, owned a small business in Bromley High Street selling china goods and cricket bats. The house was grandly known as Atlas House, but the centre of family life was a cramped basement kitchen underneath the shop. Soon Joseph Wells's cricketing days were cut short by a broken leg, and the family fortunes looked bleak.

Young 'Bertie' Wells had already shown great academic promise, but when he was thirteen his family broke up and he was forced to earn his own living. His father was bankrupt, and his mother left home to become resident housekeeper at Uppark, the great Sussex country house where she had worked as a lady's maid before her marriage. Wells was taken out of school to follow his two elder brothers into the drapery trade. After serving briefly as a pupil-teacher and a pharmacist's assistant, in 1881 he was apprenticed to a department store in Southsea, working a thirteen-hour day and sleeping in a dormitory with his fellow-apprentices. This was the unhappiest period of his life, though he would later revisit it in comic romances such as *Kipps* (1905) and *The History of Mr Polly* (1910). Kipps and Polly both manage to escape from their servitude as drapers, and in 1883, helped by his long-suffering mother, Wells cancelled his indentures and obtained a post as teaching assistant at Midhurst Grammar School near Uppark. His intellectual development, long held back, now progressed astonishingly. He passed a series of examinations in science subjects and, in September 1884, entered the Normal School of Science, South Kensington (later to become part of Imperial College of Science and Technology) on a government scholarship.

Wells was a born teacher, as many of his books would show, and at first he was an enthusiastic student. He had the good fortune to be taught biology and zoology by one of the most influential scientific thinkers of the Victorian age, Darwin's friend and supporter T. H. Huxley. Wells never forgot Huxley's teaching, but the other professors were more humdrum, and his interest in their courses rapidly waned. He scraped through second-year physics, but failed his third-year geology exam and left South Kensington in 1887 without taking a degree. He was thrilled by the theoretical framework and imaginative horizons of natural science, but impatient of practical detail and the grinding, routine tasks of laboratory work. He cut his classes and spent his time reading literature and history, satisfying the curiosity he had earlier felt while exploring the long-neglected library at Uppark. He started a college magazine, the *Science Schools Journal*, and argued for socialism in student debates.

In the summer of 1887 Wells became science master at a small private school in North Wales, but a few weeks later he was knocked down and injured by one of his pupils on the football field. Sickly and undernourished as a result of three years of student poverty, he suffered severe kidney and lung damage. After months of convalescence at Uppark he was able to return to science teaching at Henley House School, Kilburn. In 1890 he passed his University of London B.Sc. (Hons.) with a first class in zoology and obtained a post as a biology tutor for the University Correspondence College. In 1891 he married his cousin Isabel Wells, but they had little in common and soon Wells fell in love with one of his students, Amy Catherine Robbins (usually known as 'Jane'). They started living together in 1893, and married two years later when his divorce came through.

During his years as a biology tutor Wells slowly began making his way as a writer and journalist. He wrote for the

Educational Times, edited the *University Correspondent*, and in 1891 published a philosophical essay, 'The Rediscovery of the Unique', in the prestigious *Fortnightly Review*. His first book was a *Textbook of Biology* (1893). But no sooner was it published than his health again collapsed, forcing him to give up teaching and rely entirely on his literary earnings. His future seemed highly precarious, yet soon he was in regular demand as a writer of short stories and humorous essays for the burgeoning newspapers and magazines of the period. He became a fiction reviewer and, for a short period in 1895, a theatre critic.

Ever since his student days Wells had worked intermittently on a story about time-travelling and the possible future of the human race. An early version was published in the *Science Schools Journal* as 'The Chronic Argonauts', but now, after numerous redrafts and much encouragement from the poet and editor W. E. Henley, it finally took shape as *The Time Machine* (1895). Its success was instantaneous, and while it was running as a magazine serial Wells was already being spoken of as a 'man of genius'. He was celebrated as the inventor of the 'scientific romance', a combination of adventure novel and philosophical tale in which the hero becomes involved in a life-and-death struggle resulting from some unforeseen scientific development. There was now a ready market for his fiction, and *The Island of Doctor Moreau* (1896), *The Invisible Man* (1897), *The War of the Worlds* (1898), *When the Sleeper Wakes* (1899; later revised as *The Sleeper Awakes*, 1910), *The First Men in the Moon* (1901) and several other volumes followed quickly from his pen.

By the turn of the twentieth century Wells was established as a popular author in England and America, and his books were rapidly being translated into French, German, Spanish, Russian and other European languages. Already his fame had begun to eclipse that of his predecessor in scientific romance, the French author Jules Verne, who had dominated the field since the 1860s. But Wells, an increasingly self-conscious artist, had larger ambitions than to go down in history as a boys' adventure novelist like Jules Verne. *Love and Mr Lewisham* (1900) was his first attempt at realistic fiction, comic in spirit and manifestly reflecting his own experiences as a student and teacher. By the end of the Edwardian decade, when he wrote his 'Condition of England' novels *Tono-Bungay* (1909) and *The New Machiavelli* (1911), Wells had become one of the leading novelists of his day, the friend and rival of such literary figures as Arnold Bennett, Joseph Conrad, Ford Madox Ford and Henry James.

But Wells was never a devotee of art for art's sake; he was a prophetic writer with a social and political message. His first major non-fictional work was *Anticipations* (1902), a book of futurological essays setting out the possible effects of scientific and technological progress in the twentieth century. *Anticipations* brought him into contact with the Fabian Society and launched his career as a political journalist and an influential voice of the British left. During his Fabian period Wells wrote *A Modern Utopia* (1905), but failed in his attempt to challenge the bureaucratic, reformist outlook of the Society's leaders such as Bernard Shaw (a lifelong friend and rival) and Beatrice Webb. Wells's Edwardian scientific romances such as *The Food of the Gods* (1904) and *The War in the Air* (1908), though full of humorous touches, are propagandist in intent. In other 'future war' stories of this period he predicted the tank and the atomic bomb.

Success as an author brought about great changes in his personal life. Ill-health had forced him to leave London for the Kent coast in 1898, but in the long run the only legacy of his footballing injury was the diabetes that affected him in old age. He commissioned a house, Spade House, overlooking the English Channel at Sandgate, from the architect C. F. A. Voysey, and here his and Jane's two sons were born – George Philip or 'Gip', who became a zoology professor and collaborated with his father and Julian Huxley on the biology encyclopedia *The Science of Life* (1930), and Frank, who worked in the film industry. Wells gave generous support to his parents and to his eldest brother, who was a fellow-fugitive from the drapery trade. Increasingly, however, he looked for emotional fulfilment outside the family, and his sexual affairs became notorious. He had a daughter in 1909 with Amber Reeves, a leading young Fabian economist, and in 1914 the novelist and critic Rebecca West gave birth to his son Anthony West, whose troubled childhood would later be reflected in his own novel *Heritage* (1955) and in his biography of his father.

As Wells's personal life became the gossip of literary London, his roles as imaginative writer and political journalist or prophet came increasingly into conflict. *Ann Veronica* (1909) was an example of topical, controversial fiction, dramatizing and commenting on such issues as women's rights, sexual equality and contemporary morals. It was the first of Wells's 'discussion novels' in which his personal relationships were often very thinly disguised. His later fiction takes a great variety of forms, but it all belongs to the broad category of the novel of ideas. At one extreme is the realistic reporting of *Mr Britling Sees It Through* (1916) – still valuable and unique as a portrayal of the English 'home front' in the First World War – while at the other extreme are brief fables such as *The Undying Fire* (1919) and *The Croquet Player* (1936), political allegories about world events each cast in the form of a prophetic dialogue.

Wells was by no means an experimental novelist like his younger contemporaries James Joyce and Virginia Woolf, but he was often technically innovative, and in some of his books the boundaries between fiction and non-fiction begin to break down. Sometimes he would take a classic from an earlier, pre-modern epoch as his literary model: *A Modern Utopia* (1905), for example, refers back to Sir Thomas More's *Utopia* and Plato's *Republic*. His bestselling historical works *The Outline of History* (1920) and *A Short History of the World* (1922) break with historical conventions by looking forward to the next stage in history. These works were written in order to draw the lessons of the First World War and to ensure that, if possible, its carnage would never be repeated; Wells saw history as a 'race between education and catastrophe'. The same concerns led to his future-history novel *The Shape of Things to Come* (1933), later rewritten for the cinema as *Things to Come*, an epic science-fiction film produced in 1936 by Alexander Korda. Both novel and film contain dire warnings about the inevitable outbreak and disastrous consequences of the Second World War.

By the 1920s, Wells was not only a famous author but a public figure whose name was rarely out of the newspapers. He briefly worked for the Ministry of Propaganda in 1918, producing a memorandum on war aims which anticipated the setting-up of the League of Nations. In 1922 and 1923 he stood for Parliament as a Labour candidate. He sought to influence world leaders, including two US presidents, Theodore Roosevelt and Franklin D. Roosevelt. His meeting with Lenin in the Kremlin in 1920 and his interview in 1934 with Lenin's successor Josef Stalin were publicized all over the world. His high-pitched, piping voice was often heard on BBC radio. In 1933 he was elected president of International PEN, the writers' organization campaigning for intellectual freedom. In the same year his books were publicly burnt by the Nazis in Berlin, and he was banned from visiting Fascist Italy. His ideas strongly influenced the Pan-European Union, the pressure group advocating European unity between the wars.

But Wells became convinced that nothing less than global unity was needed if humanity was not to destroy itself. In *The Open Conspiracy* (1928) and other books he outlined his theories of world citizenship and world government. As the Second World War drew nearer he felt that his mission had been a failure and his warnings had gone unheeded. His last great campaign, for which he tried to obtain international support, was for human rights. The proposal set out in his Penguin Special *The Rights of Man* (1940) helped to bring about the United Nations declaration of 1948. He spent the war years at his house in Hanover Terrace, Regent's Park, and was awarded a D.Sc. by London University in 1943. His last book, *Mind at the End of Its Tether* (1945), was a despairing, pessimistic work, even bleaker in its prospects for mankind than *The Time Machine* fifty years earlier. He died at Hanover Terrace on 13 August 1946. He was restless and tireless to the end, a prophet eternally dissatisfied with himself and with humanity. 'Some day', he had written in a whimsical 'Auto-Obituary' three years earlier, 'I shall write a book, a *real* book.' He had published over fifty works of fiction and, in total, some 150 books and pamphlets.

                                                    Patrick Parrinder

Introduction

Mr Polly has a problem. His ideas are bigger than his vocabulary. He is forever obliged to squeeze the English language into eccentric (but still very English) shapes. Inarticulate he is not. Nor does he mis-speak, as the contemporary politician would put it. It is merely that to get them to express what Mr Polly means, his words must be pummelled into idiosyncratic eloquence.

Hence such expressive locutions as: 'intrudacious', 'meditatious', 'jawbacious' and 'retrospectatiousness'. In his higher linguistic flights Mr Polly stuffs two or more meanings into one word, creating 'macaronics'. He is, he protests, 'no fiancianier' (that is: he wants a fiancée, and doesn't know how to invest the little nest egg his father has left him). 'You've merely antiseparated me', he coolly informs his employer, on being dismissed before he could, himself, resign his post (thanks, again, to said nest egg). At times, his linguistic inventaciousness verges on the chaotic. The Pollyistic etymology of 'hysterial catechunations' for the Larkins girls' cackle is mysterious. But even when opaque, Alfred Polly remains a lexical adventurer. There are manglers of language (fictional and historical) whose transgressions brand-name them for posterity. One thinks of [Mrs] Malaprop(ism), [Sam] Weller(ism), [Professor] Spooner-(ism), [President] Bush(ism). It is a sad omission that the term [Mr] Polly(ism) has not been similarly dignified.

For those of a biographous inclination (as Polly would say – hereafter in the text, 'APWS') Wells's runaway, unhappily married, impecunious shopkeeper hero can plausibly be seen as a comic self-portrait of the artist as a middle-aged man

– with a dash of the artist's father, Joe Wells, thrown in. Wells
Sr (an unhappily married, impecunious shopkeeper), 'always
seemed poised to flee when things got difficult'.[1] Young
H. G. Wells inherited little from his father other than the same
propensity to bolt when the going got difficult, domestically.
He wrote *The History of Mr Polly* in France, having eloped
from his second wife (having divorced the first) with a new (and
pregnant) lover. Difficult indeed.

Like his author, Alfred Polly is born into the basement
level of the respectable, mid-Victorian, middle-class – a precarious hair's width above the 'abyss', that awful sub-basement
where live (if it can be called life) the 'workers' – Morlocks,
as Wells elsewhere calls them, subterranean and horrible
humanoids. Above all else, that foothold in respectability must
be preserved. For inhabitants of this uneasy class the white
collar (even if it is, like Mr Polly's, a cheap thing made of
glossed paper) is as sacred an object as the aspidistra in the
front room.

Generically, Alfred is one of Edwardian England's 'little men'
(pursued by a mysteriously invisible 'lill dog' – a mongrel hound
of heaven invisible to all eyes but those of Polly). There are
many of Mr Polly's kind in British literature: Bob Cratchit, Mr
Wemmick, Mr Pooter, Leonard Bast, Billy Liar, the platoon of
indomitable 'gumps' played on screen by Sir Norman Wisdom,
and the butler, Mr Stevens, in Kazuo Ishiguro's *Remains of the
Day* – to name a few.

'Bertie' Wells (as he was known in childhood) anatomized
homo parvus a couple of years earlier, in Chapter 3 of *The War
in the Air* (1908):

> Bert Smallways was a vulgar little creature, the sort of pert,
> limited soul that the old civilization of the early twentieth century
> produced by the million in every country of the world. He had
> lived all his life in narrow streets, and between mean houses he
> could not look over, and in a narrow circle of ideas from which
> there was no escape. He thought the whole duty of man was to
> be smarter than his fellows, get his hands, as he put it, 'on the

dibs', and have a good time. He was, in fact, the sort of man who
had made England and America what they were.

It is, of course, a self-portrait – not of what H. G. Wells became
but of what destiny intended him to be.

'The great force of material fate' has placed Polly in a station
in life from which only the egregiously fortunate (such as Kipps,
with his out-of-the-blue £26,000 bequest), the outrageously
criminal (such as the huckster pharmacist, Teddy Ponderevo,
in *Tono-Bungay*), or the accidentally heroic (Mr Polly, as it
emerges) can escape. The others are, as the apprentice draper
Minton puts it in *Kipps* (1905): 'In a blessed drainpipe, and
we've got to crawl along it till we die.'[2]

For the vast majority of little men a horrible enlightenment
awaits at the end of the pipe when, confronting oblivion, they
contemplate what their existence, 'subspecious aeternitatatous'
(APWS), has meant. 'The end!' thinks Mr Polly, as he looks
death in the eye (the razor that will free him of his mortal coil
in his hand):

> It seemed to him now that life had never begun for him, never!
> It was as if his soul had been cramped and his eyes bandaged
> from the hour of his birth. Why had he lived such a life? Why
> had he submitted to things, blundered into things? Why had he
> never insisted on the things he thought beautiful and the things
> he desired, never sought them, fought for them, taken any risk
> for them, died rather than abandon them? They were things that
> mattered, Safety did not matter. A living did not matter unless
> there were things to live for ... (p. 142)

Polly, it turns out, is one of the lucky few. He contrives to live
before it is too late. What saves him is that he discovers, as did
Wells (rather earlier in life), a great secret: 'If the world does
not please you, *you can change it*' (p. 159). 'A kind of second
French Revolution' is possible – even for little men. For Mr
Polly it will not be the kind of 'Great Change' chronicled in
Wells's scientific romance *In the Days of the Comet* (1906)

where a benign green ray from outer space solves all sublunar problems, creating a utopia of plenty, ease and free love for all. Mr Polly's revolution is strictly personal. He saves himself: the world will go on in its old, unsaved way. But he is its slave no longer. He has changed *his* world.

How does Polly pull it off? Not by the pious subservience to his betters prescribed by Samuel Smiles's *Self Help*: doing your duty in the prescribed manner of Mrs Craik's *John Halifax, Gentleman*. Polly kicks against the pricks. Nor is Polly emancipated from his class destiny by the kind of crash-course in the codes of middle-class life, which – with a few months of Professor Higgins's tutoring – transforms Eliza Doolittle from guttersnipe into a well-spoken 'lady' (give or take a 'bloody' or two).

Shaw and Wells, comrades in socialism and literature, never agreed about how the 'great change' they both prophesied for English society was to be achieved. The Irish sage eventually put his faith in biology. 'Creative Evolution' would, in its own time, do what man could not. Wells was always less patient. He wanted change now, not eons hence for his unregarded descendants, as distant from him as he was from the orangutan.

Polly's liberation is brought about by old books, new technology and his own suburban brand of terrorism. His early revolutionary stirrings manifest themselves in a taste for forbidden literature: 'Rabooloose', and 'Bocashieu' (where, one wonders, did a draper's assistant come across un-Bowdlerized copies of those libertine texts?). Polly's first constructive moves towards escape from the Kippsian drainpipe come with the purchase of a 'safety bicycle' – i.e. one equipped with Mr Dunlop's newly invented pneumatic tyres, enabling the machine and its intrepid rider to whiz over Mr McAdam's newly paved roads at dizzying speeds and vast distances. Wells was keenly aware of the liberations made available to wage-slaves by two-wheeled locomotion (as momentous as that of the four-wheeled variety – the 'quadricycle' as he originally called it – currently rolling off the production lines of Henry Ford's Rouge River factory in America).

The bicycle, it has been claimed, did more for the emancipation of the lower classes in Edwardian England than the Communist Manifesto. Wells's little men are typically, like his emblematically named hero Hoopdriver in *The Wheels of Chance* (1896), 'cyclacious coves' (APWS). The Time Machine is, objectively regarded, a super bicycle with a saddle, handle-bars, wheels and some scientifically magical gadgets to propel it through the chronosphere.

It is while spinning more mundanely through the country-side ('exploratious menanderings') on his gleaming roadster that Polly encounters the 'golden girl' sitting on the wall (a wall which, it later transpires, he will never cross). Christabel is, in truth, just a toffee-nosed 13-year-old upper-class brat, parked at boarding school while her parents rule India for its absent empress. For young Polly, intoxicated with the romances of William Morris, he is a knight mounted on his steed ('my friskiacious palfry') and she his lady Gudrun ('Gurdrum'). At her feet, as she dangles some interestingly brown-stockinged legs above his head, he feels 'like one of those old knights . . . who rode about the country looking for dragons and beautiful maidens and chivalresque adventures' (p. 80). Alas, Polly's Pre-Raphaelite vision turns to dust. Christabel is, he discovers, secretly laughing at him. He is not her knight, but an underbred jester – the amusement of an idle hour, irredeemably 'down-stairs'. It cuts him to the heart. On the rebound, he puts his cycling dreams away, accepts his destiny and marries his depressingly unpneumatic cousin, Miriam. Why? Because, as his outlaw uncle Pentstemon says (echoing Dr Moreau) it is the law of the universe: 'It's natr'l – like poaching, or drinking, or wind on the stummik' (p. 113).

Fifteen years of sterile marriage, windy stomach and penuri-ous shopkeeping ensue – years as meaningless as those of a convict doing time on the treadmill. At the moment of truth, when the novel commences, the proprietor of Polly's general outfitter's store is demented by impending bankruptcy, a cold easterly wind, marital incompatibility and chronic dyspepsia. Irritable bowel syndrome is, for Wells (as it was for Thomas Carlyle), as tellingly symptomatic as the entrails of the Roman chicken. Polly is at the end of his tether – at that stage described

in *Ann Veronica* (1909) where 'one main idea' possesses the
heroine: 'She must get away from home, she must assert herself
at once as a person or perish.' An assertion easier, probably,
for the Ibsenite New Woman than the Wellsian Little Man.
At his climax of petty-bourgeois do-or-die, Polly reaches for
the revolutionist's tool. Not dynamite (sadly unavailable in a
British seaside town in 1903), but the paraffin can. One Sunday,
while godly citizens (such as his wife) are at church and the
ungodly (it being, thank the Lord, after six o'clock) in the pub,
Mr Polly torches his shop.

Flames not being, as he would say, controllacious, he also
succeeds in incinerating the fire station next door and most of
the High Street of Sandgate ('Fishbourne' in the novel. Wells
had recently moved out of the Kent seaside town, after nine
years' residence – the novel is not a flattering valediction). Like
other dynamitards – Mr Verloc, in *The Secret Agent* (1907),
for example (a book dedicated by Conrad to Wells) – Polly's
revolutionary plans go badly awry. As the fire rages, he is
inspired by inherent human decency (not being 'one of your
Herculaceous sort', p. 174) to rescue his neighbour's ancient
mother from the inferno. As a result, he finds himself hailed a
hero by the townsfolk whose town, did they but know it, he
has laid waste. Prudently he does not enlighten them.

It was Polly's 'altruistic' intention to cut his throat after his
'bit of arson' leaving his wife, Miriam, with a double insurance
payment to remember him fondly by. That plan also goes awry.
The cut-throat razor, he discovers, is amazingly painful when
it actually cuts throats. And while he is steeling himself to the
necessary second assault on his windpipe, his trousers catch fire
and altruism entirely slips his mind.

Having received his hero's acclaim from the grateful citizens
of Fishbourne, Polly slips away, to go 'on the tramp'. He 'clears
out' (drops out, as a later generation would say). From one
aspect it is divorce, Edwardian style. Miriam will have the fire
insurance to compensate the loss of an unloving and unloved
spouse. She thrives. So does he. Life on the road – as a bachelor
once more – regenerates Polly. His skin bronzes, his beard
sprouts (no more need of cut-throat razor or paper-collar), his

stomach settles, his spirit soars. He finds his journey's end in the riverside Potwell Inn, with its fat, superannuated and amiable Circe, Flo (it is perhaps worth noting that Wells's maternal grandmother was an innkeeper).

Here occurs Mr Polly's third, and decisive, moment of liberation with his epic battle against the satanic 'Uncle Jim'. Polly resolves to stand his ground and fight this monster – 'strategiously' but none the less courageously. He triumphs and will live on, we apprehend, enjoying sunsets, catching dace, washing bottles, ferrying the odd traveller across the river. A happy little man.

Wells's own 'great change' (not to say his divorce in 1895) was achieved less violently than that of his hero. Born in 1866, the son of a talented professional cricketer turned untalented shopkeeper and an 'upper'-servant mother turned shrew, young Bertie Wells should, like his elder brothers, have aspired no higher than thriving in 'trade' had he known his place in life. The 'lucky moment' of long childhood illness opened the world of books to him. He was, it was clear, a precociously brilliant little boy. But that, in the 1870s, was no passport to social promotion. Meritocracy was a century away – unless, of course, you had the good fortune to be born American. Being cleverer than most of the 'gentlemen scholars' in England would not help young Wells any more than it had helped his 'player' father to be a more talented sportsman than the 'gentlemen' cricketers of his time. 'Place' was not that easily overcome.

Leaving school at thirteen, Bertie Wells was apprenticed first as a chemist, then, when that went wrong, as a draper's assistant. He rebelled. There are no more moving letters he wrote than those to his mother in 1883, beseeching her to let him break the indentures she had (at great sacrifice) paid for. He would, he threatened, kill himself did she not allow him to free himself. He wanted more out of life than counter-jumping with the prospect of his own modest 'establishment' if he were lucky.

The British school system was, at this period, recruiting trainee teachers from the lower classes – teachers required to deal with the masses of lower-class pupils enrolled by the 1870

Universal Education Act. The government programme offered
the bookish young Wells (as it would, a little later, D. H.
Lawrence) a narrow opening into higher education and 'the
professions'. In 1884, after a couple of years as a pupil teacher,
Wells went on a scholarship to the Normal School of Science
in South Kensington. There he was exposed both to the great
metropolis and to the full force of late Victorian scientific discovery, principally from T. H. Huxley – 'Darwin's Bulldog'.
'The year I spent in Huxley's class,' he later wrote, 'was, beyond
all question, the most educational year of my life.'[3]

The rest is literary history. Illness (happily again) put an end
to his teaching career. Although he never got a degree, his
'scientific romances', beginning with *The Time Machine* (1895),
proved hugely and lastingly popular. He mined the vein (which
he largely invented) profitably with *The Island of Doctor
Moreau*, *The Invisible Man*, *The War of the Worlds* – all now
classics of the genre.

By the time he wrote *The History of Mr Polly* (1910) Wells
was evolving into a different, or at least more versatile,
kind of novelist. It entailed a turn from cosmically huge
visions to the comically depicted comedy of small lives. Heroes
(typically drapery or chemist's assistants) with names like
Artie Kipps, George Ponderevo, Bert Smallways and, of
course, 'Elfrid' Polly populate these mid-career narratives.
Hovering over them is a draper's assistant that almost was:
Bertie Wells.

The main action of *The History of Mr Polly* is set – as we
can best calculate – around 1903 when Wells, like Polly, was
37 – 'mezzo caminaceous' (APWS). The great stabilities of the
Victorian era had not quite passed. Nor had World War One
yet arrived to kill them off utterly. Wells, of course, saw the
cataclysm coming and described it, with eerie prescience, in
The War in the Air (1908). The imminent mother of all wars is
alluded to, parenthetically, in *The History of Mr Polly* (see note
to page 131). But for the most part the narrative is set in that
Edenic interval of twentieth-century British life, which Philip
Larkin nostalgically lyricizes in his poem, 'MCMXIV':

> And the shut shops, the bleached
> Established names on the sunblinds,
> The farthings and sovereigns,
> And dark-clothed children at play
> Called after kings and queens,
> The tin advertisements
> For cocoa and twist, and the pubs
> Wide open all day;

Before its proprietor burns his shop down, one of those 'bleached names' would be: 'Alfred Polly – Outfitters'. He discovers his Eden, as the ferryman (symbolic figure) at one of those 'wide open all day' pubs, the Potwell Inn.

The last chapter of *The History of Mr Polly* pictures the hero sitting, in pastoral bliss, in the garden of the inn, Flo by his side. 'It was', we are told, 'one of those evenings serenely luminous, amply and atmospherically still' (p. 206). They talk desultorily about things. And then they lapse into contented silence, 'lost in a smooth, still quiet of the mind. A bat flitted by. 'Time we was going in, O' Party,' said Mr Polly, standing up. 'Supper to get. It's as you say, we can't sit here for ever.' (p. 209). Nor could Larkin's 'innocent' moment of British history last for ever. Polly's idyll would, in a few short years, be blasted to pieces in Flanders fields. But while it lasted, the Edwardian moment was lovely.

The amount Wells wrote, between 1903 and 1911, is prodigious in volume and bewildering in its variety. It comprises 'new woman' fiction (*Ann Veronica*), science fiction (*In the Days of the Comet*), 'modern utopias' (rather a lot of them), books of gigantic prophecy (*Anticipations*), invasion fantasies (*The War in the Air*), a surging stream of pamphlets and higher journalism, and – of course – the comedies of ordinary life, such as *The History of Mr Polly*.

One thing connects everything Wells turned his writing hand to at this period: its preoccupation with 'ideas'. He is (with Aldous Huxley close behind) the greatest novelist of ideas of the twentieth century. It is, unfairly perhaps, a second division of British literature. The notion that the novel (Lawrence's 'bright book of life') should be a mere 'vehicle' for extraneous thinking is generally thought to be objectionable. As Lawrence explained: 'If you try to nail anything down in the novel, either it kills the novel, or the novel gets up and walks away with the nail.'

We hate (or, at least, downgrade) fiction that (to paraphrase Keats) has a 'palpable design on us'. Wells's novels are hobnailed with ideas and practically mug the reader with their palpable designs. When he wrote *The History of Mr Polly* (in 1909), Wells was exploding with thought: some of it wholly contradictory. He himself was amused by the turmoil in the Wellsian brainbox – so much so that he could laugh at himself. At the end of Chapter 3, for example, we are told that 'all the elements' of Polly's troubles:

> had been adequately diagnosed by a certain high-browed, spectacled gentleman living at Highbury, wearing a gold pince-nez, and writing for the most part in the beautiful library of the Climax Club. This gentleman did not know Mr Polly personally, but he had dealt with him generally as 'one of those ill-adjusted units that abound in a society that has failed to develop a collective intelligence and a collective will for order commensurate with its complexities'. (p. 45)

Who, one may wonder, is this sage? Physically – as the toweringly high brow and pince-nez clearly signal – it is Sidney Webb, philosopher king of the Fabians. But the wisdom about 'a collective intelligence and a collective will for order' is (who else?) H. G. Wells, from his 1908 tract, *First and Last Things* (Book III, sect. 3):

> Socialism is to me no more and no less than the awakening of a collective consciousness in humanity, a collective will and a collective mind out of which finer individualities may arise forever in a perpetual series of fresh endeavours and fresh achievements for the race.

Wells had just moved to a new house in Highbury, in 1909, and the Reform Club (to which he was elected in 1905) was his HQ when in town. No one among his acquaintance could have failed to pick up the in-joke. It is extended (rather too long, one might think) with a huge self-mocking Wellsian excursus in the following chapter. The point of it all is clear. H. G. Wells is a blooming idiot and a gasbag. Who says? H. G. Wells, that's who.

The major influence in Wells's thoughts about political reform in the years in the run up to writing *The History of Mr Polly* was the Fabian Society. He was invited to join this lobby group of the country's most intellectual (and least effectual) socialists in 1903. They grandly named their movement after the patient Roman general who waited before attacking Hannibal. Wells was many things, often all at once – but never patient. Fabius, after all, did eventually strike – the Fabians, it seemed, never would. The time was never quite propitious. Wells took on the 'Old Gang' – notably Sidney and Beatrice Webb, and G. B. Shaw – and tried, by sheer bludgeoning force of mind, to bring them round to his more activist view of things. He failed and, after five years' struggle, Wells resigned the movement in disgust, just before writing *The History of Mr Polly*.

His personal life was, over the same period, similarly turbulent and ruptured. He had divorced his first wife, Isabel, in 1895, after four years of marriage. He promptly married his second wife, Jane. He believed, throughout life, in 'open union' – free love for freethinkers like himself (but not, alas, his wives). At the time of writing *The History of Mr Polly*, his mistress, Amber Reeves, had just borne him a daughter (in 1914, Rebecca West would bear him a son). H. G. Wells had, unsurprisingly, earned the public reputation of a philanderer. His writing provocatively advocated the freedoms he practised in his personal (but hardly private) life.

All of which makes it surprising that Wells is so reticent about sex in *The History of Mr Polly*. It is, of course, hinted at. The hero's adolescent taste for Rabelais, Boccaccio and Sterne is a clear hint that he has sexual appetites. There must, presumably, have been sexual relations between Mr and Mrs Polly, but there are no offspring (did he use contraceptives?).

Apart from one passing moment when the fall of her dress suggests a fullness of form she does not possess, Miriam has no physical attractions for her spouse. But neither, as we are given to understand, do any others of the female sex (apart from the untouchable Christabel).

Uncle Jim, as we apprehend, has sexual designs of a peculiarly filthy kind on his cousin's daughter little Polly. He is a monster. She is nine. Too young for her namesake saviour. (Interestingly, Christabel was also pre-pubescent: a besotted Mr Polly asks her to wait five years for him.) Mr Polly, as far as the narrative divulges, is as sexually inactive and 'unphiloprogenitous' (APWS) as a worker bee. Strange.

The tamping down of what he elsewhere called 'the red blaze of sex' in *The History of Mr Polly* may have been prudent. Wells, at the time of writing this novel, was under sustained fire as an opponent of marriage and a corrupter of the young. The *Spectator* led the pack. Wells was also having trouble with publishers. Macmillan had turned down the immediately preceding work, *Ann Veronica*, on the grounds of its 'sexual interest'. With *The History of Mr Polly*, Wells moved to a new publisher, Thomas Nelson. They were Scottish, rather strait-laced, and specialized in educational text books. Mr Polly, of course, is no model of uxorious 'rectitudinousness' (APWS). He deserts his wife and lives with another woman. But the ample Flo is, we gather, too old to serve as his mistress (as little Polly is too young). When the couple adjourn indoors, at the end of the narrative, it is, we may confidently assume, to separate bedrooms. The *Spectator*, in its review of the novel (7 May 1910), declared itself well pleased by the reform in Mr Wells's morals (at least as they were proclaimed in his fiction):

> We felt it a duty to speak plainly of the influence that must be exerted by the immoral sophistries of *Ann Veronica*. We are glad to be able to notice a novel by Mr Wells which is free from reproach.

Mrs Grundy, in other words, approved.

The History of Mr Polly offers the reader a rather bumpy narrative ride with frequent and abrupt changes of pace and

focus. At least half of its length is taken up with a funeral, a
wedding and a fist fight. While skipping over decades of Mr
Polly's marital history, Wells will linger, at inordinate length,
on what precisely his hero had on a particular day for lunch
(cold meat and pickles, usually). A vast looping flashback (was
Wells spoofing his friend Conrad?) takes up the first third of
the novel. Fifteen married years happen largely offstage. The
reader is kept waiting most of the novel for Polly's liberation
to happen.

The final phase of the novel – in which the hero finally
transforms himself from a wretched tradesman into a happy
tramp – is worth the wait. There was, at the time Wells was
writing *The History of Mr Polly* (1909) and in the year it was
published (1910), a lively literary debate about 'vagabondage'.
The most romantic view of life on the open road is found in the
novels of Jeffrey Farnol, notably *The Broad Highway* (1910),
whose 'ante scriptum' paints a paradisal picture of vagrancy:

> As I sat of an early summer morning in the shade of a tree, eating
> fried bacon with a tinker, the thought came to me that I might
> some day write a book of my own: a book that should treat of
> the roads and by-roads, of trees, and wind in lonely places, of
> rapid brooks and lazy streams, of the glory of dawn, the glow
> of evening, and the purple solitude of night; a book of wayside
> inns and sequestered taverns; a book of country things and ways
> and people. And the thought pleased me much.

It pleased enough Edwardian readers (few of whom, one
suspects, were homeless) to make Farnol a bestselling author.
Farnol's romanticism is satirized in another novel of 1910,
E. M. Forster's *Howards End*, where Leonard Bast – en-
thused by the writings of Farnol (we deduce) – makes a practical experiment and finds the reality of the broad highway a
singularly depressing experience.

Wells took the more realistic – although still romantically
tinged – line expressed in another bestseller of the period,
W. H. Davies's *The Autobiography of a Supertramp* (1908).
G. B. Shaw, who had been instrumental in getting the book

published, wrote in his preface to it that Davies's account of life on the road:

> made me realize what a slave of convention I have been all my life. When I think of the way I worked tamely for my living when Mr Davies, a free knight of the highway, lived like a pet bird on titbits, I feel that I have been duped out of my natural liberty.[4]

It is 'natural liberty' that Mr Polly, in his modest way, achieves.

It is likely also that Wells was thinking of such other contemporary classics of tramping as Josiah Flynt's *My Life* (1908) and Bart Kennedy's *A Sailor Tramp* (1902 – a favourite text of Mr Polly's, we are told). It would be interesting, too, to know if the greatest laureate of the twentieth-century tramp, Charlie Chaplin, read *Mr Polly*. The influence can certainly be felt.

The literary undergrowth that once surrounded *The History of Mr Polly* has largely died away. But for its contemporaries (not least Wells) it was a novel that conducted a heated conversation with other fiction of the time. One notes, for example, the glancing allusion (see note to p. 131) to William Le Queux's 1906 apocalyptic docu-fantasy, *The Invasion of 1910* (1906), a work that Wells had recently skilfully recast as *The War in the Air* (1908). When Polly forlornly tells Christabel, 'I am a Nobody', most contemporary readers would certainly have recalled Pooter, the nondescript hero of the Grossmiths' *Diary of a Nobody* (1892).

Most aggressively, *The History of Mr Polly* represents a cheerful rewrite of Hardy's anything but cheerful *Jude the Obscure* (1895) and of George Gissing's similarly depressive *Demos* (1886). Wells thought Hardy's novel 'one of the greatest books of his time'.[5] Gissing was an admired friend; Wells dashed to his deathbed, in France in 1903, to pay a novelist's final respects to a fellow novelist. But his vision of the 'Unclassed' (as Gissing called them) is in every respect more optimistic. Wells's heroes do not – like Jude Fawley or Richard Mutimer or Edwin Reardon – go under. They triumph.

Wells inclined to the 'jolly' view of life projected in Jerome

K. Jerome's *Three Men in a Boat* (1889) – a comedy directly
alluded to in the adventures of the 'Three P's' (which includes a
hilariously incompetent boating episode). There were, however,
limits to his jollity. Readers in 1910 would have picked up the
ironic echoes of Richard le Gallienne's 1896 bestseller, *The
Quest of the Golden Girl* (see note to p. 67). The fluffy story
of a young man's walking tour in search of the ideal bride
had offended Wells when he reviewed it on its first appearance.
Golden Girls (as Wells was only too well aware in 1909) are
not easily come by – and discarding them, once the glisten has
faded, is pure hell.

Why read *The History of Mr Polly* when novels like Le
Queux's, Le Gallienne's and even (sadly) most of Gissing's are
forgotten? For the same thing, one would argue, that Mr Polly
eventually finds life worth living for – 'fun'. It is, even for
readers of a later century, a superbly funny novel. Much of its
comedy comes through the ear. Few writers have been able
to reproduce the dialects of their time more hilariously than
H. G. Wells. His expertise is evident from Polly's explosive
opening outburst:

> 'Hole!' said Mr Polly, and then for a change, and with greatly
> increased emphasis: ''*Ole!*' He paused, and then broke out with
> one of his private and peculiar idioms. 'Oh! *Beastly* Silly Wheeze
> of a hole!' (p. 7)

to the sidesplitting sound-reproduction of the hero's wedding
service:

> The officiating clergy sighed deeply, began, and married them
> wearily and without any hitch.
>   'D'bloved we gath'd gether sighto' Gard 'n face this con'gation
> join gather Man Wom Ho Mat'mony which is on'bl state stooted
> by Gard in times mans in 'cency . . .'
>   Mr Polly's thoughts wandered wide and far, and once again
> something like a cold hand touched his heart, and he saw a sweet
> face in sunshine under the shadow of trees.
>   Someone was nudging him. It was Johnson's finger diverting

his eyes to the crucial place in the Prayer Book to which they had
come.

'Wiltou lover, cumfer, oner keeper sickness and health? . . .'

'Say "I will".'

Mr Polly moistened his lips. 'I will,' he said hoarsely. (p. 103)

Vladimir Nabokov, unsurprisingly, was an admirer of this
aspect of Wells's genius as, one can intuit, were James Joyce
and Kingsley Amis. Not that the technique ('cacography'
as it has been called) originates with Wells. One can trace it
back through the nineteenth-century 'Cockney Novelists'
(J. E. Milliken, Edwin Pugh, William Pett Ridge) to Thackeray's
Yellowplush Papers (composed by a comically illiterate, but
indomitably talkative, footman) and, ultimately, to Shakespeare's Dogberry and Verges.

But the 'font et origino' (APWS) of Pollyism is, one need
hardly be told, Dickens. Not the Dickens of *Pickwick Papers*,
but of the novel that most closely draws on the novelist's early
life (and which most closely parallels that of his disciple, Wells)
– *Great Expectations*. One of the many in-jokes in *The History
of Mr Polly* is the hero's instinctive but inexplicable dislike
for the Great Inimitable. Mr Polly, we are told, otherwise an
omnivorous devourer of fiction 'never took at all kindly to
Dickens' (p. 120).

Why not? Because – as he must be dimly aware – Dickens
had his number. There is a moment in *Great Expectations*
(Chapter 27) in which Joe Gargery comes up to town to see
Pip, now a gentleman in lodging with his fellow gent, Herbert
Pocket. 'Have you seen anything of London, yet?' asks Herbert
condescendingly, intending to be kind to the country bumpkin:

> 'Why yes, Sir,' said Joe, 'me and Wopsel went off straight to look
> at the Blacking Ware'us. But we didn't find that it come up to its
> likeness in the red bills at the shop doors: which I meantersay,'
> added Joe in an explanatory manner, 'as it is there drawd too
> architectooralooral.'
>
> I really believe Joe would have prolonged this word (mightily
> expressive to my mind of some architecture that I know) into a

perfect Chorus, but for his attention being providentially attracted by his hat which was toppling.

What is significant is not Joe's *lapsus linguae* but that, as Pip recognizes, his illiterate friend has hit the nail on the head better than he could, with all his newly acquired education. It is the essence of the characteristic Polly coinage. Wrong, but magnificently the *mot juste*.

Ideas, even ideas as radioactively 'advanced' as those of H. G. Wells, have a short half-life. So much has society changed (greater change than even Wells foresaw) that most of the British population under forty will have little more sense of what a draper's assistant is than a pterodactyl. Sadly, even the 'genteel' proletarianisms of Polly and his class are nowadays only normally heard among citizens over the age of fifty. In a few years that richly nuanced dialect will be as dead as Sanskrit. Wells has left one of its finer monuments. And, as a bonus, *The History of Mr Polly* is a novel that remains enjoyable for its 'fun'. Enjoy.

John Sutherland

NOTES

1. Norman and Jean MacKenzie, *The Time Traveller: The Life of H. G. Wells* (London: 1987), p. 7.
2. H. G. Wells, *Kipps* (London: 1905), p. 54.
3. MacKenzie, *The Time Traveller*, 57.
4. W. H. Davies, *Autobiography of a Supertramp* (London: 1908), p. xii.
5. David C. Smith, *H. G. Wells: Desperately Mortal* (London: 1986), p. 39.

Further Reading

The standard biography of Wells (essential to an understanding of the autobiographical elements in *The History of Mr Polly*) is the MacKenzies' *The Time Traveller*. Smith's volume is also informative, as is Wells's *Experiment in Autobiography*. West's book, Michael Coren's *The Invisible Man: The Life and Liberties of H. G. Wells* (London, 1993) and Michael Foot's *H. G.: The History of Mr Wells* (London, 1995) all proved controversial on publication – mainly for their contentions about the author's political and anthropological views. Useful contextual material can be found in Parrinder's *Critical Heritage* and in J. R. Hammond's *An H. G. Wells Companion* (London, 1979). Of particular interest to the study of *The History of Mr Polly* is Royal Gettman's *George Gissing and H. G. Wells* (London, 1960) and Harris Wilson's *Arnold Bennett and H. G. Wells* (London, 1960).

P. P.

Note on the Text

Wells began writing *The History of Mr Polly* in Sandgate, Kent, in May 1909; its composition overlapped with the completion of *Ann Veronica*, published later that year. *Mr Polly* was published in 1910 by Thomas Nelson and Sons in Britain and Duffield & Co. in the United States. Shortly after the book was completed, Wells, like his creation, moved away from Kent: *The New Machiavelli*, his next novel, published later in 1911, also tells the story of a man who runs away from an unsatisfactory career and an unhappy marriage. In *Experiment in Autobiography* (1934), Wells places Polly in the category of 'caricature-individualities', rather than characters, such as Hoopdriver in *The Wheels of Chance* (1896) and Kipps in *Kipps* (1905), and speculates that the book's appeal may not endure if Polly's 'bookish illiteracy' becomes inexplicable to better educated future generations. Wells admits nonetheless in the Preface to the 1924 Atlantic Edition that *Mr Polly* is 'his happiest book and the one he cares for most'; he gives further insight into the material for the book in 'Drawn from Life? H. G. Wells and Mr Polly', in the *Strand Magazine* (August 1928).

The copy text used here is from Volume XVII of the Atlantic edition of the Works of H. G. Wells (London: T. Fisher Unwin, and New York: Scribner's, 1924). The British and American first editions have been consulted to ensure accuracy in preparation of the current text, as have the Essex (1927), which largely reprints the Atlantic text, and Penguin editions (1946) (although these both introduce errors not otherwise present in earlier editions). The typesetter of the Nelson edition seems to

have been baffled in places by the punctuation and capitalization of phonetic cockney: apostrophes for missing letters in
the 1924 text are more sensibly placed. In both first editions,
Mr Polly's age is mistakenly given as thirty-seven the first time
it is mentioned and thirty-five later on. The Atlantic text cor-
rects this and a small number of misprints, also making several
small corrections and changes, such as altering the name of
the Johnsons' maid from Bessie to Betsey. The American first
edition is a little freer of errors than the British; in this version
the title of Chapter 5, 'Romance', is replaced by 'Mr Polly takes
a Vacation'. In revising the text for the Atlantic edition, Wells
seems to have become more conscious in the intervening twelve
years of the novel's historical setting, substituting 'technically
a "wing-poke"' with 'what was called in those days a "wing-
poke"'.

A handful of obvious errors in the Atlantic ('head' for 'heap',
'populous' for 'popular') have been corrected in the present
text, as listed below. The Atlantic begins a new paragraph with
'Perhaps he would get quite a lot of work' on p. 160: in this
instance, the first edition has been followed. Both 'dulness' and
'dullness' occur in the 1924 text: this has been made consistent
throughout. 'Gray' in the Atlantic has been re-anglicized to
'grey', and 'medieval' preferred to 'mediaeval'. 'Shakespeare'
which appears in the first edition, and in other volumes in the
Atlantic edition, has been preferred to the Atlantic's archaic
'Shakespear'. The Atlantic text favours the more transatlantic
'burned' over the first edition's 'burnt'; the present edition has
restored the original spelling, and the slightly peculiar looking
'cosey' and 'nosey' in the Atlantic have also been restored to
their more familiar spellings. Titles of books have also been
italicized where they are not in the copy text, as appropriate.
The Atlantic typesetter has standardized some of Wells's upper-
case comic emphases from the first edition ('Infancy', 'Cousin',
'Man', 'Treat'), somewhat flattening the comic effect of Wells's
style; where appropriate, these have been restored (such
changes are not recorded in the list of emendations below).

The first edition uses commas more sparingly than the Atlantic, even to the detriment of syntax; with only a handful of

corrections, the Atlantic punctuation has thus largely been followed throughout. Housestyling of punctuation and spelling
has been implemented to make the text more accessible to the
reader: single quotation marks (for doubles) with doubles inside
singles as needed; end punctuation placed outside end quotation
marks when appropriate; spaced N-dashes (for the heavier,
longer M-dash) and M-dashes (for double length 2M-dash); 'iz'
spellings (e.g. recognize, not recognise), and 'judgement' rather
than 'judgment'; no full stop after personal titles (Dr, Mr, Mrs)
or chapter titles, which may not follow the capitalization of the
copy text. Accents have been removed from commonly used
foreign words such as 'role', and commas deleted before the
last item of a list. Apostrophes following proper names ending
in 's' have been standardized as, for example, 'Parsons's', rather
than 'Parsons''. In keeping with modern practice and with
house style, hyphenation has been reduced ('gas lamp', 'motor
car', 'dining room'; 'tablecloth', 'wallpaper', 'gasworks', 'downstream'). Words now commonly printed as one, ('someone',
'goodbye', 'upstairs', 'suchlike', 'weekday', 'today') are done
so here. I have retained Wells's spelling of 'Ginn' for 'Djinn'.

SOURCES OF SUBSTANTIVE
EMENDATIONS

N=Nelson, D=Duffield, A=Atlantic

Page:line	Reading adopted	Reading rejected
22:2	further (N)	farther (A)
28:37	heap (N, D)	head (A)
48:2	castors (A, D)	casters (A)
69:28	populous (N)	popular (A)
79:11	Heaven (N)	heaven (A)
82:4	Booom (N)	Boom (A)
93:18	clenched (N)	clinched (A, D)
112:20	disappear (N, D)	disappeared (A)
119:33	beauty! (N, D)	beauty. (A)

124:24	satirize it (N)	satirise it (D), satirise. (A)
134:9	Jujitsu (N)	Jiu-jitsu (A)
142:15	now again? (N, D)	now again (A)
145:30	Hinks's (N)	Hink's (A), Hinks' (D)
147:29	(kiking) (N)	kiking (A), kicking (D)
150:10	wun't (N)	won't (A)

The manuscript for *The History of Mr Polly* can be found in the H. G. Wells archive at the University of Illinois at Champaign-Urbana; Christopher Rolfe's 'From Puttenhanger to Polly: A Note on H. G. Wells's Comic Masterpiece', in *The Wellsian* 5 (1982), provides some useful information about the novel's composition.

I would like to thank the staffs of the British and Durham University Libraries for their assistance in the preparation of the text and Notes for this edition. Dr John Partington supplied some helpful material for the text; I would also like to thank Helen Cornford and Lindeth Vasey at Penguin, and Professor Patrick Parrinder.

Simon J. James

THE HISTORY OF
MR POLLY

Preface to Volume XVII
of the Atlantic Edition
(1924)

Two stories of very unequal value, *The History of Mr Polly*[1] and *Bealby*, are printed together in this volume. Mr Polly was invented in 1909–10; *Bealby* was written in the gloom of impending war and is a desperate attempt to keep cheerful. A small but influential group of critics maintain that *The History of Mr Polly* is the writer's best book. He does not agree with them in that, but certainly it is his happiest book and the one he cares for most. It has many affinities with *Kipps*, but it is done with a surer hand. *Bealby*, as the music hall people say, 'gets the laugh' once or twice, but it betrays a writer intensely irritated by his world; the pompous statesman who falls downstairs, the old popularity-hunting general, a character planned to reflect upon rather than rival Colonel Newcome, Miss Madeleine Philips and the caravan party are all most unlovingly drawn. And Captain Douglas flies off at last, to his army manoeuvres in France and hard work – like an author flying from the end of an irritating task. All the characters in *Bealby* are pelted with derision and misfortune. 'Take that!' says the author as Shonts is torn to pieces and the caravan upsets. But *The History of Mr Polly* is warm with a pervading affection, and even Miriam is left in peace and contentment at last to distribute eggs beyond refreshment to her unwary customers.

Contents

CHAPTER I
BEGINNINGS AND
THE BAZAAR

I

'Hole!' said Mr Polly, and then for a change, and with greatly increased emphasis: ''*Ole!*' He paused, and then broke out with one of his private and peculiar idioms. 'Oh! *Beastly* Silly Wheeze of a hole!'

He was sitting on a stile between two threadbare-looking fields, and suffering acutely from indigestion.

He suffered from indigestion now nearly every afternoon in his life, but as he lacked introspection he projected the associated discomfort upon the world. Every afternoon he discovered afresh that life as a whole, and every aspect of life that presented itself, was 'beastly'. And this afternoon, lured by the delusive blueness of a sky that was blue because the March wind was in the east, he had come out in the hope of snatching something of the joyousness of spring. The mysterious alchemy of mind and body refused, however, to permit any joyousness in the spring.

He had had a little difficulty in finding his cap before he came out. He wanted his cap – the new golf cap – and Mrs Polly must needs fish out his old soft brown felt hat. ''*Ere*'s your 'at,' she said, in a tone of insincere encouragement.

He had been routing among the piled newspapers under the kitchen dresser, and had turned quite hopefully and taken the thing. He put it on. But it didn't feel right. Nothing felt right. He put a trembling hand upon the crown and pressed it on his head, and tried it askew to the right, and then askew to the left.

Then the full sense of the offered indignity came home to

him. The hat masked the upper sinister quarter of his face, and he spoke with a wrathful eye regarding his wife from under the brim. In a voice thick with fury he said, 'I s'pose you'd like me to wear that silly Mud Pie[1] for ever, eh? I tell you I won't. I'm sick of it. I'm pretty near sick of everything, comes to that. . . . Hat!'

He clutched it with quivering fingers. 'Hat!' he repeated. Then he flung it to the ground, and kicked it with extraordinary fury across the kitchen. It flew up against the door and dropped to the ground with its ribbon band half off.

'Shan't go out!' he said, and sticking his hands into his jacket pockets, discovered the missing cap in the right one.

There was nothing for it but to go straight upstairs without a word, and out, slamming the shop door hard.

'Beauty!' said Mrs Polly at last to a tremendous silence, picking up and dusting the rejected headdress. 'Tantrums,' she added. 'I 'aven't patience.' And moving with the slow reluctance of a deeply offended woman, she began to pile together the simple apparatus of their recent meal, for transportation to the scullery sink.

The repast she had prepared for him did not seem to her to justify his ingratitude. There had been the cold pork from Sunday, and some nice cold potatoes, and Rashdall's Mixed Pickles,[2] of which he was inordinately fond. He had eaten three gherkins, two onions, a small cauliflower head and several capers, with every appearance of appetite, and indeed with avidity; and then there had been cold suet pudding to follow, with treacle, and then a nice bit of cheese. It was the pale, hard sort of cheese he liked; red cheese he declared was indigestible. He had also had three big slices of greyish baker's bread, and had drunk the best part of the jugful of beer. . . . But there seems to be no pleasing some people.

'Tantrums!' said Mrs Polly at the sink, struggling with the mustard on his plate, and expressing the only solution of the problem that occurred to her.

And Mr Polly sat on the stile and hated the whole scheme of life – which was at once excessive and inadequate of him. He hated Fishbourne, he hated Fishbourne High Street, he hated

his shop and his wife and his neighbours – every blessed neighbour – and with indescribable bitterness he hated himself.

'Why did I ever get in this silly Hole?' he said. 'Why did I
ever?'

He sat on the stile, and looked with eyes that seemed blurred
with impalpable flaws at a world in which even the spring buds
were wilted, the sunlight metallic, and the shadows mixed with
blue-black ink.

To the moralist I know he might have served as a figure of
sinful discontent, but that is because it is the habit of moralists
to ignore material circumstances – if, indeed, one may speak
of a recent meal as a circumstance – seeing that Mr Polly
was circum.[3] Drink, indeed, our teachers will criticize nowadays both as regards quantity and quality, but neither church
nor state nor school will raise a warning finger between a man
and his hunger and his wife's catering. So on nearly every day
in his life Mr Polly fell into a violent rage and hatred against
the outer world in the afternoon, and never suspected that
it was this inner world to which I am with such masterly delicacy alluding, that was thus reflecting its sinister disorder upon
the things without. It is a pity that some human beings are not
more transparent. If Mr Polly, for example, had been transparent,[4] or even passably translucent, then perhaps he might
have realized, from the Laocoon[5] struggle he would have
glimpsed, that indeed he was not so much a human being as a
civil war.

Wonderful things must have been going on inside Mr Polly.
Oh! wonderful things. It must have been like a badly managed
industrial city during a period of depression; agitators, acts of
violence, strikes, the forces of law and order doing their best,
rushings to and fro, upheavals, the 'Marseillaise', tumbrils, the
rumble and the thunder of the tumbrils. . . .

I do not know why the east wind aggravates life to unhealthy
people. It made Mr Polly's teeth seem loose in his head, and his
skin feel like a misfit, and his hair a dry stringy exasperation. . . .

Why cannot doctors give us an antidote to the east wind?

'Never have the sense to get your hair cut till it's too long,'
said Mr Polly, catching sight of his shadow, 'you blighted,

desgenerated[6] Paintbrush! Ugh!' and he flattened down the projecting tails with an urgent hand.

2

Mr Polly's age was exactly thirty-five years and a half. He was a short, compact figure, and a little inclined to a localized embonpoint. His face was not unpleasing; the features fine, but a trifle too large about the lower half of his face, and a trifle too pointed about the nose to be classically perfect. The corners of his sensitive mouth were depressed. His eyes were ruddy brown and troubled, and the left one was round with more of wonder in it than its fellow. His complexion was dull and yellowish. That, as I have explained, on account of those civil disturbances. He was, in the technical sense of the word, clean-shaved, with a small fallow patch under the right ear and a cut on the chin. His brow had the little puckerings of a thoroughly discontented man, little wrinklings and lumps, particularly over his right eye, and he sat with his hands in his pockets, a little askew on the stile, and swung one leg.

'Hole!' he repeated presently.

He broke into a quavering song: 'Roöötten Beëëastly Silly Hole!'

His voice thickened with rage, and the rest of his discourse was marred by an unfortunate choice of epithets.

He was dressed in a shabby black morning coat and vest; the braid that bound these garments was a little loose in places. His collar was chosen from stock and with projecting corners, what was called in those days a 'wing-poke'; that and his tie, which was new and loose and rich in colouring, had been selected to encourage and stimulate customers – for he dealt in gentlemen's outfitting. His golf cap, which was also from stock and aslant over his eye, gave his misery a desperate touch. He wore brown leather boots – because he hated the smell of blacking.

Perhaps after all it was not simply indigestion that troubled him.

Behind the superficialities of Mr Polly's being moved a larger and vaguer distress. The elementary education he had acquired[7]

had left him with the impression that arithmetic was a fluky
science and best avoided in practical affairs, but even the
absence of book-keeping and a total inability to distinguish
between capital and interest, could not blind him for ever to
the fact that the little shop in the High Street was not paying.
An absence of returns, a constriction of credit, a depleted till –
the most valiant resolves to keep smiling could not prevail for
ever against these insistent phenomena. One might bustle about
in the morning before dinner and in the afternoon after tea and
forget that huge dark cloud of insolvency that gathered and
spread in the background, but it was part of the desolation of
these afternoon periods, those grey spaces of time after meals
when all one's courage had descended to the unseen battles of
the pit, that life seemed stripped to the bone and one saw with
a hopeless clearness.

Let me tell the history of Mr Polly from the cradle to these
present difficulties.

First the infant, mewling and puking in its nurse's arms.[8]

There had been a time when two people had thought Mr Polly
the most wonderful and adorable thing in the world, had kissed
his toenails, saying myum, myum! and marvelled at the exquisite softness and delicacy of his hair, had called to one another
to remark the peculiar distinction with which he bubbled, had
disputed whether the sound he had made was just da, da, or
truly and intentionally dadda, had washed him in the utmost
detail, and wrapped him up in soft warm blankets, and smothered him with kisses. A regal time that was, and four-and-thirty
years ago; and a merciful forgetfulness barred Mr Polly from
ever bringing its careless luxury, its autocratic demands and
instant obedience, into contrast with his present condition of
life. These two people had worshipped him from the crown of
his head to the soles of his exquisite feet. And also they had fed
him rather unwisely, for no one had ever troubled to teach his
mother anything about the mysteries of a child's upbringing
– though, of course, the monthly nurse and the charwoman
gave some valuable hints – and by his fifth birthday the perfect

rhythms of his nice new interior were already darkened with
perplexity. . . .

His mother died when he was seven. He began only to have
distinctive memories of himself in the time when his education
had already begun.

I remember seeing a picture of Education – in some place. I
think it was Education, but quite conceivably it represented the
Empire teaching her Sons, and I have a strong impression that
it was a wall painting upon some public building in Manchester
or Birmingham or Glasgow, but very possibly I am mistaken
about that. It represented a glorious woman, with a wise and
fearless face, stooping over her children, and pointing them to
far horizons. The sky displayed the pearly warmth of a summer
dawn, and all the painting was marvellously bright as if with
the youth and hope of the delicately beautiful children in the
foreground. She was telling them, one felt, of the great prospect
of life that opened before them, of the splendours of sea and
mountain they might travel and see, the joys of skill they might
acquire, of effort and the pride of effort, and the devotions and
nobilities it was theirs to achieve. Perhaps even she whispered
of the warm triumphant mystery of love that comes at last to
those who have patience and unblemished hearts. . . . She was
reminding them of their great heritage as English children,
rulers of more than one-fifth of mankind, of the obligation to
do and be the best that such a pride of empire entails, of their
essential nobility and knighthood, and of the restraints and
charities and disciplined strength that is becoming in knights
and rulers. . . .

The education of Mr Polly did not follow this picture very
closely. He went for some time to a National School, which
was run on severely economical lines to keep down the rates,
by a largely untrained staff; he was set sums to do that he did
not understand, and that no one made him understand; he was
made to read the Catechism and Bible with the utmost industry
and an entire disregard of punctuation or significance; caused to
imitate writing copies and drawing copies; given object lessons
upon sealing wax and silkworms and potato bugs and ginger
and iron and suchlike things; taught various other subjects his

mind refused to entertain; and afterwards, when he was about twelve, he was jerked by his parents to 'finish off' in a private school of dingy aspect and still dingier pretensions, where there were no object lessons, and the studies of book-keeping and French were pursued (but never effectually overtaken) under the guidance of an elderly gentleman, who wore a nondescript gown and took snuff, wrote copperplate, explained nothing, and used a cane with remarkable dexterity and gusto.

Mr Polly went into the National School at six, and he left the private school at fourteen, and by that time his mind was in much the same state that you would be in, dear reader, if you were operated upon for appendicitis by a well-meaning, boldly enterprising, but rather overworked and underpaid butcher boy, who was superseded towards the climax of the operation by a left-handed clerk of high principles but intemperate habits – that is to say, it was in a thorough mess. The nice little curiosities and willingness of a child were in a jumbled and thwarted condition, hacked and cut about – the operators had left, so to speak, all their sponges and ligatures in the mangled confusion – and Mr Polly had lost much of his natural confidence, so far as figures and sciences and languages and the possibilities of learning things were concerned. He thought of the present world no longer as a wonderland of experiences, but as geography and history, as the repeating of names that were hard to pronounce, and lists of products and populations and heights and lengths, and as lists and dates – oh! and Boredom indescribable. He thought of religion as the recital of more or less incomprehensible words that were hard to remember, and of the Divinity as of a limitless Being having the nature of a schoolmaster and making infinite rules, known and unknown, rules that were always ruthlessly enforced, and with an infinite capacity for punishment and – most horrible of all to think of – limitless powers of espial. (So to the best of his ability he did not think of that unrelenting eye.) He was uncertain about the spelling and pronunciation of most of the words in our beautiful but abundant and perplexing tongue – that especially was a pity, because words attracted him, and under happier conditions he might have used them well – he was always doubtful whether

it was eight sevens or nine eights that was sixty-three[9] (he knew
no method for settling the difficulty), and he thought the merit
of a drawing consisted in the care with which it was 'lined in'.
'Lining in' bored him beyond measure.

But the indigestions of mind and body that were to play so
large a part in his subsequent career were still only beginning.
His liver and his gastric juice, his wonder and imagination kept
up a fight against the things that threatened to overwhelm soul
and body together. Outside the regions devastated by the school
curriculum he was still intensely curious. He had cheerful phases
of enterprise, and about thirteen he suddenly discovered reading
and its joys. He began to read stories voraciously, and books
of travel, provided they were also adventurous. He got these
chiefly from the local institute, and he also 'took in' irregularly,
but thoroughly, one of those inspiring weeklies that dull people
used to call 'penny dreadfuls',[10] admirable weeklies crammed
with imagination that the cheap boys' 'comics' of today have
replaced. At fourteen, when he emerged from the valley of the
shadow[11] of education, there survived something – indeed it
survived still, obscured and thwarted, at five-and-thirty – that
pointed, not with a visible and prevailing finger like the finger
of that beautiful woman in the picture, but pointed nevertheless,
to the idea that there was interest and happiness in the world.
Deep in the being of Mr Polly, deep in that darkness, like a
creature which has been beaten about the head and left for
dead but still lives, crawled a persuasion that over and above
the things that are jolly and 'bits of all right', there was beauty,
there was delight; that somewhere – magically inaccessible,
perhaps, but still somewhere – were pure and easy and joyous
states of body and mind.

He would sneak out on moonless winter nights and stare up
at the stars, and afterwards find it difficult to tell his father
where he had been.

He would read tales about hunters and explorers, and
imagine himself riding mustangs as fleet as the wind across
the prairies of Western America, or coming as a conquering
and adored white man into the swarming villages of Central
Africa. He shot bears with a revolver – a cigarette in the other

hand – and made a necklace of their teeth and claws for the chief's beautiful young daughter. Also he killed a lion with a pointed stake, stabbing through the beast's heart as it stood over him.

He thought it would be splendid to be a diver and go down into the dark green mysteries of the sea.

He led stormers against well-nigh impregnable forts, and died on the ramparts at the moment of victory. (His grave was watered by a nation's tears.)

He rammed and torpedoed ships, one against ten.

He was beloved by queens in barbaric lands, and reconciled whole nations to the Christian faith.

He was martyred, and took it very calmly and beautifully – but only once or twice after the Revivalist week. It did not become a habit with him.

He explored the Amazon, and found, newly exposed by the fall of a great tree, a rock of gold.

Engaged in these pursuits he would neglect the work immediately in hand, sitting somewhat slackly on the form and projecting himself in a manner tempting to a schoolmaster with a cane. . . . And twice he had books confiscated.

Recalled to the realities of life, he would rub himself or sigh as the occasion required, and resume his attempts to write as good as copperplate. He hated writing; the ink always crept up his fingers, and the smell of ink offended him. And he was filled with unexpressed doubts. *Why* should writing slope down from right to left? *Why* should downstrokes be thick and upstrokes thin? *Why* should the handle of one's pen point over one's right shoulder?

His copy books towards the end foreshadowed his destiny and took the form of commercial documents. *'Dear Sir,'* they ran, *'Referring to your esteemed order of the 26th ult.,*[12] *we beg to inform you,'* and so on.

The compression of Mr Polly's mind and soul in the educational institutions of his time was terminated abruptly by his father, between his fourteenth and fifteenth birthday. His father – who had long since forgotten the time when his son's little limbs seemed to have come straight from God's hand, and when he had kissed five minute toenails in a rapture of loving tenderness – remarked—

'It's time that dratted boy did something for a living.'

And a month or so later Mr Polly began that career in business that led him at last to the sole proprietorship of a bankrupt outfitter's shop – and to the stile on which he was sitting.

3

Mr Polly was not naturally interested in hosiery and gentlemen's outfitting. At times, indeed, he urged himself to a spurious curiosity about that trade, but presently something more congenial came along and checked the effort. He was apprenticed in one of those large, rather low-class establishments which sell everything from pianos and furniture to books and millinery, a department store, in fact the Port Burdock Drapery Bazaar at Port Burdock, one of the three townships that are grouped round the Port Burdock naval dockyards. There he remained six years. He spent most of the time inattentive to business, in a sort of uncomfortable happiness, increasing his indigestion.

On the whole he preferred business to school; the hours were longer, but the tension was not nearly so great. The place was better aired, you were not kept in for no reason at all, and the cane was not employed. You watched the growth of your moustache with interest and impatience, and mastered the beginnings of social intercourse. You talked and found there were things amusing to say. Also you had regular pocket money, and a voice in the purchase of your clothes, and presently a small salary. And there were girls! And friendship! In the retrospect Port Burdock sparkled with the facets of quite a cluster of remembered jolly times.

('Didn't save much money, though,' said Mr Polly.)

The first apprentices' dormitory was a long, bleak room with six beds, six chests of drawers and looking glasses, and a number of boxes of wood or tin; it opened into a still longer and bleaker room of eight beds, and this into a third apartment with yellow-grained paper and American cloth tables,[13] which was the dining room by day, and the men's sitting and smoking room after nine. Here Mr Polly, who had been an only child, first tasted the joys of social intercourse. To begin with, there were attempts to bully him on account of his refusal to consider face-washing a diurnal duty, but two fights with the apprentices next above him established a useful reputation for choler, and the presence of girl apprentices in the shop somehow raised his standard of cleanliness to a more acceptable level. He didn't, of course, have very much to do with the feminine staff in his department, but he spoke to them casually as he traversed foreign parts of the Bazaar, or got out of their way politely, or helped them to lift down heavy boxes, and on such occasions he felt their scrutiny. Except in the course of business or at meal times the men and women of the establishment had very little opportunity of meeting; the men were in their rooms and the girls in theirs. Yet these feminine creatures, at once so near and so remote, affected him profoundly. He would watch them going to and fro, and marvel secretly at the beauty of their hair, or the roundness of their necks, or the warm softness of their cheeks, or the delicacy of their hands. He would fall into passions for them at dinner time, and try to show devotions by his manner of passing the bread and margarine at tea. There was a very fair-haired, fair-skinned apprentice in the adjacent haberdashery to whom he said 'good morning' every morning, and for a period it seemed to him the most significant event in his day. When she said, 'I do hope it will be fine tomorrow,' he felt it marked an epoch. He had had no sisters, and was innately disposed to worship womankind. But he did not betray as much to Platt and Parsons.

To Platt and Parsons he affected an attitude of seasoned depravity towards the creatures. Platt and Parsons were his contemporary apprentices in departments of the drapery shop, and the three were drawn together into a close friendship by the fact that all their names began with P. They decided they were the three P's, and went about together of an evening with the bearing of desperate dogs. Sometimes when they had money they went into public houses and had drinks. Then they would become more desperate than ever, and walk along the pavement

under the gas lamps arm in arm singing. Platt had a good tenor
voice and had been in a church choir, and so he led the singing.
Parsons had a serviceable bellow, which roared and faded and
roared again very wonderfully. Mr Polly's share was an extraordinary lowing noise, a sort of flat recitative which he called
'singing seconds'. They would have sung catches if they had
known how to do it, but as it was they sang melancholy music
hall songs about dying soldiers and the old folks far away.

They would sometimes go into the quieter residential quarters of Port Burdock, where policemen and other obstacles were
infrequent, and really let their voices soar like hawks, and feel
very happy. The dogs of the district would be stirred to hopeless
emulation, and would keep it up for long after the three P's had
been swallowed up by the night. One jealous brute of an Irish
terrier made a gallant attempt to bite Parsons, but was beaten
by numbers and solidarity.

The three P's took the utmost interest in each other, and
found no other company so good. They talked about everything
in the world; and would go on talking in their dormitory after
the gas was out, until the other men were reduced to throwing
boots. They skulked from their departments in the slack hours
of the afternoon to gossip in the packing room of the warehouse. On Sundays and Bank Holidays they went for long
walks together, talking.

Platt was white-faced and dark, and disposed to undertones
and mystery, and a curiosity about society and the *demi-monde*.
He kept himself *au courant* by reading a penny paper of infinite
suggestion called *Modern Society*. Parsons was of an ampler
build, already promising fatness, with curly hair and a lot of
rolling, rollicking, curly features, and a large, blob-shaped nose.
He had a great memory, and a real interest in literature. He
knew great portions of Shakespeare and Milton by heart, and
would recite them at the slightest provocation. He read everything he could get hold of, and if he liked it he read it aloud; it
did not matter who else liked it. At first Mr Polly was disposed
to be suspicious of this literature, but he was carried away by
Parsons's enthusiasm. The three P's went to a performance of
Romeo and Juliet at the Port Burdock Theatre Royal, and hung

over the gallery fascinated. After that they made a sort of password of, 'Do you bite your thumbs at Us, Sir?'[14] To which the countersign was, 'We bite our Thumbs.'

For weeks the glory of Shakespeare's Verona lit Mr Polly's life. He walked as though he carried a sword at his side and swung a mantle from his shoulders. He went through the grimy streets of Port Burdock with his eye on the first-floor windows – looking for balconies. A ladder in the yard flooded his mind with romantic ideas. Then Parsons discovered an Italian writer, whose name Mr Polly rendered as 'Bocashieu';[15] and after some excursions into that author's remains, the talk of Parsons became infested with the word 'amours', and Mr Polly would stand in front of his hosiery fixtures trifling with paper and string, and thinking of perennial picnics under dark olive trees in the everlasting sunshine of Italy.

And about that time it was that all three P's adopted turn-down collars and large, loose, artistic silk ties, which they tied very much on one side, and wore with an air of defiance; and a certain swashbuckling carriage.

And then came the glorious revelation of that great French-man whom Mr Polly called 'Rabooloose'.[16] The three P's thought the birth feast of Gargantua the most glorious piece of writing in the world – and I am not certain they were wrong; and on wet Sunday evenings, when there was danger of hymn-singing, they would get Parsons to read it aloud.

Towards the several members of the YMCA[17] who shared the dormitory, the three P's always maintained a sarcastic and defiant attitude.

'We have got a perfect right to do what we like in our corner,' Platt maintained. 'You do what you like in yours.'

'But the language,' objected Morrison, the white-faced, earnest-eyed improver,[18] who was leading a profoundly religious life under great difficulties.

'*Language*, man!' roared Parsons; 'why, it's *LITERA-TURE!*'

'Sunday isn't the time for Literature.'

'It's the only time we've got. And besides—'

The horrors of religious controversy would begin. . . .

Mr Polly stuck loyally by the three P's, but in the secret places of his heart he was torn. A fire of conviction burned in Morrison's eyes and spoke in his urgent, persuasive voice. He lived the better life manifestly: chaste in word and deed, industrious, studiously kindly. When the junior apprentice had sore feet and homesickness, Morrison washed the feet and comforted the heart; and he helped other men to get through with their work when he might have gone early – a superhuman thing to do. No one who has not worked for endless days of interminable hours, with scarce a gleam of rest or liberty between the toil and the sleep, can understand how superhuman. Polly was secretly a little afraid to be left alone with this man and the power of the spirit that was in him. He felt watched.

Platt, also struggling with things his mind could not contrive to reconcile, said, 'That confounded hypocrite.'

'He's no hypocrite,' said Parsons; 'he's no hypocrite, O' Man. But he's got no blessed *Joy de Vive*[19] – that's what's wrong with him. Let's go down to the Harbour Arms and see some of those blessed old captains getting drunk.'

'Short of sugar, O' Man,'[20] said Mr Polly, slapping his trouser pocket.

'Oh, *carm* on,' said Parsons; 'always do it on tuppence for a bitter.'

'Lemme get my Pipe on,' said Platt, who had recently taken to smoking with great ferocity. 'Then I'm with you.'

(Pause and struggle.)

'Don't ram it down, O' Man,' said Parsons, watching with knitted brows; 'don't ram it down. Give it Air. Seen my stick, O' Man? Right O.'

And, leaning on his cane, he composed himself in an attitude of sympathetic patience towards Platt's incendiary efforts.

4

Jolly days of companionship they were for the incipient bankrupt on the stile to look back upon.

The interminable working hours of the Bazaar had long since

faded from his memory – except for one or two conspicuous rows and one or two larks – but the rare Sundays and holidays shone out like diamonds among pebbles. They shone with the mellow splendour of evening skies reflected in calm water, and athwart them all went old Parsons bellowing an interpretation of life, gesticulating, appreciating, and making appreciate, expounding books, talking of that mystery of his, the 'Joy de Vive'.

There were some particularly splendid walks on Bank Holidays. The three P's would start on Sunday morning early, and find a room in some modest inn and talk themselves asleep, and return singing through the night, or having an 'argy bargy' about the stars, on Monday evening. They would come over the hill out of the pleasant English countryside in which they had wandered and see Port Burdock spread out below, a network of interlacing streetlamps and shifting tram lights against the black, beacon-gemmed immensity of the harbour waters.

'Back to the collar, O' Man,' Parsons would say. There is no satisfactory plural to 'O' Man', so he always used it in the singular.

'Don't mention it,' said Platt.

And once they got a boat for the whole summer day, and rowed up past the moored ironclads[21] and the black old hulks and the various shipping of the harbour, past a white troopship, and past the trim front and the slips and interesting vistas of the dockyard to the shallow channels and rocky, weedy wildernesses of the upper harbour. And Parsons and Mr Polly had a great dispute and quarrel that day as to how far a big gun could shoot.

The country over the hills behind Port Burdock is all that an old-fashioned, scarcely disturbed English countryside should be. In those days the bicycle was still rare and costly, and the motor car had yet to come and stir up rural serenities. The three P's would take footpaths haphazard across fields, and plunge into unknown winding lanes between high hedges of honeysuckle and dogrose. Greatly daring, they would follow green bridle paths through primrose-studded undergrowths, or wander waist-deep in the bracken of beech woods. About twenty miles from Port Burdock there came a region of hop gardens and hoast-crowned[22] farms; and further on, to be reached only by cheap tickets on Bank Holiday times, was a sterile ridge of very clean roads and red sandpits and pines, and gorse and heather. The three P's could not afford to buy bicycles, and they found boots the greatest item of their skimpy expenditure. They threw appearances to the winds at last, and got ready-made working-men's hobnails.[23] There was much discussion and strong feeling over this step in the dormitory, and the three P's were held to have derogated from the dignity of the emporium.

There is no countryside like the English countryside for those who have learned to love it; its firm yet gentle lines of hill and dale, its ordered confusion of features, its deer parks and downland, its castles and stately houses, its hamlets and old churches, its farms and ricks and great barns and ancient trees, its pools and ponds and shining threads of rivers, its flower-starred hedgerows, its orchards and woodland patches, its village greens and kindly inns. Other countrysides have their pleasant aspects, but none such variety, none that shine so steadfastly throughout the year. Picardy is pink and white and pleasant in the blossom time; Burgundy goes on with its sun-shine and wide hillside and cramped vineyards, a beautiful tune repeated and repeated; Italy gives salitas[24] and wayside chapels, and chestnuts and olive orchards; the Ardennes has its woods and gorges – Touraine and the Rhineland, the wide Campagna with its distant Apennines, and the neat prosperity and mountain backgrounds of South Germany all clamour their especial merits at one's memory. And there are the hills and fields of Virginia, like an England grown very big and slovenly, the woods and big river sweeps of Pennsylvania, the trim New England landscape, a little bleak and rather fine, like the New England mind, and the wide, rough country roads and hills and woodland of New York State. But none of these change scene and character in three miles of walking, nor have so mellow a sunlight nor so diversified a cloudland nor confess the perpetual refreshment of the strong soft winds that blow from off the sea, as our mother England does.

It was good for the three P's to walk through such a land and forget for a time that indeed they had no footing in it all, that they were doomed to toil behind counters in such places as Port Burdock for the better part of their lives. They would forget the customers and shopwalkers and department buyers and everything, and become just happy wanderers in a world of pleasant breezes and songbirds and shady trees.

The arrival at the inn was a great affair. No one, they were convinced, would take them for drapers, and there might be a pretty serving-girl or a jolly old landlady, or what Parsons called a 'bit of character' drinking in the bar.

There would always be weighty inquiries as to what they could have, and it would work out always at cold beef and pickles, or fried ham and eggs and shandygaff,[25] two pints of beer and two bottles of ginger beer foaming in a huge round-bellied jug.

The glorious moment of standing lordly in the inn doorway and staring out at the world, the swinging sign, the geese upon the green, the duckpond, a waiting wagon, the church tower, a sleepy cat, the blue heavens, with the sizzle of the frying audible behind one! The keen smell of the bacon! The trotting of feet bearing the repast; the click and clatter as the tableware is finally arranged! A clean white cloth! 'Ready, Sir!' or 'Ready, Gentlemen!' Better hearing that than 'Forward, Polly! Look sharp!'

The going in! The sitting down! The falling to!

'Bread, O' Man?'

'Right-o!' Don't bag all the crust, O' Man.'

Once a simple-mannered girl in a pink print dress stayed and talked with them as they ate; led by the gallant Parsons they professed to be all desperately in love with her, and courted her to say which she preferred of them, it was so manifest she did prefer one and so impossible to say which it was held her there, until a distant maternal voice called her away. Afterwards, as they left the inn, she waylaid them at the orchard corner and gave them, a little shyly, three yellow-green apples – and wished them to come again some day, and vanished, and reappeared looking after them as they turned the corner, waving a white handkerchief. All the rest of that day they disputed over the signs of her favour, and the next Sunday they went there again.

But she had vanished, and a mother of forbidding aspect afforded no explanations.

If Platt and Parsons and Mr Polly live to be a hundred, they will none of them forget that girl as she stood with a pink flush upon her, faintly smiling and yet earnest, parting the branches of the hedgerows and reaching down, apple in hand. . . .

And once they went along the coast, following it as closely as possible, and so came at last to Fishbourne, that easternmost suburb of Brayling and Hampstead-on-the-Sea.

Fishbourne[26] seemed a very jolly little place to Mr Polly that afternoon. It has a clean sandy beach, instead of the mud and pebbles and coaly defilements of Port Burdock, a row of six bathing-machines,[27] and a shelter on the Parade in which the three P's sat after a satisfying but rather expensive lunch that had included celery. Rows of verandahed villas proffered apartments; they had feasted in a hotel with a porch painted white, and gay with geraniums above; and the High Street, with the old church at the head, had been full of an agreeable afternoon stillness.

'Nice little place for business,' said Platt sagely from behind his big pipe.

It stuck in Mr Polly's memory.

5

Mr Polly was not so picturesque a youth as Parsons. He lacked richness in his voice, and went about in those days with his hands in his pockets looking quietly speculative.

He specialized in slang and the misuse of English, and he played the role of an appreciative stimulant to Parsons. Words attracted him curiously, words rich in suggestion, and he loved a novel and striking phrase. His school training had given him little or no mastery of the mysterious pronunciation of English, and no confidence in himself. His schoolmaster indeed had been both unsound and variable. New words had terror and fascination for him; he did not acquire them, he could not avoid them, and so he plunged into them. His only rule was not to be misled by the spelling. That was no guide anyhow. He avoided every recognized phrase in the language, and mispronounced everything in order that he should be suspected of whim rather than of ignorance.

'Sesquippledan,' he would say. 'Sesquippledan verboo-juice.'[28]

'Eh?' said Platt.

'Eloquent Rapsodooce.'[29]

'Where?' asked Platt.

'In the warehouse, O' Man. All among the tablecloths and blankets. Carlyle. He's reading aloud. Doing the High Froth. Spuming! Windmilling! Waw, waw! It's a sight worth seeing. He'll bark his blessed knuckles one of these days on the fixtures, O' Man.'

He held an imaginary book in one hand and waved an eloquent gesture. 'So too shall every Hero inasmuch as notwithstanding for evermore come back to Reality,' he parodied the enthusiastic Parsons, 'so that in fashion and thereby, upon things and not *under* things articulariously He stands.'[30]

'I should laugh if the Governor dropped on him,' said Platt. 'He'd never hear him coming.'

'The O' Man's drunk with it – fair drunk,' said Polly. '*I* never did. It's worse than when he got on to Raboloose.'

CHAPTER 2
THE DISMISSAL
OF PARSONS

Suddenly Parsons got himself dismissed.

He got himself dismissed under circumstances of peculiar violence, that left a deep impression on Mr Polly's mind. He wondered about it for years afterwards, trying to get the rights of the case.

Parsons's apprenticeship was over; he had reached the status of an Improver, and he dressed the window of the Manchester[1] department. By his own standards he dressed it wonderfully. 'Well, O' Man,' he used to say, 'there's one thing about my position here – I *can* dress a window.'

And when trouble was under discussion he would hold that 'little Fluffums' – which was the apprentices' name for Mr Garvace, the senior partner and managing director of the Bazaar – would think twice before he got rid of the only man in the place who could make a windowful of Manchester goods *tell*.

Then, like many a fellow artist, he fell a prey to theories.

'The art of window-dressing is in its Infancy, O' Man – in its blooming Infancy. All balance and stiffness like a blessed Egyptian picture. No Joy in it, no blooming Joy! Conventional. A shop-window ought to get hold of people, *grip* 'em as they go along. It stands to reason. Grip!'

His voice would sink to a kind of quiet bellow. '*Do* they grip?'

Then, after a pause, a savage roar: '*Naw!*'

'He's got a Heavy on,' said Mr Polly. 'Go it, O' Man; let's have some more of it.'

'Look at old Morrison's dress-stuff windows! Tidy, tasteful, correct, I grant you, but Bleak!' He let out the word reinforced to a shout: 'Bleak!'

'Bleak!' echoed Mr Polly.

'Just pieces of stuff in rows, rows of tidy little puffs, perhaps one bit just unrolled, quiet tickets.'

'Might as well be in church, O' Man,' said Mr Polly.

'A window ought to be exciting,' said Parsons; 'it ought to make you say, "'El-*lo*!" when you see it.'

He paused, and Platt watched him over a snorting pipe.

'Rockcockyo,'[2] said Mr Polly.

'We want a new school of window-dressing,' said Parsons, regardless of the comment. 'A New School! The Port Burdock school. Day after tomorrow I change the Fitzallan Street stuff. This time it's going to be a change. I mean to have a crowd or bust!'

And as a matter of fact he did both.

His voice dropped to a note of self-reproach. 'I've been timid, O' Man. I've been holding myself in. I haven't done myself Justice. I've kept down the simmering, seething, teeming ideas. . . . All that's over now.'

'Over,' gulped Polly.

'Over for good and all, O' Man.'

2

Platt came to Polly, who was sorting up collar boxes. 'O' Man's doing his Blooming Window.'

'What window?'

'What he said.'

Polly remembered.

He went on with his collar boxes with his eye on his senior, Mansfield. Mansfield was presently called away to the counting house, and instantly Polly shot out by the street door, and made a rapid transit along the street front past the Manchester window, and so into the silk room door. He could not linger long, but he gathered joy, a swift and fearful joy, from his brief inspection of Parsons's unconscious back. Parsons had his tail coat off, and was working with vigour; his habit of pulling his waistcoat straps to their utmost brought out all the agreeable promise of corpulence in his youthful frame. He was blowing excitedly and running his fingers through his hair, and then moving with all the swift eagerness of a man inspired. All about his feet and knees were scarlet blankets, not folded, not formally unfolded, but – the only phrase is – shied about. And a great bar sinister[3] of roller towelling stretched across the front of the window on which was a ticket, and the ticket said in bold, black letters: 'LOOK!'

So soon as Mr Polly got into the silk department and met Platt he knew he had not lingered nearly long enough outside.

'Did you see the boards at the back?' said Platt.

Mr Polly hadn't. 'The High Egrugious[4] is fairly On,' he said, and dived down to return by devious subterranean routes to the outfitting department.

Presently the street door opened and Platt, with an air of intense devotion to business assumed to cover his adoption of that unusual route, came in and made for the staircase down to the warehouse. He rolled up his eyes at Polly. 'Oh, *Lor*!' he said, and vanished.

Irresistible curiosity seized Polly. Should he go through the shop to the Manchester department, or risk a second transit outside?

He was impelled to make a dive at the street door.

'Where are you going?' asked Mansfield.

'Lill dog,' said Polly, with an air of lucid explanation, and left him to get any meaning he could from it.

Parsons was worth the subsequent trouble. Parsons really was extremely rich. This time Polly stopped to take it in.

Parsons had made a huge asymmetrical pile of thick white and red blankets twisted and rolled to accentuate their woolly softness heaped up in a warm disorder, with large window tickets inscribed in blazing red letters: 'Cosy Comfort at Cut Prices', and 'Curl up and Cuddle below Cost'. Regardless of the daylight, he had turned up the electric light[5] on that side of the window to reflect a warm glow upon the heap, and be-hind, in pursuit of contrasted bleakness, he was now hanging long strips of grey silesia[6] and chilly-coloured linen dustering.

It was wonderful, but—

Mr Polly decided that it was time he went in. He found Platt in the silk department, apparently on the verge of another plunge into the exterior world. 'Cosy Comfort at Cut Prices,' said Polly. 'Allittritions Artful Aid.'[7]

He did not dare go into the street for the third time, and he was hovering feverishly near the window when he saw the governor, Mr Garvace – that is to say, the managing director of the Bazaar – walking along the pavement after his manner, to assure himself all was well with the establishment he guided.

Mr Garvace was a short, stout man, with that air of modest pride that so often goes with corpulence, choleric and decisive in manner, and with hands that looked like bunches of fingers. He was red-haired and ruddy, and after the custom of such complexions, hairs sprang from the tip of his nose. When he wished to bring the power of the human eye to bear upon an assistant, he projected his chest, knitted one brow, and partially closed the left eyelid.

An expression of speculative wonder overspread the countenance of Mr Polly. He felt he must *see*. Yes, whatever happened, he must *see*.

'Wanttospeak to Parsons, Sir,' he said to Mr Mansfield, and deserted his post hastily, dashed through the intervening departments, and was in position behind a pile of Bolton sheeting as the governor came in out of the street.

'What on earth do you think you are doing with that window, Parsons?' began Mr Garvace.

Only the legs of Parsons and the lower part of his waistcoat and an intervening inch of shirt were visible. He was standing inside the window on the steps, hanging up the last strip of his background from the brass rail along the ceiling. Within, the Manchester shop window was cut off by a partition rather like the partition of an old-fashioned church pew from the general space of the shop. There was a panelled barrier, that is to say, with a little door like a pew door in it. Parsons's face appeared, staring with round eyes at his employer.

Mr Garvace had to repeat his question.

'Dressing it, Sir – on new lines.'

'Come out of it,' said Mr Garvace.

Parsons stared, and Mr Garvace had to repeat his command.

Parsons, with a dazed expression, began to descend the steps slowly.

Mr Garvace turned about. 'Where's Morrison? Morrison!'

Morrison appeared.

'Take this window over,' said Mr Garvace, pointing his bunch of fingers at Parsons. 'Take all this muddle out and dress it properly.'

Morrison advanced and hesitated.

'I beg your pardon, Sir,' said Parsons, with an immense politeness, 'but this is *my* window.'

'Take it all out,' said Mr Garvace, turning away.

Morrison advanced. Parsons shut the door with a click that arrested Mr Garvace.

'Come out of that window,' he said. 'You can't dress it. If you want to play the fool with a window—'

'This window's All Right,' said the genius in window-dressing, and there was a little pause.

'Open the door and go right in,' said Mr Garvace to Morrison.

'You leave that door alone, Morrison,' said Parsons.

Polly was no longer even trying to hide behind the stack of Bolton sheetings. He realized he was in the presence of forces too stupendous to heed him.

'Get him out,' said Mr Garvace.

Morrison seemed to be thinking out the ethics of his position. The idea of loyalty to his employer prevailed with him. He laid his hand on the door to open it; Parsons tried to disengage his hand. Mr Garvace joined his effort to Morrison's. Then the heart of Polly leaped, and the world blazed up to wonder and splendour. Parsons disappeared behind the partition for a moment, and reappeared instantly, gripping a thin cylinder of rolled huckaback.[8] With this he smote at Morrison's head. Morrison's head ducked under the resounding impact, but he clung on and so did Mr Garvace. The door came open, and then Mr Garvace was staggering back, hand to head, his autocratic, his sacred baldness, smitten. Parsons was beyond all control – a strangeness, a marvel. Heaven knows how the artistic struggle had strained that richly endowed temperament. 'Say I can't dress a window, you thundering old Humbug,' he said, and hurled the huckaback at his master. He followed this up by pitching first a blanket, then an armful of silesia, then a window support out of the window into the shop. It leaped into Polly's mind that Parsons hated his own effort and was glad to demolish it. For a crowded second his attention was concentrated upon Parsons, infuriated, active, like a figure of earthquake with its coat off, shying things headlong.

Then he perceived the back of Mr Garvace and heard his gubernatorial voice crying to no one in particular and everybody in general, 'Get him out of the window. He's mad. He's dangerous. Get him out of the window.'

Then a crimson blanket was for a moment over the head of Mr Garvace, and his voice, muffled for an instant, broke out into unwonted expletive.

Then people had arrived from all parts of the Bazaar. Luck, the ledger clerk, blundered against Polly and said, 'Help him!' Somerville from the silks vaulted the counter, and seized a chair by the back. Polly lost his head. He clawed at the Bolton sheeting[9] before him, and if he could have detached a piece he would certainly have hit somebody with it. As it was he simply upset the pile. It fell away from Polly, and he had an impression of somebody squeaking as it went down. It was the sort of impression one disregards. The collapse of the pile of goods just sufficed to end his subconscious efforts to get something to hit somebody with, and his whole attention focussed itself upon the struggle in the window. For a splendid instant Parsons towered up over the active backs that clustered about the shop window door, an active whirl of gesture, tearing things down and throwing them, and then he went under. There was an instant's furious struggle, a crash, a second crash, and the crack of broken plate glass. Then a stillness and heavy breathing.

Parsons was overpowered. . . .

Polly, stepping over scattered pieces of Bolton sheeting, saw his transfigured friend with a dark cut, that was not at present bleeding, on the forehead, one arm held by Somerville and the other by Morrison.

'You – you – you – you annoyed me,' said Parsons, sobbing for breath.

3

There are events that detach themselves from the general stream of occurrences and seem to partake of the nature of revelations. Such was this Parsons affair. It began by seeming grotesque; it ended disconcertingly. The fabric of Mr Polly's daily life was torn, and beneath it he discovered depths and terrors.

Life was not altogether a lark.

The calling in of a policeman seemed at the moment a pantomime touch. But when it became manifest that Mr Garvace was in a fury of vindictiveness, the affair took on a different complexion. The way in which the policeman made a note of everything and aspirated nothing[10] impressed the sensitive mind of Polly profoundly. Polly presently found himself straightening up ties to the refrain of ''E then 'It you on the 'Ead—'Ard.'

In the dormitory that night Parsons became heroic. He sat on the edge of the bed with his head bandaged, packing very slowly and insisting over and over again, 'He ought to have left my window alone, O' Man. He didn't ought to have touched my window.'

Polly was to go to the police court in the morning as a witness. The terror of that ordeal almost overshadowed the tragic fact that Parsons was not only summoned for assault, but 'swapped', and packing his box. Polly knew himself well enough to know he would make a bad witness. He felt sure of one fact only – namely, that ''E then 'It 'Im on the 'Ead—'Ard'. All the rest danced about in his mind now, and how it would dance about on the morrow Heaven only knew. Would there be a cross-examination? Is it perjoocery[11] to make a slip? People did sometimes perjuice themselves. Serious offence.

Platt was doing his best to help Parsons and inciting public opinion against Morrison. But Parsons would not hear of anything against Morrison. 'He was all right, O' Man – according to his lights,' said Parsons. 'It isn't him I complain of.'

He speculated on the morrow. 'I shall 'ave to pay a fine,' he said. 'No good trying to get out of it. It's true I hit him. I hit him' – he paused and seemed to be seeking an exquisite accuracy. His voice sank to a confidential note – 'on the head – about here.'

He answered the suggestion of a bright junior apprentice in a corner of the dormitory. 'What's the Good of a Cross summons,'[12] he replied, 'with old Corks the chemist and Mottishead the house agent and all that lot on the Bench? Humble Pie,[13] that's my meal tomorrow, O' Man. Humble Pie.'

Packing went on for a time.

'But, Lord! what a Life it is!' said Parsons, giving his deep notes scope. 'Ten-thirty-five a man trying to do his Duty, mistaken perhaps, but doing his best; ten-forty, Ruined. Ruined!' He lifted his voice to a shout: 'Ruined!' and dropped it to 'Like an earthquake.'

'Heated altaclation,'[14] said Polly.

'Like a blooming earthquake,' said Parsons, with the notes of a rising wind.

He meditated gloomily upon his future, and a colder chill invaded Polly's mind. 'Likely to get another crib, ain't I? – with assaulted the guv'nor on my reference. . . . I suppose, though, he won't give me refs. Hard enough to get a crib at the best of times,' said Parsons.

'You ought to go round with a show, O' Man,' said Mr Polly.

Things were not so dreadful in the police court as Mr Polly had expected. He was given a seat with other witnesses against the wall of the court, and after an interesting larceny case Parsons appeared and stood, not in the dock, but at the table. By that time Mr Polly's legs, which had been tucked up at first under his chair out of respect to the court, were extended straight before him, and his hands were in his trousers pockets. He was inventing names for the four magistrates on the bench, and had got to 'the Grave and Reverend Signor with the palatial

Boko',[15] when his thoughts were recalled to gravity by the sound of his name. He rose with alacrity, and was fielded by an expert policeman from a brisk attempt to get into the vacant dock. The clerk to the Justices repeated the oath with incredible rapidity.

'Right-o,' said Mr Polly, but quite respectfully, and kissed the book.

His evidence was simple and quite audible after one warning from the superintendent of police to 'speak up'. He tried to put in a good word for Parsons by saying he was 'naturally of a choleraic[16] disposition', but the start and the slow grin of enjoyment upon the face of 'the Grave and Reverend Signor with the palatial Boko' suggested that the word was not so good as he had thought it. The rest of the bench was frankly puzzled, and there were hasty consultations.

'You mean 'E 'as a 'Ot temper,' said the presiding magistrate.

'I mean 'E 'as a 'Ot temper,' replied Polly, magically incapable of aspirates for the moment.

'You don't mean 'E ketches cholera?'

'I mean – he's easily put out.'

'Then why can't you say so?' said the presiding magistrate.

Parsons was bound over.

He came for his luggage while everyone was in the shop, and Garvace would not let him invade the business to say goodbye. When Mr Polly went upstairs for margarine and bread and tea, he slipped on into the dormitory at once to see what was happening further in the Parsons case. But Parsons had vanished. There was no Parsons, no trace of Parsons. His cubicle was swept and garnished. For the first time in his life Polly had a sense of irreparable loss.

A minute or so after Platt dashed in.

'Ugh!' he said, and then discovered Polly. Polly was leaning out of the window, and did not look round. Platt went up to him.

'He's gone already,' said Platt. 'Might have stopped to say goodbye to a chap.'

There was a little pause before Polly replied. He thrust his finger into his mouth and gulped.

'Bit on that beastly tooth of mine,' he said, still not looking at Platt. 'It's made my eyes water something chronic. Anyone might think I'd been Piping my Eye,[17] by the look of me.'

CHAPTER 3

CRIBS

Port Burdock was never the same place for Mr Polly after Parsons had left it. There were no chest notes in his occasional letters, and little of the 'Joy de Vive' got through by them. Parsons had gone, he said, to London, and found a place as warehouseman in a cheap outfitting shop near St Paul's Churchyard, where references were not required. It became apparent as time passed that new interests were absorbing him. He wrote of Socialism and the rights of man, things that had no appeal for Mr Polly. He felt strangers had got hold of his Parsons, were at work upon him, making him into someone else, something less picturesque.... Port Burdock became a dreariness full of faded memories of Parsons, and work a bore. Platt revealed himself alone as a tiresome companion, obsessed by romantic ideas about intrigues and vices and 'society women'.

Mr Polly's depression manifested itself in a general slackness. A certain impatience in the manner of Mr Garvace presently got upon his nerves. Relations were becoming strained. He asked for a rise of salary to test his position, and gave notice to leave when it was refused.

It took him two months to place himself in another situation, and during that time he had quite a disagreeable amount of loneliness, disappointment, anxiety and humiliation.

He went at first to stay with a married cousin who had a house at Easewood. His widowed father had recently given up the music and bicycle shop (with the post of organist at the parish church) that had sustained his home, and was

living upon a small annuity as a guest of his cousin, and growing a little tiresome on account of some mysterious internal
discomfort that the local practitioner diagnosed as imagination. He had aged with unusual rapidity and become ex-
cessively irritable, but the cousin's wife was a born manager,
and contrived to get along with him. Our Mr Polly's status
was that of a guest pure and simple; but after a fortnight of
congested hospitality, in which he wrote nearly a hundred
variants of:

> Sir, – *Reffering to your advt. in the 'Christian World' for an
> Improver in Gents' outfitting, I beg to submit myself for the
> situation. Have had six years' experience.* . . .

and upset a penny bottle of ink over a toilet cover and the
bedroom carpet, his cousin took him for a walk and pointed
out the superior advantages of apartments in London from
which to swoop down upon the briefly yawning vacancy.

'Helpful,' said Mr Polly; 'very helpful, O' Man, indeed. I
might have gone on here for weeks,' and packed.

He got a room in an institution that was partly a benevolent
hostel for men in his circumstances and partly a high-minded
but forbidding coffee house, and a centre for Pleasant Sunday
Afternoons. Mr Polly spent a critical but pleasant Sunday afternoon in a back seat inventing such phrases as:

'Soulful Owner of the Exorbiant Largenial Development.'[1]
An Adam's Apple being in question.

'Earnest Joy.'

'Exultant, Urgent Loogoobuosity.'[2]

A manly young curate, marking and misunderstanding his
preoccupied face and moving lips, came and sat by him and
entered into conversation with the idea of making him feel more
at home. The conversation was awkward and disconnected
for a minute or so, and then suddenly a memory of the Port
Burdock Bazaar occurred to Mr Polly, and with a baffling
whisper of 'Lill dog', and a reassuring nod, he rose up and
escaped, to wander out relieved and observant into the varied
London streets.

He found the collection of men he met waiting about in wholesale establishments in Wood Street and St Paul's Churchyard (where they interview the buyers who have come up from the country) interesting and stimulating, but far too strongly charged with the suggestion of his own fate to be really joyful. There were men in all degrees between confidence and distress, and in every stage between extravagant smartness and the last stages of decay. There were sunny young men full of an abounding and elbowing energy before whom the soul of Polly sank into hate and dismay. 'Smart Juniors,' said Polly to himself, 'full of Smart Juniosity. The Shoveacious Cult.'[3] There were hungry-looking individuals of thirty-five or so, that he decided must be 'Proletelerians' – he had often wanted to find someone who fitted that attractive word. Middle-aged men, 'too old at Forty', discoursed in the waiting rooms on the outlook in the trade; it had never been so bad, they said, while Mr Polly wondered if 'Dejuiced' was a permissible epithet. There were men with an overweening sense of their importance, manifestly annoyed and angry to find themselves still disengaged, and inclined to suspect a plot, and men so faint-hearted one was terrified to imagine their behaviour when it came to an interview. There was a fresh-faced young man with an unintelligent face who seemed to think himself equipped against the world beyond all misadventure by a collar of exceptional height, and another who introduced a note of gaiety by wearing a flannel shirt and a check suit of remarkable virulence. Every day Mr Polly looked round to mark how many of the familiar faces had gone, and the deepening anxiety (reflecting his own) on the faces that remained, and every day some new type joined the drifting shoal. He realized how small a chance his poor letter from Easewood ran against this hungry cluster of competitors at the fountainhead.

At the back of Mr Polly's mind while he made his observations was a disagreeable flavour of a dentist's parlour. At any moment his name might be shouted, and he might have to haul himself into the presence of some fresh specimen of employer, and to repeat once more his passionate protestation of interest in the business, his possession of capacity for zeal – zeal on behalf of anyone who would pay him a salary of twenty-six pounds a year.

The prospective employer would unfold his ideals of the employee. 'I want a smart, willing young man, thoroughly willing, who won't object to take trouble. I don't want a slacker, the sort of fellow who has to be pushed up to his work and held there. I've got no use for him.'

At the back of Mr Polly's mind, and quite beyond his control, the insubordinate phrasemaker would be proffering such combinations as 'Chubby Chops', or 'Chubby Charmer', as suitable for the gentleman, very much as a hat salesman proffers hats.

'I don't think you'd find much slackness about *me*, Sir,' said Mr Polly brightly, trying to disregard his deeper self.

'I want a young man who means getting on.'

'Exactly, Sir. Excelsior.'

'I beg your pardon?'

'I said excelsior, Sir. It's a sort of motto of mine. From Longfellow.[4] Would you want me to serve through?'

The chubby gentleman explained and reverted to his ideals, with a faint air of suspicion. 'Do *you* mean getting on?' he asked.

'I hope so, Sir,' said Mr Polly.

'Get on or get out, eh?'

Mr Polly made a rapturous noise, nodded appreciation, and said indistinctly, '*Quite* my style.'

'Some of my people have been with me twenty years,' said the employer. 'My Manchester buyer came to me as a boy of twelve. You're a Christian?'

'Church of England,' said Mr Polly.

'H'm,' said the employer, a little checked. 'For good all round business work, I should have preferred a Baptist. Still —'

He studied Mr Polly's tie, which was severely neat and businesslike, as became an aspiring outfitter. Mr Polly's conception of his own pose and expression was rendered by that uncontrollable phrasemonger at the back as 'Obsequies Deference'.[5]

'I am inclined,' said the prospective employer in a conclusive manner, 'to look up your reference.'

Mr Polly stood up abruptly.

'Thank you,' said the employer, and dismissed him.

'Chump chops! How about chump chops?' said the phrase-monger with an air of inspiration.

'I hope then to hear from you, Sir,' said Mr Polly in his best salesman manner.

'If everything is satisfactory,' said the prospective employer.

2

A man whose brain devotes its hinterland to making odd phrases and nicknames out of ill-conceived words, whose conception of life is a lump of auriferous rock to which all the value is given by rare veins of unbusinesslike joy, who reads Boccaccio and Rabelais and Shakespeare with gusto, and uses 'Stertoraneous Shover' and 'Smart Junior' as terms of bitterest opprobrium, is not likely to make a great success under modern business conditions. Mr Polly dreamt always of picturesque and mellow things, and had an instinctive hatred of the strenuous life. He would have resisted the spell of ex-President Roosevelt, or General Baden Powell, or Mr Peter Keary, or the late Dr Samuel Smiles quite easily – I doubt if even Mr St Loe Strachey could have inspired him; and he loved Falstaff and Hudibras and coarse laughter, and the Old England of Washington Irving and the memory of Charles the Second's courtly days.[6] His progress was necessarily slow. He did not get rises; he lost situations; there was something in his eye employers did not like; he would have lost his places oftener if he had not been at times an exceptionally brilliant salesman, rather carefully neat, and a slow but very fair window-dresser.

He went from situation to situation, he invented a great wealth of nicknames, he conceived enmities and made friends – but none so richly satisfying as Parsons. He was frequently, but mildly and discursively, in love; and sometimes he thought of that girl who had given him a yellow-green apple. He had an idea amounting to a flattering certainty whose youthful freshness it was had stirred her to self-forgetfulness. And sometimes he thought of Fishbourne sleeping prosperously in the sun. And he had moods of discomfort and lassitude and ill-temper, due to the beginnings of indigestion.

Various forces and suggestions came into his life and swayed him for longer and shorter periods.

He went to Canterbury and came under the influence of Gothic architecture. There was a blood affinity between Mr Polly and the Gothic; in the Middle Ages he would, no doubt, have sat upon a scaffolding and carved out penetrating and none too flattering portraits of church dignitaries upon the capitals; and when he strolled, with his hands behind his back, along the cloisters behind the cathedral, and looked at the rich grass plot in the centre, he had the strangest sense of being at home – far more than he had ever been at home before. 'Portly capons,'[7] he used to murmur to himself, under the impression that he was naming a characteristic type of medieval churchman.

He liked to sit in the nave during the service, and look through the great gates at the candles and choristers, and listen to the organ-sustained voices, but the transepts he never penetrated because of the charge for admission. The music and the long vista of the fretted roof filled him with a vague and mystical happiness that he had no words, even mispronounceable words, to express. But some of the smug monuments in the aisles got a wreath of epithets; 'metrorious urnfuls', 'funererial claims', 'dejected angelosity',[8] for example. He wandered about the precincts, and speculated about the people who lived in the ripe and cosy houses of grey stone that cluster there so comfortably. Through green doors in high stone walls he caught glimpses of level lawns and blazing flowerbeds; mullioned windows revealed shaded reading-lamps and disciplined shelves of brown bound books. Now and then a dignitary in gaiters would pass him ('Portly capon'), or a drift of white-robed choirboys cross a distant arcade and vanish in a doorway, or the pink and cream of some girlish dress flit like a butterfly across the cool still spaces of the place. Particularly he responded to the ruined arches of the Benedictines' Infirmary and the view of Bell Harry Tower[9] from the school-building. He was stirred to read the *Canterbury Tales*, but he could not get on with Chaucer's old-fashioned English, it fatigued his attention, and he would have given all the storytelling very readily for a few adventures on the road. He wanted these nice people to live more and yarn less. He appreciated the wife of Bath very keenly. He would have liked to have known that woman.

At Canterbury too, he first, to his knowledge, saw Americans.

His shop did a good class trade in Westgate Street, and he would see them go by on the way to stare at Chaucer's 'Chequers'[10] and then turn down Mercery Lane to Prior Goldstone's gate. It impressed him that they were always in a kind of quiet hurry, and very determined and methodical people – much more so than any English he knew.

'Cultured Rapacacity,' he tried.

'Vorocious Return to the Heritage.'[11]

He would expound them incidentally to his attendant apprentices. He had overheard a little lady putting her view to a friend near the Christchurch gate. The accent and intonation had hung in his memory, and he would reproduce them more or less accurately. 'Now, does this Marlowe monument[12] really and truly *matter?*' he had heard the little lady inquire. 'We've no time for side shows and second-rate stunts, Mamie. We want just the Big Simple Things of the place, just the Broad Elemental Canterbury Praposition. What is it saying to us? I want to get right hold of that, and then have tea in the very room that Chaucer did, and hustle to get that four-eighteen train back to London. . . .'

He would go over these specious phrases, finding them full of an indescribable flavour. 'Just the Broad Elemental Canterbury Praposition,' he would repeat. . . .

He would try to imagine Parsons confronted with Americans. For his own part, he knew himself to be altogether inadequate. . . .

Canterbury was the most congenial situation Mr Polly ever found during these wander years, albeit a very desert so far as companionship went.

3

It was after Canterbury that the universe became really disagreeable to Mr Polly. It was brought home to him not so much
vividly as with a harsh ungainly insistence that he was a failure
in his trade. It was not the trade he ought to have chosen,
though what trade he ought to have chosen was by no means
clear.

He made great but irregular efforts, and produced a forced
smartness that, like a cheap dye, refused to stand sunshine. He
acquired a sort of parsimony also, in which acquisition he was
helped by one or two phases of absolute impecuniosity. But he
was hopeless in competition against the naturally gifted, the
born hustlers, the young men who meant to get on.

He left the Canterbury place very regretfully. He and another
commercial gentleman took a boat one Sunday afternoon at
Sturry-on-the-Stour, when the wind was in the west, and sailed
it very happily eastward for an hour. They had never sailed a
boat before, and it seemed a simple and wonderful thing to do.
When they turned, they found the river too narrow for tacking,
and the tide running out like a sluice. They battled back to
Sturry in the course of six hours (at a shilling the first hour and
sixpence for each hour afterwards), rowing a mile in an hour
and a half or so, until the turn of the tide came to help them,
and then they had a night walk to Canterbury, and found
themselves remorselessly locked out.

The Canterbury employer was an amiable, religious-spirited
man, and he would probably not have dismissed Mr Polly if
that unfortunate tendency to phrase things had not shocked
him. 'A Tide's a Tide, Sir,' said Mr Polly, feeling that things
were not so bad. 'I've no lune-attic power to alter *that*.'

It proved impossible to explain to the Canterbury employer
that this was not a highly disrespectful and blasphemous
remark.

'And besides, what good are you to me this morning, do you
think?' said the Canterbury employer, 'with your arms pulled
out of their sockets?'

So Mr Polly resumed his observations in the Wood Street

warehouses once more, and had some dismal times. The shoal of fish waiting for the crumbs of employment seemed larger than ever.

He took counsel with himself. Should he 'chuck' the out-fitting? It wasn't any good for him now, and presently, when he was older and his youthful smartness had passed into the dullness of middle age, it would be worse. What else could he do?

He could think of nothing. He went one night to a music hall and developed a vague idea of a comic performance; the comic men seemed violent rowdies, and not at all funny; but when he thought of the great pit of the audience yawning before him, he realized that his was an altogether too delicate talent for such a use. He was impressed by the charm of selling vegetables by auction in one of those open shops near London Bridge, but admitted upon reflection his general want to technical know-ledge. He made some inquiries about emigration, but none of the colonies were in want of shop assistants without capital. He kept up his attendance in Wood Street.

He subdued his ideal of salary by the sum of five pounds a year, and was taken into a driving establishment in Clapham, which dealt chiefly in ready-made suits, fed its assistants in an underground dining room, and kept open until twelve on Saturdays. He found it hard to be cheerful there. His fits of indigestion became worse, and he began to lie awake at night and think. Sunshine and laughter seemed things lost for ever; picnics, and shouting in the moonlight.

The chief shopwalker took a dislike to him and nagged him. 'Nar, then, Polly!' 'Look alive, Polly!' became the burden of his days. 'As Smart a chap as you could have,' said the chief shopwalker, 'but no *Zest*. No *Zest*! No *Vim*! What's the matter with you?'

During his night vigils Mr Polly had a feeling. . . . A young rabbit must have very much the feeling when, after a youth of gambolling in sunny woods and furtive jolly raids upon the growing wheat and exciting triumphant bolts before ineffectual casual dogs, it finds itself at last for a long night of floundering effort and perplexity in a net – for the rest of its life.

He could not grasp what was wrong with him. He made enormous efforts to diagnose his case. Was he really just a 'lazy slacker' who ought to 'buck up'? He couldn't find it in him to believe it. He blamed his father a good deal – it is what fathers are for – in putting him to a trade he wasn't happy to follow, but he found it impossible to say what he ought to have followed. He felt there had been something stupid about his school, but just where that came in he couldn't say. He made some perfectly sincere efforts to 'buck up' and 'shove' ruthlessly. But that was infernal – impossible. He had to admit himself miserable with all the misery of a social misfit, and with no clear prospect of more than the most incidental happiness ahead of him. And for all his attempts at self-reproach and self-discipline he felt at bottom that he wasn't at fault.

As a matter of fact all the elements of his troubles had been adequately diagnosed by a certain high-browed, spectacled gentleman living at Highbury, wearing a gold pince-nez, and writing for the most part in the beautiful library of the Climax Club. This gentleman did not know Mr Polly personally, but he had dealt with him generally as 'one of those ill-adjusted units that abound in a society that has failed to develop a collective intelligence and a collective will for order commensurate with its complexities'.[13]

But phrases of that sort had no appeal for Mr Polly.

CHAPTER 4

MR POLLY AN ORPHAN

I

Then a great change was brought about in the life of Mr Polly by the death of his father. His father died suddenly – the local practitioner still clung to his theory that it was imagination he suffered from, but compromised in the certificate with the appendicitis that was then so fashionable – and Mr Polly found himself heir to a debatable number of pieces of furniture in the house of his cousin near Easewood Junction, a family Bible, an engraved portrait of Garibaldi and a bust of Mr Gladstone,[1] an invalid gold watch, a gold locket formerly belonging to his mother, some minor jewellery and bric-à-brac, a quantity of nearly valueless old clothes, and an insurance policy and money in the bank amounting altogether to the sum of three hundred and fifty-five pounds.

Mr Polly had always regarded his father as an immortal, as an eternal fact; and his father, being of a reserved nature in his declining years, had said nothing about the insurance policy. Both wealth and bereavement therefore took Mr Polly by surprise, and found him a little inadequate. His mother's death had been a childish grief and long forgotten, and the strongest affection in his life had been for Parsons. An only child of sociable tendencies turns his back a good deal upon home; and the aunt who had succeeded his mother was an economist and furniture-polisher, a knuckle-rapper and sharp silencer: no friend for a slovenly little boy. He had loved other little boys and girls transitorily; none had been frequent and familiar enough to strike deep roots in his heart; and he had grown up with a tattered and dissipated affectionateness that was becoming wildly shy. His father had always been a stranger, an irritable stranger with exceptional powers of intervention and comment, and an air of being disappointed about his offspring. It was shocking to lose him; it was like an unexpected hole in the universe, the writing of 'Death' upon the sky; but it did not at first tear Mr Polly's heartstrings so much as rouse him to a pitch of vivid attention.

He came down to the cottage at Easewood in response to an urgent telegram, and found his father already dead. His Cousin Johnson received him with much solemnity, and ushered him upstairs to look at a stiff, straight, shrouded form with a face unwontedly quiet and, it seemed by reason of its pinched nostrils, scornful.

'Looks peaceful,' said Mr Polly, disregarding the scorn to the best of his ability.

'It was a merciful relief,' said Mr Johnson.

There was a pause.

'Second – second Departed I've ever seen – not counting mummies,' said Mr Polly, feeling it necessary to say something.

'We did all we could.'

'No doubt of it, O' Man,' said Mr Polly.

A second long pause followed, and then, to Mr Polly's great relief, Johnson moved towards the door.

Afterwards Mr Polly went for a solitary walk in the evening light, and as he walked, suddenly his dead father became real to him. He thought of things far away down the perspective of memory – of jolly moments when his father had skylarked with a wildly excited little boy; of a certain annual visit to the Crystal Palace pantomime, full of trivial glittering incidents and wonders; of his father's dread back while customers were in the old, minutely known shop. It is curious that the memory which seemed to link him nearest to the dead man was the memory of a fit of passion. His father had wanted to get a small sofa up the narrow winding staircase from the little room behind the shop to the bedroom above, and it had jammed. For a time his father had coaxed, and then groaned like a soul in torment, and given way to blind fury; had sworn, kicked and struck at the offending piece of furniture, and finally, with an

immense effort, wrenched it upstairs, with considerable incidental damage to lath and plaster and one of the castors.
That moment when self-control was altogether torn aside, the
shocked discovery of his father's perfect humanity, had left
a singular impression on Mr Polly's queer mind. It was as if
something extravagantly vital had come out of his father and
laid a warmly passionate hand upon his heart. He remembered
that now very vividly, and it became a clue to endless other
memories that had else been dispersed and confusing.

A weakly wilful being, struggling to get obdurate things
round impossible corners – in that symbol Mr Polly could
recognize himself and all the trouble of humanity.

He hadn't had a particularly good time, poor old chap; and
now it was all over – finished. . . .

Johnson was the sort of man who derives great satisfaction
from a funeral; a melancholy, serious, practical-minded man of
five-and-thirty, with great powers of advice. He was the up-line
ticket clerk[2] at Easewood Junction, and felt the responsibilities
of his position. He was naturally thoughtful and reserved, and
greatly sustained in that by an innate rectitude of body and an
overhanging and forward inclination of the upper part of his
face and head. He was pale but freckled, and his dark grey eyes
were deeply set. His lightest interest was cricket, but he did not
take that lightly. His chief holiday was to go to a cricket match,
which he did as if he was going to church; and he watched
critically, applauded sparingly, and was darkly offended by
any unorthodox play. His convictions upon all subjects were
taciturnly inflexible. He was an obstinate player of draughts
and chess, and an earnest and persistent reader of *The British
Weekly*.[3] His wife was a pink, short, wilfully smiling, managing,
ingratiating, talkative woman, who was determined to be pleasant, and take a bright, hopeful view of everything, even when
it was not really bright and hopeful. She had large, blue, expressive eyes and a round face, and she always spoke of her
husband as Harold. She addressed sympathetic and considerate
remarks about the deceased to Mr Polly in notes of brisk
encouragement. 'He was really quite cheerful at the end,' she
said several times, with congratulatory gusto; 'quite cheerful.'

She made dying seem almost agreeable.

Both these people were resolved to treat Mr Polly very well, and to help his exceptional incompetence in every possible way; and after a simple supper of ham and bread and cheese and pickles and cold apple tart and small beer had been cleared away, they put him into the armchair almost as though he was an invalid, and sat on chairs that made them look down upon him, and opened a directive discussion of the arrangements for the funeral. After all, a funeral is a distinct social opportunity, and rare when you have no family and few relations, and they did not want to see it spoiled and wasted.

'You'll have a hearse, of course,' said Mrs Johnson; 'not one of them combinations, with the driver sitting on the coffin. Disrespectful, I think they are. I can't fancy how people can bring themselves to be buried in combinations.' She flattened her voice in a manner she used to intimate aesthetic feeling. 'I *do* like them glass hearses,' she said. 'So refined and nice they are.'

'Podger's hearse you'll have,' said Johnson conclusively; 'it's the best in Easewood.'

'Everything that's right and proper,' said Mr Polly.

'Podger's ready to come and measure at any time,' said Johnson.

'Then you'll want a mourners' carriage or two, according to whom you're going to invite,' said Mr Johnson.

'Didn't think of inviting anyone,' said Mr Polly.

'Oh, you'll *have* to ask a few friends,' said Mr Johnson. 'You can't let your father go to his grave without asking a few friends.'

'Funeral baked meats, like,'⁴ said Mr Polly.

'Not baked; but of course you'll have to give them something. Ham and chicken's very suitable. You don't want a lot of cooking, with the ceremony coming into the middle of it. I wonder who Alfred ought to invite, Harold? Just the immediate relations. One doesn't want a Great Crowd of People, and one doesn't want not to show respect.'

'But he hated our relations – most of them.'

'He's not hating them *now*,' said Mr Johnson; 'you may be

sure of that. It's just because of that I think they ought to come, all of them – even your Aunt Mildred.'

'Bit vulturial,⁵ isn't it?' said Mr Polly unheeded.

'Wouldn't be more than twelve or thirteen people if they *all* came,' said Mr Johnson.

'We could have everything put out ready in the back room, and the gloves and whisky in the front room; and while we were all at the – ceremony, Bessie could bring it all into the front room on a tray, and put it out nice and proper. There'd have to be whisky, and sherry-or-port for the ladies. . . .'

'Where'll you get your mourning?' asked Johnson abruptly.

Mr Polly had not yet considered this by-product of sorrow. 'Haven't thought of it yet, O' Man.'

A disagreeable feeling spread over his body, as though he was blackening as he sat. He hated black garments.

'I suppose I must *have* mourning,' he said.

'*Well!*' said Johnson, with a solemn smile.

'Got to see it through,' said Mr Polly indistinctly.

'If I were you,' said Johnson, 'I should get ready-made trousers. That's all you really want. And a black satin tie, and a top hat with a deep mourning band. And gloves.'

'Jet cuff links he ought to have – as chief mourner,' said Mrs Johnson.

'Not obligatory,' said Johnson.

'It shows respect,' said Mrs Johnson.

'It shows respect, of course,' said Johnson.

And then Mrs Johnson went on with the utmost gusto to the details of the 'casket', while Mr Polly sat more and more deeply and droopingly into the armchair, assenting with a note of protest to all they said. After he had retired for the night he remained for a long time perched on the edge of the sofa, which was his bed, staring at the prospect before him. 'Chasing the o' man about to the last,' he said.

He hated the thought and elaboration of death as a healthy animal must hate it. His mind struggled with unwonted social problems.

'Got to put 'em away somehow, I suppose,' said Mr Polly. 'Wish I'd looked him up a bit more while he was alive.'

2

Bereavement came to Mr Polly before the realization of opulence and its anxieties and responsibilities. That only dawned upon him on the morrow – which chanced to be Sunday – as he walked with Johnson before church time about the tangle of struggling building enterprise that constituted the rising urban district of Easewood. Johnson was off duty that morning, and devoted the time very generously to the admonitory discussion of Mr Polly's worldly outlook.

'Don't seem to get the hang of the business somehow,' said Mr Polly. 'Too much blooming humbug in it for my way of thinking.'

'If I were you,' said Mr Johnson, 'I should push for a first-class place in London – take almost nothing and live on my reserves. That's what I should do.'

'Come the Heavy,' said Mr Polly.

'Get a better-class reference.'

There was a pause. 'Think of investing your money?' asked Johnson.

'Hardly got used to the idea of having it yet, O' Man.'

'You'll have to do something with it. Give you nearly twenty pounds a year if you invest it properly.'

'Haven't seen it yet in that light,' said Mr Polly defensively.

'There's no end of things you could put it into.'

'It's getting it out again I shouldn't feel sure of. I'm no sort of Fiancianier.[6] Sooner back horses.'

'I wouldn't do that if I were you.'

'Not my style, O' Man.'

'It's a nest-egg,' said Johnson.

Mr Polly made an indeterminate noise.

'There's building societies,' Johnson threw out in a speculative tone. Mr Polly, with detached brevity, admitted there were.

'You might lend it on mortgage,' said Johnson. 'Very safe form of investment.'

'Shan't think anything about it – not till the o' man's underground,' said Mr Polly, with an inspiration.

They turned a corner that led towards the junction.

'Might do worse,' said Johnson, 'than put it into a small shop.'

At the moment this remark made very little appeal to Mr Polly. But afterwards it developed. It fell into his mind like some obscure seed and germinated.

'These shops aren't in a bad position,' said Johnson.

The row he referred to gaped in the late painful stage in building before the healing touch of the plasterer assuages the roughness of the brickwork. The space for the shop yawned an oblong gap below, framed above by an iron girder; 'Windows and fittings to suit tenant', a board at the end of the row promised; and behind was the door space and a glimpse of stairs going up to the living rooms above. 'Not a bad position,' said Johnson, and led the way into the establishment. 'Room for fixtures there,' he said, pointing to the blank wall.

The two men went upstairs to the little sitting room (or best bedroom it would have to be) above the shop. Then they descended to the kitchen below.

'Rooms in a new house always look a bit small,' said Johnson.

They came out of the house again by the prospective back door, and picked their way through builders' litter across the yard space to the road again. They drew nearer the junction to where a pavement and shops already open and active formed the commercial centre of Easewood. On the opposite side of the way the side door of a flourishing little establishment opened, and a man and his wife and a small boy in a sailor suit came into the street. The wife was a pretty woman in brown, with a floriferous straw hat, and the group was altogether very Sundayfied and shiny and spick and span. The shop itself had a large plate glass window whose contents were now veiled by a buff blind on which was inscribed in scrolly letters: 'Rymer, Pork Butcher and Provision Merchant', and then with voluptuous elaborations, 'The World Famed Easewood Sausage'.

Greetings were exchanged between Mr Johnson and this distinguished comestible.

'Off to church already?' said Johnson.

'Walking across the fields to Little Dorington,' said Mr Rymer.

'Very pleasant walk,' said Johnson.

'Very,' said Mr Rymer.

'Hope you'll enjoy it,' said Mr Johnson.

'That chap's done well,' said Johnson, *sotto voce*,[7] as they went on. 'Came here with nothing – practically, four years ago. And as thin as a lath. Look at him now!

'He's worked hard, of course,' said Johnson, improving the occasion.

Thought fell between the cousins for a space.

'Some men can do one thing,' said Johnson, 'and some another. . . . For a man who sticks to it there's a lot to be done in a shop.'

3

All the preparations for the funeral ran easily and happily under Mrs Johnson's skilful hands. On the eve of the sad occasion she produced a reserve of black sateen, the kitchen steps, and a box of tin tacks, and decorated the house with festoons and bows of black in the best possible taste. She tied up the knocker with black crape, and put a large bow over the corner of the steel engraving of Garibaldi, and swathed the bust of Mr Gladstone that had belonged to the deceased with inky swathings. She turned round the two vases that had views of Tivoli and the Bay of Naples, so that these rather brilliant landscapes were hidden and only the plain blue enamel showed, and she anticipated the long contemplated purchase of a tablecloth for the front room, and substituted a violet-purple cover for the now very worn and faded raptures and roses in plushette that had hitherto done duty there. Everything that loving consideration could do to impart a dignified solemnity to her little home was done.

She had released Mr Polly from the irksome duty of issuing invitations, and as the moments of assembly drew near she sent him and Mr Johnson out into the narrow, long strip of garden at the back of the house, to be free to put a finishing touch or so to her preparations. She sent them out together because she had a queer little persuasion at the back of her mind that Mr

Polly wanted to bolt from his sacred duties, and there was no way out of the garden except through the house.

Mr Johnson was a steady, successful gardener, and particularly good with celery and peas. He walked slowly along the narrow path down the centre, pointing out to Mr Polly a number of interesting points in the management of peas, wrinkles neatly applied and difficulties wisely overcome, and all that he did for the comfort and propitiation of that fitful but rewarding vegetable. Presently a sound of nervous laughter and raised voices from the house proclaimed the arrival of the earlier guests, and the worst of that anticipatory tension was over.

When Mr Polly re-entered the house he found three entirely strange young women with pink faces, demonstrative manners and emphatic mourning engaged in an incoherent conversation with Mrs Johnson. All three kissed him with great gusto after the ancient English fashion. 'These are your Cousins Larkins,' said Mrs Johnson. 'That's Annie' (unexpected hug and smack), 'that's Miriam' (resolute hug and smack), 'and that's Minnie' (prolonged hug and smack).

'Right-o,' said Mr Polly, emerging a little crumpled and breathless from the hearty introduction. 'I see.'

'Here's Aunt Larkins,' said Mrs Johnson, as an elderly and stouter edition of the three young women appeared in the doorway.

Mr Polly backed rather faint-heartedly, but Aunt Larkins was not to be denied. Having hugged and kissed her nephew resoundingly, she gripped him by the wrists and scanned his features. She had a round, sentimental, freckled face. 'I should 'ave known 'im anywhere,' she said, with fervour.

'Hark at Mother!' said the cousin called Annie. 'Why, she's never set eyes on him before.'

'I should 'ave known 'im anywhere,' said Mrs Larkins, 'for Lizzie's child. You've got her eyes! It's a Resemblance! And as for never seeing 'im—I've *dandled* him, Miss Imperence. I've dandled him.'

'You couldn't dandle him now, Ma!' Miss Annie remarked, with a shriek of laughter.

All the sisters laughed at that. 'The things you say, Annie!' said Miriam, and for a time the room was full of mirth.

Mr Polly felt it incumbent upon him to say something. 'My dandling days are over,' he said.

The reception of this remark would have convinced a far more modest character than Mr Polly that it was extremely witty.

Mr Polly followed it up by another one almost equally good. 'My turn to dandle,' he said, with a sly look at his aunt, and convulsed everyone.

'Not me,' said Mrs Larkins, taking his point, '*thank* you,' and achieved a climax.

It was queer, but they seemed to be easy people to get on with anyhow. They were still picking little ripples and giggles of mirth from the idea of Mr Polly dandling Aunt Larkins when Mr Johnson, who had answered the door, ushered in a stooping figure, who was at once hailed by Mrs Johnson as 'Why! Uncle Pentstemon!'[8] Uncle Pentstemon was rather a shock. His was an aged rather than venerable figure. Time had removed the hair from the top of his head and distributed a small dividend of the plunder in little bunches carelessly and impartially over the rest of his features; he was dressed in a very big, old frock-coat and a long, cylindrical top hat, which he had kept on; he was very much bent, and he carried a rush basket, from which protruded coy intimations of the lettuces and onions he had brought to grace the occasion. He hobbled into the room, re-sisting the efforts of Johnson to divest him of his various encumbrances, halted, and surveyed the company with an expression of profound hostility, breathing hard. Recognition quickened in his eyes.

'*You* here?' he said to Aunt Larkins, and then, 'You *would* be. . . . These your gals?'

'They are,' said Aunt Larkins, 'and better gals —'

'That Annie?' asked Uncle Pentstemon, pointing a horny thumbnail.

'Fancy your remembering her name!'

'She mucked up my mushroom bed, the baggage!' said Uncle Pentstemon ungenially, 'and I give it to her to rights. Trounced

her I did – fairly. *I* remember her. Here's some green stuff for
you, Grace. Fresh it is, and wholesome. I shall be wanting the
basket back, and mind you let me have it. . . . Have you nailed
him down yet? Ah! You always was a bit in front of what was
needful.'

His attention was drawn inward by a troublesome tooth, and
he sucked at it spitefully. There was something potent about
this old man that silenced everyone for a moment or so. He
seemed a fragment from the ruder agricultural past of our race,
like a lump of soil among things of paper. He put his packet
of earthy vegetables very deliberately on the new violet tablecloth, removed his hat carefully, and dabbled his brow, and
wiped out his hat brim with an abundant crimson and yellow
pocket handkerchief.

'I'm glad you were able to come, Uncle,' said Mrs Johnson.

'Oh, I *came*,' said Uncle Pentstemon. 'I *came*.'

He turned on Mrs Larkins. 'Gals in service?' he asked.

'They aren't, and they won't be,' said Mrs Larkins.

'No,' he said, with infinite meaning, and turned his eye on
Mr Polly.

'You Lizzie's boy?' he said.

Mr Polly was spared much self-exposition by the tumult
occasioned by further arrivals.

'Ah! here's May Punt!' said Mrs Johnson, and a small woman
dressed in the borrowed mourning of a large woman, and
leading a very small, fair-haired, sharp-nosed, observant little
boy – it was his first funeral – appeared, closely followed by
several friends of Mrs Johnson who had come to swell the
display of respect, and who left only vague, confused impressions upon Mr Polly's mind. (Aunt Mildred, who was an
unexplained family scandal, had declined Mrs Johnson's hospitality to the relief of everyone who understood – as Mrs
Johnson intimated – though who understood, and what, as my
headmaster used to say, Mr Polly could form no idea.)

Everybody was in profound mourning, of course – mourning
in the modern English style, with the dyer's handiwork only
too apparent, and hats and jackets of the current cut. There
was very little crape, and the costumes had none of the goodness

and specialization and genuine enjoyment of mourning for
mourning's sake that a similar Continental gathering would
have displayed. Still that congestion of strangers in black sufficed to stun and confuse Mr Polly's impressionable mind. It
seemed to him much more extraordinary than anything he had
expected.

'Now, gals,' said Mrs Larkins, 'see if you can help,' and the
three daughters became confusingly active between the front
room and the back.

'I hope everyone'll take a glass of sherry and a biscuit,' said
Mrs Johnson. 'We don't stand on ceremony,' and a decanter
appeared in the place of Uncle Pentstemon's vegetables.

Uncle Pentstemon had refused to be relieved of his hat;
he sat stiffly down on a chair against the wall, with that venerable headdress between his feet, watching the approach of anyone jealously. 'Don't you go squashing my hat,' he said.
Conversation became confused and general. Uncle Pentstemon
addressed himself to Mr Polly.

'You're a little chap,' he said; 'a puny little chap. I never did
agree to Lizzie marrying him, but I suppose bygones must be
bygones now. I suppose they made you a clerk or something.'

'Outfitter,' said Mr Polly.

'I remember. Them girls pretend to be dressmakers.'

'They *are* dressmakers,' said Mrs Larkins across the room.

'I *will* take a glass of sherry,' he remarked; and then mildly
to Mr Polly, 'They 'old to it, you see.'

He took the glass Mrs Johnson handed him, and poised it
critically between a horny finger and thumb. 'You'll be paying
for this,' he said to Mr Polly. 'Here's *to* you. . . . Don't you go
treading on my hat, young woman. You brush your skirts
against it and you take a shillin' off its value. It ain't the sort of
'at you see nowadays.'

He drank noisily.

The sherry presently loosened everybody's tongue, and the
opening coldness passed.

'There ought to have been a *postmortem*,'[9] Polly heard
Mrs Punt remarking to one of Mrs Johnson's friends, and
Miriam and another were lost in admiration of Mrs Johnson's

decorations. 'So very nice and refined,' they were both repeating
at intervals.

The sherry and biscuits were still being discussed when Mr
Podger, the undertaker, arrived, a broad, cheerfully sorrowful,
clean-shaven little man, accompanied by a melancholy-faced
assistant. He conversed for a time with Johnson in the passage
outside. The sense of his business stilled the rising waves of
chatter and carried off everyone's attention in the wake of his
heavy footsteps to the room above.

4

Things crowded upon Mr Polly. Everyone, he noticed, took
sherry with a solemn avidity, and a small portion even was
administered sacramentally to the Punt boy. There followed
a distribution of black kid gloves, and much trying-on and
humouring of fingers. '*Good* gloves,' said one of Mrs Johnson's
friends. 'There's a little pair there for Willie,' said Mrs Johnson
triumphantly. Everyone seemed gravely content with the amaz-
ing procedure of the occasion. Presently Mr Podger was picking
Mr Polly out as Chief Mourner to go with Mrs Johnson, Mrs
Larkins and Annie in the first mourning carriage.

'Right-o,' said Mr Polly, and repented instantly of the alacrity
of the phrase.

'There'll have to be a walking party,' said Mrs Johnson cheerfully. 'There's only two coaches. I dare say we can put in six in
each, but that leaves three over.'

There was a generous struggle to be pedestrian, and the two
other Larkins girls, confessing coyly to tight new boots and
displaying a certain eagerness, were added to the contents of
the first carriage.

'It'll be a squeeze,' said Annie.

'*I* don't mind a squeeze,' said Mr Polly.

He decided privately that the proper phrase for the result of
that remark was 'Hysterial catechunations'.[10]

Mr Podger re-entered the room from a momentary super-
vision of the bumping business that was now proceeding down
the staircase.

'Bearing up,' he said cheerfully, rubbing his hands together. 'Bearing up!'

That stuck very vividly in Mr Polly's mind, and so did the close-wedged drive to the churchyard, bunched in between two young women in confused dull and shiny black, and the fact that the wind was bleak and that the officiating clergyman had a cold, and sniffed between his sentences. The wonder of life! The wonder of everything! What had he expected that this should all be so astoundingly different?

He found his attention converging more and more upon the Larkins cousins. The interest was reciprocal. They watched him with a kind of suppressed excitement and became risible with his every word and gesture. He was more and more aware of their personal quality. Annie had blue eyes, and a red, attractive mouth, a harsh voice, and a habit of extreme liveliness that even this occasion could not suppress; Minnie was fond, extremely free about the touching of hands and suchlike endearments; Miriam was dark and quieter than her sisters and regarded him earnestly. Mrs Larkins was very happy in her daughters, and they had the naive affectionateness of those who see few people and find a strange cousin a wonderful outlet. Mr Polly had never been very much kissed, and it made his mind swim. He did not know for the life of him whether he liked or disliked all or any of the Larkins cousins. It was rather attractive to make them laugh anyhow; they laughed at anything.

There they were tugging at his mind, and the funeral tugging at his mind too, and the sense of himself as Chief Mourner in a brand-new silk hat with a broad mourning band. He watched the ceremony and missed his responses, and strange feelings twisted at his heartstrings.

5

Mr Polly walked back to the house because he wanted to be alone. Miriam and Minnie would have accompanied him, but finding Uncle Pentstemon beside the Chief Mourner they went on in front.

'You're wise,' said Uncle Pentstemon.

'Glad you think so,' said Mr Polly, rousing himself to talk.

'I likes a bit of walking before a meal,' said Uncle Pentstemon, and made a kind of large hiccup. 'That sherry rises,' he remarked. 'Grocer's stuff, I expect.'

He went on to ask how much the funeral might be costing, and seemed pleased to find Mr Polly didn't know.

'In that case,' he said impressively, 'it's pretty certain to cost more'n you expect, my boy.'

He meditated for a time. 'I've seen a mort of undertakers,'[11] he declared; 'a mort of undertakers.'

The Larkins girls attracted his attention.

'Lets lodgin's and chars,' he commented. 'Leastways she goes out to cook dinners. And *look* at 'em! Dressed up to the nines. If it ain't borryd clothes, that is. And they goes out to work at a factory!'

'Did you know my father much, Uncle Pentstemon?' asked Mr Polly.

'Couldn't stand Lizzie throwin' herself away like that,' said Uncle Pentstemon, and repeated his hiccup on a larger scale.

'That *weren't* good sherry,' said Uncle Pentstemon, with the first note of pathos Mr Polly had detected in his quavering voice.

The funeral in the rather cold wind had proved wonderfully appetizing, and every eye brightened at the sight of the cold collation that was now spread in the front room. Mrs Johnson was very brisk, and Mr Polly, when he re-entered the house, found the party sitting down.

'Come along, Alfred,' cried the hostess cheerfully. 'We can't very well begin without you. Have you got the bottled beer ready to open, Bessie? Uncle, you'll have a drop of whisky, I expect.'

'Put it where I can mix for myself; I can't bear wimmin's mixing,' said Uncle Pentstemon, placing his hat very carefully out of harm's way on the bookcase.

There were two cold boiled chickens, which Johnson carved with great care and justice, and a nice piece of ham, some brawn, and a steak and kidney pie, a large bowl of salad and several sorts of pickles, and afterwards some cold apple tart, jam roll, and a good piece of Stilton cheese, lots of bottled beer, some lemonade for the ladies, and milk for Master Punt: a very bright and satisfying meal. Mr Polly found himself seated between Mrs Punt, who was much preoccupied with Master Punt's table manners, and one of Mrs Johnson's school friends, who was exchanging reminiscences with Mrs Johnson of school-days and news of how various common friends had changed and married. Opposite him was Miriam and another of the early Johnson circle, and also he had brawn to carve, and there was hardly room for the helpful Bessie to pass behind his chair, so that altogether his mind would have been amply distracted from any mortuary broodings, even if a wordy warfare about the education of the modern young woman had not sprung up between Uncle Pentstemon and Mrs Larkins, and threatened for a time, in spite of a word or so in season[12] from Johnson, to wreck all the harmony of the sad occasion.

The general effect was after this fashion:

First an impression of Mrs Punt on the right, speaking in a refined undertone: 'You didn't, I suppose, Mr Polly, think to 'ave your poor dear father *postmortemed*?'

Lady on the left side, breaking in: 'I was just reminding Grace of the dear dead days beyond recall.'[13]

Attempted reply to Mrs Punt: 'Didn't think of it for a moment. Can't give you a piece of this brawn, can I?'

Fragment from the left: 'Grace and Beauty they used to call us, and we used to sit at the same desk.'

Mrs Punt, breaking out suddenly: 'Don't *swaller* your fork, Willie – You see, Mr Polly, I used to have a young gentleman, a medical student, lodging with me —'

Voice from down the table with a large softness: ''Am, Elfred? I didn't give you very much 'am.'

Bessie became evident at the back of Mr Polly's chair, struggling wildly to get past. Mr Polly did his best to be helpful. 'Can you get past? Lemme sit forward a bit. Urr-oo! Right-o!'

Lady to the left going on valiantly and speaking to everyone who cared to listen, while Mrs Johnson beamed beside her: 'There she used to sit as bold as brass, and the fun she used to make of things no one *could* believe – knowing her now. She used to make faces at the mistress through the —'

Mrs Punt, keeping steadily on: 'The contents of the stummik at any rate *ought* to be examined.'

Voice of Mrs Johnson: 'Elfrid, pass the mustid down.'

Miriam, leaning across the table: 'Elfrid!'

'Once she got us all kept in. The whole school!'

Miriam, more insistently: 'Elfrid!'

Uncle Pentstemon, raising his voice defiantly: 'Trounce 'er again I would if she did as much now. That I would. Dratted mischief!'

Miriam, catching Mr Polly's eye: 'Elfrid! This lady knows Canterbury. I been telling her you been there.'

Mr Polly: 'Glad you know it.'

The lady, shouting: 'I like it.'

Mrs Larkins, raising her voice: 'I won't 'ave my girls spoken of, not by nobody, old *or* young.'

POP! imperfectly located.

Mr Johnson, at large: '*Ain't* the beer up! It's the 'eated room.'

Bessie: ''Scuse me, Sir, passing so soon again, but –' Rest inaudible. Mr Polly, accommodating himself: 'Urr-oo! Right? Right-o!'

The knives and forks, probably by some secret common agreement, clash and clatter together, and drown every other sound.

'Nobody 'ad the least idea 'ow 'e died – nobody. . . . Willie, don't *golp* so. You ain't in a 'urry, are you? You don't want to ketch a train, or anything – golping like that!'

'D'you remember, Grace, 'ow one day we 'ad writing lesson . . .'

'Nicer girls no one ever 'ad – though I say it who shouldn't.'

Mrs Johnson, in a shrill, clear, hospitable voice: 'Harold, won't Mrs Larkins 'ave a teeny bit more fowl?'

Mr Polly was rising to the situation. 'Or some brawn, Mrs Larkins?' Catching Uncle Pentstemon's eye: 'Can't send *you* some brawn, Sir?'

'Elfrid!'

Loud hiccup from Uncle Pentstemon, momentary consternation, followed by giggle from Annie.

The narration at Mr Polly's elbow pursued a quiet but relentless course. 'Directly the new doctor came in, he said, "Everything must be took out and put in spirits – everything."'

Willie – audible ingurgitation.

The narration on the left was flourishing up to a climax. 'Ladies, she sez, dip their pens *in* their ink and keep their noses out of it.'

'Elfrid!' persuasively.

'Certain people may cast snacks[14] at other people's daughters, never having had any of their own, though two poor souls of wives dead and buried through their goings on —'

Johnson, ruling the storm: 'We don't want old scores dug up on such a day as this —'

'Old scores you may call them, but worth a dozen of them that put them to their rest, poor dears.'

'Elfrid!' with a note of remonstrance.

'If you choke yourself, my lord, not another mouthful do you 'ave. No nice puddin'! Nothing!'

'And kept us in, she did, every afternoon for a week!'

It seemed to be the end, and Mr Polly replied, with an air of being profoundly impressed, 'Really!'

'Elfrid!' a little disheartened.

'And then they 'ad it! They found he'd swallowed the very key to unlock the drawer —'

'Then don't let people go casting snacks!'

'*Who's* casting snacks?'

'Elfrid! This lady wants to know, 'ave the Prossers left Canterbury?'

'No wish to make myself disagreeable, not to God's 'umblest worm —'

'Alf, you aren't very busy with that brawn up there!'

And so on for the hour.

The general effect upon Mr Polly at the time was at once confusing and exhilarating; but it led him to eat copiously and carelessly, and long before the end, when after an hour and a quarter a movement took the party, and it pushed away its cheese plates and rose sighing and stretching from the remains of the repast, little streaks and bands of dyspeptic irritation and melancholy were darkening the serenity of his mind.

He stood between the mantelshelf and the window – the blinds were up now – and the Larkins sisters clustered about him. He battled with the oncoming depression, and forced himself to be extremely facetious about two noticeable rings on Annie's hand. 'They ain't real,' said Annie coquettishly. 'Got 'em out of a prize packet.'

'Prize packet in trousers, I expect,' said Mr Polly, and awakened inextinguishable laughter.

'Oh, the Things you say!' said Minnie, slapping his shoulder.

Something he had quite extraordinarily forgotten came into his head.

'Bless my heart!' he cried, suddenly serious.

'What's the matter?' asked Johnson.

'Ought to have gone back to shop three days ago. They'll make no end of a row!'

'Lor, you *are* a Treat!' said Cousin Annie, and screamed with laughter at a delicious idea. 'You'll get the Chuck,' she said.

Mr Polly made a convulsive grimace at her.

'I'll die!' she said. 'I don't believe you care a bit.'

Feeling a little disorganized by her hilarity and a shocked expression that had come to the face of Cousin Miriam, he made some indistinct excuse and went out through the back room and scullery into the little garden. The cool air and a very slight drizzle of rain was a relief – anyhow. But the black mood of the replete dyspeptic had come upon him. His soul darkened hopelessly. He walked with his hands in his pockets down the path between the rows of exceptionally cultured peas, and unreasonably, overwhelmingly, he was smitten by sorrow for his father. The heady noise and muddle and confused excitement of the feast passed from him like a curtain drawn away. He thought of that hot and angry and struggling creature who had tugged and sworn so foolishly at the sofa upon the twisted staircase, and who was now lying still and hidden at the bottom of a wall-sided, oblong pit, beside the heaped gravel that would presently cover him. The stillness of it! the wonder of it! the infinite reproach! Hatred for all these people – all of them – possessed Mr Polly's soul.

'Hen-witted gigglers,' said Mr Polly.

He went down to the fence, and stood with his hands on it, staring away at nothing. He stayed there for what seemed a long time. From the house came a sound of raised voices that subsided, and then Mrs Johnson calling for Bessie.

'Gowlish gusto,' said Mr Polly. 'Jumping it in. Funererial Games.[15] Don't hurt him, of course. Doesn't matter to *him*. . . .'

Nobody missed Mr Polly for a long time.

When at last he reappeared among them his eye was almost grim, but nobody noticed his eye. They were looking at watches, and Johnson was being omniscient about trains. They seemed to discover Mr Polly afresh just at the moment of parting, and said a number of more or less appropriate things. But Uncle Pentstemon was far too worried about his rush basket, which had been carelessly mislaid, he seemed to think with larcenous intentions, to remember Mr Polly at all. Mrs Johnson had tried to fob him off with a similar but inferior basket – his own had one handle mended with string according to a method of peculiar virtue and inimitable distinction known only to himself – and the old gentleman had taken her attempt as the gravest reflection upon his years and intelligence. Mr Polly was left very largely to the Larkins trio. Cousin Minnie became shameless, and kept kissing him goodbye – and then finding out it wasn't time to go. Cousin Miriam seemed to think her silly, and caught Mr Polly's eye sympathetically. Cousin Annie ceased to giggle, and lapsed into a nearly sentimental state. She said with real feeling that she had enjoyed the funeral more than words could tell.

CHAPTER 5
ROMANCE

I

Mr Polly returned to Clapham from the funeral celebrations prepared for trouble, and took his dismissal in a manly spirit.

'You've merely antiseparated me[1] by a hair,' he said politely.

And he told them in the dormitory that he meant to take a little holiday before his next crib, though a certain inherited reticence suppressed the fact of the legacy.

'You'll do that all right,' said Ascough, the head of the boot shop. 'It's quite the fashion just at present. Six Weeks in Wonderful Wood Street. They're running excursions. . . .'

'A little holiday'; that was the form his sense of wealth took first – it made a little holiday possible. Holidays were his life, and the rest merely adulterated living. And now he might take a little holiday and have money for railway fares and money for meals, and money for inns. But – He wanted someone to take the holiday with.

For a time he cherished a design of hunting up Parsons, getting him to throw up his situation, and going with him to Stratford-on-Avon and Shrewsbury, and the Welsh mountains and the Wye, and a lot of places like that, for a really gorgeous, careless, illimitable old holiday of a month. But, alas! Parsons had gone from the St Paul's Churchyard outfitter's long ago, and left no address.

Polly tried to think he would be almost as happy wandering alone, but he knew better. He had dreamt of casual encounters with delightfully interesting people by the wayside – even romantic encounters. Such things happened in Chaucer and 'Bocashiew'; they happened with extreme facility in Mr

Richard le Gallienne's very detrimental book, *The Quest of the Golden Girl*,[2] which he had read at Canterbury; but he had no confidence they would happen in England – to him.

When, a month later, he came out of the Clapham side door at last into the bright sunshine of a fine London day, with a dazzling sense of limitless freedom upon him, he did nothing more adventurous than order the cabman to drive to Waterloo, and there take a ticket to Easewood.

He wanted – what *did* he want most in life? I think his distinctive craving is best expressed as fun – fun in companionship. He had already spent a pound or two upon three select feasts to his fellow assistants, sprat suppers they were, and there had been a great and very successful Sunday pilgrimage to Richmond, by Wandsworth and Wimbledon's open common, a trailing garrulous company walking about a solemnly happy host, to wonderful cold meat and salad at the Roebuck, a bowl of punch, punch! and a bill to correspond; but now it was a weekday, and he went down to Easewood with his bag and portmanteau in a solitary compartment, and looked out of the window upon a world in which every possible congenial seemed either toiling in a situation or else looking for one with a gnawing and hopelessly preoccupying anxiety. He stared out of the window at the exploitation roads of suburbs and rows of houses all very much alike, either emphatically and impatiently TO LET, or full of rather busy unsocial people. Near Wimbledon he had a glimpse of golf links, and saw two elderly gentlemen, who, had they chosen, might have been gentlemen of grace and leisure, addressing themselves to smite hunted little white balls great distances with the utmost bitterness and dexterity. Mr Polly could not understand them.

Every road, he remarked as freshly as though he had never observed it before, was bordered by inflexible palings or iron fences or severely disciplined hedges. He wondered if perhaps abroad there might be beautifully careless, unenclosed highroads. Perhaps after all the best way of taking a holiday is to go abroad.

He was haunted by the memory of what was either a halfforgotten picture or a dream; a carriage was drawn up by the wayside and four beautiful people, two men and two women graciously dressed, were dancing a formal ceremonious dance, full of bows and curtseys, to the music of a wandering fiddler they had encountered. They had been driving one way and he walking another – a happy encounter with this obvious result. They might have come straight out of happy Theleme, whose motto is: 'Do what thou wilt.'[3] The driver had taken his two sleek horses out; they grazed unchallenged; and he sat on a stone clapping time with his hands while the fiddler played. The shade of the trees did not altogether shut out the sunshine, the grass in the wood was lush and full of still daffodils, the turf they danced on was starred with daisies.

Mr Polly, dear heart! firmly believed that things like that could and did happen – somewhere. Only it puzzled him that morning that he never saw them happening. Perhaps they happened south of Guilford! Perhaps they happened in Italy. Perhaps they ceased to happen a hundred years ago. Perhaps they happened just round the corner – on weekdays when all good Mr Pollys are safely shut up in shops. And so dreaming of delightful impossibilities until his heart ached for them, he was rattled along in the suburban train to Johnson's discreet home and the briskly stimulating welcome of Mrs Johnson.

2

Mr Polly translated his restless craving for joy and leisure into Harold Johnsonese by saying that he meant to look about him for a bit before going into another situation. It was a decision Johnson very warmly approved. It was arranged that Mr Polly should occupy his former room and board with the Johnsons in consideration of a weekly payment of eighteen shillings. And the next morning Mr Polly went out early and reappeared with a purchase, a safety bicycle[4] which he proposed to study and master in the sandy lane below the Johnsons' house. But over the struggles that preceded his mastery it is humane to draw a veil.

And also Mr Polly bought a number of books; Rabelais for his own, and *The Arabian Nights*, the works of Sterne, a pile of *Tales from Blackwood*,[5] cheap in a second-hand book-shop, the plays of William Shakespeare, a second-hand copy of Belloc's *Path to Rome*,[6] an odd volume of *Purchas his Pilgrimes*[7] and *The Life and Death of Jason*.[8]

'Better get yourself a good book on book-keeping,' said Johnson, turning over perplexing pages.

A belated spring, to make up for lost time, was now advancing with great strides. Sunshine and a stirring wind were poured out over the land, fleets of towering clouds sailed upon urgent tremendous missions across the blue sea of heaven, and presently Mr Polly was riding a little unstably along unfamiliar Surrey roads, wondering always what was round the next corner, and marking the blackthorn and looking out for the first white flower buds of the may. He was perplexed and distressed, as indeed are all right-thinking souls, that there is no may in early May.

He did not ride at the even pace sensible people use, who have marked out a journey from one place to another, and settled what time it will take them. He rode at variable speeds, and always as though he was looking for something that missing left life attractive still, but a little wanting in significance. And sometimes he was so unreasonably happy he had to whistle and sing, and sometimes he was incredibly, but not at all painfully, sad. His indigestion vanished with air and exercise, and it was quite pleasant in the evening to stroll about the garden with Johnson and discuss plans for the future. Johnson was full of ideas. Moreover, Mr Polly had marked the road that led to Stamton, that rising populous suburb; and as his bicycle legs grew strong his wheel, with a sort of inevitableness, carried him towards a row of houses in a back street in which his Larkins cousins made their home together.

He was received with great enthusiasm.

The street was a dingy little street, a *cul-de-sac* of very small houses in a row, each with an almost flattened bow window and a blistered brown door with a black knocker. He poised his bright new bicycle against the window, and knocked and stood waiting, and felt himself in his straw hat and black serge suit a very pleasant and prosperous-looking figure. The door

was opened by Cousin Miriam. She was wearing a blueish print
dress that brought out a kind of sallow warmth in her skin,
and although it was nearly four o'clock in the afternoon her
sleeves were tucked up, as if for some domestic task, above
her elbows, showing her rather slender but very shapely yellowish arms. The loosely pinned bodice confessed a delicately
rounded neck.

For a moment she regarded him with suspicion and a faint
hostility, and then recognition dawned in her eyes.

'Why!' she said, 'it's Cousin Elfrid!'

'Thought I'd look you up,' he said.

'Fancy you coming to see us like this!' she answered.

They stood confronting one another for a moment, while
Miriam collected herself for the unexpected emergency.

'Exploratious menanderings,'[9] said Mr Polly, indicating the
bicycle.

Miriam's face betrayed no appreciation of the remark.

'Wait a moment,' she said, coming to a rapid decision, 'and
I'll tell Ma.'

She closed the door on him abruptly, leaving him a little
surprised in the street. 'Ma!' he heard her calling, and a swift
speech followed, the import of which he didn't catch. Then she
reappeared. It seemed but an instant, but she was changed; the
arms had vanished into sleeves, the apron had gone, a certain
pleasing disorder of the hair had been at least reproved.

'I didn't mean to shut you out,' she said, coming out upon
the step. 'I just told Ma. How are you, Elfrid? You *are* looking
well. I didn't know you rode a bicycle. Is it a new one?'

She leaned upon his bicycle. 'Bright it is!' she said. 'What a
trouble you must have to keep it clean!'

Mr Polly was aware of a rustling transit along the passage, and of the house suddenly full of hushed but strenuous
movement.

'It's plated mostly,' said Mr Polly.

'What d'you carry in that little bag thing?' she asked, and
then branched off to: 'We're all in a mess today, you know. It's
my cleaning-up day today. I'm not a bit tidy, I know, but I *do*
like to 'ave a go in at things now and then. *They'd* leave

everything, I believe. If I let 'em. . . . You got to take us as you
find us, Elfrid. Mercy we wasn't all out.' She paused. She was
talking against time. 'I *am* glad to see you again,' she repeated.

'Couldn't keep away,' said Mr Polly gallantly. 'Had to come
over and see my pretty cousins again.'

Miriam did not answer for a moment. She coloured deeply.
'You *do say* things!' she said.

She stared at Mr Polly, and his unfortunate sense of fitness
made him nod his head towards her, regard her firmly with
a round brown eye, and add impressively: 'I don't say *which*
of them.'

Her answering expression made him realize for an instant
the terrible dangers he trifled with. Avidity flared up in her eyes.
Minnie's voice came happily to dissolve the situation.

''Ello, Elfrid!' she said from the door-step.

Her hair was just passably tidy, and she was a little effaced
by a red blouse, but there was no mistaking the genuine bright-
ness of her welcome.

He was to come in to tea, and Mrs Larkins, exuberantly
genial in a floriferous but dingy flannel dressing-gown, appeared
to confirm that. He brought in his bicycle and put it in a narrow,
empty, dingy passage, and everyone crowded into a small, untidy kitchen, whose table had been hastily cleared of the debris
of the midday repast.

'You must come in 'ere,' said Mrs Larkins, 'for Miriam's
turning out the front room. I never did see such a girl for
cleanin' up. Miriam's 'Oliday's a scrub. You've caught us on
the 'Op, as the sayin' is, but Welcome all the same. Pity Annie's
at work today; she won't be 'ome till seven.'

Miriam put chairs and attended to the fire; Minnie edged up
to Mr Polly and said, 'I *am* glad to see you again, Elfrid,' with
a warm contiguous intimacy that betrayed a broken tooth.
Mrs Larkins got out tea-things, and descanted on the noble
simplicity of their lives, and how he 'mustn't mind our simple
ways'. They enveloped Mr Polly with a geniality that intoxicated his amiable nature; he insisted upon helping to lay the
things, and created enormous laughter by pretending not to
know where plates and knives and cups ought to go. 'Who'm I

going to sit next?' he said, and developed voluminous amusement by attempts to arrange the plates so that he could rub elbows with all three. Mrs Larkins had to sit down in the windsor chair by the grandfather clock (which was dark with dirt, and not going) to laugh at her ease at his well-acted perplexity.

They got seated at last, and Mr Polly struck a vein of humour in telling them how he learned to ride the bicycle. He found the mere repetition of the word 'wabble' sufficient to produce almost inextinguishable mirth.

'No foreseeing little accidentulous misadventures,' he said, 'none whatever.'

(Giggle from Minnie.)

'Stout elderly gentleman – shirtsleeves – large straw wastepaper basket sort of hat – starts to cross the road – going to the oil shop – prodic refreshment of oilcan—'

'Don't say you run 'im down,' said Mrs Larkins, gasping. 'Don't say you run 'im down, Elfrid!'

'Run 'im down! Not me, Madam; I never run anything down. Wabble. Ring the bell. Wabble, wabble—'

(Laughter and tears.)

'No one's going to run him down. Hears the bell! Wabble. Gust of wind. Off comes the hat smack into the wheel. Wabble. *Lord! what's* going to happen? Hat across the road, old gentleman after it, bell, shriek. He ran into me. Didn't ring his bell, hadn't *got* a bell – just ran into me. Over I went clinging to his venerable head. Down he went with me clinging to him. Oilcan blump, blump into the road.'

(Interlude while Minnie is attended to for crumb in the windpipe.)

'Well, what happened to the old man with the oilcan?' said Mrs Larkins.

'We sat about among the debreece[10] and had a bit of an argument. I told him he oughtn't to come out wearing such a dangerous hat – flying at things. Said if he couldn't control his hat, he ought to leave it at home. High old jawbacious[11] argument we had, I tell you. "I tell you, Sir –" "I tell *you*, Sir." Waw-waw-waw. Infuriacious. But that's the sort of thing that's constantly happening, you know – on a bicycle. People run into you, hens, and cats, and dogs, and things. Everything seems to have its mark on you; everything.'

'*You* never run into anything.'

'Never. Swelpme,'[12] said Mr Polly very solemnly.

'Never, 'e say!' squealed Minnie. 'Hark at 'im!' and relapsed into a condition that urgently demanded back-thumping. 'Don't be so silly,' said Miriam, thumping hard.

Mr Polly had never been such a social success before. They hung upon his every word – and laughed. What a family they were for laughter! And he loved laughter. The background he apprehended dimly; it was very much the sort of background his life had always had. There was a threadbare tablecloth on the table, and the slop basin and teapot did not go with the cups and saucers, the plates were different again, the knives worn down, the butter lived in a greenish glass dish of its own. Behind was a dresser hung with spare and miscellaneous crockery, with a work box and an untidy work basket; there was an ailing musk plant in the window, and the tattered and blotched wallpaper was covered by bright-coloured grocers' almanacs. Feminine wrappings hung from pegs upon the door, and the floor was covered with a varied collection of fragments of oilcloth. The windsor chair he sat in was unstable – which presently afforded material for humour. 'Steady, old nag,' he said; 'Whoa, my friskiacious palfrey!'[13]

'The things he says! You never know what he won't say next!'

3

'You ain't talkin' of goin'!' cried Mrs Larkins.

'Supper at eight.'

'Stay to supper with *us*, now you '*ave* come over,' said Mrs Larkins, with corroborating cries from Minnie. ''Ave a bit of a walk with the gals, and then come back to supper. You might all go and meet Annie while I straighten up, and lay things out.'

'You're not to go touching the front room, mind,' said Miriam.

'*Who's* going to touch yer front room?' said Mrs Larkins, apparently forgetful for a moment of Mr Polly.

Both girls dressed with some care while Mrs Larkins sketched the better side of their characters, and then the three young people went out to see something of Stamton. In the streets their risible mood gave way to a self-conscious propriety that was particularly evident in Miriam's bearing. They took Mr Polly to the Stamton wreckery-ation ground[14] – that at least was what they called it – with its handsome custodian's cottage, its asphalt paths, its Jubilee drinking-fountain, its clumps of wallflower and daffodils, its charmingly artistic notice boards with green borders and 'art' lettering, and so to the new cemetery and a distant view of the Surrey hills, and round by the gasworks to the canal, to the factory that presently disgorged a surprised and radiant Annie.

' 'El-*lo!*' said Annie.

It is very pleasant to every properly constituted mind to be a centre of amiable interest for one's fellow-creatures; and when one is a young man conscious of becoming mourning and a certain wit, and the fellow-creatures are three young and ardent and sufficiently expressive young women who dispute for the honour of walking by one's side, one may be excused a secret exaltation. They did dispute.

'I'm going to 'ave 'im now,' said Annie. 'You two've been 'aving 'im all the safternoon. Besides, I've got something to say to 'im.'

She had something to say to him. It came presently.

'I say,' she said abruptly. 'I *did* get them rings out of a prize packet.'

'What rings?' asked Mr Polly.

'What you saw at your poor father's funeral. You made out they meant something. They didn't – straight.'

'Then some people have been very remiss about their chances,' said Mr Polly, understanding.

'They haven't had any chances,' said Annie. 'I don't believe in making oneself too free with people.'

'Nor me,' said Mr Polly.

'I may be a bit larky and cheerful in my manner,' Annie admitted. 'But it don't *mean* anything. I ain't that sort.'

'Right-o,' said Mr Polly.

4

It was past ten when Mr Polly found himself riding back towards Easewood in a broad moonlight, and with a little Japanese lantern dangling from his handlebar, making a fiery circle of pinkish light on and roundabout his front wheel. He was mightily pleased with himself and the day. There had been four-ale[15] to drink at supper mixed with ginger beer, very free and jolly in a jug. No shadow fell upon the agreeable excitement of his mind until he faced the anxious and reproachful face of Johnson, who had been sitting up for him, smoking and trying to read the odd volume of *Purchas his Pilgrimes* – about the monk who went into Sarmatia and saw those limitless Tartar carts that carried tents.

'Not had an accident, Elfrid?' said Johnson.

The weakness of Mr Polly's character came out in his reply.

'Not much,' he said. 'Pedal got a bit loose in Stamton, O' Man. Couldn't ride it; so I looked up the cousins while I waited.'

'Not the Larkins lot?'

'Yes.'

Johnson yawned hugely, and asked for and was given friendly particulars.

'Well,' he said, 'better get to bed. I been reading that book of yours; rum stuff. Can't make it out quite. Quite out of date, I should say, if you asked me.'

'That's all right, O' Man,' said Mr Polly.

'Not a bit of use for anything that I can see.'

'Not a bit.'

'See any shops in Stamton?'

'Nothing to speak of,' said Mr Polly. 'Goo'-night, O' Man.'

Before and after this brief conversation his mind ran on his cousins very warmly and prettily in the vein of high spring. Mr Polly had been drinking at the poisoned fountains of English

literature, fountains so unsuited to the needs of a decent clerk
or shopman, fountains charged with the dangerous suggestion
that it becomes a man of gaiety and spirit to make love gallantly
and rather carelessly. It seemed to him that evening to be handsome and humorous and practicable to make love to all his
cousins. It wasn't that he liked any of them particularly, but he
liked something about them. He liked their youth and feminin-
ity, their resolute high spirits, and their interest in him.

They laughed at nothing and knew nothing, and Minnie had
lost a tooth, and Annie screamed and shouted; but they were
interesting, intensely interesting.

And Miriam wasn't so bad as the others. He had kissed them
all, and had been kissed in addition several times by Minnie –
'oscoolatory exercises'.[16]

He buried his nose in his pillow and went to sleep – to dream
of anything rather than getting on in the world, as a sensible
young man in his position ought to have done.

5

And now Mr Polly began to lead a double life. With the Johnsons he professed to be inclined, but not so conclusively inclined
as to be inconvenient, to get a shop for himself – to be, to use
the phrase he preferred, 'looking for an opening'. He would
ride off in the afternoon upon that research, remarking that he
was going to 'cast a strategetical eye' on Chertsey or Weybridge.
But if not all roads, still a great majority of them led by however devious ways to Stamton, and to laughter and increasing
familiarity. Relations developed with Annie and Minnie and
Miriam. Their various characters were increasingly interesting. The laughter became perceptibly less abundant, something
of the fizz had gone from the first opening, still these visits
remained wonderfully friendly and upholding. Then back he
would come to grave but evasive discussions with Johnson.

Johnson was really anxious to get Mr Polly 'into something'.
His was a reserved, honest character, and he would really have
preferred to see his lodger doing things for himself than receive
his money for housekeeping. He hated waste, anybody's waste,

much more than he desired profit. But Mrs Johnson was all for Mr Polly's loitering. She seemed much the more human and likeable of the two to Mr Polly.

He tried at times to work up enthusiasm for the various avenues to wellbeing his discussion with Johnson opened. But they remained disheartening prospects. He imagined himself wonderfully smartened up, acquiring style and value in a London shop; but the picture was stiff and unconvincing. He tried to rouse himself to enthusiasm by the idea of his property increasing by leaps and bounds, by twenty pounds a year or so, let us say, each year, in a well-placed little shop, the corner shop Johnson favoured. There was a certain picturesque interest in imagining cutthroat economies, but his heart told him there would be little in practising them.

And then it happened to Mr Polly that real Romance came out of dreamland into his life, intoxicated and gladdened him with sweetly beautiful suggestions – and left him. She came and left him as that dear lady leaves so many of us, alas! not sparing him one jot or one tittle of the hollowness of her retreating aspect.

It was all the more to Mr Polly's taste that the thing should happen as things happen in books.

In a resolute attempt not to get to Stamton that day, he had turned due southward from Easewood towards a country where the abundance of bracken jungles, lady's smock, stitchwort, bluebells, and grassy stretches by the wayside under shady trees does much to compensate the lighter type of mind for the absence of promising 'openings'. He turned aside from the road, wheeled his machine along a faintly marked attractive trail through bracken until he came to a heap of logs against a high old stone wall with a damaged coping and wallflower plants already gone to seed. He sat down, balanced the straw hat on a convenient lump of wood, lit a cigarette, and abandoned himself to agreeable musings and the friendly observation of a cheerful little brown and grey bird his stillness presently encouraged to approach him.

'This is All Right,' said Mr Polly softly to the little brown and grey bird. 'Business – later.'

He reflected that he might go on in this way for four or five years, and then be scarcely worse off than he had been in his father's lifetime.

'Vile Business,' said Mr Polly.

Then Romance appeared. Or to be exact, Romance became audible.

Romance began as a series of small but increasingly vigorous movements on the other side of the wall, then a voice murmuring, then as a falling of little fragments on the other side and as ten pink fingertips, scarcely apprehended before Romance became startlingly and emphatically a leg, remained for a time a fine, slender, actively struggling limb, brown-stockinged, and wearing a brown toe-worn shoe, and then. . . . A handsome, red-haired girl wearing a short dress of blue linen was sitting astride the wall, panting, considerably disarranged by her climbing, and as yet unaware of Mr Polly. . . .

His fine instincts made him turn his head away and assume an attitude of negligent contemplation, with his ears and mind alive to every sound behind him.

'Goodness!' said a voice, with a sharp note of surprise.

Mr Polly was on his feet in an instant. 'Dear me! Can I be of any assistance?' he said, with deferential gallantry.

'I don't know,' said the young lady, and regarded him calmly with clear blue eyes. 'I didn't know there was anyone here,' she added.

'Sorry,' said Mr Polly, 'if I am intrudacious.[17] I didn't know you didn't want me to be here.'

She reflected for a moment on the word.

'It isn't that,' she said, surveying him. 'I oughtn't to get over the wall,' she explained. 'It's out of bounds; at least in term time. But this being holidays —'

Her manner placed the matter before him.

'Holidays is different,' said Mr Polly.

'I don't want to actually *break* the rules,' she said.

'Leave them behind you,' said Mr Polly, with a catch of the breath, 'where they are safe.' And marvelling at his own wit and daring, and indeed trembling within himself, he held out a hand for her.

She brought another brown leg from the unknown, and arranged her skirt with a dexterity altogether feminine.

'I think I'll stay on the wall,' she decided. 'So long as some of me's in bounds —'

She continued to regard him with an irresistible smile of satisfaction. Mr Polly smiled in return.

'You bicycle?' she said.

Mr Polly admitted the fact, and she said she did too.

'All my people are in India,'[18] she explained. 'It's beastly rot – I mean it's frightfully dull being left here alone.'

'All *my* people,' said Mr Polly, 'are in Heaven!'

'I say!'

'Fact,' said Mr Polly. 'Got nobody.'

'And that's why –' She checked her artless comment on his mourning. 'I say,' she said in a sympathetic voice, 'I *am* sorry. I really am. Was it a fire, or a ship – or something?'

Her sympathy was very delightful. He shook his head. 'The ordinary tables of mortality,' he said. 'First one, and then another.'

Behind his outward melancholy, delight was dancing wildly.

'Are *you* lonely?' asked the girl.

Mr Polly nodded.

'I was just sitting there in melancholic rectrospectatiousness,' he said, indicating the logs; and again a swift thoughtfulness swept across her face.

'There's no harm in our talking,' she reflected.

'It's a kindness. Won't you get down?'

She reflected, and surveyed the turf below and the scene around, and him.

'I'll stay on the wall,' she said, 'if only for bounds' sake.'

She certainly looked quite adorable on the wall. She had a fine neck and pointed chin that was particularly admirable from below, and pretty eyes and fine eyebrows are never so pretty as when they look down upon one. But no calculation of that sort, thank Heaven, was going on beneath her ruddy shock of hair.

6

'Let's talk,' she said, and for a time they were both tongue-tied.

Mr Polly's literary proclivities had taught him that under such circumstances a strain of gallantry was demanded. And something in his blood repeated that lesson.

'You make me feel like one of those old knights,' he said, 'who rode about the country looking for dragons and beautiful maidens and chivalresque adventures.'

'Oh!' she said. 'Why?'

'Beautiful maiden,' he said.

She flushed under her freckles with the quick bright flush those pretty red-haired people have. 'Nonsense!' she said.

'You are. I'm not the first to tell you that. A beautiful maiden imprisoned in an enchanted school.'

'*You* wouldn't think it enchanted.'

'And here am I – clad in steel. Well, not exactly, but my fiery warhorse is, anyhow. Ready to absquatulate all the dragons, and rescue you.'

She laughed, a jolly laugh, that showed delightfully gleaming teeth. 'I wish you could *see* the dragons,' she said, with great enjoyment. Mr Polly felt they were a sun's distance from the world of every day.

'Fly with me!' he dared.

She stared for a moment, and then went off into peals of laughter. 'You *are* funny!' she said. 'Why, I haven't known you five minutes.'

'One doesn't – in this medevial world. My mind is made up, anyhow.'

He was proud and pleased with his joke, and quick to change his key neatly. 'I wish one could,' he said.

'I wonder if people ever did.'

'If there were people like you.'

'We don't even know each other's names,' she remarked, with a descent to matters of fact.

'Yours is the prettiest name in the world.'

'How do you know?'

'It must be – anyhow.'

'It *is* rather pretty, you know. It's Christabel.'

'What did I tell you?'

'And yours?'

'Poorer than I deserve. It's Alfred.'

'*I* can't call you Alfred.'

'Well, Polly.'

'It's a girl's name!'

For a moment he went out of tune. 'I wish it was,' he said, and could have bitten out his tongue at the Larkins sound of it.

'I shan't forget it,' she remarked consolingly.

'I say,' she said, in the pause that followed, 'why are you riding about the country on a bicycle?'

'I'm doing it because I like it.'

She sought to estimate his social status on her limited basis of experience. He stood leaning with one hand against the wall, looking up at her and tingling with daring thoughts. He was a littleish man, you must remember, but neither mean-looking nor unhandsome in those days, sunburnt by his holiday and now warmly flushed. He had an inspiration to simple speech that no practised trifler with love could have bettered. 'There *is* love at first sight,' he said, and said it sincerely.

She stared at him with eyes round and big with excitement.

'I think,' she said slowly, and without any signs of fear or retreat, 'I ought to get back over the wall.'

'It needn't matter to you,' he said; 'I'm just a nobody.[19] But I know you are the best and most beautiful thing I've ever spoken to.' His breath caught against something. 'No harm in telling you that,' he said.

'I should have to go back if I thought you were serious,' she said after a pause, and they both smiled together.

After that they talked in a fragmentary way for some time. The blue eyes surveyed Mr Polly with kindly curiosity from under a broad, finely modelled brow, much as an exceptionally intelligent cat might survey a new sort of dog. She meant to find out all about him. She asked questions that riddled the honest knight in armour below, and probed ever nearer to the hateful secret of the shop and his normal servitude. And when he made a flourish and mispronounced a word, a thoughtful shade passed like the shadow of a cloud across her face.

'Booom!' came the sound of a gong.

'Lordy!' cried the girl, and flashed a pair of brown legs at him and was gone.

Then her pink fingertips reappeared, and the top of her red hair. 'Knight,' she cried from the other side of the wall. 'Knight there!'

'Lady!' he answered.

'Come again tomorrow.'

'At your command. But—'

'Yes?'

'Just one finger.'

'What do you mean?'

'To kiss.'

The rustle of retreating footsteps and silence. . . .

But after he had waited next day for twenty minutes she reappeared, a little out of breath with the effort to surmount the wall, and head first this time. And it seemed to him she was lighter and more daring and altogether prettier than the dreams and enchanted memories that had filled the interval.

7

From first to last their acquaintance lasted ten days, but into that time Mr Polly packed ten years of dreams.

'He don't seem,' said Johnson, 'to take a serious interest in anything. That shop at the corner's bound to be snapped up if he don't look out.'

The girl and Mr Polly did not meet on every one of those ten days; one was Sunday and she could not come, and on the eighth the school reassembled and she made vague excuses. All their meetings amounted to this, that she sat on the wall, more or less in bounds as she expressed it, and let Mr Polly fall in love with her and try to express it below. She sat in a state of irresponsible exaltation, watching him, and at intervals prodding a vivisecting[20] point of encouragement into him, with that

strange passive cruelty which is natural and proper in her sex
and age.

And Mr Polly fell in love, as though the world had given
way beneath him and he had dropped through into another,
into a world of luminous clouds and of a desolate, hopeless
wilderness of desiring and of wild valleys of unreasonable
ecstasy, a world whose infinite miseries were finer and in some
inexplicable way sweeter than the purest gold of the daily life,
whose joys – they were indeed but the merest remote glimpses
of joy – were brighter than a dying martyr's vision of heaven.
Her smiling face looked down upon him out of the sky, her
careless pose was the living body of life. It was senseless, it was
utterly foolish, but all that was best and richest in Mr Polly's
nature broke like a wave and foamed up at the girl's feet, and
died, and never touched her. And she sat on the wall and
marvelled at him, and was amused, and once, suddenly moved
and wrung by his pleading, she bent down rather shamefacedly
and gave him a freckled, tennis-blistered little paw to kiss. And
she looked into his eyes and suddenly felt a perplexity, a curious
swimming of the mind that made her recoil and stiffen, and
wonder afterwards and dream. . . .

And then with some instinct of self-protection she went and
told her three best friends, great students of character all, of
this remarkable phenomenon she had discovered on the other
side of the wall.

'Look here,' said Mr Polly, 'I'm wild for the love of you! I
can't keep up this gesticulatious game[21] any more. I'm not a
Knight. Treat me as a human man. You may sit up there smiling,
but I'd die in torments to have you mine for an hour. I'm
nobody and nothing. But look here! Will you wait for me five
years? You're just a girl yet, and it wouldn't be hard.'

'Shut up!' said Christabel, in an aside he did not hear, and
something he did not see touched her hand.

'I've always been just dilletentytating[22] about till now, but I
could work. I've just woke up. Wait till I've got a chance with
the money I've got.'

'But you haven't got much money!'

'I've got enough to take a chance with, some sort of chance.

I'd find a chance. I'll do that, anyhow. I'll go away. I mean what I say. I'll stop trifling and shirking. If I don't come back it won't matter. If I do—'

Her expression had become uneasy. Suddenly she bent down towards him.

'Don't!' she said in an undertone.

'Don't – what?'

'Don't go on like this! You're different. Go on being the knight who wants to kiss my hand as his – what did you call it?' The ghost of a smile curved her face. 'Gurdrum!'[23]

'But—'

Then through a pause they both stared at each other, listening.

A muffled tumult on the other side of the wall asserted itself.

'Shut *up*, Rosie!' said a voice.

'I tell you I will see! I can't half hear. Give me a leg up!'

'You Idiot! He'll see you. You're spoiling everything.'

The bottom dropped out of Mr Polly's world. He felt as people must feel who are going to faint.

'You've got someone –' he said, aghast.

She found life inexpressible to Mr Polly. She addressed some unseen hearers. 'You filthy little Beasts!' she cried, with a sharp note of agony in her voice, and swung herself back over the wall and vanished. There was a squeal of pain and fear, and a swift, fierce altercation.

For a couple of seconds he stood agape.

Then a wild resolve to confirm his worst sense of what was on the other side of the wall made him seize a log, put it against the stones, clutch the parapet with insecure fingers, and lug himself to a momentary balance on the wall.

Romance and his goddess had vanished.

A red-haired girl with a pigtail was wringing the wrist of a schoolfellow, who shrieked with pain and cried, 'Mercy! mercy! O-o-o! Christabel!'

'You Idiot!' cried Christabel. 'You giggling Idiot!'

Two other young ladies made off through the beech trees from this outburst of savagery.

Then the grip of Mr Polly's fingers gave, and he hit his chin against the stones and slipped clumsily to the ground again, scraping his cheek against the wall, and hurting his shin against the log by which he had reached the top. Just for a moment he crouched against the wall.

He swore, staggered to the pile of logs, and sat down.

He remained very still for some time, with his lips pressed together.

'Fool!' he said at last. 'You Blithering Fool!' and began to rub his shin as though he had just discovered his bruises.

Afterwards he found his face was wet with blood – which was none the less red stuff from the heart because it came from slight abrasions.

CHAPTER 6
MIRIAM

I

It is an illogical consequence of one human being's ill-treatment that we should fly immediately to another, but that is the way with us. It seemed to Mr Polly that only a human touch could assuage the smart of his humiliation. Moreover, it had, for some undefined reason, to be a feminine touch, and the number of women in his world was limited.

He thought of the Larkins family – the Larkins whom he had not been near now for ten long days. Healing people they seemed to him now – healing, simple people. They had good hearts, and he had neglected them for a mirage. If he rode over to them he would be able to talk bosh, and laugh, and forget the whirl of memories and thoughts that was spinning round and round so unendurably in his brain.

'Law!' said Mrs Larkins, 'come in! You're quite a stranger, Elfrid!'

'Been seeing to business,' said the unveracious Polly.

'None of 'em ain't at 'ome, but Miriam's just out to do a bit of shopping. Won't let me shop, she won't, because I'm so keerless. She's a wonderful manager, that girl. Minnie's got some work at the carpet place. 'Ope it won't make 'er ill again. She's the loving delikit sort, is Minnie. . . . Come into the front parlour. It's a bit untidy, but you got to take us as you find us. Wot you been doing to your face?'

'Bit of a scraze[1] with the bicycle,' said Mr Polly.

''Ow?'

'Trying to pass a carriage on the wrong side, and he drew up and ran me against a wall.'

Mrs Larkins scrutinized it. 'You ought to 'ave someone look after your scrazes,' she said. 'That's all red and rough. It ought to be cold-creamed. Bring your bicycle into the passage and come in.'

She 'straightened up a bit'. That is to say, she increased the dislocation of a number of scattered articles, put a work basket on the top of several books, swept two or three dogs'-eared numbers of *The Lady's Own Novelist* from the table into the broken armchair, and proceeded to sketch together the tea-things with various such interpolations as: 'Law, if I ain't for-got the butter!' All the while she talked of Annie's good spirits and cleverness with her millinery, and of Minnie's affection, and Miriam's relative love of order and management. Mr Polly stood by the window uneasily, and thought how good and sincere was the Larkins's tone. It was well to be back again.

'You're a long time finding that shop of yours,' said Mrs Larkins.

'Don't do to be too precipitous,' said Mr Polly.

'No,' said Mrs Larkins, 'once you got it you got it. Like choosing a 'usband. You better see you got it good. I kept Larkins 'esitating two years, I did, until I felt sure of him. A 'ansom man 'e was, as you can see by the looks of the girls, but 'ansom is as 'ansom does. You'd like a bit of jam to your tea, I expect? I 'ope they'll keep *their* men waiting when the time comes. I tell them if they think of marrying, it only shows they don't know when they're well off. Here's Miriam!'

Miriam entered with several parcels in a net, and a peevish expression. 'Mother,' she said, 'you might 'ave prevented my going out with the net with the broken handle. I've been cutting my fingers with the string all the way 'ome.' Then she discovered Mr Polly and her face brightened.

''Ello, Elfrid!' she said. 'Where you been all this time?'

'Looking round,' said Mr Polly.

'Found a shop?'

'One or two likely ones. But it takes time.'

'You've got the wrong cups, Mother.'

She went into the kitchen, disposed of her purchases, and returned with the right cups. 'What you done to your face,

Elfrid?' she asked, and came and scrutinized his scratches. 'All rough it is.'

He repeated his story of the accident, and she was sympathetic in a pleasant, homely way.

'You *are* quiet today,' she said, as they sat down to tea.

'Meditatious,'[2] said Mr Polly.

Quite by accident he touched her hand on the table, and she answered his touch.

'Why not?' thought Mr Polly, and looking up, caught Mrs Larkins's eye and flushed guiltily. But Mrs Larkins, with unusual restraint, said nothing. She made a grimace, enigmatical, but in its essence friendly.

Presently Minnie came in with some vague grievance against the manager of the carpet-making place about his method of estimating piecework. Her account was redundant, defective, and highly technical, but redeemed by a certain earnestness. 'I'm never within sixpence of what I reckon to be,' she said. 'It's a bit too 'ot.' Then Mr Polly, feeling that he was being conspicuously dull, launched into a description of the shop he was looking for and the shops he had seen. His mind warmed up as he talked.

'Found your tongue again,' said Mrs Larkins.

He had. He began to embroider the subject and work upon it. For the first time it assumed picturesque and desirable qualities in his mind. It stimulated him to see how readily and willingly they accepted his sketches. Bright ideas appeared in his mind from nowhere. He was suddenly enthusiastic.

'When I get this shop of mine I shall have a cat. Must make a home for a cat, you know.'

'What, to catch the mice?' said Mrs Larkins.

'No – sleep in the window. A venerable signor of a cat. Tabby. Cat's no good if it isn't tabby. Cat I'm going to have, and a canary! Didn't think of that before, but a cat and a canary seem to go, you know. Summer weather I shall sit at breakfast in the little room behind the shop, sun streaming in the window to rights, cat on a chair, canary singing, and – Mrs Polly. . . .'

''Ello!' said Mrs Larkins.

'Mrs Polly frying an extra bit of bacon. Bacon singing, cat singing, canary singing, kettle singing. Mrs Polly—'

'But who's Mrs Polly going to be?' said Mrs Larkins.

'Figment of imagination, M'am,' said Mr Polly. 'Put in to fill up picture. No face to figure – as yet. Still, that's how it will be, I can assure you. I think I must have a bit of garden. Johnson's the man for a garden, of course,' he said, going off at a tangent, 'but I don't mean a fierce sort of garden. Earnest industry. Anxious moments. Fervous digging.[3] Shan't go in for that sort of garden, M'am. No! Too much Backache for me. My garden will be just a patch of 'sturtiums and sweetpea. Red-bricked yard, clothesline. Trellis put up in odd time. Humorous wind vane.[4] Creeper up the back of the house.'

'Virginia creeper?' asked Miriam.

'Canary creeper,'[5] said Mr Polly.

'You *will* 'ave it nice,' said Miriam desirously.

'Rather,' said Mr Polly. 'Ting-a-ling-a-ling. Shop!'

He straightened himself up, and they all laughed.

'Smart little shop,' he said. 'Counter. Desk. All complete. Umbrella stand. Carpet on the floor. Cat asleep on the counter. Ties and hose on a rail over the counter. All right.'

'I wonder you don't set about it right off,' said Miriam.

'Mean to get it exactly right, M'am,' said Mr Polly.

'Have to have a Tom cat,' said Mr Polly, and paused for an expectant moment. 'Wouldn't do to open shop one morning, you know, and find the window full of kittens. Can't sell kittens. . . .'

When tea was over he was left alone with Minnie for a few minutes, and an odd intimation of an incident occurred that left Mr Polly rather scared and shaken. A silence fell between them – an uneasy silence. He sat with his elbows on the table looking at her. All the way from Easewood to Stamton his erratic imagination had been running upon neat ways of proposing marriage. I don't know why it should have done, but it had. It was a kind of secret exercise that had not had any definite aim at the time, but which now recurred to him with extraordinary force. He couldn't think of anything in the world that wasn't the gambit to a proposal. It was almost irresistibly fascinating to think how immensely a few words from him would excite and revolutionize Minnie. She was sitting at the table with a work basket among the tea-things, mending a glove in order to avoid her share of clearing away.

'I like cats,' said Minnie, after a thoughtful pause. 'I'm always saying to Mother, I wish we 'ad a cat. But we couldn't 'ave a cat 'ere – not with no yard.'

'Never had a cat myself,' said Mr Polly. 'No!'

'I'm fond of them,' said Minnie.

'I like the look of them,' said Mr Polly. 'Can't exactly call myself fond.'

'I expect I shall get one some day. When about you get your shop.'

'I shall have my shop all right before long,' said Mr Polly. 'Trust me. Canary-bird and all.'

She shook her head. 'I shall get a cat first,' she said. 'You never mean anything you say.'

'Might get 'em together,' said Mr Polly, with his sense of a neat thing outrunning his discretion.

'Why! 'ow do you mean?' said Minnie, suddenly alert.

'Shop and cat thrown in,' said Mr Polly in spite of himself, and his head swam, and he broke out into a cold sweat as he said it.

He found her eyes fixed on him with an eager expression. 'Mean to say – ?' she began, as if for verification. He sprang to his feet, and turned to the window. 'Little dog!' he said, and moved doorward hastily. 'Eating my bicycle tyre, I believe,' he explained. And so escaped.

He saw his bicycle in the hall and cut it dead.[6]

He heard Mrs Larkins in the passage behind him as he opened the front door.

He turned to her. 'Thought my bicycle was on fire,' he said. 'Outside. Funny fancy! All right reely. Little dog outside. . . . Miriam ready?'

'What for?'

'To go and meet Annie.'

Mrs Larkins stared at him. 'You're stopping for a bit of supper!'

'If I may,' said Mr Polly.

'You're a rum un,' said Mrs Larkins, and called: 'Miriam!'

Minnie appeared at the door of the room looking infinitely perplexed. 'There ain't a little dog anywhere, Elfrid,' she said.

Mr Polly passed his hand over his brow. 'I had a most curious sensation. Felt exactly as though something was up somewhere. That's why I said Little Dog. All right now.'

He bent down and pinched his bicycle tyre.

'You was saying something about a cat, Elfrid,' said Minnie.

'Give you one,' he answered, without looking up. 'The very day my shop is opened.'

He straightened himself up and smiled reassuringly.

'Trust me,' he said.

2

When, after imperceptible manoeuvres by Mrs Larkins, he found himself starting circuitously through the inevitable recreation ground with Miriam to meet Annie, he found himself quite unable to avoid the topic of the shop that had now taken such a grip upon him. A sense of danger only increased the attraction. Minnie's persistent disposition to accompany them had been crushed by a novel and violent and pungently expressed desire on the part of Mrs Larkins to see her do something in the house sometimes. . . .

'You really think you'll open a shop?' said Miriam.

'I hate cribs,' said Mr Polly, adopting a moderate tone. 'In a shop there's this drawback and that, but one *is* one's own Master.'

'That wasn't all talk?'

'Not a bit of it.'

'After all,' he went on, 'a little shop needn't be so bad.'

'It's a 'ome,' said Miriam.

'It's a home.'

Pause.

'There's no need to keep accounts and that sort of thing if there's no assistant. I dare say I could run a shop all right if I wasn't interfered with.'

'I should like to see you in your shop,' said Miriam. 'I expect you'd keep everything tremendously neat.'

The conversation flagged.

'Let's sit down on one of those seats over there past that notice board,' said Miriam, 'where we can see those blue flowers.'

They did as she suggested, and sat down in a corner where a triangular bed of stock and delphinium brightened the asphalted traceries of the recreation ground.

'I wonder what they call those flowers,' she said. 'I always like them. They're handsome.'

'Delphicums and larkspurs,'[7] said Mr Polly. 'They used to be in the park at Port Burdock.'

'Floriferous corner,' he added approvingly.

He put an arm over the back of the seat, and assumed a more comfortable attitude. He glanced at Miriam, who was sitting in a lax, thoughtful pose, with her eyes on the flowers. She was wearing her old dress. She had not had time to change, and the blue tones of her old dress brought out a certain warmth in her skin, and her pose exaggerated whatever was feminine in her rather lean and insufficient body, and rounded her flat chest delusively. A little line of light lay across her profile. The afternoon was full of transfiguring sunshine, children were playing noisily in the adjacent sandpit, some Judas trees were abloom in the villa gardens that bordered the recreation ground, and all the place was bright with touches of young summer colour. It all merged with the effect of Miriam in Mr Polly's mind.

Her thought found speech. 'One did ought to be happy in a shop,' she said, with a note of unusual softness in her voice.

It seemed to him that she was right. One did ought to be happy in a shop. Folly not to banish dreams that made one ache of townless woods and bracken tangles and red-haired linen-clad figures sitting in dappled sunshine upon grey and crumbling walls and looking queenly down on one with clear blue eyes. Cruel and foolish dreams they were, that ended in one's being laughed at and made a mock of. There was no mockery here.

'A shop's such a respectable thing to be,' said Miriam thoughtfully.

'*I* could be happy in a shop,' he said.

His sense of effect had made him pause.

'If I had the right company,' he added.

She became very still.

Mr Polly swerved a little from the conversational ice-run upon which he had embarked.

'I'm not such a blooming Geezer,' he said, 'as not to be able to sell goods a bit. One has to be nosy over one's buying, of course. But I shall do all right.'

He stopped, and felt falling, falling through the aching silence that followed.

'If you get the right company,' said Miriam.

'I shall get that all right.'

'You don't mean you've got someone—?'

He found himself plunging.

'I've got someone in my eye this minute,' he said.

'Elfrid!' she said, turning to him. 'You don't mean—'

Well, *did* he mean? 'I do!' he said.

'Not reely!' She clenched her hands to keep still.

He took the conclusive step.

'Well, you and me, Miriam, in a little shop, with a cat and a canary—' He tried too late to get back to a hypothetical note. 'Just suppose it!'

'You mean,' said Miriam, 'you're in love with me, Elfrid?'

What possible answer can a man give to such a question but 'Yes'!

Regardless of the public park, the children in the sandpit, and everyone, she bent forward and seized his shoulder and kissed him on the lips. Something lit up in Mr Polly at the touch. He put an arm about her and kissed her back, and felt an irrevocable act was sealed. He had a curious feeling that it would be very satisfying to marry and have a wife – only somehow he wished it wasn't Miriam. Her lips were very pleasant to him, and the feel of her in his arm.

They recoiled a little from each other, and sat for a moment flushed and awkwardly silent. His mind was altogether incapable of controlling its confusions.

'I didn't dream,' said Miriam, 'you cared – Sometimes I thought it was Annie, sometimes Minnie—'

'Always I liked you better than them,' said Mr Polly.

'I loved you, Elfrid,' said Miriam, 'since ever we met at your poor father's funeral. Leastways I *would* have done if I had thought – You didn't seem to mean anything you said.

'I can't believe it!' she added.

'Nor I,' said Mr Polly.

'You mean to marry me and start that little shop?'

'Soon as ever I find it,' said Mr Polly.

'I had no more idea when I came out with you—'

'Nor me.'

'It's like a dream.'

They said no more for a little while.

'I got to pinch myself to think it's real,' said Miriam. 'What they'll do without me at 'ome I can't imagine. When I tell them—'

For the life of him Mr Polly could not tell whether he was fullest of tender anticipations or regretful panic.

'Mother's no good at managing – not a bit. Annie don't care for housework, and Minnie's got no 'ead for it. What they'll do without me I can't imagine.'

'They'll have to do without you,' said Mr Polly, sticking to his guns.

A clock in the town began striking.

'Lor!' said Miriam, 'we shall miss Annie, sitting 'ere and lovemaking.'

She rose and made as if to take Mr Polly's arm. But Mr Polly felt that their condition must be nakedly exposed to the ridicule of the world by such a linking, and evaded her movement.

Annie was already in sight before a flood of hesitation and terrors assailed Mr Polly.

'Don't tell anyone yet a bit,' he said.

'Only Mother,' said Miriam firmly.

3

Figures are the most shocking things in the world. The pettiest little squiggles of black, looked at in the right light; and yet consider the blow they can give you upon the heart. You return from a careless holiday abroad, and turn over the page of a newspaper, and against the name of the distant, vague-conceived railway, in mortgages upon which you have embarked the bulk of your capital, you see, instead of the familiar, persistent 95–6 (varying at most to 93 *ex div.*[8]), this slightly richer arrangement of marks, 76½–78½.

It is like the opening of a pit just under your feet.

So, too, Mr Polly's happy sense of limitless resources was obliterated suddenly by a vision of this tracery:

'298'

instead of the

'350'

he had come to regard as the fixed symbol of his affluence.

It gave him a disagreeable feeling about the diaphragm, akin in a remote degree to the sensation he had when the perfidy of the red-haired schoolgirl became plain to him. It made his brow moist.

'Going down a Vorterex,' he whispered.

By a characteristic feat of subtraction he decided that he must have spent sixty-two pounds.

'Funererial baked meats,' he said, recalling possible items.

The happy dream in which he had been living, of long, warm days, of open roads, of limitless, unchecked hours, of infinite time to look about him, vanished like a thing enchanted. He was suddenly back in the hard old economic world, that exacts work, that limits range, that discourages phrasing and dispels laughter. He saw Wood Street and its fearful suspenses yawning beneath his feet.

And also he had promised to marry Miriam, and on the whole rather wanted to.

He was distraught at supper. Afterwards, when Mrs Johnson had gone to bed with a slight headache, he opened a conversation with Johnson.

'It's about time, O' Man, I saw about doing something,' he said. 'Riding about and looking at shops all very debonairious,[9] O' Man, but it's time I took one for keeps.'

'What did I tell you?' said Johnson.

'How do you think that corner shop of yours will figure out?' Mr Polly asked.

'You're really meaning it?'

'If it's a practable proposition, O' Man. Assuming it's practable, what's your idea of the figures?'

Johnson went to the chiffonier,[10] got out a letter, and tore off the back sheet. 'Let's figure it out,' he said, with solemn satisfaction. 'Let's see the lowest you could do it on.'

He squared himself to the task, and Mr Polly sat beside him like a pupil, watching the evolution of the grey, distasteful figures that were to dispose of his little hoard.

'What running expenses have we got to provide for?' said Johnson, wetting his pencil. 'Let's have them first. Rent? . . .'

At the end of an hour of hideous speculations, Johnson decided, 'It's close; but you'll have a chance.'

'M'm,' said Mr Polly. 'What more does a brave man want?'

'One thing you can do quite easily. I've asked about it.'

'What's that, O' Man?' said Mr Polly.

'Take the shop without the house above it.'

'I suppose I might put my head in to mind it,' said Mr Polly, 'and get a job with my body.'

'Not exactly that. But I thought you'd save a lot if you stayed on here – being all alone, as you are.'

'Never thought of that, O' Man,' said Mr Polly, and reflected silently upon the needlessness of Miriam.

'We were talking of eighty pounds for stock,' said Johnson. 'Of course seventy-five is five pounds less, isn't it? Not much else we can cut.'

'No,' said Mr Polly.

'It's very interesting, all this,' said Johnson, folding up the half-sheet of paper and unfolding it. 'I wish sometimes I had a business of my own instead of a fixed salary. You'll have to keep books, of course.'

'One wants to know where one is.'

'I should do it all by double entry,' said Johnson. 'A little troublesome at first, but far the best in the end.'

'Lemme see that paper,' said Mr Polly, and took it with the feeling of a man who takes a nauseating medicine, and scrutinized his cousin's neat figures with listless eyes.

'Well,' said Johnson, rising and stretching, 'Bed! Better sleep on it, O' Man.'

'Right-o!' said Mr Polly, without moving; but indeed he could as well have slept upon a bed of thorns.

He had a dreadful night. It was like the end of the annual holiday, only infinitely worse. It was like a newly arrived prisoner's backward glance at the trees and heather through the prison gates. He had to go back to harness, and he was as fitted to go in harness as the ordinary domestic cat. All night Fate, with the quiet complacency, and indeed at times the very face and gestures, of Johnson, guided him towards that undesired establishment at the corner near the station. 'O Lord!' he cried, 'I'd rather go back to cribs. I *should* keep my money, anyhow.' Fate never winced.

'Run away to sea,' whispered Mr Polly; but he knew he wasn't man enough. 'Cut my blooming throat.'

Some braver strain urged him to think of Miriam, and for a little while he lay still. . . .

'Well, O' Man?' said Johnson, when Mr Polly came down to breakfast, and Mrs Johnson looked up brightly. Mr Polly had never felt breakfast so unattractive before.

'Just a day or so more, O' Man, to turn it over in my mind,' he said.

'You'll get the place snapped up,' said Johnson.

There were times in those last few days of coyness with his destiny when his engagement seemed the most negligible of circumstances; and times – and these happened for the most part at nights, after Mrs Johnson had indulged everybody in a Welsh rarebit – when it assumed so sinister and portentous an appearance as to make him think of suicide. And there were

times too when he very distinctly desired to be married, now
that the idea had got into his head, at any cost. Also he tried to
recall all the circumstances of his proposal time after time, and
never quite succeeded in recalling what had brought the thing
off. He went over to Stamton with a becoming frequency, and
kissed all his cousins, and Miriam especially, a great deal, and
found it very stirring and refreshing. They all appeared to know;
and Minnie was tearful but resigned. Mrs Larkins met him, and
indeed enveloped him, with unwonted warmth, and there was
a big pot of household jam for tea. And he could not make up
his mind to sign his name to anything about the shop, though
it crawled nearer and nearer to him though the project had
materialized now to the tent of a draft agreement, with the
place for his signature indicated in pencil.

One morning, just after Mr Johnson had gone to the station,
Mr Polly wheeled his bicycle out into the road, went up to his
bedroom, packed his long white nightdress, a comb, and a
toothbrush in a manner that was as offhand as he could make
it, informed Mrs Johnson, who was manifestly curious, that
he was 'off for a day or two to clear his head', and fled forth-
right into the road, and mounting, turned his wheel towards
the tropics and the equator and the south coast of England,
and indeed more particularly to where the little village of
Fishbourne slumbers and sleeps.

When he returned, four days later, he astonished Johnson
beyond measure by remarking, so soon as the shop project was
reopened, 'I've took a little contraption at Fishbourne, O' Man,
that I fancy suits me better.'

He paused, and then added in a manner if possible even more
offhand, 'Oh, and I'm going to have a bit of a nuptial over at
Stamton – with one of the Larkins cousins.'

'Nuptial!' said Johnson.

'Wedding-bells, O' Man. Benedictine collapse.'[11]

On the whole Johnson showed great self-control. 'It's your
own affair, O' Man,' he said, when things had been more clearly
explained; 'and I hope you won't feel sorry when it's too late.'

But Mrs Johnson was first of all angrily silent, and then
reproachful. 'I don't see what we've done to be made fools of

like this,' she said. 'After all the trouble we've 'ad to make you comfortable and see after you – out late, and sitting up, and everything; and then you go off as sly as sly, without a word, an' get a shop behind our backs, as though you thought we meant to steal your money. I 'aven't patience with such deceitfulness, and I didn't think it of you, Elfrid. And now the letting season's 'arf gone by, and what I shall do with that room of yours I've no idea. Frank is frank, and fair play fair play; so *I* was told, any'ow, when I was a girl. Just as long as it suits you to stay 'ere you stay 'ere, and then it's off and no thank you whether we like it or not. Johnson's too easy with you. 'E sits there and doesn't say a word; and night after night 'e's been adding up and subtracting, and multiplying and dividing, and suggesting and thinkin' for you, instead of seeing to his own affairs.'

She paused for breath.

'Unfortunate amoor,'[12] said Mr Polly apologetically and indistinctly. 'Didn't expect it myself.'

4

Mr Polly's marriage followed with a certain inevitableness.

He tried to assure himself that he was acting upon his own forceful initiative, but at the back of his mind was the completest realization of his powerlessness to resist the gigantic social forces he had set in motion. He had got to marry under the will of society,[13] even as in times past it had been appointed for other sunny souls under the will of society that they should be led out by serious and unavoidable fellow-creatures and ceremoniously drowned or burnt or hung. He would have preferred infinitely a more observant and less conspicuous role, but the choice was no longer open to him. He did his best to play his part, and he procured some particularly neat check trousers to do it in. The rest of his costume, except for some bright yellow gloves, a grey and blue mixture tie, and that the broad crape band was changed for a livelier piece of silk, were the things he had worn at the funeral of his father. So nearly akin are human joy and sorrow.

The Larkins sisters had done wonders with grey sateen. The idea of orange blossom and white veils had been abandoned reluctantly on account of the expense of the cabs. A novelette in which the heroine had stood at the altar in 'a modest going-away dress' had materially assisted this decision. Miriam was frankly tearful, and so, indeed, was Annie, but with laughter as well to carry it off. Mr Polly heard Annie say something vague about never getting a chance because of Miriam always sticking about at home like a cat at a mouse hole, that became, as people say, food for thought. Mrs Larkins was from the first flushed, garrulous, and wet and smeared by copious weeping; an incredibly soaked and crumpled and used-up pocket handkerchief never left the clutch of her plump red hand. 'Goo' girls all of them,' she kept on saying in a tremulous voice; 'such Goo'-Goo'-Goo' girls!' She wetted Mr Polly dreadfully when she kissed him. Her emotion affected the buttons down the back of her bodice, and almost the last filial duty Miriam did before entering on her new life was to close that gaping orifice for the eleventh time. Her bonnet was small and ill-balanced, black adorned with red roses, and first it got over her right eye until Annie told her of it, and then she pushed it over her left eye and looked ferocious for a space, and after that baptismal kissing of Mr Polly the delicate millinery took fright and climbed right up to the back part of her head and hung on there by a pin, and flapped piteously at all the larger waves of emotion that filled the gathering. Mr Polly became more and more aware of that bonnet as time went on, until he felt for it like a thing alive. Towards the end it had yawning fits.

The company did not include Mrs Johnson, but Johnson came with a pervading surreptitiousness and backed against walls and watched Mr Polly with doubt and speculation in his large grey eye, and whistled noiselessly and doubtfully on the edge of things. He was, so to speak, to be best man *sotto voce*. A sprinkling of girls in gay hats from Miriam's place of business appeared in church, great nudgers all of them, but only two came on afterwards to the house. Mrs Punt brought her son with his ever-widening mind – it was his first wedding; and a Larkins uncle, a Mr Voules, a licensed victualler, very kindly

drove over in a high-hung dogcart from Sommershill with a
plump, well-dressed wife, to give the bride away. One or two
total strangers drifted into the church and sat down observantly
in distant seats.

This sprinkling of people seemed only to enhance the cool
brown emptiness of the church, the rows and rows of empty
pews, disengaged Prayer Books, and abandoned hassocks. It
had the effect of a preposterous misfit. Johnson consulted
with a thin-legged, short-skirted verger about the disposition
of the party. The officiating clergy appeared distantly in the
doorway of the vestry putting on his surplice, and relapsed
into a contemplative cheek-scratching that was manifestly habitual. Before the bride arrived, Mr Polly's sense of the church
found an outlet in whispered criticisms of ecclesiastical architecture with Johnson. 'Early Norman arches, eh?' he said, 'or
Perpendicular.'

'Can't say,' said Johnson.

'Telessated pavements[14] all right.'

'It's well laid anyhow.'

'Can't say I admire the altar. Scrappy rather with those
flowers.'

He coughed behind his hand and cleared his throat. At the
back of his mind he was speculating whether flight at this
eleventh hour would be criminal or merely reprehensible bad
taste. A murmur from the nudgers announced the arrival of the
bridal party.

The little procession from a remote door became one of the
enduring memories of Mr Polly's life. The verger had bustled
to meet it and arrange it according to tradition and morality.
In spite of Mrs Larkins's impassioned 'Don't take her from
me yet!' he made Miriam go first with Mr Voules, the brides-
maids followed, and then himself, hopelessly unable to disen-
tangle himself from the whispering maternal anguish of Mrs
Larkins. Mrs Voules, a compact, rounded woman with a square,
expressionless face, imperturbable dignity, and a dress of
considerable fashion, completed the procession.

Mr Polly's eyes fell first upon the bride; the sight of her filled
him with a curious stir of emotion. Alarm, desire, affection,

respect – and a queer element of reluctant dislike, all played their part in that complex eddy. The grey dress made her a stranger to him, made her stiff and commonplace; she was not even the rather drooping form that had caught his facile sense of beauty when he had proposed to her in the recreation ground. There was something, too, that did not please him in the angle of her hat; it was, indeed, an ill-conceived hat with large, aimless rosettes of pink and grey. Then his mind passed to Mrs Larkins and the bonnet that was to gain such a hold upon him; it seemed to be flag-signalling as she advanced, and to the two eager, unrefined sisters he was acquiring.

A freak of fancy set him wondering where and when in the future a beautiful girl with red hair might march along some splendid aisle –. Never mind! He became aware of Mr Voules.

He became aware of Mr Voules as a watchful, blue eye of intense forcefulness. It was the eye of a man who has got hold of a situation. He was a fat, short, red-faced man, clad in a tight-fitting tail coat of black and white check, with a coquettish bow tie under the lowest of a number of crisp little red chins. He held the bride under his arm with an air of invincible championship, and his free arm flourished a grey top hat of an equestrian type. Mr Polly instantly learned from that eye that Mr Voules knew all about his longing for flight. Its azure-rimmed pupil glowed with disciplined resolution. It said: 'I've come to give this girl away, and give her away I will. I'm here now, and things have to go on all right. So don't think of it any more' – and Mr Polly didn't. A faint phantom of a certain 'lill dog' that had hovered just beneath the threshold of conscious-ness vanished into black impossibility. Until the conclusive moment of the service was attained the eye of Mr Voules watched Mr Polly relentlessly, and then instantly he relieved guard, and blew his nose into a voluminous and richly patterned handkerchief, and sighed and looked round for the approval and sympathy of Mrs Voules, and nodded to her brightly, like one who has always foretold a successful issue to things. Mr Polly felt at last like a marionette that has dropped off its wire. But it was long before that release arrived.

He became aware of Miriam breathing close to him.

'Hallo!' he said, and feeling that was clumsy and would meet the eye's disapproval: 'Grey dress – suits you no end.'

Miriam's eyes shone under her hat-brim.

'Not reely!' she whispered.

'You're all right,' he said, with the feeling of the eye's observation and criticism stiffening his lips. He cleared his throat.

The verger's hand pushed at him from behind. Someone was driving Miriam towards the altar-rail and the clergyman. 'We're in for it,' said Mr Polly to her sympathetically. 'Where? Here? Right-o.'

He was interested for a moment or so in something indescribably habitual in the clergyman's pose. What a lot of weddings he must have seen! Sick he must be of them!

'Don't let your attention wander,' said the eye.

'Got the ring?' whispered Johnson.

'Pawned it yesterday,' answered Mr Polly, with an attempt at lightness, and then had a dreadful moment under that pitiless scrutiny while he felt in the wrong waistcoat pocket. . . .

The officiating clergy sighed deeply, began, and married them wearily and without any hitch.

'D'bloved we gath'd gether sighto' Gard 'n face this con'gation join gather Man Wom Ho Mat'mony whichis on'bl state stooted by Gard in times mans in'cency. . . .'

Mr Polly's thoughts wandered wide and far, and once again something like a cold hand touched his heart, and he saw a sweet face in sunshine under the shadow of trees.

Someone was nudging him. It was Johnson's finger diverting his eyes to the crucial place in the Prayer Book to which they had come.

'Wiltou lover, cumfer, oner keeper sickness and health? . . .'

'*Say, "I will".*'

Mr Polly moistened his lips. 'I will,' he said hoarsely.

Miriam, nearly inaudible, answered some similar demand.

Then the clergyman said: 'Who gi's Wom mad't this man?'

'Well, *I'm* doing that,' said Mr Voules in a refreshingly full voice, and looking round the church.

'Pete arf me,' said the clergyman to Mr Polly. 'Take thee Mirum wed wife—'

'Take thee Mi'm wed' wife,' said Mr Polly.

'Have hold this day ford.'

'Have hold this day ford.'

'Betworse, richypoo'.'

'Bet worse, richypoo'. . . .'

Then came Miriam's turn.

'Lego hands,' said the clergyman, 'gothering? No! On book. So! Here! Pete arf me "Wis ring Ivy wed."'

'Wis ring Ivy wed—'

So it went on, blurred and hurried, like the momentary vision of a very beautiful thing seen through the smoke of a passing train. . . .

'Now, my boy,' said Mr Voules at last, gripping Mr Polly's elbow tightly, 'you've got to sign the registry and there you are! Done!'

Before him stood Miriam, a little stiffly, the hat with a slight rake across her forehead, and a kind of questioning hesitation in her face. Mr Voules urged him past her.

It was astounding. She was his wife!

And for some reason Miriam and Mrs Larkins were sobbing, and Annie was looking grave. Hadn't they, after all, wanted him to marry her? Because if that was the case—!

He became aware for the first time of the presence of Uncle Pentstemon in the background but approaching, wearing a tie of a light mineral blue colour, and grinning and sucking enigmatically and judicially round his principal tooth.

5

It was in the vestry that the force of Mr Voules's personality began to show at its true value. He seemed to open out, like the fisherman's Ginn[15] from the pot, and spread over everything directly the restraints of the ceremony were at an end.

'Ceremony,' he said to the clergyman, 'excellent, excellent.' He also shook hands with Mrs Larkins, who clung to him for a space, and kissed Miriam on the cheek. 'First kiss for me,' he said, 'anyhow.'

He led Mr Polly to the register by the arm, and then got

chairs for Mrs Larkins and his wife. He then turned on Miriam. 'Now, young people,' he said. 'One! or *I* shall again.'

'That's right,' said Mr Voules. 'Same again, Miss.'

Mr Polly was overcome with modest confusion, and turning, found a refuge from this publicity in the arms of Mrs Larkins. Then in a state of profuse moisture he was assaulted and kissed by Annie and Minnie, who were immediately kissed upon some indistinctly stated grounds by Mr Voules, who then kissed the entirely impassive Mrs Voules, and smacked his lips and remarked, 'Home again safe and sound.' Then, with a strange harrowing cry, Mrs Larkins seized upon and bedewed Miriam with kisses. Annie and Minnie kissed each other, and Johnson went abruptly to the door of the vestry and stared into the church, no doubt with ideas of sanctuary in his mind.[16] 'Like a bit of a kiss round sometimes,' said Mr Voules, and made a kind of hissing noise with his teeth, and suddenly smacked his hands together with great *éclat* several times. Meanwhile the clergyman scratched his cheek with one hand and fiddled the pen with the other, and the verger coughed protestingly.

'The dogcart's just outside,' said Mr Voules. 'No walking home today for the bride, M'am.'

'Not going to drive us?' cried Annie.

'The happy pair, Miss. *Your* turn soon.'

'Get out!' said Annie. 'I shan't marry – ever.'

'You won't be able to help it. You'll have to do it, just to disperse the crowd.' Mr Voules laid his hand on Mr Polly's shoulder. 'The bridegroom gives his arm to the bride. Hands across, and down the middle. Prump, Prump, Perump-pump-pump-pump-perump.'

Mr Polly found himself and the bride leading the way towards the western door.

Mrs Larkins passed close to Uncle Pentstemon, sobbing too earnestly to be aware of him. 'Such a goo'-goo'-goo' girl,' she sobbed.

'Didn't think I'd come, did you?' said Uncle Pentstemon; but she swept past him, too busy with the expression of her feelings to observe him.

'She didn't think I'd come, I lay,' said Uncle Pentstemon, a little foiled, but effecting an auditory lodgement upon Johnson.

'I don't know,' said Johnson, uncomfortable. 'I suppose you were asked. How are you getting on?'

'I was *arst*,' said Uncle Pentstemon, and brooded for a moment.

'I goes about seeing wonders,' he added, and then in a sort of enhanced undertone, 'One of 'er girls gettin' married. That's what I means by wonders. Lord's goodness! Wow!'

'Nothing the matter?' asked Johnson.

'Got it in the back for a moment. Going to be a change of weather, I suppose,' said Uncle Pentstemon. 'I brought 'er a nice present, too, what I got in this passel. Vallyble old tea caddy that uset' be my mother's. What I kep' my baccy in for years and years – till the hinge at the back got broke. It ain't been no use to me particular since, so thinks I, drat it! I may as well give it to 'er as not. . . .'

Mr Polly found himself emerging from the western door.

Outside, a crowd of half a dozen adults and about fifty children had collected, and hailed the approach of the newly wedded couple with a faint, indeterminate cheer. All the children were holding something in little bags, and his attention was caught by the expression of vindictive concentration upon the face of a small, big-eared boy in the foreground. He didn't for the moment realize what these things might import. Then he received a stinging handful of rice in the ear, and a great light shone.

'Not yet, you young fool,' he heard Mr Voules saying behind him, and then a second handful spoke against his hat.

'Not yet,' said Mr Voules, with increasing emphasis, and Mr Polly became aware that he and Miriam were the focus of two crescents of small boys, each with the light of massacre in his eyes and a grubby fist clutching into a paper bag for rice, and that Mr Voules was warding off probable discharges with a large red hand.

The dogcart was in charge of a loafer, and the horse and the whip were adorned with white favours, and the back seat was confused, but not untenable, with hampers. 'Up we go,' said Mr Voules. 'Old birds in front and young ones behind.' An ominous group of ill-restrained rice-throwers followed them up as they mounted.

'Get your handkerchief for your face,' said Mr Polly to his bride, and took the place next the pavement with considerable heroism, held on, gripped his hat, shut his eyes, and prepared for the worst. 'Off!' said Mr Voules, and a concentrated fire came stinging Mr Polly's face.

The horse shied, and when the bridegroom could look at the world again it was manifest the dogcart had just missed an electric tram by a hair's breadth, and far away outside the church railings the verger and Johnson were battling with an active crowd of small boys for the life of the rest of the Larkins family. Mrs Punt and her son had escaped across the road, the son trailing and stumbling at the end of a remorseless arm; but Uncle Pentstemon, encumbered by the tea caddy, was the centre of a little circle of his own, and appeared to be dratting them all very heartily. Remoter, a policeman approached with an air of tranquil unconsciousness.

'Steady, you idiot, stead-y!' cried Mr Voules; and then over his shoulder, 'I brought that rice. I like old customs. – Whoa! stead-y.'

The dogcart swerved violently, and then, evoking a shout of groundless alarm from a cyclist, took a corner, and the rest of the wedding party was hidden from Mr Polly's eyes.

6

'We'll get the stuff into the house before the old gal comes along,' said Mr Voules, 'if you'll hold the hoss.'

'How about the key?' asked Mr Polly.

'I got the key, coming.'

And while Mr Polly held the sweating horse and dodged the foam that dripped from its bit, the house absorbed Miriam and Mr Voules altogether. Mr Voules carried in the various hampers he had brought with him, and finally closed the door behind him.

For some time Mr Polly remained alone with his charge in the little blind alley outside the Larkins's house, while the

neighbours scrutinized him from behind their blinds. He reflected that he was a married man, that he must look very like
a fool, that the head of a horse is a silly shape and its eye a
bulger; he wondered what the horse thought of him, and
whether it really liked being held and patted on the neck, or
whether it only submitted out of contempt. Did it know he
was married? Then he wondered if the clergyman had thought
him much of an ass, and whether the individual lurking
behind the lace curtains of the front room next door was a man
or a woman. A door opened over the way, and an elderly
gentleman in a kind of embroidered fez appeared smoking a
pipe, with a quiet, satisfied expression. He regarded Mr Polly
for some time with mild but sustained curiosity. Finally he
called: 'Hi!'

'Hallo!' said Mr Polly.

'You needn't 'old that 'orse,' said the old gentleman.

'Spirited beast,' said Mr Polly. 'And,' – with some faint
analogy to ginger beer in his mind – 'he's up today.'

' 'E won't turn 'isself round,' said the old gentleman, 'any'ow.
And there ain't no way through for 'im to go.'

'*Verbum sap*,'[17] said Mr Polly, and abandoned the horse and
turned to the door. It opened to him just as Mrs Larkins, on
the arm of Johnson, followed by Annie, Minnie, two friends,
Mrs Punt and her son, and at a slight distance Uncle Pentstemon, appeared round the corner.

'They're coming,' he said to Miriam, and put an arm about
her and gave her a kiss.

She was kissing him back, when they were startled violently
by the shying of two empty hampers into the passage. Then Mr
Voules appeared holding a third.

'Here! you'll have plenty of time for that presently,' he said;
'get these hampers away before the old girl comes. I got a cold
collation here to make her sit up. My eye!'

Miriam took the hampers, and Mr Polly, under compulsion
from Mr Voules, went into the little front room. A profuse pie
and a large ham had been added to the modest provision of
Mrs Larkins, and a number of select-looking bottles shouldered
the bottle of sherry and the bottle of port she had got to grace

the feast. They certainly went better with the iced wedding cake in the middle. Mrs Voules, still impassive, stood by the window regarding these things with faint approval.

'Makes it look a bit thicker, eh?' said Mr Voules, and blew out both his cheeks, and smacked his hands together violently several times. 'Surprise the old girl no end.'

He stood back and smiled and bowed with arms extended as the others came clustering at the door.

'Why, Un-cle Voules!' cried Annie, with a rising note.

It was his reward.

And then came a great wedging and squeezing and crowding into the little room. Nearly everyone was hungry, and eyes brightened at the sight of the pie and the ham and the convivial array of bottles. 'Sit down, everyone,' cried Mr Voules. 'Leaning against anything counts as sitting, and makes it easier to shake down the grub!'

The two friends from Miriam's place of business came into the room among the first, and then wedged themselves so hopelessly against Johnson in an attempt to get out again to take off their things upstairs, that they abandoned the attempt. Amid the struggle Mr Polly saw Uncle Pentstemon relieve himself of his parcel by giving it to the bride. 'Here!' he said, and handed it to her. 'Weddin' present,' he explained, and added with a confidential chuckle, '*I* never thought I'd 'ave to give one – ever.'

'Who says steak and kidney pie?' bawled Mr Voules. 'Who says steak and kidney pie? You 'ave a drop of old Tommy,[18] Martha. That's what you want to steady you. . . .

'Sit down, everyone, and don't all speak at once. Who says steak and kidney pie? . . .'

'Vociceratious,' whispered Mr Polly. 'Convivial vociferations.'[19]

'Bit of 'am with it,' shouted Mr Voules, poising a slice of ham on his knife. 'Anyone 'ave a bit of 'am with it? Won't that little man of yours, Mrs Punt – won't 'e 'ave a bit of 'am? . . .

'And now, ladies and gentlemen,' said Mr Voules, still standing and dominating the crammed roomful, 'now you got your plates filled, and something I can warrant you good in your glasses, wot about drinking the 'ealth of the bride?'

'Eat a bit fust,' said Uncle Pentstemon, speaking with his mouth full, amidst murmurs of applause. 'Eat a bit fust.'

So they did, and the plates clattered and the glasses clinked.

Mr Polly stood shoulder to shoulder with Johnson for a moment. 'In for it,' said Mr Polly cheeringly.

'Cheer up, O' Man, and peck a bit. No reason why *you* shouldn't eat, you know.'

The Punt boy stood on Mr Polly's boots for a minute, struggling violently against the compunction of Mrs Punt's grip.

'Pie,' said the Punt boy, 'pie!'

'You sit 'ere and 'ave 'am, my lord!' said Mrs Punt, prevailing. 'Pie you can't 'ave and you won't.'

'Lor' bless my heart, Mrs Punt!' protested Mr Voules, 'let the boy 'ave a bit if he wants it – wedding and all!'

'You 'aven't 'ad 'im sick on your 'ands, Uncle Voules,' said Mrs Punt. 'Else you wouldn't want to humour his fancies as you do. . . .'

'I can't help feeling it's a mistake, O' Man,' said Johnson, in a confidential undertone. 'I can't help feeling you've been Rash. Let's hope for the best.'

'Always glad of good wishes, O' Man,' said Mr Polly. 'You'd better have a drink or something. Anyhow, sit down to it.'

Johnson subsided gloomily, and Mr Polly secured some ham and carried it off, and sat himself down on the sewing machine on the floor in the corner to devour it. He was hungry, and a little cut off from the rest of the company by Mrs Voules's hat and back, and he occupied himself for a time with ham and his own thoughts. He became aware of a series of jangling concussions on the table. He craned his neck, and discovered that Mr Voules was standing up and leaning forward over the table in the manner distinctive of after dinner speeches, tapping upon the table with a black bottle. 'Ladies and gentlemen,' said Mr Voules, raising his glass solemnly in the empty desert of sound he had made, and paused for a second or so. 'Ladies and gentlemen – the Bride.' He searched his mind for some suitable wreath of speech, and brightened at last with discovery. 'Here's luck to her!' he said at last.

'Here's Luck!' said Johnson hopelessly but resolutely, and raised his glass. Everybody murmured, 'Here's Luck.'

'Luck!' said Mr Polly, unseen in his corner, lifting a forkful of ham.

'That's all right,' said Mr Voules, with a sigh of relief at having brought off a difficult operation. 'And now, who's for a bit more pie?'

For a time conversation was fragmentary again. But presently Mr Voules rose from his chair again, and produced a silence by renewed hammering; he had subsided with a contented smile after his first oratorical effort. 'Ladies and gents,' he said, 'fill up for a second toast: the happy Bridegroom!' He stood for half a minute searching his mind for the apt phrase that came at last in a rush. 'Here's (hic) luck to *him*,' said Mr Voules.

'Luck to him!' said everyone; and Mr Polly, standing up behind Mrs Voules, bowed amiably, amidst enthusiasm.

'He may say what he likes,' said Mrs Larkins, 'he's *got* luck. That girl's a treasure of treasures, and always has been ever since she tried to nurse her own little sister being but three at the time and fell the full flight of stairs from top to bottom, no hurt that any outward eye 'as ever seen but always ready and helping, always tidying and busy. A treasure I must say, and a treasure I will say, giving no more than her due. . . .'

She was silenced altogether by a rapping sound that would not be denied. Mr Voules had been struck by a fresh idea, and was standing up and hammering with the bottle again.

'The third Toast, ladies and gentlemen,' he said; 'fill up, please. The Mother of the Bride. I – er . . . Uoo . . .'Ere! . . . Ladies and gem, 'Ere's Luck to 'er! . . .'

7

The dingy little room was stuffy and crowded to its utmost limit, and Mr Polly's skies were dark with the sense of irreparable acts. Everybody seemed noisy and greedy, and doing foolish things. Miriam, still in that unbecoming hat – for presently they had to start off to the station together – sat just beyond Mrs Punt and her son, doing her share in the hospitalities, and

ever and again glancing at him with a deliberately encouraging
smile. Once she leaned over the back of the chair to him and
whispered cheeringly, 'Soon be together now.' Next to her sat
Johnson, profoundly silent, and then Annie, talking vigorously
to a friend. Uncle Pentstemon was eating voraciously opposite,
but with a kindling eye for Annie. Mrs Larkins sat next Mr
Voules. She was unable to eat a mouthful, she declared, it would
choke her; but ever and again Mr Voules wooed her to swallow
a little drop of liquid refreshment.

There seemed a lot of rice upon everybody, in their hats and
hair and the folds of their garments.

Presently Mr Voules was hammering the table for the fourth
time in the interests of the Best Man. . . .

All feasts come to an end at last, and the break-up of things
was precipitated by alarming symptoms on the part of Master
Punt. He was taken out hastily after a whispered consultation;
and since he had got into the corner between the fireplace and
the cupboard, that meant everyone moving to make way for
him. Johnson took the opportunity to say, 'Well, so long,' to
anyone who might be listening, and disappear. Mr Polly found
himself smoking a cigarette and walking up and down outside
in the company of Uncle Pentstemon, while Mr Voules replaced
bottles in hampers, and prepared for departure, and the
womenkind of the party crowded upstairs with the bride. Mr
Polly felt taciturn, but the events of the day had stirred the
mind of Uncle Pentstemon to speech. And so he spoke, discursively and disconnectedly, a little heedless of his listener, as
wise old men will.

'They do say,' said Uncle Pentstemon, 'one funeral makes
many. This time it's a wedding. But it's all very much of a
muchness. . . .

''Am *do* get in my teeth nowadays,' said Uncle Pentstemon,
'I can't understand it. 'Tisn't like there was nubblicks[20] or
strings or such in 'am. It's a plain food, sure-ly.

'You *got* to get married,' said Uncle Pentstemon, resuming
his discourse. 'That's the way of it. Some has. Some hain't. I
done it long before I was your age. It hain't for me to blame
you. You can't 'elp being the marrying sort any more than me.

It's nat'ral – like poaching, or drinking, or wind on the stummik. You can't 'elp it, and there you are! As for the good of it, there ain't no particular good in it as I can see. It's a toss-up. The hotter come, the sooner cold; but they all gets tired of it sooner or later. . . . I hain't no grounds to complain. Two I've 'ad and buried, and might 'ave 'ad a third, and never no worrit with kids – never. . . .

'You done well not to 'ave the big gal. I will say that for ye. She's a gadabout grinny,[21] she is, if ever was. A gadabout grinny. Mucked up my mushroom bed to rights, she did, and I 'aven't forgot it. Got the feet of a centipede, she 'as – all over everything, and neither with your leave nor by your leave. Like a stray 'en in a pea patch. Cluck! cluck! Trying to laugh it off. *I* laughed 'er off, I did. Dratted lumpin' baggage! . . .'

For a while he mused malevolently upon Annie, and routed out a reluctant crumb from some coy sitting-out place in his tooth.

'Wimmin's a toss-up,' said Uncle Pentstemon. 'Prize packets they are, and you can't tell what's in 'em till you took 'em 'ome and undone 'em. Never was a bachelor married yet that didn't buy a pig in a poke. Never! Marriage seems to change the very natures in 'em through and through. You can't tell what they won't turn into – nohow.

'I seen the nicest girls go wrong,' said Uncle Pentstemon, and added with unusual thoughtfulness, 'Not that I mean *you* got one of that sort.'

He sent another crumb on to its long home with a sucking, encouraging noise.

'The wust sort's the grizzler,' Uncle Pentstemon resumed. 'If ever I'd 'ad a grizzler, I'd up and 'it 'er on the 'ead with sumpthin' pretty quick. I don't think I *could* abide a grizzler,' said Uncle Pentstemon. 'I'd liefer 'ave a lump-about like that other gal. I would indeed. I lay I'd make 'er stop laughing after a bit for all 'er airs. And mind where her clumsy great feet went. . . .

'A man's got to tackle 'em, whatever they be,' said Uncle Pentstemon, summing up the shrewd observation of an old-world lifetime. 'Good or bad,' said Uncle Pentstemon, raising his voice fearlessly, 'a man's got to tackle 'em.'

8

At last it was time for the two young people to catch the train
for Waterloo *en route* for Fishbourne. They had to hurry, and
as a concluding glory of matrimony they travelled second
class,[22] and were seen off by all the rest of the party except the
Punts, Master Punt being now beyond any question unwell.

'Off!' The train moved out of the station.

Mr Polly remained waving his hat and Mrs Polly her handkerchief until they were hidden under the bridge. The dominating
figure to the last was Mr Voules. He had followed them along
the platform, waving the equestrian grey hat and kissing his
hand to the bride.

They subsided into their seats.

'Got a compartment to ourselves, anyhow,' said Mrs Polly,
after a pause.

Silence for a moment.

'The rice 'e must 'ave bought. Pounds and pounds!'

Mr Polly felt round his collar at the thought.

'Ain't you going to kiss me, Elfrid, now we're alone together?'

He roused himself to sit forward, hands on knees, cocked
his hat over one eye, and assumed an expression of avidity
becoming to the occasion.

'Never!' he said. 'Ever!' and feigned to be selecting a place to
kiss with great discrimination.

'Come here,' he said, and drew her to him.

'Be careful of my 'at,' said Mrs Polly, yielding awkwardly.

CHAPTER 7

THE LITTLE SHOP
AT FISHBOURNE

I

For fifteen years Mr Polly was a respectable shopkeeper in
Fishbourne.

Years they were in which every day was tedious, and when
they were gone it was as if they had gone in a flash. But now
Mr Polly had good looks no more. He was, as I have described
him in the beginning of this story, thirty-seven, and fattish in a
not very healthy way, dull and yellowish about the complexion,
and with discontented wrinkles round his eyes. He sat on the stile
above Fishbourne and cried to the heavens above him: 'Oh,
Roöötten Beëëastly Silly Hole!' And he wore a rather shabby
black morning coat and vest, and his tie was richly splendid,
being from stock, and his golf cap aslant over one eye.

Fifteen years ago, and it might have seemed to you that the
queer little flower of Mr Polly's imagination might be altogether
withered and dead, and with no living seed left in any part of
him. But, indeed, it still lived as an insatiable hunger for bright
and delightful experiences, for the gracious aspect of things, for
beauty. He still read books when he had a chance – books that
told of glorious places abroad and glorious times, that wrung
a rich humour from life, and contained the delight of words
freshly and expressively grouped. But, alas! there are not many
such books, and for the newspapers and the cheap fiction that
abounded more and more in the world, Mr Polly had little
taste. There was no epithet in them. And there was no one to
talk to, as he loved to talk. And he had to mind his shop.

It was a reluctant little shop from the beginning.

He had taken it to escape the doom of Johnson's choice, and

because Fishbourne had a hold upon his imagination. He had disregarded the ill-built, cramped rooms behind it in which he would have to lurk and live, and the relentless limitations of its dimensions, the inconvenience of an underground kitchen that must necessarily be the living room in winter – the narrow yard behind giving upon the yard of the Royal Fishbourne Hotel – the tiresome sitting and waiting for custom, the restricted prospects of trade. He had visualized himself and Miriam first as at breakfast on a clear, bright, winter morning, amidst a tremendous smell of bacon, and then as having muffins for tea. He had also thought of sitting on the beach on Sunday afternoons, and of going for a walk in the country behind the town and picking marguerites and poppies. But, in fact, Miriam and he were usually extremely cross at breakfast, and it did not run to muffins at tea. And she didn't think it looked well, she said, to go trapesing about the country on Sundays.

It was unfortunate that Miriam never took to the house from the first. She did not like it when she saw it, and liked it less as she explored it. 'There's too many stairs,' she said, 'and the coal being indoors will make a lot of work.'

'Didn't think of that,' said Mr Polly, following her round.

'It'll be a hard house to keep clean,' said Miriam.

'White paint's all very well in its way,' said Miriam, 'but it shows the dirt something fearful. Better 'ave 'ad it nicely grained.'

'There's a kind of place here,' said Mr Polly, 'where we might have some flowers in pots.'

'Not me,' said Miriam. 'I've 'ad trouble enough with Minnie and 'er musk. . . .'

They stayed for a week in a cheap boarding house before they moved in. They had bought some furniture in Stamton, mostly second-hand, but with new cheap cutlery and china and linen, and they supplemented this from the Fishbourne shops. Miriam, relieved from the hilarious associations of home, developed a meagre and serious quality of her own, and went about with knitted brows pursuing some ideal of ''aving everything right'. Mr Polly gave himself to the arrangement of the shop with a certain zest, and whistled a great deal, until Miriam appeared and said that it went through her head. So soon as he had taken the shop he had filled the window with aggressive posters, announcing in no measured terms that he was going to open; and, now he was getting his stuff put out, he was resolved to show Fishbourne what window-dressing could do. He meant to give them boater straws, imitation Panamas, bathing dresses with novelties in stripes, light flannel shirts, summer ties, and ready-made flannel trousers for men, youths, and boys. Incidentally he watched the small fishmonger over the way, and had a glimpse of the china dealer next door, and wondered if a friendly nod would be out of place. And on the first Sunday in this new life he and Miriam arrayed themselves with great care, he in his wedding-funeral hat and coat and she in her going-away dress, and went processionally to church – a more respectable-looking couple you could hardly imagine – and looked about them.

Things began to settle down next week into their places. A few customers came, chiefly for bathing-suits and hat guards, and on Saturday night the cheapest straw hats and ties, and Mr Polly found himself more and more drawn towards the shop door and the social charm of the street. He found the china dealer unpacking a crate at the edge of the pavement, and remarked that it was a fine day. The china dealer gave a reluctant assent, and plunged into the crate in a manner that presented no encouragement to a loquacious neighbour.

'Zealacious commerciality,'[1] whispered Mr Polly to that unfriendly back view. . . .

2

Miriam combined earnestness of spirit with great practical incapacity. The house was never clean nor tidy, but always being frightfully disarranged for cleaning or tidying up, and she cooked because food had to be cooked, and with a sound moralist's entire disregard of the quality or the consequences. The food came from her hands done rather than improved, and looking as uncomfortable as savages clothed under duress by a missionary with a stock of outsizes. Such food is too apt to

behave resentfully, rebel, and work Obi.[2] She ceased to listen
to her husband's talk from the day she married him, and ceased
to unwrinkle the kink in her brow at his presence, giving herself
up to mental states that had a quality of preoccupation. And
she developed an idea, for which, perhaps, there was legitimate
excuse, that he was lazy. He seemed to stand about a great deal,
to read – an indolent habit – and presently to seek company
for talking. He began to attend the bar parlour of the God's
Providence Inn with some frequency, and would have done so
regularly in the evening if cards, which bored him to death, had
not arrested conversation. But the perpetual foolish variation
of the permutations and combinations of two-and-fifty cards
taken five at a time, and the meagre surprises and excitements
that ensue, had no charm for Mr Polly's mind, which was at
once too vivid in its impressions and too easily fatigued.

It was soon manifest the shop paid only in the most exacting
sense, and Miriam did not conceal her opinion that he ought
to bestir himself and 'do things', though what he was to do was
hard to say. You see, when you have once sunken your capital
in a shop you do not very easily get it out again. If customers
will not come to you cheerfully and freely, the law sets limits
upon the compulsion you may exercise. You cannot pursue
people about the streets of a watering place, compelling them
either by threats or importunity to buy flannel trousers.
Additional sources of income for a tradesman are not always
easy to find. Wintershed, at the bicycle and gramophone shop
to the right, played the organ in the church, and Clamp of the
toy-shop was pew opener and so forth; Gambell, the greengrocer, waited at table and his wife cooked, and Carter, the
watchmaker, left things to his wife while he went about the
world winding clocks; but Mr Polly had none of these arts, and
wouldn't, in spite of Miriam's quietly persistent protests, get
any other. And on summer evenings he would ride his bicycle
about the country, and if he discovered a sale where there were
books, he would as often as not waste half the next day in going
again to acquire a job lot of them haphazard, and bring them
home tied about with string, and hide them from Miriam under
the counter in the shop. That is a heartbreaking thing for any

wife with a serious investigatory turn of mind to discover. She was always thinking of burning these finds, but her natural turn for economy prevailed with her.

The books he read during those fifteen years! He read everything he got except theology, and, as he read, his little unsuccessful circumstances vanished and the wonder of life returned to him; the routine of reluctant getting up, opening shop, pretending to dust it with zest, breakfasting with a shop egg underdone or overdone, or a herring raw or charred, and coffee made Miriam's way, and full of little particles, the return to the shop, the morning paper, the standing, standing at the door saying 'How do!' to passers-by, or getting a bit of gossip, or watching unusual visitors, all these things vanished as the auditorium of a theatre vanishes when the stage is lit. He acquired hundreds of books at last – old, dusty books, books with torn covers and broken covers, fat books whose backs were naked string and glue – an inimical litter to Miriam.

There was, for example, the voyages of La Perouse,[3] with many careful, explicit woodcuts and the frankest revelations of the ways of the eighteenth-century sailorman, homely, adventurous, drunken, incontinent, and delightful, until he floated, smooth and slow, with all sails set and mirrored in the glassy water, until his head was full of the thought of shining, kindly, brown-skinned women, who smiled at him and wreathed his head with unfamiliar flowers. He had, too, a piece of a book about the lost palaces of Yucatan, those vast terraces buried in primordial forest, of whose makers there is now no human memory. With La Perouse he linked *The Island Nights' Entertainments*, and it never palled upon him that in the dusky stabbing of the 'Island of Voices'[4] something poured over the stabber's hands 'like warm tea'.[5] Queer, incommunicable joy it is, the joy of the vivid phrase that turns the statement of the horridest fact to beauty!

And another book which had no beginning for him was the second volume of the travels of the Abbés Huc and Gabet.[6] He followed those two sweet souls from their lessons in Thibetan under Sandura the Bearded (who called them donkeys, to their infinite benefit, and stole their store of butter) through a

hundred misadventures to the very heart of Lhasa; and it was
a thirst in him that was never quenched to find the other volume
and whence they came, and who in fact they were. He read
Fenimore Cooper and *Tom Cringle's Log* side by side with
Joseph Conrad,[7] and dreamt of the many-hued humanity of the
East and West Indies until his heart ached to see those sun-
soaked lands before he died. Conrad's prose had a pleasure for
him that he was never able to define, a peculiar, deep-coloured
effect. He found, too, one day, among a pile of soiled sixpenny
books at Port Burdock, to which place he sometimes rode on
his ageing bicycle, Bart Kennedy's *A Sailor Tramp*,[8] all written
in vivid jerks, and had for ever after a kindlier and more understanding eye for every burly rough who slouched through Fishbourne High Street. Sterne he read with a wavering appreciation
and some perplexity, but except for the *Pickwick Papers*, for
some reason that I do not understand, he never took at all kindly
to Dickens. Yet he liked Lever, and Thackeray's *Catherine*, and
all Dumas until he got to the *Vicomte de Bragelonne*.[9] I am
puzzled by his insensibility to Dickens, and I record it, as a
good historian should, with an admission of my perplexity. It
is much more understandable that he had no love for Scott.[10]
And I suppose it was because of his ignorance of the proper
pronunciation of words that he infinitely preferred any prose
to any metrical writing.

A book he browsed over with a recurrent pleasure was
Waterton's *Wanderings in South America*.[11] He would even
amuse himself by inventing descriptions of other birds in the
Watertonian manner, new birds that he invented, birds with
peculiarities that made him chuckle when they occurred to
him. He tried to make Rusper, the ironmonger, share this joy
with him. He read Bates, too, about the Amazon;[12] but when
he discovered that you could not see one bank from the other,
he lost, through some mysterious action of the soul that again
I cannot understand, at least a tithe of the pleasure he had
taken in that river. But he read all sorts of things; a book of old
Keltic stories collected by Joyce charmed him, and Mitford's
Tales of Old Japan,[13] and a number of paper-covered volumes,
Tales from Blackwood, he had acquired at Easewood, remained

a stand-by. He developed a quite considerable acquaintance with the plays of William Shakespeare, and in his dreams he wore cinque cento or Elizabethan clothes, and walked about a stormy, ruffling, taverning, teeming world. Great land of sublimated things, thou World of Books, happy asylum, refreshment, and refuge from the world of every day! . . .

The essential thing of those fifteen long years of shopkeeping is Mr Polly, well athwart the counter of his rather ill-lit shop, lost in a book, or rousing himself with a sigh to attend to business.

And meanwhile he got little exercise; indigestion grew with him until it ruled all his moods; he fattened and deteriorated physically, great moods of distress invaded and darkened his skies, little things irritated him more and more, and casual laughter ceased in him. His hair began to come off until he had a large bald space at the back of his head. Suddenly, one day it came to him – forgetful of those books and all he had lived and seen through them – that he had been in his shop for exactly fifteen years, that he would soon be forty, and that his life during that time had not been worth living, that it had been in apathetic and feebly hostile and critical company, ugly in detail and mean in scope, and that it had brought him at last to an outlook utterly hopeless and grey.

3

I have already had occasion to mention, indeed I have quoted, a certain high-browed gentleman living at Highbury, wearing a golden pince-nez, and writing for the most part in that very beautiful room, the library of the Climax Club.[14] There he wrestles with what he calls 'social problems' in a bloodless but at times, I think one must admit, an extremely illuminating manner. He has a fixed idea that something called a collective 'intelligence' is wanted in the world, which means in practice that you and I and everyone have to think about things frightfully hard and pool the results, and oblige ourselves to be shamelessly and persistently clear and truthful, and support and respect (I suppose) a perfect horde of professors and writers and artists and ill-groomed, difficult people, instead of using our brains in a moderate and sensible manner to play golf and bridge (pretending a sense of humour prevents our doing anything else with them), and generally taking life in a nice, easy, gentlemanly way, confound him! Well, this dome-headed monster of intellect alleges that Mr Polly was unhappy entirely through that.

'A rapidly complicating society,' he writes, 'which, as a whole, declines to contemplate its future or face the intricate problems of its organization, is in exactly the position of a man who takes no thought of dietary or regimen, who abstains from baths and exercise and gives his appetites free play. It accumulates useless and aimless lives, as a man accumulates fat and morbid products in his blood; it declines in its collective efficiency and vigour, and secretes discomfort and misery. Every phase of its evolution is accompanied by a maximum of avoidable distress and inconvenience and human waste. . . .

'Nothing can better demonstrate the collective dullness of our community, the crying need for a strenuous, intellectual renewal, than the consideration of that vast mass of useless, uncomfortable, under-educated, under-trained, and altogether pitiable people we contemplate when we use that inaccurate and misleading term, the Lower Middle Class. A great proportion of the lower middle class should properly be assigned to the unemployed and the unemployable. They are only not that, because the possession of some small hoard of money, savings during a period of wage-earning, an insurance policy or such like capital, prevents a direct appeal to the rates. But they are doing little or nothing for the community in return for what they consume; they have no understanding of any relation of service to the community, they have never been trained nor their imaginations touched to any social purpose. A great proportion of small shopkeepers, for example, are people who have, through the inefficiency that comes from inadequate training and sheer aimlessness, or through improvements in machinery or the drift of trade, been thrown out of employment, and who set up in needless shops as a method of eking out the savings upon which they count. They contrive to make sixty or seventy percent of their expenditure, the rest is drawn from the shrinking capital. Essentially their lives are failures, not the sharp and tragic failure of the labourer who gets out of work and starves, but a slow, chronic process of consecutive small losses which may end, if the individual is exceptionally fortunate, in an impoverished deathbed before actual bankruptcy or destitution supervenes. Their chances of ascendant means are less in their shops than in any lottery that was ever planned. The secular development of transit and communications has made the organization of distributing businesses upon large and economical lines inevitable; except in the chaotic confusions of newly opened countries, the day when a man might earn an independent living by unskilled, or practically unskilled, retailing has gone for ever. Yet every year sees the melancholy procession towards petty bankruptcy and imprisonment for debt go on, and there is no statesmanship in us to avert it. Every issue of every trade journal has its four or five columns of abridged bankruptcy proceedings, nearly every item in which means the final collapse of another struggling family upon the resources of the community, and continually a fresh supply of superfluous artisans and shop-assistants, coming out of employment with savings or "help" from relations, of widows with a husband's insurance money, of the ill-trained sons of parsimonious fathers, replaces the fallen in the ill-equipped, jerry-built shops that everywhere abound. . . .'

I quote these fragments from a gifted if unpleasant contemporary for what they are worth. I feel this has to come in here as the broad aspect of this History. I come back to Mr Polly, sitting upon his gate and swearing in the east wind, and so returning I have a sense of floating across unbridged abysses between the general and the particular. There, on the one hand, is the man of understanding seeing clearly – I suppose he sees clearly – the big process that dooms millions of lives to thwarting and discomfort and unhappy circumstances, and giving us no help, no hint, by which we may get that better 'collective will and intelligence' which would dam that stream of human failure; and on the other hand, Mr Polly, sitting on his gate, untrained, unwarned, confused, distressed, angry, seeing nothing except that he is, as it were, netted in greyness and discomfort – with life dancing all about him; Mr Polly with a capacity for joy and beauty at least as keen and subtle as yours or mine.

4

I have hinted that our Mother England had equipped Mr Polly for the management of his internal concerns no whit better than she had for the direction of his external affairs. With a careless generosity she affords her children a variety of foods unparalleled in the world's history, including many condiments and preserved preparations novel to the human economy. And Miriam did the cooking. Mr Polly's system, like a confused and ill-governed democracy, had been brought to a state of perpetual clamour and disorder, demanding now evil and unsuitable internal satisfactions such as pickles and vinegar and the crackling on pork, and now vindictive external expressions, such as war and bloodshed throughout the world. So that Mr Polly had been led into hatred and a series of disagreeable quarrels with his landlord, his wholesalers, and most of his neighbours.

Rumbold, the china dealer next door, seemed hostile from the first for no apparent reason, and always unpacked his crates with a full back to his new neighbour, and from the first Mr Polly resented and hated that uncivil breadth of expressionless humanity, wanted to prod it, kick it, satirize it. But you cannot satirize a back, if you have no friend to nudge while you do it.

At last Mr Polly could stand it no longer. He approached and prodded Rumbold.

' 'Ello!' said Rumbold, suddenly erect and turned about.

'Can't we have some other point of view?' said Mr Polly. 'I'm tired of the end elevation.'

'Eh?' said Mr Rumbold, frankly puzzled.

'Of all the vertebracious animals man alone raises his face to the sky, O' Man. Well, why avert it?'

Rumbold shook his head with a helpless expression.

'Don't like so much Arreary Pensy.'[15]

Rumbold, distressed, in utter obscurity.

'In fact, I'm sick of your turning your back on me, see?'

A great light shone on Rumbold. '*That's* what you're talking about!' he said.

'That's it,' said Polly.

Rumbold scratched his ear with the three strawy jampots he held in his hand. 'Way the wind blows, I expect,' he said. 'But what's the fuss?'

'No fuss!' said Mr Polly. 'Passing remark. I don't like it, O' Man, that's all.'

'Can't help it, if the wind blows my stror,' said Mr Rumbold, still far from clear about it.

'It isn't ordinary civility,' said Mr Polly.

'Got to unpack 'ow it suits me. Can't unpack with the stror blowing into one's eyes.'

'Needn't unpack like a pig rooting for truffles, need you?'

'Truffles?'

'Needn't unpack like a pig.'

Mr Rumbold apprehended something.

'Pig!' he said, impressed. 'You calling me a pig?'

'It's the side I seem to get of you.'

''Ere,' said Mr Rumbold, suddenly fierce, and shouting and making his points with gesticulated jampots, 'you go indoors. I don't want no row with you, and I don't want you to row with me. I don't know what you're after, but I'm a peaceful man – teetotaller, too, and a good thing if *you* was. See? You go indoors!'

'You mean to say – I'm asking you civilly to stop unpacking – with your back to me.'

'Pig ain't civil and you ain't sober. You go indoors and lemme go on unpacking. You – you're excited.'[16]

'D'you mean –!' Mr Polly was foiled.

He perceived an immense solidity about Rumbold.

'Get back to your shop and lemme get on with my business,' said Mr Rumbold. 'Stop calling me pigs. See? Sweep your pavemint.'

'I came here to make a civil request.'

'You came 'ere to make a row. I don't want no truck with

you. See? I don't like the looks of you. See? And I can't stand
'ere all day arguing. See?'

Pause of mutual inspection.

It occurred to Mr Polly that probably he was to some extent
in the wrong.

Mr Rumbold, blowing heavily, walked past him, deposited
the jampots in his shop with an immense affectation that there
was no Mr Polly in the world, returned, turned a scornful back
on Mr Polly, and dived to the interior of the crate. Mr Polly
stood baffled. Should he kick this solid mass before him? Should
he administer a resounding kick?

No!

He plunged his hands deeply into his trousers pockets, began
to whistle, and returned to his own doorstep with an air of
profound unconcern. There, for a time, to the tune of 'Men of
Harlech', he contemplated the receding possibility of kicking
Mr Rumbold hard. It would be splendid – and for the moment
satisfying. But he decided not to do it. For indefinable reasons
he could not do it. He went indoors and straightened up his
dress ties very slowly and thoughtfully. Presently he went to
the window and regarded Mr Rumbold obliquely. Mr Rumbold
was still unpacking. . . .

Mr Polly had no human intercourse thereafter with Rumbold
for fifteen years. He kept up a Hate.

There was a time when it seemed as if Rumbold might go, but
he had a meeting of his creditors and then went on unpacking as
before, obtusely as ever.

5

Hinks, the saddler, two shops farther down the street, was a
different case. Hinks was the aggressor – practically.

Hinks was a sporting man in his way, with that taste for
checks in costume and tight trousers which is, under Providence, so mysteriously and invariably associated with equestrian proclivities. At first Mr Polly took to him as a character,
became frequent in the God's Providence Inn under his guidance, stood and was stood drinks, and concealed a great ignor-

ance of horses until Hinks became urgent for him to play billiards or bet.

Then Mr Polly took to evading him, and Hinks ceased to conceal his opinion that Mr Polly was in reality a softish sort of flat.[17]

He did not, however, discontinue conversation with Mr Polly. He would come along to him whenever he appeared at his door and converse about sport and women and fisticuffs and the pride of life with an air of extreme initiation, until Mr Polly felt himself the faintest underdeveloped simulacrum of man that had ever hovered on the verge of non-existence.

So he invented phrases for Hinks's clothes, and took Rusper, the ironmonger, into his confidence upon the weaknesses of Hinks. He called him the 'chequered Careerist',[18] and spoke of his patterned legs as 'shivery shakys'.[19] Good things of this sort are apt to get round to people.

He was standing at his door one day, feeling bored, when Hinks appeared down the street, stood still, and regarded him with a strange, malignant expression for a space.

Mr Polly waved a hand in a rather belated salutation.

Mr Hinks spat on the pavement and appeared to reflect. Then he came towards Mr Polly portentously and paused, and spoke between his teeth in an earnest, confidential tone.

'You been flapping your mouth about me, I'm told,' he said.

Mr Polly felt suddenly spiritless. 'Not that I know of,' he answered.

'Not that you know of, be blowed! You been flapping your mouth.'

'Don't see it,' said Mr Polly.

'Don't see it, be blowed! You go flapping your silly mouth about me, and I'll give you a poke in the eye. See?'

Mr Hinks regarded the effect of this coldly but firmly, and spat again.

'Understand me?' he inquired.

'Don't recollect,' began Mr Polly.

'Don't recollect, be blowed! You flap your mouth a damn sight too much. This place gets more of your mouth than it wants. . . . Seen this?'

And Mr Hinks, having displayed a freckled fist of extraordinary size and pugginess in an ostentatiously familiar manner to
Mr Polly's close inspection by sight or smell, turned it about
this way and that, shaking it gently for a moment or so, replaced
it carefully in his pocket as if for future use, receded slowly and
watchfully for a pace, and then turned away as if to other
matters, and ceased to be, even in outward seeming, a friend. . . .

6

Mr Polly's intercourse with all his fellow-tradesmen was tar-
nished sooner or later by some such adverse incident, until not
a friend remained to him, and loneliness made even the shop
door terrible. Shops bankrupted all about him, and fresh people
came, and new acquaintances sprang up, but sooner or later a
discord was inevitable – the tension under which these badly
fed, poorly housed, bored and bothered neighbours lived made
it inevitable. The mere fact that Mr Polly had to see them every
day, that there was no getting away from them, was in itself
sufficient to make them almost unendurable to his frettingly
active mind.

Among other shopkeepers in the High Street there was
Chuffles, the grocer, a small, hairy, silently intent polygamist,
who was given rough music by the youth of the neighbourhood because of a scandal about his wife's sister,[20] and who
was nevertheless totally uninteresting, and Tonks, the second
grocer, an old man with an older, very enfeebled wife, both
submerged by piety. Tonks went bankrupt, and was succeeded
by a branch of the National Provision Company, with a young
manager exactly like a fox, except that he barked. The toy
and sweetstuff shop was kept by an old woman of repellent
manners, and so was the little fish shop at the end of the
street. The Berlin wool[21] shop, having gone bankrupt, became
a newspaper shop, then fell to a haberdasher in consumption,
and finally to a stationer; the three shops at the end of the street
wallowed in and out of insolvency in the hands of a bicycle
repairer and dealer, a gramophone dealer, a tobacconist, a six-
penny-halfpenny bazaar keeper, a shoemaker, a greengrocer,

and the exploiter of a cinematograph peepshow[22] – but none of them supplied friendship to Mr Polly.

These adventurers in commerce were all more or less distraught souls, driving without intelligible comment before the gale of fate. The two milkmen of Fishbourne were brothers who had quarrelled about their father's will and started in opposition to each other. One was stone deaf and no use to Mr Polly, and the other was a sporting man with a natural dread of epithet, who sided with Hinks. So it was all about him; on every hand, it seemed, were uncongenial people, uninteresting people, or people who conceived the deepest distrust and hostility towards him – a magic circle of suspicious, preoccupied, and dehumanized humanity. So the poison in his system poisoned the world without.

But Boomer, the wine merchant, and Tashingford, the chemist, be it noted, were fraught with pride, and held themselves to be a cut above Mr Polly. They never quarrelled with him, preferring to bear themselves from the outset as though they had already done so.

As his internal malady grew upon Mr Polly, and he became more and more a battleground of fermenting foods and warring juices, he came to hate the very sight, as people say, of every one of these neighbours. There they were, every day and all the days, just the same, echoing his own stagnation. They pained him all round the top and back of his head; they made his legs and arms weary and spiritless. The air was tasteless by reason of them. He lost his human kindliness.

In the afternoons he would hover in the shop, bored to death with his business and his home and Miriam, and yet afraid to go out because of his inflamed and magnified dislike and dread of these neighbours. He could not bring himself to go out and run the gauntlet of the observant windows and the cold and estranged eyes.

One of his last friendships was with Rusper, the ironmonger. Rusper took over Worthington's shop about three years after Mr Polly opened. He was a tall, lean, nervous, convulsive man, with an upturned, back-thrown, oval head, who read newspapers and *The Review of Reviews*[23] assiduously, had belonged

to a Literary Society somewhere once, and had some defect
of the palate that at first gave his lightest word a charm and
interest for Mr Polly. It caused a peculiar clinking sound, as
though he had something between a giggle and a gas meter[24] at
work in his neck.

His literary admirations were not precisely Mr Polly's literary
admirations; he thought books were written to enshrine Great
Thoughts, and that art was pedagogy in fancy dress; he had no
sense of phrase or epithet or richness of texture, but still he
knew there were books. He did know there were books, and
he was full of large, windy ideas of the sort he called 'Modern
(kik) Thought', and seemed needlessly and helplessly concerned
about '(kik) the Welfare of the Race'.[25]

Mr Polly would dream about that (kik) at nights.

It seemed to that undesirable mind of his that Rusper's head
was the most egg-shaped head he had ever seen; the similarity
weighed upon him, and when he found an argument growing
warm with Rusper he would say, 'Boil it some more, O' Man;
boil it harder!' or 'Six minutes at least,' allusions Rusper could
never make head or tail of, and got at last to disregard as a part
of Mr Polly's general eccentricity. For a long time that little
tendency threw no shadow over their intercourse, but it contained within it the seeds of an ultimate disruption.

Often during the days of this friendship Mr Polly would leave
his shop and walk over to Mr Rusper's establishment and stand
in his doorway and inquire, 'Well, O' Man, how's the Mind of
the Age working?' and get quite an hour of it; and sometimes
Mr Rusper would come into the outfitter's shop with 'Heard
the (kik) latest?' and spend the rest of the morning.

Then Mr Rusper married; and he married, very inconsider-
ately, a woman who was totally uninteresting to Mr Polly. A
coolness grew between them from the first intimation of her
advent. Mr Polly couldn't help thinking when he saw her that
she drew her hair back from her forehead a great deal too
tightly, and that her elbows were angular. His desire not to
mention these things in the apt terms that welled up so richly
in his mind made him awkward in her presence, and that gave
her an impression that he was hiding some guilty secret from

her. She decided he must have a bad influence upon her husband, and she made it a point to appear whenever she heard
him talking to Rusper.

One day they became a little heated about the German peril.[26]

'I lay (kik) they'll invade us,' said Rusper.

'Not a bit of it. William's not the Xerxiacious sort.'[27]

'You'll see, O' Man.'

'Just what I shan't do.'

'Before (kik) five years are out.'

'Not it.'

'Yes.'

'No.'

'Yes.'

'Oh, boil it hard!' said Mr Polly.

Then he looked up and saw Mrs Rusper standing behind the
counter, half hidden by a trophy of spades and garden shears
and a knife cleaning machine, and by her expression he knew
instantly that she understood.

The conversation paled, and presently Mr Polly withdrew.

After that estrangement increased steadily.

Mr Rusper ceased altogether to come over to the outfitter's,
and Mr Polly called upon the ironmonger only with the completest air of casualty. And everything they said to each other
led now to flat contradiction and raised voices. Rusper had
been warned in vague and alarming terms that Mr Polly insulted
and made game of him, he couldn't discover exactly where; and
so it appeared to him now that every word of Mr Polly's might
be an insult meriting his resentment, meriting it none the less
because it was masked and cloaked.

Soon Mr Polly's calls upon Mr Rusper ceased also; and
then Mr Rusper, pursuing incomprehensible lines of thought,
became afflicted with a specialized shortsightedness that applied only to Mr Polly. He would look in other directions
when Mr Polly appeared, and his large, oval face assumed an
expression of conscious serenity and deliberate happy unaware-
ness that would have maddened a far less irritable person than
Mr Polly. It evoked a strong desire to mock and ape, and
produced in his throat a cough of singular scornfulness, more

particularly when Mr Rusper also assisted with an assumed
unconsciousness that was all his own.

Then one day Mr Polly had a bicycle accident.

His bicycle was now very old, and it is one of the concomi-
tants of a bicycle's senility that its freewheel should one day
obstinately cease to be free. It corresponds to that epoch in
human decay when an old gentleman loses an incisor tooth. It
happened just as Mr Polly was approaching Mr Rusper's shop,
and the untoward chance of a motor car trying to pass a wagon
on the wrong side gave Mr Polly no choice but to get on to the
pavement and dismount. He was always accustomed to take
his time and step off his left pedal at its lowest point, but the
jamming of the freewheel gear made that lowest moment a
transitory one, and the pedal was lifting his foot for another
revolution before he realized what had happened. Before he
could dismount according to his habit the pedal had to make a
revolution, and before it could make a revolution Mr Polly
found himself among the various sonorous things with which
Mr Rusper adorned the front of his shop – zinc dustbins, household pails, lawnmowers, rakes, spades, and all manner of
clattering things. Before he got among them he had one of
those agonizing moments of helpless wrath and suspense that
seem to last ages, in which one seems to perceive everything
and think of nothing but words that are better forgotten. He
sent a column of pails thundering across the doorway, and
dismounted with one foot in a sanitary dustbin, amidst an
enormous uproar of falling ironmongery.

'Put all over the place!' he cried, and found Mr Rusper
emerging from his shop with the large tranquillities of his
countenance puckered to anger, like the frowns in the brow
of a reefing sail. He gesticulated speechlessly for a moment.

'(kik) Jer doing?' he said at last.

'Tin mantraps!' said Mr Polly.

'Jer (kik) doing?'

'Dressing all over the pavement as though the blessed town
belonged to you! Ugh!'

And Mr Polly, in attempting a dignified movement, realized
his entanglement with the dustbin for the first time. With a low,

embittering expression, he kicked his foot about in it for a moment very noisily, and finally sent it thundering to the kerb. On its way it struck a pail or so. Then Mr Polly picked up his bicycle and proposed to resume his homeward way. But the hand of Mr Rusper arrested him.

'Put it (kik) all (kik) back (kik).'

'Put it (kik) back yourself.'

'You got (kik) put it back.'

'Get out of the (kik) way.'

Mr Rusper laid one hand on the bicycle handle, and the other gripped Mr Polly's collar urgently. Whereupon Mr Polly said 'Leggo!' and again, 'D'you *hear*? Leggo!' and then drove his elbow with considerable force into the region of Mr Rusper's midriff. Whereupon Mr Rusper, with a loud, impassioned cry resembling 'Woo kik' more than any other combination of letters, released the bicycle handle, seized Mr Polly by the cap and hair, and bore his head and shoulders downwards. Thereat Mr Polly, emitting such words as everyone knows and nobody prints, butted his utmost into the concavity of Mr Rusper, entwined a leg about him, and, after terrific moments of sway-ing instability, fell headlong beneath him amidst the bicycle and pails. There on the pavement these inexpert children of a pacific age, untrained in arms and uninured to violence, abandoned themselves to amateurish and absurd efforts to hurt and injure one another – of which the most palpable consequences were dusty backs, ruffled hair, and torn and twisted collars. Mr Polly by accident got his finger into Mr Rusper's mouth, and strove earnestly for some time to prolong that aperture in the direction of Mr Rusper's ear before it occurred to Mr Rusper to bite him (and even then he didn't bite very hard), while Mr Rusper concentrated his mind almost entirely on an effort to rub Mr Polly's face on the pavement. (And their positions bristled with chances of the deadliest sort!) They didn't, from first to last, draw blood.

Then it seemed to each of them that the other had become endowed with many hands and several voices and great accessions of strength. They submitted to fate and ceased to struggle. They found themselves torn apart and held up by outwardly scandalized and inwardly delighted neighbours, and invited to explain what it was all about.

'Got to (kik) puttem all back,' panted Mr Rusper, in the expert grasp of Hinks. 'Merely asked him to (kik) puttem all back.'

Mr Polly was under restraint of little Clamp of the toyshop, who was holding his hands in a complex and uncomfortable manner that he afterwards explained to Wintershed was a combination of something romantic called 'Jujitsu'[28] and something else still more romantic called the 'Police Grip'.[29]

'Pails,' explained Mr Polly, in breathless fragments. 'All over the road. Pails. Bungs up the street with his pails. Look at them!'

'Deliber (kik) lib (kik) liberately rode into my goods (kik). Constantly (kik) annoying me (kik)!' said Mr Rusper.

They were both tremendously earnest and reasonable in their manner. They wished everyone to regard them as responsible and intellectual men acting for the love of right and the enduring good of the world. They felt they must treat this business as a profound and publicly significant affair. They wanted to explain and orate and show the entire necessity of everything they had done. Mr Polly was convinced he had never been so absolutely correct in all his life as when he planted his foot in the sanitary dustbin, and Mr Rusper considered his clutch at Mr Polly's hair as the one faultless impulse in an otherwise undistinguished career. But it was clear in their minds they might easily become ridiculous if they were not careful, if for a second they stepped over the edge of the high spirit and pitiless dignity they had hitherto maintained. At any cost they perceived they must not become ridiculous.

Mr Chuffles, the scandalous grocer, joined the throng about the principal combatants, mutely, as became an outcast, and with a sad, distressed, helpful expression picked up Mr Polly's bicycle. Gambell's summer errand boy, moved by example, restored the dustbin and pails to their self-respect.

''E ought – 'E ought (kik) pick them up,' protested Mr Rusper.

'What's it all about?' said Mr Hinks for the third time,

shaking Mr Rusper gently. ''As 'e been calling you names?'

'Simply ran into his pails – as anyone might,' said Mr Polly, 'and out he comes and scrags me.'

'(kik) Assault!' said Mr Rusper.

'He assaulted *me*,' said Mr Polly.

'Jumped (kik) into my dus'bin,' said Mr Rusper. 'That assault? Or isn't it?'

'You better drop it,' said Mr Hinks.

'Great pity they can't be'ave better, both of 'em,' said Mr Chuffles, glad for once to find himself morally unassailable.

'Anyone see it begin?' said Mr Wintershed.

'*I* was in the shop,' said Mrs Rusper suddenly, from the doorstep, piercing the little group of men and boys with the sharp horror of a woman's voice. 'If a witness is wanted, I suppose I've got a tongue. I suppose I got a voice in seeing my own husband injured. My husband went out and spoke to Mr Polly, who was jumping off and on his bicycle all among our pails and things, and immediately 'e butted him in the stomach – immediately – most savagely – butted him. Just after his dinner, too, and him far from strong. I could have screamed. But Rusper caught hold of him right away, I will say that for Rusper—'

'I'm going', said Mr Polly suddenly, releasing himself from the Anglo-Japanese grip and holding out his hands for his bicycle.

'Teach you (kik) to leave things alone,' said Mr Rusper, with an air of one who has given a lesson.

The testimony of Mrs Rusper continued relentlessly in the background.

'You'll hear of me through a summons,' said Mr Polly, preparing to wheel his bicycle.

'(kik) Me too,' said Mr Rusper.

Someone handed Mr Polly a collar. 'This yours?'

Mr Polly investigated his neck. 'I suppose it is. Anyone seen a tie?'

A small boy produced a grimy strip of spotted blue silk.

'Human life isn't safe with you,' said Mr Polly as a parting shot.

'(kik) Yours isn't,' said Mr Rusper.

And they got small satisfaction out of the Bench, which refused altogether to perceive the relentless correctitude of the behaviour of either party, and reproved the eagerness of Mrs Rusper – speaking to her gently, firmly but exasperatingly as 'My Good Woman', and telling her to 'Answer the Question! Answer the Question!'

'Seems a Pity,' said the chairman, when binding them over to keep the peace, 'you can't behave like Respectable Tradesmen. Seems a Great Pity. Bad Example to the Young and all that. Don't do any Good to the town, don't do any Good to your-selves, don't do any manner of Good, to have all the Tradesmen in the Place scrapping about the Pavement of an Afternoon. Think we're letting you off very easily this time, and hope it will be a Warning to you. Don't expect Men of your Position to come up before us. Very Regrettable Affair. Eh?'

He addressed the latter inquiry to his two colleagues.

'Exactly, exactly,' said the colleague to the right.

'Err (kik),' said Mr Rusper.

7

But the disgust that overshadowed Mr Polly's being as he sat upon the stile had other and profounder justification than his quarrel with Rusper and the indignity of appearing before the county bench. He was, for the first time in his business career, short with his rent for the approaching quarter day; and, so far as he could trust his own handling of figures, he was sixty or seventy pounds on the wrong side of solvency. And that was the outcome of fifteen years of passive endurance of dullness throughout the best years of his life. What would Miriam say when she learned this, and was invited to face the prospect of exile – Heaven knows what sort of exile – from their present home? She would grumble and scold and become limply unhelpful, he knew, and none the less so because he could not help things. She would say he ought to have worked harder, and a hundred such exasperating, pointless things. Such thoughts as these require no aid from undigested cold pork and cold potatoes and pickles to darken the soul, and with these aids his soul was black indeed.

'May as well have a bit of a walk,' said Mr Polly at last, after nearly intolerable meditations, and sat round and put a leg over the stile.

He remained still for some time before he brought over the other leg.

'Kill myself,' he murmured at last.

It was an idea that came back to his mind nowadays with a continually increasing attractiveness, more particularly after meals. Life, he felt, had no further happiness for him. He hated Miriam, and there was no getting away from her, whatever might betide. And for the rest, there was toil and struggle, toil and struggle with a failing heart and dwindling courage, to sustain that dreary duologue. 'Life's insured,' said Mr Polly; 'place is insured. I don't see it does any harm to her or anyone.'

He stuck his hands in his pockets. 'Needn't hurt much,' he said. He began to elaborate a plan.

He found it was quite interesting elaborating his plan. His countenance became less miserable and his pace quickened.

There is nothing so good in all the world for melancholia as walking, and the exercise of the imagination in planning something presently to be done, and soon the wrathful wretchedness had vanished from Mr Polly's face. He would have to do the thing secretly and elaborately, because otherwise there might be difficulties about the life insurance. He began to scheme how he could circumvent that difficulty. . . .

He took a long walk, for, after all, what is the good of hurrying back to shop when you are not only insolvent but very soon to die? His dinner and the east wind lost their sinister hold upon his soul, and when at last he came back along the Fishbourne High Street his face was unusually bright and the craving hunger of the dyspeptic was returning. So he went into the grocer's and bought a ruddily decorated tin of a brightly pink fish-like substance known as 'Deep Sea Salmon'. This he was resolved to consume, regardless of cost, with vinegar and salt and pepper as a relish to his supper.

He did, and since he and Miriam rarely talked, and Miriam thought honour and his recent behaviour demanded a hostile silence, he ate fast and copiously and soon gloomily. He ate alone, for she refrained, to mark her sense of his extravagance. Then he prowled into the High Street for a time, thought it an infernal place, tried his pipe and found it foul and bitter, and retired wearily to bed.

He slept for an hour or so, and then woke up to the contemplation of Miriam's hunched back and the riddle of life, and this bright and attractive idea of ending for ever and ever and ever all the things that were locking him in, this bright idea that shone like a baleful star above all the reek and darkness of his misery....

CHAPTER 8

MAKING AN END
TO THINGS

I

Mr Polly designed his suicide with considerable care and a quite remarkable altruism.

His passionate hatred for Miriam vanished directly the idea of getting away from her for ever became clear in his mind. He found himself full of solicitude then for her welfare. He did not want to buy his release at her expense. He had not the remotest intention of leaving her unprotected, with a painfully dead husband and a bankrupt shop on her hands. It seemed to him that he could contrive to secure for her the full benefit of both his life insurance and his fire insurance if he managed things in a tactful manner. He felt happier than he had done for years scheming out this undertaking, albeit it was, perhaps, a larger and somberer kind of happiness than had fallen to his lot before. It amazed him to think he had endured his monotony of misery and failure for so long.

But there were some queer doubts and questions in the dim, half-lit background of his mind that he had very resolutely to ignore.

'Sick of it,' he had to repeat to himself aloud to keep his determination clear and firm. His life was a failure; there was nothing more to hope for but unhappiness. Why shouldn't he?

His project was to begin the fire with the stairs that led from the ground floor to the underground kitchen and scullery. This he would soak with paraffin, and assist with firewood and paper and a brisk fire in the coal cellar underneath. He would smash a hole or so in the stairs to ventilate the blaze, and have a good pile of boxes and paper, and a convenient chair or so,

in the shop above. He would have the paraffin can upset, and
the shop lamp, as if awaiting refilling, at convenient distances
in the scullery ready to catch. Then he would smash the house
lamp on the staircase – a fall with that in his hand was to be
the ostensible cause of the blaze – and he would cut his throat
at the top of the kitchen stairs, which would then become his
funeral pyre. He would do all this on Sunday evening while
Miriam was at church, and it would appear that he had fallen
downstairs with the lamp and been burned to death. There was
really no flaw whatever that he could see in the scheme. He was
quite sure he knew how to cut his throat, deep at the side and
not to saw at the windpipe, and he was reasonably sure it
wouldn't hurt him very much. And then everything would be
at an end.

There was no particularly hurry to get the thing done, of
course, and meanwhile he occupied his mind with possible
variations of the scheme. . . .

It needed a particularly dry and dusty east wind, a Sunday
dinner of exceptional virulence, a conclusive letter from Konk,
Maybrick, Ghool and Gabbitas, his principal and most urgent
creditors, and a conversation with Miriam, arising out of
arrears of rent and leading on to mutual character sketching,
before Mr Polly could be brought to the necessary pitch of
despair to carry out his plans. He went for an embittering walk,
and came back to find Miriam in a bad temper over the tea
things, with the brewings of three-quarters of an hour in the
pot and hot buttered muffins gone leathery. He sat eating in
silence with his resolution made.

'Coming to church?' said Miriam after she had cleared away.

'Rather. I got a lot to be grateful for,' said Mr Polly.

'You got what you deserve,' said Miriam.

'Suppose I have,' said Mr Polly, and went and stared out of
the back window at a despondent horse in the hotel yard.

He was still standing there when Miriam came downstairs
dressed for church. Something in his immobility struck home
to her. 'You'd better come to church than mope,' she said.

'I shan't mope,' he answered.

She remained still. Her presence irritated him. He felt that in another moment he should say something absurd to her, make some last appeal for that understanding she had never been able to give. 'Oh! *go* to church,' he said.

In another moment the outer door slammed upon her. 'Good riddance!' said Mr Polly.

He turned about. 'I've had my whack,' he said.

He reflected. 'I don't see she'll have any cause to holler,' he said. 'Beastly Home! Beastly Life!'

For a space he remained thoughtful. 'Here goes!' he said at last.

2

For twenty minutes Mr Polly busied himself about the house, making his preparations very neatly and methodically.

He opened the attic windows, in order to make sure of a good draught through the house, and drew down the blinds at the back and shut the kitchen door to conceal his arrangements from casual observation. At the end he would open the door on the yard and so make a clean, clear draught right through the house. He hacked at, and wedged off, the tread of a stair. He cleared out the coals from under the staircase, and built a neat fire of firewood and paper there; he splashed about paraffin and arranged the lamps and can even as he had designed, and made a fine, inflammable pile of things in the little parlour behind the shop. 'Looks pretty arsonical,' he said, as he surveyed it all. 'Wouldn't do to have a caller now. Now for the stairs!'

'Plenty of time,' he assured himself, and took the lamp which was to explain the whole affair, and went to the head of the staircase between the scullery and the parlour. He sat down in the twilight, with the unlit lamp beside him, and surveyed things. He must light the fire in the coal cellar under the stairs, open the back door, then come up them very quickly and light the paraffin puddles[1] on each step, then sit down here again and cut his throat. He drew his razor from his pocket and felt the edge. It wouldn't hurt much, and in ten minutes he would be indistinguishable ashes in the blaze.

And this was the end of life for him!

The end! And it seemed to him now that life had never begun for him, never! It was as if his soul had been cramped and his eyes bandaged from the hour of his birth. Why had he lived such a life? Why had he submitted to things, blundered into things? Why had he never insisted on the things he thought beautiful and the things he desired, never sought them, fought for them, taken any risk for them, died rather than abandon them? They were the things that mattered. Safety did not matter. A living did not matter unless there were things to live for....

He had been a fool, a coward and a fool; he had been fooled, too, for no one had ever warned him to take a firm hold upon life, no one had ever told him of the littleness of fear or pain or death. But what was the good of going through it now again? It was over and done with.

The clock in the back parlour pinged the half-hour.

'Time!' said Mr Polly, and stood up.

For an instant he battled with an impulse to put it all back, hastily, guiltily, and abandon this desperate plan of suicide for ever.

But Miriam would smell the paraffin!

'No way out this time, O' Man,' said Mr Polly, and went slowly downstairs, matchbox in hand.

He paused for five seconds, perhaps, to listen to noises in the yard of the Royal Fishbourne Hotel before he struck his match. It trembled a little in his hand. The paper blackened, and an edge of blue flame ran outward and spread. The fire burned up readily, and in an instant the wood was crackling cheerfully.

Someone might hear. He must hurry.

He lit a pool of paraffin on the scullery floor, and instantly a nest of wavering blue flame became agog for prey. He went up the stairs three steps at a time, with one eager blue flicker in pursuit of him. He seized the lamp at the top. 'Now!' he said, and flung it smashing. The chimney broke, but the glass receiver stood the shock and rolled to the bottom, a potential bomb. Old Rumbold would hear that and wonder what it was. . . . He'd know soon enough!

Then Mr Polly stood hesitating, razor in hand, and then sat down. He was trembling violently, but quite unafraid.

He drew the blade lightly under one ear. 'Lord!' but it stung like a nettle!

Then he perceived a little blue thread of flame running up his leg. It arrested his attention, and for a moment he sat, razor in hand, staring at it. It must be paraffin! On his trousers that had caught fire on the stairs. Of course his legs were wet with paraffin! He smacked the flicker with his hand to put it out, and felt his leg burn as he did so. But his trousers still charred and glowed. It seemed to him necessary that he must put this out before he cut his throat. He put down the razor beside him to smack with both hands very eagerly. And as he did so a thin, tall, red flame came up through the hole in the stairs he had made and stood still, quite still, as it seemed, and looked at him. It was a strange-looking flame, a flattish, salmon colour, redly streaked. It was so queer and quiet-mannered that the sight of it held Mr Polly agape.

'Whuff!' went the can of paraffin below, and boiled over with stinking white fire. At the outbreak, the salmon-coloured flames shivered and ducked and then doubled and vanished, and instantly all the staircase was noisily ablaze.

Mr Polly sprang up and backwards, as though the uprushing tongues of fire were a pack of eager wolves.

'Good Lord!' he cried, like a man who wakes up from a dream.

He swore sharply, and slapped again at a recrudescent flame upon his leg.

'What the Deuce shall I do? I'm soaked with the confounded stuff!'

He had nerved himself for throat-cutting, but this was fire!

He wanted to delay things, to put the fire out for a moment while he did his business. The idea of arresting all this hurry with water occurred to him.

There was no water in the little parlour and none in the shop. He hesitated for a moment whether he should not run upstairs to the bedroom and get a ewer of water to throw on the flames. At this rate Rumbold's would be ablaze in five minutes. Things

were going all too fast for Mr Polly. He ran towards the staircase door, and its hot breath pulled him up sharply. Then he
dashed out through the shop. The catch of the front door
was sometimes obstinate; it was now, and instantly he became
frantic. He rattled and stormed and felt the parlour already
ablaze behind him. In another moment he was in the High
Street with the door wide open.

The staircase behind him was crackling now like horsewhips
and pistol shots.

He had a vague sense that he wasn't doing as he had proposed, but the chief thing was his sense of that uncontrolled
fire within. What was he going to do? There was the fire brigade
station next door but one.

The Fishbourne High Street had never seemed so empty.

Far off, at the corner by the God's Providence Inn, a group of
three stiff hobbledehoys[2] in their black, neat clothes conversed
intermittently with Taplow, the policeman.

'Hi!' bawled Mr Polly to them. 'Fire! Fire!' and, struck by a
horrible thought, he thought of Rumbold's deaf mother-in-law
upstairs, began to bang and kick and rattle with the utmost
fury at Rumbold's shop door.

'Hi!' he repeated, 'Fire!'

3

That was the beginning of the great Fishbourne fire, which
burned its way sideways into Mr Rusper's piles of crates and
straw, and backwards to the petrol and stabling[3] of the Royal
Fishbourne Hotel, and spread from that basis until it seemed
half Fishbourne would be ablaze. The east wind, which had
been gathering in strength all that day, fanned the flames; everything was dry and ready, and the little shed beyond Rumbold's,
in which the local fire brigade kept its manual,[4] was alight
before the Fishbourne fire hose could be saved from disaster.
In a marvellously short time a great column of black smoke,
shot with red streamers, rose out of the middle of the High
Street, and all Fishbourne was alive with excitement.

Much of the more respectable elements of Fishbourne society

was in church or chapel; many, however, had been tempted by
the blue sky and the hard freshness of spring to take walks
inland, and there had been the usual disappearance of loungers
and conversationalists from the beach and the back streets
when, at the hour of six, the shooting of bolts and the turning
of keys had ended the British Ramadan,[5] that weekly interlude
of drought our law imposes. The youth of the place were scattered on the beach or playing in backyards, under threat if their
clothes were dirtied; and the adolescent were disposed in pairs
among the more secluded corners to be found upon the outskirts
of the place. Several godless youths, seasick, but fishing steadily,
were tossing upon the sea in old Tarbold the infidel's boat, and
the Clamps were entertaining cousins from Port Burdock. Such
few visitors as Fishbourne could boast in the spring were at
church or on the beach. To all these that column of smoke did
in a manner address itself. 'Look here!' it said, 'this, within
limits, is your affair; what are you going to do?'

The three hobbledehoys, had it been a weekday and they in
working clothes, might have felt free to act, but the stiffness of
black was upon them, and they simply moved to the corner by
Rusper's to take a better view of Mr Polly beating at his door.
The policeman was a young, inexpert constable with far too
lively a sense of the public house. He put his head inside the
Private Bar, to the horror of everyone there. But there was no
breach of the law, thank Heaven! 'Polly's and Rumbold's on
fire!' he said, and vanished again. A window opened in the top
storey over Boomer's shop, and Boomer, captain of the fire
brigade, appeared, staring out with a blank expression. Still
staring, he began to fumble with his collar and tie; manifestly
he had to put on his uniform. Hinks's dog, which had been
lying on the pavement outside Wintershed's, woke up, and
having regarded Mr Polly suspiciously for some time, growled
nervously and went round the corner into Granville Alley. Mr
Polly continued to beat and kick at Rumbold's door.

Then the public houses began to vomit forth the less desirable
elements of Fishbourne society; boys and men were moved to
run and shout, and more windows went up as the stir increased.
Tashingford, the chemist, appeared, at his door, in shirtsleeves

and an apron, with his photographic plate holders in his hand. And then, like a vision of purpose, came Mr Gambell, the greengrocer, running out of Gayford's alley and buttoning on his jacket as he ran. His great brass fireman's helmet was on his head, hiding it all but the sharp nose, the firm mouth, the intrepid chin. He ran straight to the fire station and tried the door, and turned about and met the eye of Boomer still at his upper window. 'The key!' cried Mr Gambell, 'the key!'

Mr Boomer made some inaudible explanation about his trousers and half a minute.

'Seen old Rumbold?' cried Mr Polly, approaching Mr Gambell.

'Gone over Downford for a walk,' said Mr Gambell. 'He told me! But look 'ere! We 'aven't got the key!'

'Lord!' said Mr Polly, and regarded the china shop with open eyes. He knew the old woman must be there alone. He went back to the shop front, and stood surveying it in infinite perplexity. The other activities in the street did not interest him. A deaf old lady somewhere upstairs there! Precious moments passing! Suddenly he was struck by an idea, and vanished from public vision into the open door of the Royal Fishbourne Tap.

And now the street was getting crowded, and people were laying their hands to this and that.

Mr Rusper had been at home reading a number of tracts upon Tariff Reform, during the quiet of the wife's absence in church, and trying to work out the application of the whole question to ironmongery. He heard a clattering in the street, and for a time disregarded it, until a cry of 'Fire!' drew him to the window. He pencil-marked the tract of Chiozza Money's that he was reading side by side with one by Mr Holt Schooling,[6] made a hasty note, 'Bal of Trade say 12,000,000', and went to look out. Instantly he opened the window and ceased to believe the Fiscal Question the most urgent of human affairs.

'Good (kik) Gud!' said Mr Rusper.

For now the rapidly spreading blaze had forced the partition into Mr Rumbold's premises, swept across his cellar, clambered his garden wall by means of his well-tarred mushroom shed, and assailed the engine house. It stayed not to consume, but ran as a thing that seeks a quarry. Polly's shop and upper parts were already a furnace, and black smoke was coming out of Rumbold's cellar gratings. The fire in the engine house showed only as a sudden rush of smoke from the back, like something suddenly blown up. The fire brigade, still much under strength, were now hard at work in front of the latter building. They had got the door open all too late; they had rescued the fire escape and some buckets, and were now lugging out their manual, with the hose already a dripping mass of molten, flaring, stinking rubber. Boomer was dancing about and swearing and shouting; this direct attack upon his apparatus outraged his sense of chivalry. His subordinates hovered in a disheartened state about the rescued fire escape, and tried to piece Boomer's comments into some tangible instructions.

'Hi!' said Rusper from the window. '(kik) What's up?'

Gambell answered him out of his helmet. 'Hose!' he cried. 'Hose gone!'

'I (kik) got hose,' cried Rusper.

He had. He had a stock of several thousand feet of garden hose of various qualities and calibres, and now, he felt, was the time to use it. In another moment his shop door was open, and he was hurling pails, garden syringes, and rolls of garden hose out upon the pavement. '(kik) Undo it!' he cried to the gathering crowd in the roadway.

They did. Presently a hundred ready hands were unrolling and spreading and tangling up and twisting and hopelessly involving Mr Rusper's stock of hose, sustained by an unquenchable assurance that presently it would in some manner contain and convey water; and Mr Rusper on his knees, (kiking) violently, became incredibly busy with wire and brass junctions and all sorts of mysteries.

'Fix it to the (kik) bathroom tap!' said Mr Rusper.

Next door to the fire station was Mantell and Throbsons', the little Fishbourne branch of that celebrated firm, and Mr Boomer, seeking in a teeming mind for a plan of action, had determined to save this building. 'Someone telephone to the Port Burdock and Hampstead-on-Sea fire brigades,' he cried to the crowd, and then to his fellows: 'Cut away the woodwork of the fire station!' and so led the way into the blaze with a whirling hatchet that effected wonders of ventilation in no time.

But it was not, after all, such a bad idea of his. Mantell and Throbsons' was separated from the fire station in front by a covered glass passage, and at the back the roof of a big outhouse sloped down to the fire station leads. The sturdy longshoremen, who made up the bulk of the fire brigade, assailed the glass roof of the passage with extraordinary gusto, and made a smashing of glass that drowned for a time the rising uproar of the flames.

A number of willing volunteers started off to the new telephone office in obedience to Mr Boomer's request, only to be told, with cold official politeness by the young lady at the exchange, that all that had been done on her own initiative ten minutes ago. She parleyed with these heated enthusiasts for a space, and then returned to the window.

And, indeed, the spectacle was well worth looking at. The dusk was falling, and the flames were showing brilliantly at half a dozen points. The Royal Fishbourne Hotel Tap, which adjoined Mr Polly to the west, was being kept wet by the enthusiastic efforts of a string of volunteers with buckets of water, and above, at a bathroom window, the little German waiter was busy with the garden hose. But Mr Polly's establishment looked more like a house afire than most houses on fire contrive to look from start to finish. Every window showed eager, flickering flames, and flames like serpents' tongues were licking out of three large holes in the roof, which was already beginning to fall in. Behind, larger and abundantly spark-shot gusts of fire rose from the fodder that was now getting alight in the Royal Fishbourne Hotel stables. Next door to Mr Polly, Mr Rumbold's house was disgorging black smoke from the gratings that protected its underground windows, and smoke and occasional shivers of flame were also coming out of its first-floor windows. The fire station was better alight at the back than in front, and its woodwork burnt pretty briskly with peculiar greenish flickerings, and a pungent flavour. In the street an inaggressively disorderly crowd clambered over the rescued

fire escape, and resisted the attempts of the three local con-
stables to get it away from the danger of Mr Polly's tottering
facade; a cluster of busy forms danced and shouted and advised
on the noisy and smashing attempt to cut off Mantell and
Throbsons' from the fire station that was still in effectual progress. Further, a number of people appeared to be destroying
interminable red and grey snakes under the heated direction of
Mr Rusper – it was as if the High Street had a plague of worms;
and beyond again, the more timid and less active crowded in
front of an accumulation of arrested traffic. Most of the men
were in Sabbatical black, and this, and the white and starched
quality of the women and children in their best clothes, gave a
note of ceremony to the whole affair.

For a moment the attention of the telephone clerk was held by
the activities of Mr Tashingford, the chemist, who, regardless
of everyone else, was rushing across the road hurling fire gren-
ades into the fire station and running back for more, and then
her eyes lifted to the slanting outhouse roof that went up to
a ridge behind the parapet of Mantell and Throbsons'. An
expression of incredulity came into the telephone operator's
eyes, and gave place to hard activity. She flung up the window
and screamed out, 'Two people on the roof up there! Two
people on the roof!'

4

Her eyes had not deceived her. Two figures, which had emerged
from the upper staircase window of Mr Rumbold's and had
got, after a perilous paddle in his cistern, on to the fire station,
were now slowly but resolutely clambering up the outhouse
roof towards the back of the main premises of Messrs Mantell
and Throbsons'. They clambered slowly, and one urged and
helped the other, slipping and pausing ever and again amidst a
constant trickle of fragments of broken tile.

One was Mr Polly, with his hair wildly disordered, his face
covered with black smudges and streaked with perspiration,
and his trouser legs scorched and blackened; the other was an
elderly lady, quietly but becomingly dressed in black with small

white frills at her neck and wrists, and a Sunday cap of ecru
lace enlivened with a black velvet bow. Her hair was brushed
back from her wrinkled brow and plastered down tightly, meeting in a small knob behind; her wrinkled mouth bore that
expression of supreme resolution common with the toothless
aged. She was shaky, not with fear, but with the vibrations
natural to her years, and she spoke with a slow, quavering
firmness.

'I don't mind scrambling,' she said with piping inflexibility,
'but I can't jump, and I wun't jump.'

'Scramble, old lady, then, scramble!' said Mr Polly, pulling
her arm. 'It's one up and two down on these blessed tiles.'

'It's not what I'm used to,' she said.

'Stick to it,' said Mr Polly. 'Live and learn,' and got to the
ridge and grasped at her arm to pull her after him.

'I can't jump, mind ye,' she repeated, pressing her lips
together. 'And old ladies like me mustn't be hurried.'

'Well, let's get as high as possible, anyhow,' said Mr Polly,
urging her gently upwards. 'Shinning up a waterspout in your
line? Near as you'll get to Heaven.'

'I *can't* jump,' she said. 'I can do anything but jump.'

'Hold on,' said Mr Polly, 'while I give you a boost. That's –
wonderful.'

'So long as it isn't jumping. . . .'

The old lady grasped the parapet above, and there was a
moment of intense struggle.

'Urup!' said Mr Polly. 'Hold on! Gollys! where's she gone
to? . . .'

Then an ill-mended, wavering, yet very reassuring spring-side
boot appeared for an instant.

'Thought perhaps there wasn't any roof there!' he explained,
scrambling up over the parapet beside her.

'I've never been out on a roof before,' said the old lady. 'I'm
all disconnected. It's very bumpy. Especially that last bit. Can't
we sit here for a bit and rest? I'm not the girl I used to be.'

'You sit here ten minutes,' shouted Mr Polly, 'and you'll pop
like a roast chestnut. Don't understand me? *Roast Chestnut!*
ROAST CHESTNUT! POP! There ought to be a limit to

deafness. Come on round to the front and see if we can find an attic window. Look at this smoke!'

'Nasty!' said the old lady, her eyes following his gesture, puckering her face into an expression of great distaste.

'Come on!'

'Can't hear a word you say.'

He pulled her arm. 'Come on!'

She paused for a moment to relieve herself of a series of entirely unexpected chuckles. 'Sich goings on!' she said. 'I never did! Where's he going now?' and came along behind the parapet to the front of the drapery establishment.

Below, the street was now fully alive to their presence, and encouraged the appearance of their heads by shouts and cheers. A sort of free fight was going on round the fire escape, order represented by Mr Boomer and the very young policeman, and disorder by some partially intoxicated volunteers with views of their own about the manipulation of the apparatus. Two or three lengths of Mr Rusper's garden hose appeared to have twined themselves round the ladder. Mr Polly watched the struggle with a certain impatience, and glanced ever and again over his shoulder at the increasing volume of smoke and steam that was pouring up from the burning fire station. He decided to break an attic window and get in, and so try and get down through the shop. He found himself in a little bedroom, and returned to fetch his charge. For some time he could not make her understand his purpose.

'Got to come at once!' he shouted.

'I hain't 'ad sich a time for years!' said the old lady.

'We'll have to get down through the house!'

'Can't do no jumping,' said the old lady. 'No!'

She yielded reluctantly to his grasp.

She stared over the parapet. 'Runnin' and scurrying about like black beetles in a kitchen,' she said.

'We've got to hurry.'

'Mr Rumbold 'e's a very Quiet man. 'E likes everything Quiet. He'll be surprised to see me 'ere! Why! there 'e is!' She fumbled in her garments mysteriously, and at last produced a wrinkled pocket handkerchief and began to wave it.

'Oh, come ON!' cried Mr Polly, and seized her.

He got her into the attic, but the staircase, he found, was full of suffocating smoke, and he dared not venture below the next floor. He took her into a long dormitory, shut the door on those pungent and pervasive fumes, and opened the window, to discover the fire escape was now against the house, and all Fishbourne boiling with excitement as an immensely helmeted and active and resolute little figure ascended. In another moment the rescuer stared over the windowsill, heroic but just a trifle self-conscious and grotesque.

'Lawks-a-mussy!' said the old lady. 'Wonders and Wonders! Why! it's Mr Gambell! 'Iding 'is 'ead in that thing! I *never* did!'

'Can we get her out?' said Mr Gambell. 'There's not much time.'

'He might git stuck in it.'

'*You'll* get stuck in it,' said Mr Polly; 'come along!'

'Not for jumpin' I don't,' said the old lady, understanding his gestures rather than his words. 'Not a bit of it. I bain't no good at jumping, and I *wun't*.'

They urged her gently but firmly towards the window.

'You lemme do it my own way,' said the old lady at the sill. . . .

'I could do it better if 'e'd take it off.'

'Oh! *carm* on!'

'It's wuss than Carter's stile,' she said, 'before they mended it – with a cow looking at you.'

Mr Gambell hovered protectingly below. Mr Polly steered her aged limbs from above. An anxious crowd below babbled advice and did its best to upset the fire escape. Within, streamers of black smoke were pouring up through the cracks in the floor. For some seconds the world waited while the old lady gave herself up to reckless mirth again. 'Sich times!' she said. 'Poor Rumbold!'

Slowly they descended; and Mr Polly remained at the post of danger, steadying the long ladder, until the old lady was in safety below and sheltered by Mr Rumbold (who was in tears) and the young policeman from the urgent congratulations of the crowd. The crowd was full of an impotent passion to participate. Those nearest wanted to shake her hand, those remoter cheered.

'The fust fire I was ever in, and likely to be my last. It's a scurryin', 'urryin' business, but I'm real glad I haven't missed it,' said the old lady, as she was borne rather than led towards the refuge of the Temperance Hotel.

Also she was heard to remark: ''E was saying something about 'ot chestnuts. *I* haven't 'ad no 'ot chestnuts.'

Then the crowd became aware of Mr Polly awkwardly negotiating the top rungs of the fire escape. ''Ere 'e comes!' proclaimed a voice; and Mr Polly descended into the world again out of the conflagration he had lit to be his funeral pyre, moist, excited, and tremendously alive, amidst a tempest of applause. As he got lower and lower, the crowd howled like a pack of dogs at him. Impatient men, unable to wait for him, seized and shook his descending boots, and so brought him to earth with a run. He was rescued with difficulty from an enthusiast who wished to slake at his own expense and to his own accompaniment a thirst altogether heroic. He was hauled into the Temperance Hotel and flung like a sack, breathless and helpless, into the tear-wet embrace of Miriam.

5

With the dusk and the arrival of some county constabulary, and first one and presently two other fire engines from Port Burdock and Hampstead-on-Sea, the local talent of Fishbourne found itself forced back into a secondary, less responsible, and more observant role. I will not pursue the story of the fire to its ashes, nor will I do more than glance at the unfortunate Mr Rusper, a modern Laocoon,[7] vainly trying to retrieve his scattered hose amidst the tramplings and rushings of the Port Burdock experts.

In a small sitting-room of the Fishbourne Temperance Hotel a little group of Fishbourne tradesmen sat and conversed in fragments, and anon went to the window and looked out upon the smoking desolation of their houses across the way, and anon sat down again. They and their families were the guests of old Lady Bargrave, who had displayed the utmost sympathy and interest in their misfortunes. She had taken several people into her own house at Everdean, had engaged the Temperance Hotel as a temporary refuge, and personally superintended the housing of Mantell and Throbsons' homeless assistants. The Temperance Hotel became and remained extremely noisy and congested with people sitting about anywhere, conversing in fragments, and totally unable to get themselves to bed. The manager was an old soldier, and, following the best traditions of the service, saw that everyone had hot cocoa. Hot cocoa seemed to be about everywhere, and it was no doubt very heartening and sustaining to everyone. When the manager detected anyone disposed to be drooping or pensive, he exhorted that person at once to drink further hot cocoa and maintain a stout heart.

The hero of the occasion, the centre of interest, was Mr Polly. For he had not only caused the fire by upsetting a lighted lamp, scorching his trousers and narrowly escaping death, as indeed he had now explained in detail about twenty times, but he had further thought at once of that amiable but helpless old lady next door, had shown the utmost decision in making his way to her over the yard wall of the Royal Fishbourne Hotel, and had rescued her with persistence and vigour, in spite of the levity natural to her years. Everyone thought well of him and was anxious to show it, more especially by shaking his hand painfully and repeatedly. Mr Rumbold, breaking a silence of nearly fifteen years, thanked him profusely, said that he had never understood him properly, and declared he ought to have a medal. There seemed to be a widely diffused idea that Mr Polly ought to have a medal. Hinks thought so. He declared, moreover, and with the utmost emphasis, that Mr Polly had a crowded and richly decorated interior – or words to that effect. There was something apologetic in this persistence; it was as if he regretted past intimations that Mr Polly was internally defective and hollow. He also said that Mr Polly was a 'white man', albeit, as he developed it, with a liver of the deepest chromatic satisfactions.

Mr Polly wandered centrally through it all, with his face washed and his hair carefully brushed and parted, looking modest and more than a little absentminded, and wearing a pair of black dress trousers belonging to the manager of the Temperance Hotel – a larger man than himself in every way.

He drifted upstairs to his fellow-tradesmen, and stood for a time staring into the littered street, with its pools of water and extinguished gas lamps. His companions in misfortune resumed a fragmentary, disconnected conversation. They touched now on one aspect of the disaster and now on another, and there were intervals of silence. More or less empty cocoa cups were distributed over the table, mantelshelf, and piano, and in the middle of the table was a tin of biscuits, into which Mr Rumbold, sitting round-shouldered, dipped ever and again in an absentminded way, and munched like a distant shooting of coals. It added to the solemnity of the affair that nearly all of them were in their black Sunday clothes; little Clamp was particularly impressive and dignified in a wide open frock coat, a Gladstone-shaped[8] paper collar, and a large white and blue tie. They felt that they were in the presence of a great disaster, the sort of disaster that gets into the papers, and is even illustrated by blurred photographs of the crumbling ruins. In the presence of that sort of disaster all honourable men are lugubrious and sententious.

And yet it is impossible to deny a certain element of elation. Not one of those excellent men but was already realizing that a great door had opened, as it were, in the opaque fabric of destiny, that they were to get their money again that had seemed sunken for ever beyond any hope in the deeps of retail trade. Life was already in their imagination rising like a Phoenix from the flames.[9]

'I suppose there'll be a public subscription,' said Mr Clamp.

'Not for those who're insured,' said Mr Wintershed.

'I was thinking of them assistants from Mantell and Throbsons'. They must have lost nearly everything.'

'They'll be looked after all right,' said Mr Rumbold. 'Never fear.'

Pause.

'*I'm* insured,' said Mr Clamp with unconcealed satisfaction. 'Royal Salamander.'

'Same here,' said Mr Wintershed.

'Mine's the Glasgow Sun,' Mr Hinks remarked. 'Very good company.'

'You insured, Mr Polly?'

'He deserves to be,' said Rumbold.

'Ra–ther,' said Hinks. 'Blowed if he don't. Hard lines it *would* be – if there wasn't something for him.'

'Commercial and General,' answered Mr Polly over his shoulder, still staring out of the window. 'Oh! I'm all right.'

The topic dropped for a time, though manifestly it continued to exercise their minds.

'It's cleared me out of a lot of old stock,' said Mr Wintershed; 'that's one good thing.'

The remark was felt to be in rather questionable taste, and still more so was his next comment.

'Rusper's a bit sick it didn't reach '*im*.'

Everyone looked uncomfortable, and no one was willing to point the reason why Rusper should be a bit sick.

'Rusper's been playing a game of his own,' said Hinks. 'Wonder what he thought he was up to! Sittin' in the middle of the road with a pair of tweezers he was, and about a yard of wire – mending somethin'. Wonder he warn't run over by the Port Burdock engine.'

Presently a little chat sprang up upon the causes of fires, and Mr Polly was moved to tell for the one-and-twentieth time how it had happened. His story had now become as circumstantial and exact as the evidence of a police witness. 'Upset the lamp,' he said. 'I'd just lighted it. I was going upstairs, and my foot slipped against where one of the treads was a bit rotten, and down I went. Thing was aflare in a moment! . . .'

He yawned at the end of the discussion, and moved doorward.

'So long,' said Mr Polly.

'Goodnight,' said Mr Rumbold. 'You played a brave man's part! If you don't get a medal—'

He left an eloquent pause.

''Ear, 'ear!' said Mr Wintershed and Mr Clamp.

'Goo'-night, O' Man,' said Mr Hinks.

'Goo'-night, All,' said Mr Polly. . . .

He went slowly upstairs. The vague perplexity common to popular heroes pervaded his mind. He entered the bedroom and turned up the electric light. It was quite a pleasant room, one of the best in the Temperance Hotel, with a nice clean flowered wallpaper, and a very large looking glass. Miriam appeared to be asleep, and her shoulders were humped up under the clothes in a shapeless, forbidding lump that Mr Polly had found utterly loathsome for fifteen years. He went softly over to the dressing table and surveyed himself thoughtfully. Presently he hitched up the trousers. 'Miles too big for me,' he remarked. 'Funny not to have a pair of breeches of one's own. . . . Like being born again. Naked came I into the world.'[10]

Miriam stirred and rolled over, and stared at him.

'Hallo!' she said.

'Hallo.'

'Come to bed?'

'It's three.'

Pause while Mr Polly disrobed slowly.

'I been thinking,' said Miriam. 'It isn't going to be so bad after all. We shall get your insurance. We can easy begin all over again.'

'H'm,' said Mr Polly.

She turned her face away from him and reflected.

'Get a better house,' said Miriam, regarding the wallpaper pattern. 'I've always 'ated them stairs.'

Mr Polly removed a boot.

'Choose a better position where there's more doing,' murmured Miriam. . . .

'Not half so bad,' she whispered. . . .

'You *wanted* stirring up,' she said, half asleep. . . .

It dawned upon Mr Polly for the first time that he had forgotten something.

He ought to have cut his throat!

The fact struck him as remarkable, but as now no longer of

any particular urgency. It seemed a thing far off in the past, and he wondered why he had not thought of it before. Odd thing life is! If he had done it he would never have seen this clean and agreeable apartment with the electric light. . . . His thoughts wandered into a question of detail. Where could he have put down the razor? Somewhere in the little room behind the shop, he supposed, but he could not think where more precisely. Anyhow, it didn't matter now.

He undressed himself calmly, got into bed, and fell asleep almost immediately.

CHAPTER 9
THE POTWELL INN

I

But when a man has once broken through the paper walls of everyday circumstance, those unsubstantial walls that hold so many of us securely prisoned from the cradle to the grave, he has made a discovery. If the world does not please you, *you can change it*. Determine to alter it at any price, and you can change it altogether. You may change it to something sinister and angry, to something appalling, but it may be you will change it to something brighter, something more agreeable, and at the worst something much more interesting. There is only one sort of man who is absolutely to blame for his own misery, and that is the man who finds life dull and dreary. There are no circumstances in the world that determined action cannot alter, unless, perhaps, they are the walls of a prison cell, and even those will dissolve and change, I am told, into the infirmary compartment, at any rate, for the man who can fast with resolution. I give these things as facts and information, and with no moral intimations. And Mr Polly, lying awake at nights, with a renewed indigestion, with Miriam sleeping sonorously beside him, and a general air of inevitableness about his situation, saw through it, understood there was no inevitable any more, and escaped his former despair.

He could, for example, 'clear out'.

It became a wonderful and alluring phrase to him – 'Clear out!'

Why had he never thought of clearing out before?

He was amazed and a little shocked at the unimaginative and superfluous criminality in him that had turned old, cramped, and stagnant Fishbourne into a blaze and new beginnings. (I wish from the bottom of my heart I could add that he was properly sorry.) But something constricting and restrained seemed to have been destroyed by that flare. *Fishbourne wasn't the world.* That was the new, the essential fact of which he had lived so lamentably in ignorance. Fishbourne, as he had known it and hated it, so that he wanted to kill himself to get out of it, *wasn't the world.*

The insurance money he was to receive made everything humane and kindly and practicable. He would 'clear out' with justice and humanity. He would take exactly twenty-one pounds, and all the rest he would leave to Miriam. That seemed to him absolutely fair. Without him, she could do all sorts of things – all the sorts of things she was constantly urging him to do. . . .

And he would go off along the white road that led to Garchester, and on to Crogate and so to Tunbridge Wells, where there was a Toad Rock he had heard of[1] but never seen. (It seemed to him this must needs be a marvel.) And so to other towns and cities. He would walk and loiter by the way, and sleep in inns at night, and get an odd job here and there, and talk to strange people. Perhaps he would get quite a lot of work, and prosper; and if he did not do so he would lie down in front of a train, or wait for a warm night and then fall into some smooth, broad river. Not so bad as sitting down to a dentist – not nearly so bad. And he would never open a shop any more.

So the possibilities of the future presented themselves to Mr Polly as he lay awake at night.

It was springtime, and in the woods, so soon as one got out of reach of the sea wind, there would be anemones and primroses.

2

A month later a leisurely and dusty tramp, plump equatorially and slightly bald, with his hands in his pockets and his lips puckered to a contemplative whistle, strolled along the river bank between Uppingdon and Potwell. It was a profusely budding spring day, and greens such as God had never permitted in the world before in human memory (though, indeed, they come every year and we forget) were mirrored vividly in a mirror of equally unprecedented brown. For a time the wanderer stopped and stood still, and even the thin whistle died away from his lips as he watched a water vole run to and fro upon a little headland across the stream. The vole plopped into the water, and swam and dived, and only when the last ring of its disturbance had vanished did Mr Polly resume his thoughtful course to nowhere in particular.

For the first time in many years he had been leading a healthy human life, living constantly in the open air, walking every day for eight or nine hours, eating sparingly, accepting every conversational opportunity, not even disdaining the discussion of possible work. And beyond mending a hole in his coat, that he had made while negotiating barbed wire, with a borrowed needle and thread in a lodging house, he had done no real work at all. Neither had he worried about business nor about times and seasons. And for the first time in his life he had seen the Aurora Borealis.[2]

So far, the holiday had cost him very little. He had arranged it on a plan that was entirely his own. He had started with four five-pound notes and a pound divided into silver, and he had gone by train from Fishbourne to Ashington. At Ashington he had gone to the post office, obtained a registered letter envelope, and sent his four five-pound notes with a short, brotherly note addressed to himself at Gilhampton Post Office. He sent this letter to Gilhampton for no other reason in the world than that he liked the name of Gilhampton and the rural suggestion of its containing county, which was Sussex; and having so despatched it, he set himself to discover, mark down, and walk to Gilhampton, and so recover his resources. And having got to Gilhampton at last, he changed a five-pound note, bought four pound postal orders, and repeated his manoeuvre with nineteen pounds.

After a lapse of fifteen years he rediscovered this interesting world, about which so many people go incredibly blind and bored. He went along country roads while all the birds were

piping and chirruping and cheeping and singing, and looked at
fresh new things, and felt as happy and irresponsible as a boy
with an unexpected half holiday. And if ever the thought of
Miriam returned to him, he controlled his mind. He came to
country inns and sat for unmeasured hours talking of this and
that to those sage carters who rest for ever in the taps of country
inns, while the big, sleek, brass-jingling horses wait patiently
outside with their wagons. He got a job with some van people
who were wandering about the country with swings and a
steam roundabout, and remained with them three days, until
one of their dogs took a violent dislike to him, and made his
duties unpleasant. He talked to tramps and wayside labourers.
He snoozed under hedges by day, and in outhouses and hayricks
at night, and once, but only once, he slept in a casual ward.[3]
He felt as the etiolated grass and daisies must do when you
move the garden roller away to a new place.

He gathered a quantity of strange and interesting memories.

He crossed some misty meadows by moonlight and the mist
lay low on the grass, so low that it scarcely reached above his
waist, and houses and clumps of trees stood out like islands in
a milky sea, so sharply defined was the upper surface of the
mist-bank. He came nearer and nearer to a strange thing that
floated like a boat upon this magic lake, and behold, something
moved at the stern, and a rope was whisked at the prow, and
it had changed into a pensive cow, drowsy-eyed, regarding
him. . . .

He saw a remarkable sunset in a new valley near Maidstone,
a very red and clear sunset, a wide redness under a pale, cloud-
less heaven, and with the hills all round the edge of the sky a
deep purple blue and clear and flat, looking exactly as he had
seen mountains painted in pictures. He seemed transported
to some strange country, and would have felt no surprise if
the old labourer he came upon leaning silently over a gate had
addressed him in an unfamiliar tongue. . . .

Then one night, just towards dawn, his sleep upon a pile of
brushwood was broken by the distant rattle of a racing motor
car breaking all the speed regulations, and as he could not sleep
again, he got up and walked into Maidstone as the day came.

He had never been abroad in a town at four o'clock in his life before, and the stillness of everything in the bright sunrise impressed him profoundly. At one corner was a startling police-man, standing up in a doorway quite motionless like a waxen image. Mr Polly wished him 'good morning' unanswered, and went down to the bridge over the Medway, and sat on the parapet, very still and thoughtful, watching the town awaken, and wondering what he should do if it didn't, if the world of men never woke again. . . .

One day he found himself going along a road, with a wide space of sprouting bracken and occasional trees on either side, and suddenly this road became strangely and perplexingly fam-iliar. 'Lord!' he said, and turned about and stood. 'It can't be.'

He was incredulous, then left the road and walked along a scarcely perceptible track to the left, and came in half a minute to an old lichenous stone wall. It seemed exactly the bit of wall he had known so well. It might have been but yesterday he was in that place; there remained even a little pile of wood. It became absurdly the same wood. The bracken, perhaps, was not so high, and most of its fronds were still coiled up, that was all. Here he had stood, it seemed, and there she had sat and looked down upon him. Where was she now, and what had become of her? He counted the years back, and marvelled that beauty should have called to him with so imperious a voice – and signified nothing.

He hoisted himself with some little difficulty to the top of the wall, and saw far off under the beech trees two schoolgirls – small, insignificant, pigtailed creatures, with heads of blond and black, with their arms twined about each other's necks, no doubt telling each other the silliest secrets.

But that girl with the red hair – was she a countess? was she a queen? Children, perhaps? Had sorrow dared to touch her?

Had she forgotten altogether? . . .

A tramp sat by the roadside, thinking, and it seemed to the man in the passing motor car he must needs be plotting for another pot of beer. But, as a matter of fact, what the tramp was saying to himself over and over again, was a variant upon a well-known Hebrew word.

'Itchabod,'[4] the tramp was saying in the voice of one who reasons on the side of the inevitable. 'It's Fair Itchabod, O' Man. There's no going back to things like that.'

3

It was about two o'clock in the afternoon, one hot day in May, when Mr Polly, unhurrying and serene, came upon that broad bend of the river to which the little lawn and garden of the Potwell Inn run down. He stopped at the sight of the place and surveyed its deep tiled roof, nestling under big trees – you never get a decently big, decently shaped tree by the seaside – its sign towards the roadway, its sun-blistered green bench and tables, its shapely white windows and its row of upshooting hollyhock plants in the garden. A hedge separated the premises from a buttercup-yellow meadow, and beyond stood three poplars in a group against the sky, three exceptionally tall, graceful and harmonious poplars. It is hard to say what there was about them that made them so beautiful to Mr Polly, but they seemed to him to touch a pleasant scene with a distinction almost divine. He stood admiring them quietly for a long time.

At last the need for coarser aesthetic satisfactions arose in him.

'Provinder,' he whispered, drawing near to the inn. 'Cold sirloin, for choice. And nutbrown brew and wheaten bread.'

The nearer he came to the place the more he liked it. The windows on the ground floor were long and low, and they had pleasing red blinds. The green tables outside were agreeably ringed with memories of former drinks, and an extensive grape-vine spread level branches across the whole front of the place. Against the wall was a broken oar, two boathooks, and the stained and faded red cushions of a pleasure boat. One went up three steps to the glass-panelled door and peeped into a broad, low room with a bar and a beer-engine,[5] behind which were many bright and helpful-looking bottles against mirrors, and great and little pewter measures, and bottles fastened in brass wire upside down, with their corks replaced by taps, and a white china cask labelled 'Shrub',[6] and cigar boxes, and boxes of cigarettes, and a couple of Toby jugs and a beautifully coloured hunting scene framed and glazed, showing the most elegant people taking Piper's Cherry Brandy, and cards such as the law requires about the dilution of spirits and the illegality of bringing children into bars,[7] and satirical verses about swearing and asking for credit, and three very bright, red-cheeked wax apples, and a round-shaped clock.

But these were the mere background to the really pleasant thing in the spectacle, which was quite the plumpest woman Mr Polly had ever seen, seated in an armchair in the midst of all these bottles and glasses and glittering things, peacefully and tranquilly, and without the slightest loss of dignity, asleep. Many people would have called her a fat woman, but Mr Polly's innate sense of epithet told him from the outset that plump was the word. She had shapely brows and a straight, well-shaped nose, kind lines and contentment about her mouth, and beneath it the jolly chins clustered like chubby little cherubim about the feet of an Assumptioning Madonna.[8] Her plumpness was firm and pink and wholesome, and her hands, dimpled at every joint, were clasped in front of her; she seemed, as it were, to embrace herself with infinite confidence and kindliness, as one who knew herself good in substance, good in essence, and would show her gratitude to God by that ready acceptance of all that He had given her. Her head was a little on one side, not much, but just enough to speak of trustfulness, and rob her of the stiff effect of self-reliance. And she slept.

'*My* sort,' said Mr Polly, and opened the door very softly, divided between the desire to enter and come nearer, and an instinctive indisposition to break slumbers so manifestly sweet and satisfying.

She awoke with a start, and it amazed Mr Polly to see swift terror flash into her eyes. Instantly it had gone again.

'Law!' she said, her face softening with relief. 'I thought you was Jim.'

'I'm never Jim,' said Mr Polly.

'You've got his sort of hat.'

'Ah!' said Mr Polly, and leaned over the bar.

'It just came into my head you was Jim,' said the plump lady, dismissed the topic and stood up. 'I believe I was having forty winks,' she said, 'if all the truth was told. What can I do for you?'

'Cold meat?' said Mr Polly.

'There *is* cold meat,' the plump woman admitted.

'And room for it.'

The plump woman came and leaned over the bar and regarded him judicially but kindly. 'There's some cold boiled beef,' she said, and added, 'A bit of crisp lettuce?'

'New mustard,' said Mr Polly.

'And a tankard!'

'A tankard.'

They understood each other perfectly.

'Looking for work?' asked the plump woman.

'In a way,' said Mr Polly.

They smiled like old friends.

Whatever the truth may be about love, there is certainly such a thing as friendship at first sight. They liked each other's voices, they liked each other's way of smiling and speaking.

'It's such beautiful weather this spring,' said Mr Polly, explaining everything.

'What sort of work do you want?' she asked.

'I've never properly thought that out,' said Mr Polly. 'I've been looking round – for ideas.'

'Will you have your beef in the tap or outside? That's the tap.'

Mr Polly had a glimpse of an oaken settle. 'In the tap will be handier for you,' he said.

'Hear that?' said the plump lady.

'Hear what?'

'Listen.'

Presently the silence was broken by a distant howl – 'Ooooo-over!' 'Eh?' she said.

He nodded.

'That's the ferry. And there isn't a ferryman.'

'Could I?'

'Can you punt?'

'Never tried.'

'Well – pull the pole out before you reach the end of the punt, that's all. Try.'

Mr Polly went out again into the sunshine.

At times one can tell so much so briefly. Here are the facts then – bare. He found a punt and a pole, got across to the steps on the opposite side, picked up an elderly gentleman in an alpaca jacket and a pitch helmet, cruised with him vaguely for twenty minutes, conveyed him tortuously into the midst of a thicket of forget-me-not spangled sedges, splashed some water-weed over him, hit him twice with the punt pole, and finally landed him, alarmed but abusive, in treacherous soil at the edge of a hay meadow about forty yards downstream, where he immediately got into difficulties with a noisy, aggressive little white dog that was guarding a jacket.

Mr Polly returned in a complicated manner, but with perfect dignity, to his moorings.

He found the plump woman rather flushed and tearful, and seated at one of the green tables outside.

'I been laughing at you,' she said.

'What for?' asked Mr Polly.

'I ain't 'ad such a laugh since Jim come 'ome. When you 'it 'is 'ead, it 'urt my side.'

'It didn't hurt his head – not particularly.'

'Did you charge him anything?'

'Gratis,' said Mr Polly. 'I never thought of it.'

The plump woman pressed her hands to her sides and laughed silently for a space. 'You ought to 'ave charged 'im Sumpthing,' she said. 'You better come and have your cold meat before you do any more puntin'. You and me'll get on together.'

Presently she came and stood watching him eat. 'You eat better than you punt,' she said; and then, 'I dessay you could learn to punt.'

'Wax to receive and marble to retain,'[9] said Mr Polly. 'This beef is a Bit of All Right, M'am. I could have done differently if I hadn't been punting on an empty stomach. There's a leer[10] feeling as the pole goes in —'

'I've never held with fasting,' said the plump woman.

'You want a ferryman?'

'I want an odd man about the place.'

'I'm odd all right. What's the wages?'

'Not much, but you get tips and pickings. I've a sort of feeling it would suit you.'

'I've a sort of feeling it would. What's the duties? Fetch and carry? Ferry? Garden? Wash bottles? *Ceteris paribus?*'[11]

'That's about it,' said the fat woman.

'Give me a trial.'

'I've more than half a mind. Or I wouldn't have said anything about it. I suppose you're all right. You've got a sort of half-respectable look about you. I suppose you 'aven't *done* anything?'

'Bit of Arson,' said Mr Polly, as if he jested.

'So long as you haven't the habit,' said the plump woman.

'My first time, Ma'm,' said Mr Polly, munching his way through an excellent big leaf of lettuce. 'And my last.'

'It's all right if you haven't been to Prison,' said the plump woman. 'It isn't what a man's happened to do makes 'im bad. We all happen to do things at times. It's bringing it home to him and spoiling his self-respect does the mischief. You don't *look* a wrong 'un. 'Ave you been to prison?'

'Never.'

'Nor a Reformatory? Nor any Institution?'

'Not me. Do I *look* reformed?'

'Can you paint and carpenter a bit?'

'Ripe for it.'

'Have a bit of cheese?'

'If I might.'

And the way she brought the cheese showed Mr Polly that the business was settled in her mind.

He spent the afternoon exploring the premises of the Potwell Inn and learning the duties that might be expected of him, such as Stockholm tarring[12] fences, digging potatoes, swabbing out boats, helping people land, embarking, landing, and timekeeping for the hirers of two rowing boats and one Canadian canoe,[13] bailing out the said vessels and concealing their leaks and defects from prospective hirers, persuading inexperienced hirers to start downstream rather than up, repairing rowlocks

and taking inventories of returning boats with a view to sup-
plementary charges, cleaning boots, sweeping chimneys, house
painting, cleaning windows, sweeping out and sanding the Tap
and Bar, cleaning pewter, washing glasses, turpentining woodwork, whitewashing generally, plumbing and engineering,
repairing locks and clocks, waiting and tapster's work generally, beating carpets and mats, cleaning bottles and saving
corks, taking into the cellar, moving, tapping, and connecting
beer casks with their engines, blocking and destroying wasps'
nests, doing forestry with several trees, drowning superfluous
kittens, dog fancying[14] as required, assisting in the rearing of
ducklings and the care of various poultry, beekeeping, stabling,
baiting and grooming horses and asses, cleaning and 'garing'
motor cars and bicycles,[15] inflating tyres and repairing punc-
tures, recovering the bodies of drowned persons from the river
as required, and assisting people in trouble in the water, first
aid and sympathy, improvising and superintending a bathing
station for visitors, attending inquests and funerals in the interests of the establishment, scrubbing floors and all the ordinary duties of a scullion, the Ferry, chasing hens and goats
from the adjacent cottages out of the garden, making up paths
and superintending drainage, gardening generally, delivering
bottled beer and soda water siphons in the neighbourhood,
running miscellaneous errands, removing drunken and offen-
sive persons from the premises by tact or muscle, as occasion
required, keeping in with the local policeman, defending
the premises in general and the orchard in particular from
nocturnal depredators. . . .

'Can but try it,' said Mr Polly towards tea time. 'When there's
nothing else on hand I suppose I might do a bit of fishing.'

4

Mr Polly was particularly charmed by the ducklings.

They were piping about among the vegetables in the company
of their foster mother, and as he and the plump woman came
down the garden path the little creatures mobbed them, and
ran over their boots and in between Mr Polly's legs, and did

their best to be trodden upon and killed after the manner of ducklings all the world over. Mr Polly had never been near young ducklings before, and their extreme blondness and the delicate completeness of their feet and beaks filled him with admiration. It is open to question whether there is anything more friendly in the world than a very young duckling. It was with the utmost difficulty that he tore himself away to practise punting, with the plump woman coaching from the bank. Punting, he found, was difficult but not impossible, and towards four o'clock he succeeded in conveying a second passenger across the sundering flood[16] from the inn to the unknown.

As he returned, slowly indeed, but now one might almost say surely, to the peg to which the punt was moored, he became aware of a singularly delightful human being awaiting him on the bank. She stood with her legs very wide apart, her hands behind her back, and her head a little on one side, watching his gestures with an expression of disdainful interest. She had black hair and brown legs and a buff short frock and very intelligent eyes. And when he had reached a sufficient proximity she remarked, 'Hallo!'

'Hallo,' said Mr Polly, and saved himself in the nick of time from disaster.

'Silly,' said the young lady, and Mr Polly lunged nearer.

'What are you called?'

'Polly.'

'Liar!'

'Why?'

'I'm Polly.'

'Then I'm Alfred. But I meant to be Polly.'

'I was first.'

'All right. I'm going to be the ferryman.'

'I see. You'll have to punt better.'

'You should have seen me early in the afternoon.'

'I can imagine it . . . I've seen the others.'

'What others?' Mr Polly had landed now and was fastening up the punt.

'What Uncle Jim has scooted.'

'Scooted?'

'He comes and scoots them. He'll scoot you, too, I expect.'

A mysterious shadow seemed to fall athwart the sunshine and pleasantness of the Potwell Inn.

'I'm not a scooter,' said Mr Polly.

'Uncle Jim is.'

She whistled a little flatly for a moment, and threw small stones at a clump of meadowsweet that sprang from the bank. Then she remarked—

'When Uncle Jim comes back he'll cut your insides out. . . . P'r'aps, very likely, he'll let me see.'

There was a pause.

'*Who's* Uncle Jim?' Mr Polly asked in a faded voice.

'Don't know who Uncle Jim is! He'll show you. He's a scorcher, is Uncle Jim. He only came back just a little time ago, and he's scooted three men. He don't like strangers about, don't Uncle Jim. He *can* swear. He's going to teach me, soon as I can whissle properly.'

'Teach you to swear!' cried Mr Polly, horrified.

'*And* spit,' said the little girl proudly. 'He says I'm the gamest little beast he ever came across – ever.'

For the first time in his life it seemed to Mr Polly that he had come across something sheerly dreadful. He stared at the pretty thing of flesh and spirit in front of him, lightly balanced on its stout little legs and looking at him with eyes that had still to learn the expression of either disgust or fear.

'I say,' said Mr Polly, 'how old are you?'

'Nine,' said the little girl.

She turned away and reflected. Truth compelled her to add one other statement.

'He's not what I should call handsome, not Uncle Jim,' she said. 'But he's a Scorcher and no Mistake. . . . Gramma don't like him.'

5

Mr Polly found the plump woman in the big bricked kitchen lighting a fire for tea. He went to the root of the matter at once.

'I say,' he asked, 'who's Uncle Jim?'

The plump woman blanched and stood still for a moment. A stick fell out of the bundle in her hand unheeded. 'That little granddaughter of mine been saying things?' she asked faintly.

'Bits of things,' said Mr Polly.

'Well, I suppose I must tell you sooner or later. He's – It's Jim. He's the Drorback to this place, that's what he is. The Drorback. I hoped you mightn't hear so soon. . . . Very likely he's gone.'

'*She* don't seem to think so.'

''E 'asn't been near the place these two weeks and more,' said the plump woman.

'But who is he?'

'I suppose I got to tell you,' said the plump woman.

'She says he scoots people,' Mr Polly remarked after a pause.

'He's my own sister's son.' The plump woman watched the crackling fire for a space. 'I suppose I got to tell you,' she repeated.

She softened towards tears. 'I try not to think of it, and night and day he's haunting me. I try not to think of it. I've been for easy-going all my life. But I'm that worried and afraid, with death and ruin threatened and evil all about me! I don't know what to do! My own sister's son, and me a widow woman and 'elpless against his doin's!'

She put down the sticks she held upon the fender, and felt for her handkerchief. She began to sob and talk quickly.

'I wouldn't mind nothing else half so much if he'd leave that child alone. But he goes talking to her – if I leave her a moment he's talking to her, teaching her Words, and giving her ideas!'

'That's a Bit Thick,' said Mr Polly.

'Thick!' cried the plump woman; 'it's 'orrible! And what am I to do? He's been here three times now, six days, and a week, and a part of a week, and I pray to God night and day he may never come again. Praying! Back he's come, sure as fate. He takes my money and he takes my things. He won't let no man stay here to protect me or do the boats or work the ferry. The ferry's getting a scandal. They stand and shout and scream and use language. . . . If I complain they'll say I'm helpless to man-age here, they'll take away my licence, out I shall go – and it's all the living I can get – and he knows it, and he plays on it, and he don't care. And here I am. I'd send the child away, but I got nowhere to send the child. I buys him off when it comes to that, and back he comes, worse than ever, prowling round and doing evil. And not a soul to help me. Not a soul! I just hoped there might be a day or so. Before he comes back again. I was just hoping – I'm the sort that hopes.'

Mr Polly was reflecting on the flaws and drawbacks that seem to be inseparable from all the more agreeable things of life.

'Biggish sort of man, I expect?' asked Mr Polly, trying to get the situation in all its bearings.

But the plump woman did not heed him. She was going on with her fire-making, and retailing in disconnected fragments the fearfulness of Uncle Jim.

'There was always something a bit wrong with him,' she said; 'but nothing you mightn't have hoped for, not till they took him, and carried him off, and reformed him. . . .

'He was cruel to the hens and chickings, it's true, and stuck a knife into another boy; but then I've seen him that nice to a cat, nobody could have been kinder. I'm sure he didn't do no 'arm to that cat whatever anyone tries to make out of it. I'd never listen to that. . . . It was that Reformatory ruined him. They put him along of a lot of London boys full of ideas of wickedness, and because he didn't mind pain – and he don't, I *will* admit, try as I would – they made him think himself a hero. Them boys laughed at the teachers they set over them, laughed and mocked at them – and I don't suppose they *was* the best teachers in the world; I don't suppose, and I don't suppose anyone sensible does suppose that everyone who goes to be a teacher or a chaplain or a warder in a Reformatory Home goes and changes right away into an Angel of Grace from Heaven – and, oh Lord! Where was I?'

'What did they send him to the Reformatory for?'

'Playing truant and stealing. He stole right enough – stole the money from an old woman, and what was I to do when it came to the trial but say what I knew. And him like a viper alooking at me – more like a viper than a human boy. He leans on the bar and looks at me. "All right, Aunt Flo," he says; just that, and nothing more. Time after time I've dreamt of it, and now he's come. "They've Reformed me," he says, "and made me a devil, and devil I mean to be to you. So out with it," he says.'

'What did you give him last time?' asked Mr Polly.

'Three golden pounds,'[17] said the plump woman. ' "That won't last very long," he says. "But there ain't no hurry. I'll be back in a week about." If I wasn't one of the hoping sort—'

She left the sentence unfinished.

Mr Polly reflected. 'What sort of a size is he?' he asked. 'I'm not one of your Herculaceous sort, if you mean that. Nothing very wonderful bicepitally.'[18]

'You'll scoot,' said the plump woman, with conviction rather than bitterness. 'You'd better scoot now, and I'll try and find some money for him to go away again when he comes. It ain't reasonable to expect you to do anything but scoot. But I suppose it's the way of a woman in trouble to try and get help from a man, and hope and hope.'

'How long's he been about?' asked Mr Polly, ignoring his own outlook.

'Three months it is come the seventh since he come in by that very back door – and I hadn't set eyes on him for seven long years. He stood in the door watchin' me, and suddenly he let off a yelp – like a dog, and there he was grinning at the fright he'd given me. "Good old Aunity Flo," he says, "ain't you dee-lighted to see me?" he says, "now I'm Reformed." '

The plump lady went to the sink and filled the kettle.

'I never did like 'im,' she said, standing at the sink. 'And seeing him there, with his teeth all black and broken – P'r'aps I didn't give him much of a welcome at first. Not what would have been kind to him. "Lord!" I said, "it's Jim." '

' "It's Jim," he said. "Like a bad shillin' – like a damned bad shilling. Jim and trouble. You all of you wanted me Reformed, and now you got me Reformed. I'm a Reformatory Reformed Character,[19] warranted all right, and turned out as such. Ain't you going to ask me in, Aunty dear?" '

' "Come in," I said. "I won't have it said I wasn't ready to be kind to you!" '

'He comes in and shuts the door. Down he sits in that chair. "I come to torment you," he says, "you old Sumpthing!" and begins at me. . . . No 'uman being could ever have been called such things before. It made me cry out. "And now," he says, "just to show I ain't afraid of 'urting you," he says, and ups and twists my wrist.'

Mr Polly gasped.

'I could stand even his vi'lence,' said the plump woman, 'if it wasn't for the child.'

Mr Polly went to the kitchen window and surveyed his name-sake, who was away up the garden path, with her hands behind her back, and wisps of black hair in disorder about her little face, thinking, thinking profoundly, about ducklings.

'You two oughtn't to be left,' he said.

The plump woman stared at his back with hard hope in her eyes.

'I don't see that it's *my* affair,' said Mr Polly.

The plump woman resumed her business with the kettle.

'I'd like to have a look at him before I go,' said Mr Polly, thinking aloud, and added, 'somehow. Not my business, of course.'

'Lord!' he cried, with a start, at a noise in the bar, 'who's that?'

'Only a customer,' said the plump woman.

6

Mr Polly made no rash promises, and thought a great deal.

'It seems a sort of Crib,' he said, and added, 'for a chap who's looking for Trouble.'

But he stayed on, and did various things out of the list I have already given, and worked the ferry, and it was four days before he saw anything of Uncle Jim. And so resistant is the human mind to things not yet experienced, that he could easily have believed in that time that there was no such person in the world as Uncle Jim. The plump woman, after her one outbreak of confidences, ignored the subject, and little Polly seemed to have exhausted her impressions in her first communication, and

engaged her mind now, with a simple directness, in the study
and subjugation of the new human being Heaven had sent into
her world. The first unfavourable impression of his punting was
soon effaced; he could nickname ducklings very amusingly,
create boats out of wooden splinters, and stalk and fly from
imaginary tigers in the orchard, with a convincing earnestness
that was surely beyond the power of any other human being.
She conceded at last that he should be called Mr Polly, in
honour of her, Miss Polly, even as he desired.

Uncle Jim turned up in the twilight.

Uncle Jim appeared with none of the disruptive violence Mr
Polly had dreaded. He came quite softly. Mr Polly was going
down the lane behind the church that led to the Potwell Inn,
after posting a letter to the lime juice people at the post office.
He was walking slowly, after his habit, and thinking discursively. With a sudden tightening of the muscles he became aware
of a figure walking noiselessly beside him.

His first impression was of a face singularly broad above,
and with a wide, empty grin as its chief feature below, of a
slouching body and dragging feet.

''Arf a mo',' said the figure, as if in response to his start, and
speaking in a hoarse whisper. ''Arf a mo', mister. You the noo
bloke at the Potwell Inn?'

Mr Polly felt evasive. 'S'pose I am,' he replied hoarsely, and
quickened his pace.

''Arf a mo',' said Uncle Jim, taking his arm. 'We ain't doing
a (sanguinary)[20] Marathon. It ain't a (decorated) cinder track.[21]
I want a word with you, mister. See?'

Mr Polly wriggled his arm free and stopped. 'Whad is it?' he
asked, and faced the terror.

'I jest want a (decorated) word wiv you. See? – just a friendly
word or two. Just to clear up any blooming errors. That's all I
want. No need to be so (richly decorated) proud, if you *are* the
noo bloke at Potwell Inn. Not a bit of it. See?'

Uncle Jim was certainly not a handsome person. He was
short, shorter than Mr Polly, with long arms and lean, big
hands; a thin and wiry neck stuck out of his grey flannel shirt,
and supported a big head that had something of the snake

in the convergent lines of its broad, knobby brow, meanly proportioned face, and pointed chin. His almost toothless mouth seemed a cavern in the twilight. Some accident had left him with one small and active, and one large and expressionless reddish eye, and wisps of straight hair strayed from under the blue cricket cap he had pulled down obliquely over the latter. He spat between his teeth, and wiped his mouth untidily with the soft side of his fist.

'You got to blurry well shift,' he said. 'See?'

'Shift!' said Mr Polly. 'How?'

''Cos the Potwell Inn's *my* beat. See?'

Mr Polly had never felt less witty. 'How's it your beat?' he asked.

Uncle Jim thrust his face forward and shook his open hand, bent like a claw, under Mr Polly's nose. 'Not your blooming business,' he said. 'You got to shift.'

'S'pose I don't,' said Mr Polly.

'You got to shift.'

The tone of Uncle Jim's voice became urgent and confidential.

'You don't know who you're up against,' he said. 'It's a kindness I'm doing to warn you. See? I'm just one of those blokes who don't stick at things, see? I don't stick at nuffin.'

Mr Polly's manner became detached and confidential – as though the matter and the speaker interested him greatly, but didn't concern him over much. 'What do you think you'll do?' he asked.

'If you don't clear out?'

'Yes.'

'*Gaw!*' said Uncle Jim. 'You'd better! *'Ere!*' He gripped Mr Polly's wrist with a grip of steel, and in an instant Mr Polly understood the relative quality of their muscles. He breathed, an uninspiring breath, into Mr Polly's face.

'What *won't* I do,' he said, 'once I start in on you?'

He paused, and the night about them seemed to be listening. 'I'll make a mess of you,' he said, in his hoarse whisper. 'I'll do you – injuries. I'll 'urt you. I'll kick you ugly, see? I'll 'urt you in 'orrible ways – 'orrible ugly ways. . . .'

He scrutinised Mr Polly's face.

'You'll cry,' he said, 'to see yourself. See? Cry, you will.'

'You got no right,' began Mr Polly.

'Right!' His note was fierce. 'Ain't the old woman me aunt?'

He spoke still closelier. 'I'll make a gory mess of you. I'll cut bits orf you—'

He receded a little. 'I got no quarrel with *you*,' he said.

'It's too late to go tonight,' said Mr Polly.

'I'll be round tomorrer—'bout eleven. See? And if I finds you—'

He produced a blood-curdling oath.

'H'm,' said Mr Polly, trying to keep things light. 'We'll consider your suggestions.'

'You better,' said Uncle Jim, and suddenly, noiselessly, was going.

His whispering voice sank until Mr Polly could hear only the dim fragments of sentences. ''Orrible things to you—'Orrible things. ... Kick yer Ugly. ... Cut yer – liver out ... spread it all about, I will. ... See? I don't care a dead rat one way or the uvver.'

And with a curious twisting gesture of the arm, Uncle Jim receded until his face was a still, dim thing that watched, and the black shadows of the hedge seemed to have swallowed up his body altogether.

7

Next morning about half-past ten Mr Polly found himself seated under a clump of fir trees by the roadside, and about three miles and a half from the Potwell Inn. He was by no means sure whether he was taking a walk to clear his mind, or leaving that threat-marred Paradise for good and all. His reason pointed a lean, unhesitating finger along the latter course.

For, after all, the thing was not *his* quarrel.

That agreeable, plump woman – agreeable, motherly, comfortable as she might be – wasn't his affair; that child with the mop of black hair, who combined so magically the charm of mouse and butterfly and flitting bird, who was daintier than a flower and softer than a peach, was no concern of his. Good Heavens! What were they to him? Nothing! . . .

Uncle Jim, of course, *had* a claim, a sort of claim.

If it came to duty and chucking up this attractive, indolent, observant, humorous, tramping life, there were those who had a right to him, a legitimate right, a prior claim on his protection and chivalry.

Why not listen to the call of duty and go back to Miriam now? . . .

He had had a very agreeable holiday. . . .

And while Mr Polly sat thinking these things as well as he could, he knew that if only he dared to look up, the Heavens had opened, and the clear judgement on his case was written across the sky.

He knew – he knew now as much as a man can know of life. He knew he had to fight or perish.

Life had never been so clear to him before. It had always been a confused, entertaining spectacle. He had responded to this impulse and that, seeking agreeable and entertaining things, evading difficult and painful things. Such is the way of those who grow up to a life that has neither danger nor honour in its texture. He had been muddled and wrapped about and entangled, like a creature born in the jungle who has never seen sea or sky. Now he had come out of it suddenly into a great exposed place. It was as if God and Heaven waited over him, and all the earth was expectation.

'Not my business,' said Mr Polly, speaking aloud. 'Where the devil do I come in?'

And again, with something between a whine and a snarl in his voice, 'Not my blasted business!'

His mind seemed to have divided itself into several compartments, each with its own particular discussion busily in progress, and quite regardless of the others. One was busy with the detailed interpretation of the phrase, 'Kick you ugly'. There's a sort of French wrestling in which you use and guard against feet. Watch the man's eye, and as his foot comes up, grip, and over he goes – at your mercy, if you use the advantage rightly. But how do you use the advantage rightly?

When he thought of Uncle Jim the inside feeling of his body faded away rapidly to a blank discomfort. . . .

'Old cadger!²² She hadn't no business to drag me into her quarrels. Ought to go to the police and ask for help! Dragging me into a quarrel that don't concern me.

'Wish I'd never set eyes on the rotten inn!'

The reality of the case arched over him like the vault of the sky, as plain as the sweet blue heaven above and the wide spread of hill and valley about him. Man comes into life to seek and find his sufficient beauty, to serve it, to win and increase it, to fight for it, to face anything and dare anything for it, counting death as nothing so long as the dying eyes still turn to it. And fear and dullness and indolence and appetite, which, indeed, are no more than fear's three crippled brothers, who make ambushes and creep by night, are against him, to delay him, to hold him off, to hamper and beguile and kill him in that quest. He had but to lift his eyes to see all that, as much a part of his world as the driving clouds and the bending grass; but he kept himself downcast, a grumbling, inglorious, dirty, fattish little tramp, full of dreams and quivering excuses.

'Why the hell was I ever born?' he said, with the truth almost winning him.

'What do you do when a dirty man, who smells, gets you down and under, in the dirt and dust, with a knee below your diaphragm, and a large hairy hand squeezing your windpipe tighter and tighter in a quarrel that isn't, properly speaking, yours?'

'If I had a chance against him—' protested Mr Polly.

'It's no Good, you see,' said Mr Polly.

He stood up as though his decision was made, and was for an instant struck still by doubt.

There lay the road before him, going this way to the east, and that to the west.

Westward, one hour away now, was the Potwell Inn. Already things might be happening there. . . .

Eastward was the wise man's course, a road dipping between hedges to a hop garden and a wood, and presently, no doubt, reaching an inn, a picturesque church, perhaps, a village, and

fresh company. The wise man's course. Mr Polly saw himself
going along it, and tried to see himself going along it with all
the self-applause a wise man feels. But somehow it wouldn't
come like that. The wise man fell short of happiness for all his
wisdom. The wise man had a paunch, and round shoulders,
and red ears, and excuses. It was a pleasant road, and why the
wise man should not go along it merry and singing, full of
summer happiness, was a miracle to Mr Polly's mind. But,
confound it! the fact remained: the figure went slinking – slinking was the only word for it – and would not go otherwise than
slinking. He turned his eyes westward as if for an explanation,
and if the figure was no longer ignoble, the prospect was
appalling.

'One kick in the stummick would settle a chap like me,' said
Mr Polly.

'Oh, God!' cried Mr Polly, and lifted his eyes to heaven, and
said for the last time in that struggle, 'It   isn't   my   affair!'

And so saying, he turned his face towards the Potwell Inn.

He went back, neither halting nor hastening in his pace after
this last decision, but with a mind feverishly busy.

'If I get killed I get killed, and if he gets killed I get hung.
Don't seem just somehow.

'Don't suppose I shall *frighten* him off.'

8

The private war between Mr Polly and Uncle Jim for the possession of the Potwell Inn fell naturally into three chief campaigns. There was, first of all, the great campaign which ended
in the triumphant eviction of Uncle Jim from the inn premises;
there came next, after a brief interval, the futile invasions of
the premises by Uncle Jim that culminated in the Battle of the
Dead Eel; and, after some months of involuntary truce, there
was the last supreme conflict of the Night Surprise. Each of
these campaigns merits a section to itself.

Mr Polly re-entered the inn discreetly.

He found the plump woman seated in her bar, her eyes astare,
her face white and wet with tears. 'O God!' she was saying over

and over again – 'O God!' The air was full of a spirituous reek, and on the sanded boards in front of the bar were the fragments of a broken bottle, and an overturned glass.

She turned her despair at the sound of his entry, and despair gave place to astonishment.

'You come back!' she said.

'Ra-ther,' said Mr Polly.

'He's – he's mad drunk and looking for her.'

'Where is she?'

'Locked upstairs.'

'Haven't you sent to the police?'

'No one to send.'

'I'll see to it,' said Mr Polly. 'Out this way?'

She nodded.

He went to the crinkly paned window and peered out. Uncle Jim was coming down the garden path towards the house, his hands in his pockets, and singing hoarsely. Mr Polly remembered afterwards, with pride and amazement, that he felt neither faint nor rigid. He glanced round him, seized a bottle of beer by the neck as an improvised club, and went out by the garden door. Uncle Jim stopped, amazed. His brain did not instantly rise to the new posture of things. 'You!' he cried, and stopped for a moment. 'You – *scoot*!'

'*Your* job,' said Mr Polly, and advanced some paces.

Uncle Jim stood swaying with wrathful astonishment, and then darted forward with clutching hands. Mr Polly felt that if his antagonist closed, he was lost, and smote with all his force at the ugly head before him. Smash went the bottle, and Uncle Jim staggered, half stunned by the blow, and blinded with beer.

The lapses and leaps of the human mind are for ever mysterious. Mr Polly had never expected that bottle to break. In an instant he felt disarmed and helpless. Before him was Uncle Jim, infuriated and evidently still coming on, and for defence was nothing but the neck of a bottle.

For a time our Mr Polly has figured heroic. Now comes the fall again; he sounded abject terror; he dropped that ineffectual scrap of glass and turned and fled round the corner of the house.

'Bolls!' came the thick voice of the enemy behind him, as one who accepts a challenge, and bleeding but indomitable, Uncle Jim entered the house.

'Bolls!' he said, surveying the bar. 'Fightin' with bolls! I'll showim fightin' with bolls!'

Uncle Jim had learned all about fighting with bottles in the Reformatory Home. Regardless of his terror-stricken aunt, he ranged among the bottled beer and succeeded, after one or two failures, in preparing two bottles to his satisfaction by knocking off the bottom, and gripping them dagger-wise by the necks. So prepared, he went forth again to destroy Mr Polly.

Mr Polly, freed from the sense of urgent pursuit, had halted beyond the raspberry canes, and rallied his courage. The sense of Uncle Jim victorious in the house restored his manhood. He went round by the outhouses to the riverside, seeking a weapon, and found an old paddle boathook. With this he smote Uncle Jim as he emerged by the door of the tap. Uncle Jim, blaspheming dreadfully, and with dire stabbing intimations in either hand, came through the splintering paddle like a circus rider through a paper hoop, and once more Mr Polly dropped his weapon and fled.

A careless observer, watching him sprint round and round the inn in front of the lumbering and reproachful pursuit of Uncle Jim, might have formed an altogether erroneous estimate of the issue of the campaign. Certain compensating qualities of the very greatest military value were appearing in Mr Polly, even as he ran; if Uncle Jim had strength and brute courage, and the rich toughening experience a Reformatory Home affords, Mr Polly was nevertheless sober, more mobile, and with a mind now stimulated to an almost incredible nimbleness. So that he not only gained on Uncle Jim, but thought what use he might make of this advantage. The word 'strategious' flamed red across the tumult of his mind. As he came round the house for the third time, he darted suddenly into the yard, swung the door to behind himself, and bolted it, seized the zinc pig's pail that stood by the entrance to the kitchen, and had it neatly and resonantly over Uncle Jim's head, as he came belatedly in round the outhouse on the other side. One of the splintered bottles jabbed Mr Polly's ear – at the time it seemed of no importance – and then Uncle Jim was down and writhing dangerously and noisily upon the yard tiles, with his head still in the pig pail, and his bottle gone to splinters, and Mr Polly was fastening the kitchen door against him.

'Can't go on like this for ever,' said Mr Polly, whooping for breath, and selecting a weapon from among the brooms that stood behind the kitchen door.

Uncle Jim was losing his head. He was up and kicking the door, and bellowing unamiable proposals and invitations, so that a strategist emerging silently by the tap door could locate him without difficulty, steal upon him unawares, and—!

But before that felling blow could be delivered, Uncle Jim's ear had caught a footfall, and he turned. Mr Polly quailed, and lowered his broom – a fatal hesitation.

'*Now* I got you!' cried Uncle Jim, dancing forwards in a disconcerting zigzag.

He rushed to close, and Mr Polly stopped him neatly, as it were a miracle, with the head of the broom across his chest. Uncle Jim seized the broom with both hands. 'Lea go,' he said, and tugged. Mr Polly shook his head, tugged, and showed pale, compressed lips. Both tugged. Then Uncle Jim tried to get round the end of the broom; Mr Polly circled away. They began to circle about one another, both lugging hard, both intensely watchful of the slightest initiative on the part of the other. Mr Polly wished brooms were longer – twelve or thirteen feet, for example; Uncle Jim was clearly for shortness in brooms. He wasted breath in saying what was to happen shortly – sanguinary, oriental, soul-blenching things – when the broom no longer separated them. Mr Polly thought he had never seen an uglier person. Suddenly Uncle Jim flashed into violent activity, but alcohol slows movement, and Mr Polly was equal to him. Then Uncle Jim tried jerks, and, for a terrible instant, seemed to have the broom out of Mr Polly's hands. But Mr Polly recovered it with the clutch of a drowning man. Then Uncle Jim drove suddenly at Mr Polly's midriff; but again Mr Polly was ready, and swept him round in a circle. Then suddenly a wild hope filled Mr Polly. He saw the river was very near, the post to

which the punt was tied not three yards away. With a wild yell
he sent the broom home under his antagonist's ribs. 'Wooosh!'
he cried, as the resistance gave.

'Oh! *Gaw!*' said Uncle Jim, going backwards helplessly, and
Mr Polly thrust hard, and abandoned the broom to the enemy's
despairing clutch.

Splash! Uncle Jim was in the water, and Mr Polly had leaped
like a cat aboard the ferry punt, and grasped the pole.

Up came Uncle Jim spluttering and dripping. 'You (unprofit-
able matter, and printing it might lead to a Censorship of
Novels) – You know I got a weak chess!'

The pole took him in the throat and drove him backwards
and downwards.

'Lea go!' cried Uncle Jim, staggering, and with real terror in
his once awful eyes.

Splash! Down he fell backwards into a frothing mass of
water, with Mr Polly jabbing at him. Under water he turned
round, and came up again, as if in flight towards the middle of
the river. Directly his head reappeared, Mr Polly had him
between his shoulders and under again, bubbling thickly. A
hand clutched and disappeared.

It was stupendous! Mr Polly had discovered the heel of
Achilles.[23] Uncle Jim had no stomach for cold water. The broom
floated away, pitching gently on the swell. Mr Polly, infuriated
by victory, thrust Uncle Jim under again, and drove the punt
round on its chain, in such a manner that when Uncle Jim came
up for the fourth time – and now he was nearly out of his depth,
too buoyed up to walk, and apparently nearly helpless – Mr
Polly, fortunately for them both, could not reach him.

Uncle Jim made the clumsy gestures of those who struggle
insecurely in the water. 'Keep out,' said Mr Polly. Uncle Jim,
with a great effort, got a footing, emerged until his armpits were
out of water, until his waistcoat buttons showed, one by one,
till scarcely two remained, and made for the camp-sheeting.

'Keep out!' cried Mr Polly, and leaped off the punt and
followed the movements of his victim along the shore.

'I tell you I got a weak chess,' said Uncle Jim moistly. 'I 'ate
worter. This ain't fair fightin'.'

'Keep out!' said Mr Polly.

'This ain't fair fightin',' said Uncle Jim, almost weeping, and all his terrors had gone.

'Keep out!' said Mr Polly, with an accurately poised pole.

'I tell you I got to land, you Fool,' said Uncle Jim, with a sort of despairing wrathfulness, and began moving down-stream.

'You keep out,' said Mr Polly in parallel movement. 'Don't you ever land on this place again! . . .'

Slowly, argumentatively, and reluctantly, Uncle Jim waded downstream. He tried threats, he tried persuasion, he even tried a belated note of pathos; Mr Polly remained inexorable, if in secret a little perplexed as to the outcome of the situation. 'This cold's getting to my marrer!' said Uncle Jim.

'You want cooling. You keep out in it,' said Mr Polly.

They came round the bend into sight of Nicholson's ait,[24] where the backwater runs down to the Potwell Mill. And there, after much parley and several feints, Uncle Jim made a desperate effort, and struggled into clutch of the overhanging osiers[25] on the island, and so got out of the water, with the millstream between them. He emerged dripping and muddy and vindictive. 'By *Gaw*!' he said. 'I'll skin you for this!'

'You keep off, or I'll do worse to you,' said Mr Polly.

The spirit was out of Uncle Jim for the time, and he turned away to struggle through the osiers towards the mill, leaving a shining trail of water among the green-grey stems.

Mr Polly returned slowly and thoughtfully to the inn, and suddenly his mind began to bubble with phrases. The plump woman stood at the top of the steps that led up to the inn door, to greet him.

'Law!' she cried, as he drew near, ' 'asn't 'e killed you?'

'Do I look it?' said Mr Polly.

'But where's Jim?'

'Gone off.'

' 'E was mad drunk and dangerous!'

'I put him in the river,' said Mr Polly. 'That toned down his alcolaceous frenzy![26] I gave him a bit of a doing altogether.'

'Hain't he 'urt you?'

'Not a bit of it!'

'Then what's all that blood beside your ear?'

Mr Polly felt. 'Quite a cut! Funny how one overlooks things! Heated moments! He must have done that when he jabbed about with those bottles. Hallo, Kiddy! You venturing downstairs again?'

'Ain't he killed you?' asked the little girl.

'Well!'

'I wish I'd seen more of the fighting.'

'Didn't you?'

'All I saw was you running round the house, and Uncle Jim after you.'

There was a little pause. 'I was leading him on,' said Mr Polly.

'Someone's shouting at the ferry,' she said.

'Right-o. But you won't see any more of Uncle Jim for a bit. We've been having a conversazione about that.'

'I believe it *is* Uncle Jim,' said the little girl.

'Then he can wait,' said Mr Polly shortly.

He turned round and listened for the words that drifted across from the little figure on the opposite bank. So far as he could judge, Uncle Jim was making an appointment for the morrow. Mr Polly replied with a defiant movement of the punt pole. The little figure was convulsed for a moment, and then went on its way upstream – fiercely.

So it was the first campaign ended in an insecure victory.

9

The next day was Wednesday, and a slack day for the Potwell Inn. It was a hot, close day, full of the murmuring of bees.[27] One or two people crossed by the ferry; an elaborately equipped fisherman stopped for cold meat and dry ginger ale in the bar parlour; some haymakers came and drank beer for an hour, and afterwards sent jars and jugs by a boy to be replenished; that was all. Mr Polly had risen early, and was busy about the place meditating upon the probable tactics of Uncle Jim. He was no longer strung up to the desperate pitch of the first encounter. He was grave and anxious. Uncle Jim had shrunken, as all antagonists that are boldly faced shrink, after the first battle, to the negotiable, the vulnerable. Formidable he was, no doubt, but not invincible. He had, under Providence, been defeated once, and he might be defeated altogether.

Mr Polly went about the place considering the militant possibilities of pacific things – pokers, copper sticks,[28] garden implements, kitchen knives, garden nets, barbed wire, oars, clotheslines, blankets, pewter pots, stockings, and broken bottles. He prepared a club with a stocking and a bottle inside, upon the best East End model. He swung it round his head once, broke an outhouse window with a flying fragment of glass, and ruined the stocking beyond all darning. He developed a subtle scheme, with the cellar flap as a sort of pitfall; but he rejected it finally because (a) it might entrap the plump woman, and (b) he had no use whatever for Uncle Jim in the cellar. He determined to wire the garden that evening, burglar fashion, against the possibilities of a night attack.

Towards two o'clock in the afternoon three young men arrived in a capacious boat from the direction of Lammam, and asked permission to camp in the paddock. It was given all the more readily by Mr Polly because he perceived in their proximity a possible check upon the self-expression of Uncle Jim. But he did not foresee, and no one could have foreseen, that Uncle Jim, stealing craftily upon the Potwell Inn in the late afternoon, armed with a large rough-hewn stake, would have mistaken the bending form of one of those campers – who was pulling a few onions by permission in the garden – for Mr Polly's, and crept upon it swiftly and silently, and smitten its wide invitation unforgettably and unforgivably. It was an error impossible to explain; the resounding whack went up to Heaven, the cry of amazement, and Mr Polly emerged from the inn, armed with the frying pan he was cleaning, to take this reckless assailant in the rear. Uncle Jim, realizing his error, fled blaspheming into the arms of the other two campers, who were returning from the village with butcher's meat and groceries. They caught him, they smacked his face with steak and punched him with a bursting parcel of lump sugar, they held him though he bit them, and their idea of punishment was to duck him. They were hilarious, strong young stockbrokers' clerks, Territorials, and seasoned boating men;[29] they ducked him as though it was romping and all that Mr Polly had to do was to pick up lumps of sugar for them and wipe them on his sleeve and put them on a plate, and explain that Uncle Jim was a notorious bad character, and not quite right in his head.

'Got a regular Obsession the Missis is his Aunt,' said Mr Polly, expanding it. 'Perfect noosance he is.'

But he caught a glance of Uncle Jim's eye as he receded before the campers' urgency that boded ill for him, and in the night he had a disagreeable idea that perhaps his luck might not hold for the third occasion.

That came soon enough. So soon, indeed, as the campers had gone.

Thursday was the early closing day at Lammam,[30] and, next to Sunday, the busiest part of the week at the Potwell Inn. Sometimes as many as six boats all at once would be moored against the ferry punt and hiring rowboats. People could either have a complete tea, a complete tea with jam, cake, and eggs, a kettle of boiling water and find the rest, or Refreshments *à la carte* as they chose. They sat about, but usually the boiling water-ers had a delicacy about using the tables, and grouped themselves humbly on the ground. The complete tea-ers with jam and eggs got the best tablecloth, on the table nearest the steps that led up to the glass-panelled door.

The groups about the lawn were very satisfying to Mr Polly's sense of amenity. To the right were the complete tea-ers, with everything heart could desire; then a small group of three young men in remarkable green and violet and pale blue shirts, and two girls in mauve and yellow blouses, with common teas and gooseberry jam, at the green clothless table; then, on the grass down by the pollard willow,[31] a small family of hot-water-ers with a hamper, a little troubled by wasps in their jam from the nest in the tree, and all in mourning, but happy otherwise; and on the lawn to the right a ginger beer lot of 'prentices without their collars, and very jocular and happy. The young people in the rainbow shirts and blouses formed the centre of interest;

they were under the leadership of a gold-spectacled senior with a fluting voice and an air of mystery; he ordered everything, and showed a peculiar knowledge of the qualities of the Potwell jams, preferring gooseberry with much insistence. Mr Polly watched him, christened him the 'benifluous influence',[32] glanced at the 'prentices, and went inside and down into the cellar in order to replenish the stock of stone ginger beer, which the plump woman had allowed to run low during the preoccupations of the campaign. It was in the cellar that he first became aware of the return of Uncle Jim. He became aware of him as a voice, a voice not only hoarse but thick, as voices thicken under the influence of alcohol.

'Where's that muddy-faced mongrel?' cried Uncle Jim. 'Let 'im come out to me! Where's that blighted whisp with the punt pole – I got a word to say to 'im. Come out of it, you pot-bellied chunk of dirtiness, you! Come out and 'ave your ugly face wiped. I got a Thing for you. . . . '*Ear* me?

' 'E's 'iding, that's what 'e's doing,' said the voice of Uncle Jim, dropping for a moment to sorrow, and then with a great increment of wrathfulness: 'Come out of my nest, you blinking cuckoo, you, or I'll cut your silly insides out! Come out of it, you pockmarked Rat! Stealing another man's 'ome away from 'im! Come out and look me in the face, you squinting son of a Skunk! . . .'

Mr Polly took the ginger beer and went thoughtfully upstairs to the bar.

' 'E's back,' said the plump woman as he appeared. 'I knew 'e'd come back.'

'I heard him,' said Mr Polly, and looked about. 'Just gimme the old poker handle that's under the beer-engine.'

The door opened softly, and Mr Polly turned quickly. But it was only the pointed nose and intelligent face of the young man with the gilt spectacles and the discreet manner. He coughed, and the spectacles fixed Mr Polly.

'I say,' he said with quiet earnestness, 'there's a chap out here seems to *want* someone.'

'Why don't he come in?' said Mr Polly.

'He seems to want you out there.'

'What's he want?'

'I *think*,' said the spectacled young man, after a thoughtful moment, 'he appears to have brought you a present of fish.'

'Isn't he shouting?'

'He *is* a little boisterous.'

'He'd better come in.'

The manner of the spectacled young man intensified. 'I wish you'd come out and persuade him to go away,' he said. 'His language – isn't quite the thing – ladies.'

'It never was,' said the plump woman, her voice charged with sorrow.

Mr Polly moved towards the door and stood with his hand on the handle. The gold-spectacled face disappeared.

'Now, my man,' came his voice from outside, 'be careful what you're saying—'

'OO in all the World and Hereafter are you to call me me man?' cried Uncle Jim, in the voice of one astonished and pained beyond endurance, and added scornfully, 'You gold-eyed Geezer, you!'

'Tut, tut!' said the gentleman in gilt glasses. 'Restrain yourself!'

Mr Polly emerged, poker in hand, just in time to see what followed. Uncle Jim in his shirt-sleeves, and a state of ferocious decolletage, was holding something – yes! – a dead eel by means of a piece of newspaper about its tail, holding it down and back and a little sideways in such a way as to smite with it upward and hard. It struck the spectacled gentleman under the jaw with a peculiar dead thud, and a cry of horror came from the two seated parties at the sight. One of the girls shrieked piercingly, 'Horace!' and everyone sprang up. The sense of helping numbers came to Mr Polly's aid.

'Drop it!' he cried, and came down the steps waving his poker and thrusting the spectacled gentleman before him, as heretofore great heroes were wont to wield the oxhide[33] shield.

Uncle Jim gave ground suddenly, and trod upon the foot of a young man in a blue shirt, who immediately thrust at him violently with both hands.

'Lea go!' howled Uncle Jim. 'That's the Chap I'm looking for!' and pressing the head of the spectacled gentleman aside, smote hard at Mr Polly.

But at the sight of this indignity inflicted upon the spectacled gentleman a woman's heart was stirred, a pink parasol drove hard and true at Uncle Jim's wiry neck, and at the same moment the young man in the blue shirt sought to collar him, and lost his grip again.

'Suffragettes!'[34] gasped Uncle Jim, with the ferrule at his throat. 'Everywhere!' and aimed a second more successful blow at Mr Polly.

'Wup!' said Mr Polly.

But now the jam and egg party was joining in the fray. A stout, yet still fairly able-bodied gentleman in white and black checks inquired: 'What's the fellow up to? Ain't there no police here?' And it was evident that once more public opinion was rallying to the support of Mr Polly.

'Oh, come on then, all the LOT of you!' cried Uncle Jim, and backing dexterously, whirled the eel round in a destructive circle. The pink sunshade was torn from the hand that gripped it, and whirled athwart the complete but unadorned tea-things on the green table.

'Collar him! Someone get hold of his collar!' cried the gold-spectacled gentleman, retreating up the steps to the inn door as if to rally his forces.

'Stand clear, you blessed mantel ornaments!' cried Uncle Jim. 'Stand clear!' and retired backing, staving off attack by means of the whirling eel.

Mr Polly, undeterred by a sense of grave damage done to his nose, pressed the attack in front, the two young men in violet and blue skirmished on Uncle Jim's flanks, the man in white and black checks sought still further outflanking possibilities, and two of the apprentice boys ran for oars. The gold-spectacled gentleman, as if inspired, came down the wooden steps again, seized the tablecloth of the jam and egg party, lugged it from under the crockery with inadequate precautions against breakage, and advanced with compressed lips, curious lateral crouching movements, swift flashings of his glasses, and a general suggestion of bull-fighting in his pose and gestures. Uncle Jim was kept busy, and unable to plan his retreat with any strategic soundness. He was, moreover, manifestly a little nervous about the river in his rear. He gave ground in a curve, and so came right across the rapidly abandoned camp of the family in mourning, crunching teacups under his heel, over-setting the teapot, and finally tripping backwards over the ham-per. The eel flew out at a tangent from his hand, and became a mere looping relic on the sward.

'Hold him!' cried the gentleman in spectacles. 'Collar him!' and, moving forwards with extraordinary promptitude, wrap-ped the best tablecloth about Uncle Jim's arms and head. Mr Polly grasped his purpose instantly, the man in checks was scarcely slower, and in another moment Uncle Jim was no more than a bundle of smothered blasphemy, and a pair of wildly active legs.

'Duck him!' panted Mr Polly, holding on to the earthquake. 'Bes' thing – duck him.'

The bundle was convulsed by paroxysms of anger and pro-test. One boot got the hamper and sent it ten yards.

'Go in the house for a clothesline, someone,' said the gentle-man in gold spectacles. 'He'll get out of this in a moment.'

One of the apprentices ran.

'Bird nets in the garden,' shouted Mr Polly. 'In the garden.'

The apprentice was divided in his purpose.

And then suddenly Uncle Jim collapsed, and became a limp, dead-seeming thing under their hands. His arms were drawn inward, his legs bent up under his person, and so he lay.

'Fainted!' said the man in checks, relaxing his grip.

'A fit, perhaps,' said the man in spectacles.

'Keep hold!' said Mr Polly, too late.

For suddenly Uncle Jim's arms and legs flew out like springs released. Mr Polly was tumbled backwards, and fell over the broken teapot, and into the arms of the father in mourning. Something struck his head – dazingly. In another second Uncle Jim was on his feet, and the tablecloth enshrouded the head of the man in checks. Uncle Jim manifestly considered he had done all that honour required of him; and against overwhelming

numbers, and the possibility of reiterated duckings, flight is no
disgrace.

Uncle Jim fled.

Mr Polly sat up, after an interval of indeterminate length,
among the ruins of an idyllic afternoon. Quite a lot of things
seemed scattered and broken, but it was difficult to grasp it all
at once. He stared between the legs of people. He became aware
of a voice speaking slowly and complainingly.

'Someone ought to pay for those tea things,' said the father
in mourning. 'We didn't bring them 'ere to be danced on, not
by no manner of means.'

10

There followed an anxious peace for three days, and then a
rough man in a blue jersey, in the intervals of trying to choke
himself with bread and cheese and pickled onions, broke
abruptly into information.

'Jim's lagged again,[35] Missus,' he said.

'What!' said the landlady. 'Our Jim?'

'Your Jim,' said the man; and after an absolutely necessary
pause for swallowing, added, 'Stealing a 'atchet.'

He did not speak for some moments, and then he replied to
Mr Polly's inquiries: 'Yes, a 'atchet. Down Lammam way –
night before last.'

'What'd 'e steal a 'atchet for?' asked the plump woman.

' 'E said 'e wanted a 'atchet.'

'I wonder what he wanted a hatchet for,' said Mr Polly
thoughtfully.

'I dessay 'e 'ad a use for it,' said the gentleman in the blue
jersey, and he took a mouthful that amounted to conversational
suicide. There was a prolonged pause in the little bar, and Mr
Polly did some rapid thinking.

He went to the window and whistled. 'I shall stick it,' he
whispered at last. ' 'Atchets or no 'atchets.'

He turned to the man with the blue jersey, when he thought
him clear for speech again. 'How much did you say they'd given
him?' he asked.

'Three munce,' said the man in the blue jersey, and refilled anxiously, as if alarmed at the momentary clearness of his voice.

II

Those three months passed all too quickly – months of sunshine and warmth, of varied novel exertion in the open air, of congenial experiences, of interest and wholesome food and successful digestion; months that browned Mr Polly and hardened him, and saw the beginnings of his beard; months marred only by one anxiety, an anxiety Mr Polly did his utmost to suppress. The day of reckoning was never mentioned, it is true, by either the plump woman or himself, but the name of Uncle Jim was written in letters of glaring silence across their intercourse. As the term of that respite drew to an end, his anxiety increased, until at last it trenched upon his well-earned sleep. He had some idea of buying a revolver. He compromised upon a small and very foul and dirty rook rifle, which he purchased in Lammam under a pretext of bird scaring, and loaded carefully and concealed under his bed from the plump woman's eye.

September passed away, October came.

And at last came that night in October whose happenings it is so difficult for a sympathetic historian to drag out of their proper nocturnal indistinctness into the clear, hard light of positive statement. A novelist should present characters, not vivisect them[36] publicly. . . .

The best, the kindliest, if not the justest course, is surely to leave untold such things as Mr Polly would manifestly have preferred untold.

Mr Polly has declared that when the cyclist discovered him he was seeking a weapon that should make a conclusive end to Uncle Jim. That declaration is placed before the reader without comment.

The gun was certainly in the possession of Uncle Jim at that time, and no human being but Mr Polly knows how he got hold of it.

The cyclist was a literary man named Warspite, who suffered

from insomnia; he had risen and come out of his house near Lammam just before the dawn, and he discovered Mr Polly partially concealed in the ditch by the Potwell churchyard wall. It is an ordinary dry ditch full of nettles, and overgrown with elder and dog rose, and in no way suggestive of an arsenal. It is the last place in which a sensible man would look for a gun. And he says that when he dismounted to see why Mr Polly was allowing only the latter part of his person to show (and that, it would seem, by inadvertency), Mr Polly merely raised his head and advised him to 'Look out!' and added, 'He's let fly at me twice already.'

He came out under persuasion, and with gestures of extreme caution. He was wearing a white cotton nightgown of the type that has now been so extensively superseded by pyjama sleeping suits, and his legs and feet were bare, and much scratched and torn, and very muddy.

Mr Warspite takes that exceptionally lively interest in his fellow-creatures which constitutes so much of the distinctive and complex charm of your novelist all the world over, and he at once involved himself generously in the case. The two men returned at Mr Polly's initiative across the churchyard to the Potwell Inn, and came upon the burst and damaged rook rifle near the new monument to Sir Samuel Harpon at the corner by the yew.

'That must have been his third go,' said Mr Polly. 'It sounded a bit funny.'

The sight inspirited him greatly, and he explained further that he had fled to the churchyard on account of the cover afforded by tombstones from the flight of small shot. He expressed anxiety for the fate of the landlady of the Potwell Inn and her grandchild, and led the way with enhanced alacrity along the lane to that establishment.

They found the doors of the house standing open, the bar in some disorder – several bottles of whisky were afterwards found to be missing – and Blake, the village policeman, rapping patiently at the open door. He entered with them. The glass in the bar had suffered severely, and one of the mirrors was starred from a blow from a pewter pot. The till had been forced and ransacked, and so had the bureau in the minute room behind the bar.

An upper window was opened, and the voice of the landlady became audible making inquiries. They went out and parleyed with her. She had locked herself upstairs with the little girl, she said, and refused to descend until she was assured that neither Uncle Jim nor Mr Polly's gun was anywhere on the premises. Mr Blake and Mr Warspite proceeded to satisfy themselves with regard to the former condition, and Mr Polly went to his room in search of garments more suited to the brightening dawn. He returned immediately with a request that Blake and Mr Warspite would 'just come and look'. They found the apartment in a state of extraordinary confusion, the bedclothes in a ball in the corner, the drawers all open and ransacked, the chair broken, the lock of the door forced and broken, one door panel slightly scorched and perforated by shot, and the window wide open. None of Mr Polly's clothes were to be seen, but some garments which had apparently once formed part of a stoker's workaday outfit, two brownish-yellow halves of a shirt, and an unsound pair of boots, were scattered on the floor. A faint smell of gunpowder still hung in the air, and two or three books Mr Polly had recently acquired had been shied with some violence under the bed. Mr Warspite looked at Mr Blake, and then both men looked at Mr Polly. 'That's *his* boots,' said Mr Polly.

Blake turned his eyes to the window. 'Some of these tiles 'ave just got broken,' he observed.

'I got out of the window and slid down the scullery tiles,' Mr Polly answered, omitting much, they both felt, from his explanation. . . .

'Well, we better find 'im and 'ave a word with 'im,' said Blake. 'That's about my business now.'

12

But Uncle Jim had gone altogether. . . .

He did not return for some days. That, perhaps, was not very wonderful. But the days lengthened to weeks, and the weeks to months, and still Uncle Jim did not recur. A year passed, and the anxiety of him became less acute; a second healing year followed the first. One afternoon about thirty months after the Night Surprise the plump woman spoke of him.

'I wonder what's become of Jim,' she said.

'*I* wonder sometimes,' said Mr Polly.

CHAPTER 10

MIRIAM REVISITED

I

One summer afternoon, about five years after his first coming to the Potwell Inn, Mr Polly found himself sitting under the pollard willow, fishing for dace. It was a plumper, browner, and healthier Mr Polly altogether than the miserable bankrupt with whose dyspeptic portrait our novel opened. He was fat, but with a fatness more generally diffused, and the lower part of his face was touched to gravity by a small, square beard. Also he was balder.

It was the first time he had found leisure to fish, though from the very outset of his Potwell career he had promised himself abundant indulgence in the pleasures of fishing. Fishing, as the golden page of English literature testifies, is a meditative and retrospective pursuit, and the varied page of memory, disregarded so long for sake of the teeming duties I have already enumerated, began to unfold itself to Mr Polly's consideration. Speculation about Uncle Jim died for want of material, and gave place to a reckoning of the years and months that had passed since his coming to Potwell, and that to a philosophical review of his life. He began to think about Miriam, remotely and impersonally. He remembered many things that had been neglected by his conscience during the busier times, as, for example, that he had committed arson and deserted a wife. For the first time he looked these long-neglected facts in the face.

It is disagreeable to think one has committed arson, because it is an action that leads to jail. Otherwise I do not think there was a grain of regret for that in Mr Polly's composition. But deserting Miriam was in a different category. Deserting Miriam was mean.

This is a history, and not a glorification of Mr Polly, and I tell of things as they were with him. Apart from the disagreeable twinge arising from the thought of what might happen if he was found out, he had not the slightest remorse about that fire. Arson, after all, is an artificial crime. Some crimes are crimes in themselves, would be crimes without any law, the cruelties, mockery, the breaches of faith that astonish and wound, but the burning of things is in itself neither good nor bad. A large number of houses deserve to be burnt, most modern furniture, an overwhelming majority of pictures and books – one might go on for some time with the list. If our community was collectively anything more than a feeble idiot, it would burn most of London and Chicago,[1] for example, and build sane and beautiful cities in the place of these pestilential heaps of rotten private property. I have failed in presenting Mr Polly altogether if I have not made you see that he was in many respects an artless child of Nature, far more untrained, undisciplined, and spontaneous than an ordinary savage. And he was really glad, for all that little drawback of fear, that he had had the courage to set fire to his house, and fly, and come to the Potwell Inn.

But he was not glad he had left Miriam. He had seen Miriam cry once or twice in his life, and it had always reduced him to abject commiseration. He now imagined her crying. He perceived in a perplexed way that he had made himself responsible for her life. He forgot how she had spoiled his own. He had hitherto rested in the faith that she had over a hundred pounds of insurance money, but now, with his eye meditatively upon his float, he realized a hundred pounds does not last for ever. His conviction of her incompetence was unflinching; she was bound to have fooled it away somehow by this time. And then!

He saw her humping her shoulders, and sniffing in a manner he had always regarded as detestable at close quarters, but which now became harrowingly pitiful.

'Damn!' said Mr Polly, and down went his float, and he flicked a victim to destruction, and took it off the hook.

He compared his own comfort and health with Miriam's imagined distress.

'Ought to have done something for herself,' said Mr Polly, re-baiting his hook. 'She was always talking of doing things. Why couldn't she?'

He watched the float oscillating gently towards quiescence.

'Silly to begin thinking about her,' he said. 'Damn silly!'

But once he had begun thinking about her, he had to go on.

'Oh, blow!' cried Mr Polly presently, and pulled up his hook, to find another fish had just snatched at it in the last instant. His handling must have made the poor thing feel itself unwelcome.

He gathered his things together and turned towards the house.

All the Potwell Inn betrayed his influence now, for here, indeed, he had found his place in the world. It looked brighter, so bright, indeed, as to be almost skittish, with the white and green paint he had lavished upon it. Even the garden palings were striped white and green, and so were the boats; for Mr Polly was one of those who find a positive sensuous pleasure in the laying on of paint. Left and right were two large boards, which had done much to enhance the inn's popularity with the lighter-minded variety of pleasure seekers. Both marked innovations. One bore in large letters the single word 'Museum', the other was as plain and laconic with 'Omlets'. The spelling of the latter word was Mr Polly's own; but when he had seen a whole boatload of men, intent on Lammam for lunch, stop open-mouthed, and stare, and grin, and come in and ask in a marked sarcastic manner for 'omlets', he perceived that his inaccuracy had done more for the place than his utmost cunning could have contrived. In a year or so the inn was known both up and down the river by its new name of 'Omlets', and Mr Polly, after some secret irritation, smiled, and was content. And the fat woman's omelettes were things to remember.

(You will note I have changed her epithet. Time works upon us all.)

She stood upon the steps as he came towards the house, and smiled at him richly.

'Caught many?' she asked.

'Got an idea,' said Mr Polly. 'Would it put you out very much if I went off for a day or two for a bit of a holiday? There won't be much doing now until Thursday.'

2

Feeling recklessly secure behind his beard, Mr Polly surveyed the Fishbourne High Street once again. The north side was much as he had known it, except that the name of Rusper had vanished. A row of new shops replaced the destruction of the great fire. Mantell and Throbsons' had risen again upon a more flamboyant pattern, and the new fire station was in the Swiss Teutonic style, with much red paint; next door, in the place of Rumbold's, was a branch of the Colonial Tea Company, and then a Salmon and Gluckstein Tobacco Shop, and then a little shop that displayed sweets, and professed a 'Tea Room Upstairs'. He considered this as a possible place in which to prosecute inquiries about his lost wife, wavering a little between it and the God's Providence Inn down the street. Then his eye caught the name over the window. 'Polly,' he read, '& Larkins! Well, I'm – astonished!'

A momentary faintness came upon him. He walked past, and down the street, returned, and surveyed the shop again.

He saw a middle-aged, rather untidy woman standing behind the counter, who for an instant he thought might be Miriam terribly changed, and then recognized as his sister-in-law Annie, filled out, and no longer hilarious. She stared at him without a sign of recognition as he entered the shop.

'Can I have tea?' said Mr Polly.

'Well,' said Annie, 'you *can*. But our Tea Room's upstairs. . . . My sister's been cleaning it out – and it's a bit upset.'

'It *would* be,' said Mr Polly softly.

'I beg your pardon?' said Annie.

'I said *I* didn't mind. Up here?'

'I dare say there'll be a table,' said Annie, and followed him up to a room whose conscientious disorder was intensely reminiscent of Miriam.

'Nothing like turning everything upside down when you're cleaning,' said Mr Polly cheerfully.

'It's my sister's way,' said Annie impartially. 'She's gone out for a bit of air, but I dare say she'll be back soon to finish. It's a nice light room when it's tidy. Can I put you a table over there?'

'Let *me*,' said Mr Polly, and assisted.

He sat down by the open window and drummed on the table and meditated on his next step, while Annie vanished to get his tea. After all, things didn't seem so bad with Miriam. He tried over several gambits in imagination.

'Unusual name,' he said, as Annie laid a cloth before him.

Annie looked interrogation.

'Polly. Polly and Larkins. Real, I suppose?'

'Polly's my sister's name. She married a Mr Polly.'

'Widow, I presume?' said Mr Polly.

'Yes. This five years – come October.'

'Lord!' said Mr Polly, in unfeigned surprise.

'Found drowned he was. There was a lot of talk in the place.'

'Never heard of it,' said Mr Polly. 'I'm a stranger – rather.'

'In the Medway near Maidstone it was. He must have been in the water for days. Wouldn't have known him, my sister wouldn't, if it hadn't been for the name sewn in his clothes. All whitey and eat away he was.'

'Bless my heart! Must have been rather a shock for her.'

'It *was* a shock,' said Annie, and added darkly, 'But sometimes a shock's better than a long agony.'

'No doubt,' said Mr Polly.

He gazed with a rapt expression at the preparations before him. 'So I'm drowned,' something was saying inside him. 'Life insured?' he asked.

'We started the tearooms with it,' said Annie.

Why, if things were like this, had remorse and anxiety for Miriam been implanted in his soul? No shadow of an answer appeared.

'Marriage is a lottery,' said Mr Polly.

'*She* found it so,' said Annie. 'Would you like some jam?'

'I'd like an egg,' said Mr Polly. 'I'll have two. I've got a sort of feeling – As though I wanted keeping up. .... Wasn't particularly good sort, this Mr Polly?'

'He was a *wearing* husband,' said Annie. 'I've often pitied my sister. He was one of that sort—'

'Dissolute?' suggested Mr Polly faintly.

'No,' said Annie judiciously, 'not exactly dissolute. Feeble's more the word. Weak, 'e was. Weak as water. 'Ow long do you like your eggs boiled?'

'Four minutes exactly,' said Mr Polly.

'One gets talking,' said Annie.

'One does,' said Mr Polly, and she left him to his thoughts.

What perplexed him was his recent remorse and tenderness for Miriam. Now he was back in her atmosphere, all that had vanished, and the old feeling of helpless antagonism returned. He surveyed the piled furniture, the economically managed carpet, the unpleasant pictures on the wall. Why had he felt remorse? Why had he entertained this illusion of a helpless woman crying aloud in the pitiless darkness for him? He peered into the unfathomable mysteries of the heart, and ducked back to a smaller issue. *Was* he feeble? Hang it! He'd known feebler people by far.

The eggs came up. Nothing in Annie's manner invited a resumption of the discussion.

'Business brisk?' he ventured to ask.

Annie reflected. 'It is,' she said, 'and it isn't. It's like that.'

'Ah!' said Mr Polly, and squared himself to his egg. 'Was there an inquest on that chap?'

'What chap?'

'What was his name? – Polly!'

'Of course.'

'You're sure it was him?'

'What you mean?'

Annie looked at him hard, and suddenly his soul was black with terror.

'Who else could it have been – in the very clo'es 'e wore?'

'Of course,' said Mr Polly, and began his egg. He was so agitated that he only realized its condition when he was half-way through it, and Annie safely downstairs.

'Lord!' he said, reaching out hastily for the pepper. 'One of Miriam's! Management! I haven't tasted such an egg for five years. . . . Wonder where she gets them! Picks them out, I suppose.'

He abandoned it for its fellow.

Except for a slight mustiness, the second egg was very palatable indeed. He was getting to the bottom of it as Miriam came in. He looked up. 'Nice afternoon,' he said, at her stare, and perceived she knew him at once by the gesture and the voice. She went white, and shut the door behind her. She looked as though she was going to faint. Mr Polly sprang up quickly, and handed her a chair. 'My God!' she whispered, and crumpled up, rather than sat down.

'It's *you*,' she said.

'No,' said Mr Polly very earnestly, 'it isn't. It just looks like me. That's all.'

'I *knew* that man wasn't you – all along. I tried to think it was. I tried to think perhaps the water had altered your wrists and feet, and the colour of your hair.'

'Ah!'

'I'd always feared you'd come back.'

Mr Polly sat down by his egg. 'I haven't come back,' he said, very earnestly. 'Don't you think it.'

' 'Ow we'll pay back the Insurance now, I *don't* know.'

She was weeping. She produced a handkerchief, and covered her face.

'Look here, Miriam,' said Mr Polly. 'I haven't come back, and I'm not coming back. I'm – I'm a Visitant from Another World.[2] You shut up about me, and I'll shut up about myself. I came back because I thought you might be hard up, or in trouble, or some silly thing like that. Now I see you again – I'm satisfied. I'm satisfied completely. See? I'm going to absquatulate, see? Hey Presto, right away.'

He turned to his tea for a moment, finished his cup noisily, stood up.

'Don't you think you're going to see me again,' he said, 'for you ain't.'

He moved to the door.

'That *was* a tasty egg,' he said, hovered for a second, and vanished. . . .

Annie was in the shop.

'The missus has had a bit of a shock,' he remarked. 'Got some sort of fancy about a ghost. Can't make it out quite. So long!'

And he had gone.

3

Mr Polly sat beside the fat woman at one of the little green tables at the back of the Potwell Inn, and struggled with the mystery of life. It was one of those evenings serenely luminous, amply and atmospherically still, when the river bend was at its best. A swan floated against the dark green masses of the further bank, the stream flowed broad and shining to its destiny, with scarce a ripple – except where the reeds came out from the headland, and the three poplars rose clear and harmonious against the sky of green and yellow. It was as if everything lay securely within a great, warm, friendly globe of crystal sky. It was as safe and inclosed and fearless as a child that has still to be born. It was an evening full of quality, of tranquil, unqualified assurance. Mr Polly's mind was filled with the persuasion that indeed all things whatsoever must needs be satisfying and complete. It was incredible that life had ever done more than seemed to jar, that there could be any shadow in life save such velvet softness as made the setting for that silent swan, or any murmur but the ripple of the water as it swirled round the chained and gently swaying punt. And the mind of Mr Polly, exalted and made tender by this atmosphere, sought gently, but sought, to draw together the varied memories that came drifting, half submerged, across the circle of his mind.

He spoke in words that seemed like a bent and broken stick thrust suddenly into water, destroying the mirror of the shapes they sought. 'Jim's not coming back again ever,' he said. 'He got drowned five years ago.'

'Where?' asked the fat woman, surprised.

'Miles from here. In the Medway. Away in Kent.'

'Lor!' said the fat woman.

'It's right enough,' said Mr Polly.

'How d'you know?'

'I went to my home.'

'Where?'

'Don't matter. I went and found out. He'd been in the water some days. He'd got my clothes, and they'd said it was me.'

'They?'

'It don't matter. I'm not going back to them.'

The fat woman regarded him silently for some time. Her expression of scrutiny gave way to a quiet satisfaction. Then her brown eyes went to the river.

'Poor Jim,' she said. ''E 'adn't much Tact – ever.'

She added mildly, 'I can't 'ardly say I'm sorry.'

'Nor me,' said Mr Polly, and got a step nearer the thought in him. 'But it don't seem much good his having been alive, does it?'

''E wasn't much good,' the fat woman admitted. 'Ever.'

'I suppose there were things that were good to him,' Mr Polly speculated. 'They weren't *our* things.'

His hold slipped again. 'I often wonder about life,' he said weakly.

He tried again. 'One seems to start in life,' he said, 'expecting something. And it doesn't happen. And it doesn't matter. One starts with ideas that things are good and things are bad – and it hasn't much relation to what *is* good and what *is* bad. I've always been the skeptaceous sort, and it's always seemed rot to me to pretend men know good from evil. It's just what I've *never* done. No Adam's apple stuck in *my* throat, M'am. I don't own to it.'

He reflected.

'I set fire to a house – once.'

The fat woman started.

'I don't feel sorry for it. I don't believe it was a bad thing to do – any more than burning a toy, like I did once when I was a baby. I nearly killed myself with a razor. Who hasn't? – anyhow gone as far as thinking of it? Most of my time I've been half dreaming. I married like a dream almost. I've never really planned my life, or set out to live. I happened; things happened to me. It's so with everyone. Jim couldn't help himself. I shot at him, and tried to kill him. I dropped the gun and he got it. He very nearly had me. I wasn't a second too soon – ducking. . . . Awkward – that night was. . . . M'am. . . . But I don't blame him – come to that. Only I don't see what it's all up to. . . .

'Like children playing about in a nursery. Hurt themselves at times. . . .

'There's something that doesn't mind us,' he resumed presently. 'It isn't what we try to get that we get, it isn't the good we think we do is good. What makes us happy isn't our trying, what makes others happy isn't our trying. There's a sort of character people like, and stand up for, and a sort they won't. You got to work it out, and take the consequences. . . . Miriam was always trying.'

'Who was Miriam?' asked the fat woman.

'No one you know. But she used to go about with her brows knit, trying not to do whatever she wanted to do – if ever she did want to do anything—'

He lost himself.

'You can't help being fat,' said the fat woman, after a pause, trying to get up to his thoughts.

'*You* can't,' said Mr Polly.

'It helps, and it hinders.'

'Like my upside down way of talking.'

'The magistrates wouldn't 'ave kept on the licence to me if I 'adn't been fat. . . .'

'Then what have we done,' said Mr Polly, 'to get an evening like this? Lord! Look at it!' He sent his arm round the great curve of the sky.

'If I was a nigger or an Italian I should come out here and sing. I whistle sometimes, but, bless you, it's singing I've got in my mind. Sometimes I think I live for sunsets.'

'I don't see that it does you any good always looking at sunsets, like you do,' said the fat woman.

'Nor me. But I do. Sunsets and things I was made to like.'

'They don't help you,' said the fat woman thoughtfully.

'Who cares?' said Mr Polly.

A deeper strain had come to the fat woman. 'You got to die some day,' she said.

'Some things I can't believe,' said Mr Polly suddenly, 'and one is your being a skeleton. . . .' He pointed his hand towards the neighbour's hedge. 'Look at 'em – against the yellow – and they're just stingin' nettles. Nasty weeds – if you count things by their uses. And no help in the life hereafter. But just look at the look of them!'

'It isn't only looks,' said the fat woman.

'Whenever there's signs of a good sunset, and I'm not too busy,' said Mr Polly, 'I'll come and sit out here.'

The fat woman looked at him with eyes in which contentment struggled with some obscure reluctant protest, and at last turned them slowly to the black nettle pagodas against the golden sky.

'I wish we could,' she said.

'I will.'

The fat woman's voice sank nearly to the inaudible.

'Not always,' she said.

Mr Polly was some time before he replied. 'Come here always, when I'm a ghost,' he replied.

'Spoil the place for others,' said the fat woman, abandoning her moral solicitudes for a more congenial point of view.

'Not my sort of ghost wouldn't,' said Mr Polly, emerging from another long pause. 'I'd be a sort of diaphalous feeling – just mellowish and warmish like. . . .'

They said no more, but sat on in the warm twilight, until at last they could scarcely distinguish each other's faces. They were not so much thinking as lost in a smooth, still quiet of the mind. A bat flitted by.

'Time we was going in, O' Party,' said Mr Polly, standing up. 'Supper to get. It's as you say, we can't sit here for ever.'

Notes

PREFACE TO VOLUME XVII

1. *The History of Mr Polly*: If this novel is a 'history' what precisely are the historical dates of the main action? The 1949 film (starring John Mills and directed by Anthony Pelissier) grasped the nettle firmly by having Alfred's father dying in 1897 (as the date on a letter, shown on screen, indicates). With fifteen years of subsequent marriage and three years vagabondage this would put the final action in the middle of World War I – which it clearly isn't (not even Wells, prophetic as he was, foresaw that cataclysm in 1909). Certain sartorial details, such as Polly's wing-poke collar (Chapter 1) suggest a turn-of-the-century date for the later action, as do such authorial remarks as that (in the same chapter): 'In those days the bicycle was still rare and costly, and the motor car had yet to come.' Those days would seem to be the very first years of the twentieth century.

CHAPTER I
BEGINNINGS AND THE BAZAAR

1. *that silly Mud Pie*: i.e. a high-crowned soft brown hat.
2. *Rashdall's Mixed Pickles*: Presumably a reference to the most venerable manufacturer of pickled and jarred vegetables, Crosse and Blackwell, whose outlet in Soho, London, was founded in 1806. By the period of Wells's narrative they were the nationwide brand leader.
3. *was Mr Polly circum*: An unusual usage of the prefix. It evidently refers, coyly, to Mr Polly's rotundity.
4. *if Mr Polly, for example, had been transparent*: A self-regarding joke on the author's famous scientific romance, *The Invisible Man* (1897). In his *Experiment in Autobiography* (1934), Wells

ruefully noted that for younger readers he was the author of that work and nothing more.

5. *Laocoon*: In Virgil's *Aeneid*, Laocoon draws down the wrath of the gods for warning the Trojans against Greek guile. As punishment, two snakes emerge from the sea to strangle him and his sons – here emblematic of someone entangled in difficulty.

6. *desgenerated*: A reference to the evolutionary theory that suggested that humanity had reached its peak and was becoming less complex; Wells had written on the subject in his 1891 essay, 'Zoological Retrogression', and elsewhere.

7. *The elementary education he had acquired*: i.e. as a result of the elementary – or 'national' – Education Act of 1870.

8. *First the infant, mewling and puking*: Wells quotes Jaques's 'All the world's a stage' speech (*As You Like It*, II.vii.139–66) on the seven ages of man. As the novel opens, Mr Polly is in the fifth age and drearily contemplating his 'second childishness'.

9. *whether it was eight sevens or nine eights that was sixty-three*: Neither, of course.

10. *those inspiring weeklies that dull people used to call 'penny dreadfuls'*: The term 'penny dreadfuls' (or 'bloods') came into general use in the 1840s to describe Gothic tales, in eight-page, double-column instalments, luridly illustrated with woodcuts, for the working-class reader. The tale of Sweeney Todd, the demon barber, is a famous example. In the last quarter of the nineteenth century, however, penny dreadfuls came to refer more exclusively to tales for the young reader, many more of whom were literate after the 1870 Education Act. They were, genetically, the forerunner of the 'comic'. Their 'depraved' nature – as 'dull people' perceived – triggered a moral panic in the 1870s that led to the publication of 'wholesome' comics for the young, such as the Religious Tract Society's *Boy's Own Paper* (founded in 1879).

11. *valley of the shadow*: Psalms 23:4.

12. *ult*: Abbreviation of *ultimo*, meaning 'last month'.

13. *yellow-grained paper and American cloth tables*: American cloth is glossily coated, so as to be impermeable and more easily wiped.

14. *'Do you bite your thumbs at Us, Sir?'*: The mark of insult between the young bravos of the Montague and Capulet families in *Romeo and Juliet*.

15. *'Bocashieu'*: Giovanni Boccaccio (1313–75), author of the (improper as it would have been thought at the time) *Decameron*.

16. *'Rabooloose'*: François Rabelais (1490–1533), author of the (improper as it would have been thought at the time) tales of Pantagruel and Gargantua.

17. *the several members of the YMCA*: George Williams (1821–1905), a 23-year-old drapery clerk, founded the Young Men's Christian Association in Great Britain in the mid-nineteenth century. Despite the sarcasm here, young Wells found the movement's libraries a useful source of instruction. Williams was knighted, in 1894, with much fanfare and public gratitude for his work for boys.

18. *improver*: 'A person who works at a trade under an employer for the purpose of improving his or her knowledge or skill, and accepts the opportunity of such improvement wholly or in part instead of wages' (*OED*, 3).

19. *Joy de Vive*: Love of life – a mangling of the French *joie de vivre*.

20. *'Short of sugar, O' Man'*: As the context indicates, 'sugar' is slang for 'cash'. The term seems not to have survived.

21. *past the moored ironclads*: Battleships. Wells waxed sarcastically and socialistically about them in Section V of *The War in the Air* (1908):

> So it was that Bert Smallways saw the first fight of the airship and the last fight of those strangest things in the whole history of war: the ironclad battleships, which began their career with the floating batteries of the Emperor Napoleon III in the Crimean war and lasted, with an enormous expenditure of human energy and resources, for seventy years. In that space of time the world produced over twelve thousand five hundred of these strange monsters, in schools, in types, in series, each larger and heavier and more deadly than its predecessors. Each in its turn was hailed as the last birth of time, most in their turn were sold for old iron. Only about five per cent of them ever fought in a battle. Some foundered, some went ashore, and broke up, several rammed one another by accident and sank. The lives of countless men were spent in their service, the splendid genius, and patience of thousands of engineers and inventors, wealth and material beyond estimating; to their account we must put, stunted and starved lives on land, millions of children sent to toil unduly, innumerable opportunities of fine living undeveloped and lost. Money had to be found for them at any cost – that was the law of a nation's existence during that strange time. Surely they were the weirdest, most destructive and wasteful megatheria in the whole history of mechanical invention.

22. *hoast-crowned*: A dialect spelling of 'oast', a building containing a kiln for drying hops with a distinctive slanted, cone-shaped roof; a common feature of the Kent countryside.

23. *hobnails*: Heavy boots.

24. *salitas*: Salita: 'In Italy, an upward slope or incline, a stretch of rising ground' (*OED*, which gives this sentence as its first citation).

25. *fried ham and eggs and shandygaff*: An innocuous mixture of ginger beer and lemonade.

26. *Fishbourne*: In the first edition 'Foxbourne'. It is generally taken to be Sandgate, in Kent, where Wells had lived for several years before writing *The History of Mr Polly*. He subsequently (immediately before writing the novel) moved to Hampstead, in London. Hence, presumably, 'Hampstead-on-the-Sea' here.

27. *six bathing-machines*: Bathing machines were huts on wheels, brought to the edge of the water, so that the Victorian bather might change conveniently (and, most importantly, modestly) before plunging into the briny and out again.

28. *'Sesquippledan,' he would say. 'Sesquippledan verboojuice.'*: Well might Platt say 'Eh?' Polly is quoting, with hilarious inaccuracy, from the Seventh Rule in Herbert Spencer's *The Philosophy of Style* (1852):

> There seem to be several causes for this exceptional superiority of certain long words. We may ascribe it partly to the fact that a voluminous, mouth-filling epithet is, by its very size, suggestive of largeness or strength; witness the immense pomposity of *sesquipedalian verbiage*: and when great power or intensity has to be suggested, this association of ideas aids the effect.

29. *'Eloquent Rapsodooce'*: Eloquent rhapsodies.

30. *Doing the High Froth ... articulariously He stands*: Polly has been reading Thomas Carlyle's (1795–1881) *On Heroes and Hero Worship* (1841), Lecture IV:

> It is the property of every Hero, in every time, in every place and situation, that he come back to reality; that he stand upon things, and not shows of things. According as he loves, and venerates, articulately or with deep speechless thought, the awful realities of things, so will the hollow shows of things, however regular, decorous, accredited by Koreishes or Conclaves, be intolerable and detestable to him.

CHAPTER 2
THE DISMISSAL OF PARSONS

1. *Manchester*: Cotton goods.
2. *Rockockyo*: i.e. rococo. This artistic school received its name in the nineteenth century from French émigrés, who used the word to designate a highly wrought 'shellwork' style (*style rocaille*) of art and decoration.
3. *bar sinister*: A term from heraldry, indicating descent via an illegitimate line.
4. *The High Egrugious*: The 'high egregious' – i.e. something very special.
5. *the electric light*: Gas and electrical domestic lighting began to be introduced into British households in the 1880s. By the end of the century electric lights (although by no means universal) were not uncommon.
6. *grey silesia*: A kind of linen cloth, originally made in Silesia, a province of Prussia. It was not highly regarded by British textile manufacturers or discriminating consumers.
7. *Allittritions Artful Aid*: i.e. 'alliteration's artful aid', a proverbial quotation from Charles Churchill's (1731–64) poem, 'The Prophecy of Famine' (1763).
8. *rolled huckaback*: Coarse towelling.
9. *Bolton sheeting*: Fine Lanchashire cotton.
10. *aspirated nothing*: The policeman does not pronounce any of his 'h's.
11. *perjoocery*: Perjury.
12. *Cross summons*: Counter suit.
13. *Humble Pie*: To eat humble pie is to apologize after being humiliated.
14. *Heated altaclation*: Heated altercation.
15. *the Grave and Reverend Signor with the palatial Boko*: An echo of Othello's 'Most potent, grave, and reverend signors' (I.iii.76). 'Boko' may be a reference to the size of his nose.
16. *choleraic*: i.e. choleric, hot tempered – not, as Polly's lexicography implies, prone to catching cholera.
17. *Piping my Eye*: Crying. Some reprints have 'doing a blooming Pipe'. Whether the change was made by Wells (or some subeditor) is not clear.

CHAPTER 3
CRIBS

1. *Exorbiant Largenial Development*: Exorbitant development of the larynx.
2. *Urgent Loogoobusoity*: Pressing lugubriousness (?).
3. *full of Smart Juniosity. The Shoveacious Cult*: Full of young energy – willing to use their shoulders to get on in life.
4. *excelsior, Sir. It's a sort of motto of mine. From Longfellow*: i.e from Henry Wadsworth Longfellow's (1807–82) poem, 'Excelsior', an anthem to aspiration about a youth who dies after successfully scaling a mountain. Not cheerful.
5. *Obsequies Deference*: Obsequious deference. Polly, imaginatively if gloomily, combines it with 'obsequy', or funeral.
6. *ex-President Roosevelt, or General Baden Powell, or Mr Peter Keary, or the late Dr Samuel Smiles, quite easily . . . and he loved Falstaff and Hudibras and coarse laughter, and the old England of Washington Irving and the memory of Charles the Second's courtly days*: A catalogue of masculinity. Theodore Roosevelt (1858–1919) succeeded to the presidency of the United States in 1901, on the assassination of William McKinley. He was re-elected in 1904 and left office in 1909. As leader of the 'Rough Riders' in the Spanish–American War, Teddy Roosevelt was famously 'manly'. Robert Baden-Powell (1857–1941), another 'hearty', was the founder of the Boy Scout movement. The first issue of *The Scout* came out in April 1908, the same year of the first Scout Camp, as did his bestseller, *Scouting for Boys*. Among Baden-Powell's most enthusiastic supporters was the publisher Peter Keary (1865–1915). Samuel Smiles (1812–1904) was most famous as the author of the 'how to succeed in life' manual, *Self-Help* (1859). Hudibras is the Quixotic hero of Samuel Butler's (1612–80) satire of that name (1663) and (Sir John) Falstaff was Shakespeare's Rabelaisian hero. The Washington Irving (1783–1859) text referred to is, apparently, *Bracebridge Hall* (1822) and its hero, Squire Bracebridge. Charles II was, legendarily, the 'merry monarch'. The references to the death of Smiles (1904) and Roosevelt's leaving office (1909) suggest recent dates for this section of the narrative.
7. *Portly capons*: Portly capuchins – or monks – seems to be what Polly is erratically aiming at here. Capons are neutered chickens – typically plump birds.

8. *'metrorious urnfuls', 'funererial claims', 'dejected angelosity'*:
    'Meritorious urns', with a dash of 'mournful'. 'Funereal records
    (exaggerated)'. 'Angels with hanging heads'.
9. *Bell Harry Tower*: The large central tower of Canterbury
    Cathedral, completed in the late fifteenth century.
10. *Chaucer's 'Chequers'*: Where, supposedly, the pilgrims end their
    tale-telling journey in the *Canterbury Tales*. Wells knew this part
    of southern England well himself, having lived in Kent for eight
    years.
11. *'Cultured Rapacacity' . . . 'Vorocious Return to the Heritage'*:
    By the first phrase, Polly seems to mean something along the
    lines of 'cultural riches' – crossed with a commercial rapacity
    to make profit from it. The second phrase, more clearly, seems
    to mean 'true (veracious) source of our (English) literary and
    historical heritage'.
12. *this Marlowe monument*: The playwright Christopher Marlowe
    (1564–93) was the son of a Canterbury shoemaker and was
    brought up in the city. There is a monument to him outside what
    is now the Marlowe Theatre.
13. *a collective intelligence and a collective will for order, commen-
    surate with its complexities*: Wells here mocks himself, writing
    in *First and Last Things* (1908). See Introduction, p. xxii.

CHAPTER 4

MR POLLY AN ORPHAN

1. *an engraved portrait of Garibaldi, and a bust of Mr Gladstone*:
    These tributes to the Italian patriot and revolutionary Giuseppe
    Garibaldi (1807–82) and the Liberal Prime Minister (1809–98)
    suggest a somewhat radical tincture to the elder Mr Polly's polit-
    ical thinking and, perhaps, the reason why his wife Lizzie's family
    took against him.
2. *the up-line ticket clerk*: Easewood Junction has manned ticket
    offices on both sides of the main line – up to and away from
    London.
3. *The British Weekly*: An influential religious magazine, founded
    by Robertson Nicoll (1851–1923) in 1866.
4. *Funerial baked meats like*: See Hamlet's bitter: 'Thrift, thrift,
    Horatio! the funeral baked meats / Did coldly furnish forth the
    marriage tables' (I.ii.181–2). Like the Prince of Denmark, Alfred
    Polly has lost a father.

5. *Bit vulturial*: i.e. a bit like vultures, feeding on a corpse.
6. *I'm no sort of Fiancianier*: 'I'm no sort of financier' – but, with his windfall, Polly's thoughts are turning, unconsciously, to love and a fiancée.
7. *sotto voce*: In a low voice.
8. *Pentstemon*: A flower ('Bearded-tongue') with five stamens. The significance of the name is elusive.
9. *There ought to have been a postmortem*: An indirect reference to the currently famous Sir Bernard Spilsbury, pioneer of the postmortem examination. Spilsbury (1877–1947) went on to work on many famous criminal cases, most famously the 1910 Crippen trial. Over his career he carried out over 25,000 post-mortems and he kept index card details of each one.
10. *Hysterial catechunations*: Hysterical cackle.
11. *I've seen a mort of undertakers*: Mort means 'a great deal of' – here with an overtone of 'mortuary'.
12. *word or so in season*: An allusion to Isaiah 50:4.
13. *dear dead days beyond recall*: From the chorus of 'Love's Old Sweet Song' (1884), also known as 'Just a Song at Twilight', words by G. Clifton Bingham (1859–1913), music by James Lyman Molloy (1837–1909).
14. *cast snacks*: 'Cast aspersions' from 'snack' meaning 'snap' or 'bite'.
15. *Gowlish gusto ... Funererial Games*: 'Ghoulish gusto'. Polly recalls, dimly, the funeral games for Anchises, Aeneas's father, in Virgil's *Aeneid*.

CHAPTER 5
ROMANCE

1. *antiseparated me*: i.e. 'anticipated me, with this separation between us'.
2. *Mr Richard Le Gallienne's very detrimental book, The Quest of the Golden Girl*: Wells reviewed Richard le Gallienne's (1866–1947) whimsical romance about a young man's walking tour in search of the ideal bride when it first came out in 1896. Wells did not much like the book. Many late Victorian readers did.
3. *happy Theleme, whose motto is: 'Do what thou wilt'*: From Rabelais' tale of Gargantua. The hero talks of starting a new abbey at the village of Theleme whose motto will be: '*Fais ce que tu voudrais*' – do what you will.

4. *a safety bicycle*: A machine popularized in the last decade of the
    nineteenth century. They were called 'safety bicycles' because of
    their improved wheel design, tubular metal frames, chain-and-
    pedal propulsion, and pneumatic tyres (invented in 1889 by John
    Dunlop).

5. *The Arabian Nights, the works of Sterne, a pile of Tales from
    Blackwood*: Richard Burton's (1821–90) (unbowdlerized) trans-
    lation of *The Arabian Nights Entertainment* (1885), Sterne's
    (1713–68) 'improper' *Tristram Shandy* (1759–67) and a selec-
    tion of the hair-raising 'tales of terror' that *Blackwood's Maga-
    zine* specialized in. Polly's tastes are daring, we apprehend.
    Perhaps he also had a copy of Burton's translation of the *Kama
    Sutra* hidden under his mattress.

6. *a second-hand copy of Belloc's Path to Rome*: Hilaire Belloc's
    (1870–1953) religiously flavoured travel book *The Path to Rome*
    (1902), published by Wells's own publisher, Thomas Nelson.
    The dating consequences are rather perplexing. If this is 1903
    (see 'second-hand') then the fifteen years of subsequent marriage
    would put the main action of the narrative into the middle of the
    1914–18 war and after.

7. *Purchas his Pilgrimes*: i.e. *Hakluytus Post-humus, or Purchas his
    Pilgrimes. Contayning a History of the World in Sea Voyages
    and Land Travell by Englishmen and Others* (1625). Samuel
    Purchas (*c*. 1575–1626) was a major source for Coleridge's
    poetry. That Wells was reading (or thinking about) Coleridge at
    this period is further suggested by the name 'Christabel'.

8. *The Life and Death of Jason*: William Morris's (1834–96) popu-
    lar poem (containing the exploits of Jason, Medea and the
    Argonauts) published in 1867.

9. *Exploratious menanderings*: Exploratory wanderings.

10. *debreece*: Debris.

11. *jawbacious*: Garrulous.

12. *Swelpme*: 'So help me [God]'.

13. *friskiacious palfrey*: Frisky steed.

14. *Stamton wreckery-ation ground*: By the Recreation Grounds Act
    of 1859, areas of land were put aside for the leisure of the urban
    population, and paid for (after 1894) on local rates.

15. *four-ale*: So called because it cost fourpence a pint.

16. *oscoolatory exercises*: Kissing.

17. *intrudaceous*: Intrusive. Some editions have 'ubtrudaceous',
    which is rather wild even for Mr Polly.

18. *All my people are in India*: It was common practice for British

civil servants in India, fearful of the tropical climate, to send their children to English boarding schools for their education.

19. *I'm just a nobody*: Polly alludes, presumably, to *The Diary of a Nobody* (1892), by George (1847–1912) and Weedon (1854–1919) Grossmith, identifying himself with the extravagantly self-deprecating hero, Charles Pooter.

20. *vivisecting*: I.e. with the cold scientific curiosity of a vivisectionist – one of the *bête noire* types among well-thinking intellectuals of the period.

21. *gesticulatious game*: 'This game of gestures without action'.

22. *dilletentytating*: Playing the [unserious] dilettante.

23. *Gurdrum*: i.e. Gudrun, a heroine in William Morris's poem, 'The Earthly Paradise' (1868–70). Polly's thoughts are incorrigibly 'chivalresque'.

CHAPTER 6

MIRIAM

1. *Bit of a scraze*: Scrape, scratch, graze.

2. *Meditatious*: Meditative.

3. *Fervous digging*: Feverish digging.

4. *Humorous wind vane*: i.e. a wind vane with a humorous device (a cat catching a bird, perhaps) on it.

5. *Virginia creeper . . . Canary creeper*: Miriam is thinking (subconsciously) of the wedding night, Alfred of a caged bird.

6. *He saw his bicycle in the hall and cut it dead*: To 'cut' someone socially is to ignore them deliberately.

7. *Delphicums and larkspurs*: Delphiniums and larkspur. They are the same flowering (or, as Polly would say, 'floriferous') plant.

8. *ex div.*: Exclusive of dividend.

9. *debonairious*: Debonair – soon to be well dressed.

10. *chiffonier*: Chest of drawers.

11. *Benedictine collapse*: Like Benedick, the confirmed bachelor in Shakespeare's *Much Ado about Nothing* who, in spite of his opposition to matrimony, eventually surrenders to Beatrice.

12. *Unfortunate amoor*: Unlucky affair of the heart.

13. *under the will of society*: An allusion to John Locke's (1632–1704) *Second Treatise of Government* (1690, paragraph 96): 'When any number of men have, by the consent of every individual, made a community, they have thereby made that com-

munity one body, with a power to act as one body, which is only by the will and determination of the majority.'

14. *Telessated pavements*: Checkered (tesselated) paving.

15. *fisherman's Ginn*: In the 'The Fisherman and the Djinn', in *The Arabian Nights*, the Djinn is imprisoned in a small pot until freed by a fisherman.

16. *with ideas of sanctuary in his mind*: In the Middle Ages, fleeing criminals could claim sanctuary from the law in a church.

17. *verbum sap*: A word to the wise.

18. *old Tommy*: Brandy, one assumes.

19. *Convivial vociferations*: Convivial hubbub.

20. *nubblicks*: Or 'nubbles' – lumps.

21. *a gadabout grinny*: A fidgety, grinning girl.

22. *second class*: There were, at this period, three classes of coach for the rail traveller. The Pollys are splashing out on their wedding day – but not immoderately.

CHAPTER 7

THE LITTLE SHOP AT FISHBOURNE

1. *Zealacious commerciality*: A zealous commercial spirit.

2. *rebel, and work Obi*: Work bad magic (the term *Obi*, or *obeah*, is African. Polly has been reading his travel books).

3. *the voyages of La Perouse*: i.e. *The Voyage of La Pérouse* (1785–88). Captain Jean-François de Galaup de La Pérouse (1741–88) explored the coasts below the Bering Strait with a view to establishing a French market in the area.

4. *The Island Nights' Entertainments . . . Island of Voices*: R. L. Stevenson's (1850–94) 1893 collection of South Sea tales, including the *Isle of Voices* and *The Beach of Falesá*.

5. *like warm tea*: A recollection of the hero's murdering the villain in *The Beach of Falesá*: 'The blood came over my hands, I remember, hot as tea.'

6. *travels of the Abbés Huc and Gabet*: Mid-nineteenth-century travellers to China and Tibet.

7. *He read Fenimore Cooper and Tom Cringle's Log side by side with Joseph Conrad*: James Fenimore Cooper (1789–1851), author of the 'Leather-Stocking Tales'. *Tom Cringle's Log* (1833), by Michael Scott (1789–1835), was a favourite nineteenth-century nautical tale set mainly in the Caribbean. The Conrad

(1857–1924) fiction that Polly would have most relished are the
early 'Eastern World' romances, such as *Almayer's Folly* (1895)
and *An Outcast of the Islands* (1896).

8.   *Bart Kennedy's A Sailor Tramp*: Kennedy (1861–1930) wrote,
     in addition to this classic of the tramping life (1902), the autobio-
     graphical *A Man Adrift* (1899), the narrative of a wandering life,
     which would also have been much to Polly's taste.

9.   *he never took at all kindly to Dickens. Yet he liked Lever, and
     Thackeray's Catherine, and all Dumas until he got to the Vicomte
     de Bragelonne*: Charles Dickens (1812–70), the novelist most
     often regarded as the strongest influence on *The History of Mr
     Polly*; Charles Lever (1806–72), the author of rollicking 'Irish'
     tales. Thackeray's (1811–63) anti-Newgate (i.e. crime fiction)
     satire, *Catherine* (1839), is an odd choice, except, perhaps, that
     its heroine is a husband killer (a more homicidal Miriam). *The
     Viscount of Bragelonne, or Ten Years Later* (1848–50) is the last
     in the trilogy of of Alexandre Dumas' (1802–70) musketeer
     romances. Polly prefers stories of young, not ageing, heroes.

10. *It is much more understandable that he had no love for Scott*:
     Sir Walter Scott (1771–1832). I'm not sure I do understand it.

11. *Waterton's Wanderings in South America*: i.e. Charles
     Waterton's (1782–1865) *Wanderings in South America* (1825),
     a pioneer work of natural history. Among other things, Waterton
     collected a number of poisons from the region – notably curare,
     which went on to have valuable medical applications.

12. *Bates, too, about the Amazon*: The naturalist and entomologist,
     Henry Walter Bates (1825–92). Bates's work was important in
     developing theories of evolution. It is evident that in this passage
     Wells is principally remembering his own reading, at a formative
     stage of his early career.

13. *a book of old Keltic stories collected by Joyce charmed him, and
     Mitford's Tales of Old Japan*: i.e. P. W. Joyce (1827–1914), *Old
     Celtic Romances* (1879) and Algernon Mitford (1837–1916,
     sometime Foreign Office diplomatist in Peking and Japan), *Tales
     of Old Japan* (1871).

14. *a certain high-browed gentleman living at Highbury, wearing a
     golden pince-nez, and writing for the most part in that very
     beautiful room, the library of the Climax Club*: Identifiably
     Sidney Webb (1859–1947), political thinker, founder (with his
     wife Beatrice) of the Fabian Society and the London School
     of Economics and, recently, a doctrinal opponent of (erstwhile
     fellow-Fabian) H. G. Wells. Wells mischievously puts his own

views in the mouth of Webb. Wells was himself elected to the Reform Club in 1905, and did much of his writing there.

15. *Arreary Pensy*: i.e. *arrière pensée*, French for 'afterthought' although, of course, Mr Polly is thinking more of *derrières* – or backsides.

16. *You – you're excited*: i.e. drunk.

17. *softish sort of flat*: i.e. easily duped, or hoodwinked.

18. *chequered Careerist*: i.e. someone with a chequered career behind him – and checkered trousers around his behind.

19. *shivery shakys*: i.e. shaking shanks.

20. *silently intent polygamist ... wife's sister*: An allusion to the 'deceased wife's sister act' (permitting marriage between those so related) passed, after decades of lobbying, in 1906.

21. *Berlin wool*: Fine, coloured, knitting wool.

22. *cinematograph peepshow*: The earliest cinematograph apparatus, in the early 1900s, supplied images to just one viewer. These 'what the butler saw' machines were soon replaced by cinema theatres, with projected images on to a large screen.

23. *The Review of Reviews*: Founded by W. T. Stead (1849–1912) in 1890. In March 1895 it declared (presciently): 'H. G. Wells is a man of genius.'

24. *gas meter*: Penny-slot gas meters were introduced in 1890. Incandescent gas-mantles were introduced in 1885 and held their own, for decades, against the nearly simultaneous electric light.

25. *the Welfare of the Race*: Rusper (as was Wells) is evidently a eugenicist, a follower of Sir Francis Galton (1822–1911). Wells uses the phrase 'welfare of the race' prominently in his 1905 tract, *A Modern Utopia*.

26. *the German peril*: A reference, apparently, to William Le Queux's (1864–1927) alarmist (and wildly popular) fantasy of Britain being overrun, imminently, by Germany, *The Invasion of 1910* (1906).

27. *William's not the Xerxiacious sort*: Wilhelm II was crowned the German Kaiser (or emperor) in 1888 and famously wanted a 'place in the sun' for the German people. To which end, under the Tirpitz Plan, he built up the German military machine. As Wells's *The War in the Air* (1908) indicates, he for one did think Wilhelm belligerent. Xerxes became king of Persia at the death of his father, Darius the Great, in 485 BC and (vainly) continued the family project of conquering Greece.

28. *Jujitsu*: This weaponless martial art became very popular in the early twentieth century. It was developed by Jigoro Kano in the

late 1800s. In 1904 Yoshiaki Yamashita, one of Kano's students, travelled to the US and taught Jujitsu to President Theodore Roosevelt and West Point cadets. Wells was a huge admirer of Roosevelt.

29. *Police Grip*: A grip in which the arms are locked by pinning one arm behind the back.

CHAPTER 8

MAKING AN END TO THINGS

1. *paraffin puddles*: The paraffin (kerosene) stove first appeared in 1892 when a Swede, Frans Wilhelm Lindqvist, registered his 'Sootless Kerosene Stove'. The design burned paraffin gas, which was vaporized from the liquid fuel in tubes forming the burner head.

2. *hobbledehoys*: 'A youth at the age between boyhood and manhood, a stripling; *esp.* a clumsy or awkward youth' (*OED*, 1).

3. *the petrol and stabling*: i.e. servicing both cars and horse-drawn vehicles.

4. *kept its manual*: i.e. its hand-operated pumps and devices.

5. *had ended the British Ramadan*: The ninth month of the Muslim year, imposing fasting on the faithful during daylight hours. Here it is an allusion to the English liquor licensing laws that controlled Sunday drinking. In 1910, Fishbourne's public houses would only be permitted to be open, on a Sunday, from one o'clock to three o'clock and six o'clock to ten o'clock (all p.m.).

6. *the tract of Chiozza Money's that he was reading side by side with one by Mr Holt Schooling*: i.e. Leo Chiozza Money (1870–1904), a writer on economic matters, Liberal MP and lobbyist for free trade. J. Holt Schooling (1859–1927) was a proponent of protectionism and tariff reform. Chalk and cheese economists.

7. *Mr Rusper, a modern Laocoon*: See Chapter 1, note 5.

8. *Gladstone-shaped*: An upright collar with flared sides.

9. *Phoenix from the flames*: In Egyptian mythology, the phoenix burns itself to death, and is reborn from the ashes.

10. *Naked came I into the world*: Polly echoes Job (another unhappily married man): 'Naked came I out of my mother's womb, and naked shall I return thither' (Job 1:21).

CHAPTER 9

THE POTWELL INN

1. *there was a Toad Rock he had heard of*: The village of Rusthall lies about a mile to the west of Tunbridge Wells. Tourists are drawn to the 'Toad Rock' there, a natural rock formation which looks like a sitting toad, standing on an outcrop of sandstone.
2. *Aurora Borealis*: The Northern Lights, a natural phenomenon caused by the collision of ions from the sun with the earth's magnetic field.
3. *a casual ward*: i.e. the workhouse, which offers overnight bed and board for the vagrant and destitute.
4. *Itchabod*: i.e. 'Ichabod' – 'the glory has departed' (1 Samuel 4:19–22).
5. *beer-engine*: 'A machine for drawing or pumping up beer from the casks to the bar' (*OED*).
6. *Shrub*: A drink made from gin or rum, mixed with fruit juice, sugar and spice.
7. *the illegality of bringing children into bars*: As the law stood in 1910, children under fourteen were not allowed into the bar areas of public houses.
8. *an Assumptioning Madonna*: i.e. a representation of the Virgin Mary being assumed into heaven.
9. *Wax to receive and marble to retain*: From Byron's (1788–1824) poem *Beppo* (1818) (stanza 34): 'His heart was one of those which most enamour us / Wax to receive, and marble to retain.'
10. *leer*: Suspicious.
11. *Ceteris paribus*: Other things being equal.
12. *Stockholm tarring*: Stockholm tar is made from pinewood resin and normally used in shipbuilding.
13. *Canadian canoe*: Now more usually known as a kayak.
14. *dog fancying*: Dog breeding.
15. *cleaning and 'garing' motor cars and bicycles*: This seems to mean 'greasing' or, possibly, waxing.
16. *across the sundering flood*: An arch allusion to William Morris's romance, *The Sundering Flood* (1898).
17. *Three golden pounds*: Three golden guinea coins, presumably.
18. *Herculaceous sort ... Nothing very wonderful bicepitally*: Not like Hercules. Not very well developed around the biceps. The first modern bodybuilder, Eugen Sandow (1867–1925), had recently begun his career as a 'strongman' with famously

impressive biceps. Wells refers directly to Sandow in Chapter 7 of *A Modern Utopia*.

19. *I'm a Reformatory Reformed Character*: The reformatory system of penal education for young people was founded, in 1852, by Thomas Barwick Lloyd Baker (1807–86), lawyer and philanthropist. He based part of the stern regime on his own Eton schooldays. Like others with working-class associations, Wells evidently did not think much of reformatories.

20. *sanguinary*: i.e. 'bloody' (later 'blurry' and 'decorated').

21. *cinder track*: A track used for running on at athletics grounds.

22. *Old cadger*: i.e. trickster.

23. *the heel of Achilles*: In Greek mythology, Achilles was invulnerable except at the heel of one foot: hence, a point of weakness.

24. *Nicholson's ait*: An 'ait' is a small island in the middle of a stream.

25. *osiers*: Willows.

26. *his alcolaceous frenzy*: His alcohol-fuelled fury.

27. *full of the murmuring of bees*: An allusion to Alfred Lord Tennyson's (1809–92) alliterative lines in 'Come Down, O Maid' in *The Princess* (1847): 'Myriads of rivulets hurrying thro' the lawn, / The moan of doves in immemorial elms, / And murmuring of innumerable bees.'

28. *copper sticks*: Used for stirring laundry in a large washing pot, or copper.

29. *Territorials, and seasoned boating men*: i.e. part-time soldiers. The Volunteer Movement was begun in 1859 as a response to alarm about revolutions in Europe. It evolved into the 'The Territorial Force', as it was called, in 1908. A significant dating reference, suggesting that Wells has brought the action up nearly to the time of writing, 1909.

30. *early closing day at Lammam*: In order to prevent the exploitation of shopworkers, and compensate for Saturday opening, shopkeepers were obliged to close up for one half-weekday (traditionally Thursday afternoon). The law operated until well into the second half of the twentieth century.

31. *pollard willow*: To pollard a tree is to cut back its branches to encourage more bushy growth.

32. *benifluous influence*: Benign influence.

33. *oxhide*: In Homer's *The Iliad*, the heroes' shields are made from oxhide: famously, Ajax's contains seven layers.

34. *Suffragettes*: The suffragette movement, a pressure group aiming to get women the vote, was formed by Emmeline and Christabel

Pankhurst in 1903. They were, in frustration, obliged to use ever more 'direct' (and occasionally violent) methods, as Jim here implies.

35. *Jim's lagged again*: i.e. he's back in prison.

36. *A novelist should present characters, not vivisect them*: An allusion to Wells's long-standing debate with his friend, Henry James (1843–1916), on the 'Art of Fiction'. Wells favoured a broader brush and lighter touch in his characterizations.

CHAPTER 10

MIRIAM REVISITED

1. *burn most of London and Chicago*: Cities traditionally associated with conflagration. The Great Fire of London was in 1666, that of Chicago in 1871.

2. *Visitant from Another World*: Wells had satirized the late-Victorian craze for spiritualism in his 1900 novel *Love and Mr Lewisham*; Polly is asking Miriam to think of him as a ghost.

J. S.
S. J. J.

READ MORE IN PENGUIN

In every corner of the world, on every subject under the sun, Penguin represents quality and variety – the very best in publishing today.

For complete information about books available from Penguin – including Puffins, Penguin Classics and Arkana – and how to order them, write to us at the appropriate address below. Please note that for copyright reasons the selection of books varies from country to country.

In the United Kingdom: Please write to *Dept. EP, Penguin Books Ltd, Bath Road, Harmondsworth, West Drayton, Middlesex UB7 0DA*

In the United States: Please write to *Consumer Services, Penguin Putnam Inc., 405 Murray Hill Parkway, East Rutherford, New Jersey 07073-2136.* VISA and MasterCard holders call 1-800-631-8571 to order Penguin titles

In Canada: Please write to *Penguin Books Canada Ltd, 10 Alcorn Avenue, Suite 300, Toronto, Ontario M4V 3B2*

In Australia: Please write to *Penguin Books Australia Ltd, 487 Maroondah Highway, Ringwood, Victoria 3134*

In New Zealand: Please write to *Penguin Books (NZ) Ltd, Private Bag 102902, North Shore Mail Centre, Auckland 10*

In India: Please write to *Penguin Books India Pvt Ltd, 11 Community Centre, Panchsheel Park, New Delhi 110017*

In the Netherlands: Please write to *Penguin Books Netherlands bv, Postbus 3507, NL-1001 AH Amsterdam*

In Germany: Please write to *Penguin Books Deutschland GmbH, Metzlerstrasse 26, 60594 Frankfurt am Main*

In Spain: Please write to *Penguin Books S. A., Bravo Murillo 19, 1°B, 28015 Madrid*

In Italy: Please write to *Penguin Italia s.r.l., Via Vittorio Emanuele 45/a, 20094 Corsico, Milano*

In France: Please write to *Penguin France, 12, Rue Prosper Ferradou, 31700 Blagnac*

In Japan: Please write to *Penguin Books Japan Ltd, Iidabashi KM-Bldg, 2-23-9 Koraku, Bunkyo-Ku, Tokyo 112-0004*

In South Africa: Please write to *Penguin Books South Africa (Pty) Ltd, P.O. Box 751093, Gardenview, 2047 Johannesburg*

PENGUIN CLASSICS

KIPPS   H.G. WELLS

'It is vulgarly imagined that to have money is to have no troubles at all'

Orphaned at an early age, raised by his aunt and uncle, and apprenticed for seven years to a draper, Artie Kipps is stunned to discover upon reading a newspaper advertisement that he is the grandson of a wealthy gentleman – and the inheritor of his fortune. Thrown dramatically into the upper classes, he struggles desperately to learn the etiquette and rules of polite society. But as he soon discovers, becoming a 'true gentleman' is neither as easy nor as desirable as it at first appears.

Telling the hilarious tale of one man's struggle for self-improvement, Kipps is a brilliantly witty satire upon social pretension. Part of a brand-new Penguin series of H. G. Wells's works, this edition includes a newly established text, a full biographical essay on Wells, a further reading list and detailed notes. The introduction, by David Lodge, places the work in its literary and social context, considers earlier drafts and provides a detailed biography of Wells.

'The best novel in the last forty years' Henry James

Introduced by David Lodge
Textual Editing by Simon J. James
Notes by Simon J. James

PENGUIN CLASSICS

LOVE AND MR LEWISHAM   H.G. WELLS

'He was no common Student, he was a man with a Secret Life'

Young, impoverished and ambitious, science student Mr Lewisham is
locked in a struggle to further himself through academic achievement.
But when his former sweetheart, Ethel Henderson, re-enters his life his
strictly regimented existence is thrown into chaos by the resurgence of old
passion. Driven by overwhelming desire, he pursues Ethel passionately,
only to find that while she returns his love she also hides a dark secret. For
she is involved in a plot of trickery that goes against his firmest beliefs,
working as an assistant to her stepfather – a cynical charlatan 'mystic' who
earns his living by deluding the weak-willed with sly trickery.

A biting critique on the spiritualist craze sweeping the nation, *Love and
Mr Lewisham* is also an exploration of one man's conflict between love
and ambition. Part of a brand-new Penguin series of H. G. Wells's works,
this edition includes a newly established text, a full biographical essay on
Wells, a further reading list and detailed notes. The introduction, by
Gillian Beer, considers the book as the first of Wells's satires on social
pretension in Edwardian England.

Introduction by Gillian Beer
Textual Editing by Simon J. James
Notes by Simon J. James

PENGUIN CLASSICS

THE NEW MACHIAVELLI   H.G. WELLS

'Men are egotistical even in devotion'

A successful author and Liberal MP with a loving and benevolent wife, Richard Remington appears to be a man to envy. But underneath his superficial contentment, he is far from happy with either his marriage or the politics of his party. *The New Machiavelli* describes the disarray into which his life is thrown, when he meets the young and beautiful Isabel Rivers and becomes tormented by desire. At first, he struggles to resist and remain focused upon his familiar political, personal and social life. But as he soon learns, it is harder than he could have imagined to turn his back on love.

Based on Wells's own experiences, this is a vivid and unfailingly candid account of the damage wrought by a scandalous society affair, and the overwhelming power of passion. Part of a brand-new Penguin series of H. G. Wells's works, this edition includes a newly established text, a full biographical essay on Wells, a further reading list and detailed notes. Michael Foot's introduction considers the novel's liberal politics, and describes Wells's own strong support for the suffragette movement.

Introduced by Michael Foot
Textual Editing by Simon J. James
Notes by John Partington

PENGUIN CLASSICS

TONO-BUNGAY H.G. WELLS

'I never really determined whether my uncle regarded Tono-Bungay as a fraud'

Presented as a miraculous cure-all, Tono-Bungay is in fact nothing other than a pleasant-tasting liquid with no positive effects. Nonetheless, when the young George Ponderevo is employed by his Uncle Edward to help market this ineffective medicine, he finds his life overwhelmed by its sudden success. Soon, the worthless substance is turned into a formidable fortune, as society becomes convinced of the merits of Tono-Bungay through a combination of skilled advertising and public credulity. As the newly rich George discovers, however, there is far more to class in England than merely the possession of wealth.

An acerbic account of human gullibility and a damning indictment of the British class-system, *Tono-Bungay* remains one of the greatest of all satires on the power of advertising and the press. Part of a brand-new Penguin series of H. G. Wells's works, this edition includes a newly established text, a full biographical reading list and detailed notes. The introduction, by Edward Mendelson, explores the many ways in which the work satirises the fictions and delusions that shape modern life.

Introduced by Edward Mendelson
Textual Editing by Edward Mendelson and Patrick Parrinder
Notes by Edward Mendelson

PENGUIN CLASSICS

ANN VERONICA H.G. WELLS

'There was a pause, and then the front door slammed ... Ann Veronica realized that she was alone with the world'

Twenty-one, passionate and headstrong, Ann Veronica Stanley is determined to live her own life. When her father forbids her from attending a fashionable Ball, she decides she has no choice but to leave he family home and make a fresh start in London. There, she finds a world of intellectuals, socialists and suffragettes – a place where, as a student in Biology at Imperial College, she can be truly free. But when she meets the brilliant Capes, a married academic, and quickly falls in love, she soon finds that freedom comes at a price.

A fascinating description of the women's suffrage movement, *Ann Veronica* offers an optimistic depiction of one woman's sexual awakening and search for independence. Part of a brand-new Penguin series of H. G. Wells's works, this edition includes a newly established text, a full biographical essay on Wells, a further reading list and detailed notes. The introduction, by Margaret Drabble, considers the relevance of the novel to Wells's personal life.

Introduced by Margaret Drabble
Textual Editing by Sita Schutt
Notes by Sita Schutt

PENGUIN CLASSICS

THE INVISIBLE MAN   H.G. WELLS

'"It's very simple," said the voice. "I'm an invisible man"'

With his face swaddled in bandages, his eyes hidden behind dark glasses and his hands covered even indoors, Griffin – the new guest at *The Coach and Horses* – is at first assumed to be a shy accident-victim. But the true reason for his disguise is far more chilling: he has developed a process that has made him invisible, and is locked in a struggle to discover the antidote. Forced from the village, and driven to murder, he seeks the aid of an old friend, Kemp. The horror of his fate has affected his mind, however – and when Kemp refuse to help, he resolves to wreak his revenge.

Depicting one man's transformation and descent into brutality, *The Invisible Man* is a riveting exploration of science's power to corrupt. Part of a brand-new Penguin series of H. G. Wells's works, this edition includes a newly established text, a full biographical essay on Wells, a further reading list and detailed notes. Christopher Priest's introduction considers the novel's impact upon modern literature.

Introduced by Christopher Priest
Textual Editing by Patrick Parrinder
Notes by Andy Sawyer

PENGUIN CLASSICS

THE SLEEPER AWAKES   H.G. WELLS

'"It is no dream," he said, "no dream." And he bowed his face upon his hands'

A troubled insomniac in 1890s England falls suddenly into a sleep-like trance, from which he does not awake for over two hundred years. During his centuries of slumber, however, investments are made that make him the richest and most powerful man on Earth. But when he comes out of his trance he is horrified to discover that the money accumulated in his name is being used to maintain a hierarchal society in which most are poor, and more than a third of all people are enslaved. Oppressed and uneducated, the masses cling desperately to one dream – that the sleeper will awake, and lead them all to freedom.

Wildly imaginative and compelling, *The Sleeper Awakes* is a fascinating and prescient account of a future dominated by capitalist greed and mechanical force. Part of a brand-new Penguin series of H. G. Wells's works, this edition includes a newly established text and detailed notes. The introduction, by Patrick Parrinder, outlines the development of Wells's political philosophy.

Introduced by Patrick Parrinder
Textual Editing by Patrick Parrinder
Notes by Andy Sawyer

PENGUIN CLASSICS

THE FIRST MEN IN THE MOON   H.G. WELLS

'I fell and fell and fell for evermore into the abyss of the sky'

When penniless businessman Mr Bedford retreats to the Kent coast to write a play, he meets by chance the brilliant Dr Cavor, an absent-minded scientist on the brink of developing a material that blocks gravity. Cavor soon succeeds in his experiments, only to tell a stunned Bedford the invention makes possible one of the oldest dreams of humanity: a journey to the moon. With Bedford motivated by money, and Cavor by the desire for knowledge, the two embark on the expedition. But neither are prepared for what they find – a world of freezing nights, boiling days and sinister alien life, on which they may be trapped forever.

The First Men in the Moon is one of the first and greatest science fiction novels. Part of a brand-new Penguin series of H. G. Wells's works, this edition includes a newly established text, a full biographical essay on Wells, a further reading list and detailed notes. China Mieville's introduction places the novel in literary context, and reveals it as a skilled critique of Imperialism.

Introduced by China Mieville
Textual Editing by Patrick Parrinder
Notes by Steven McLean
